A World Apart
Kate Alexandra

Contents

A note on spellings   VI

Dedication   VII

Introduction   VIII

1. Chapter One   2

2. Chapter Two.   8

3. Chapter Three   19

4. Chapter Four   34

5. Chapter Five   44

6. Chapter Six   53

7. Chapter Seven   58

8. Chapter Eight   68

9. Chapter Nine   75

10. Chapter Ten   81

11. Chapter Eleven   92

12. Chapter Twelve   98

13.	Chapter Thirteen	103
14.	Chapter Fourteen	111
15.	Chapter Fifteen	123
16.	Chapter Sixteen	139
17.	Chapter Seventeen	150
18.	Chapter Eighteen	159
19.	Chapter Nineteen	176
20.	Chapter Twenty	204
21.	Chapter Twenty-One	222
22.	Chapter Twenty-Two	228
23.	Chapter Twenty-Three	235
24.	Chapter Twenty-Four	255
25.	Chapter Twenty-Five	266
26.	Chapter Twenty-Six	281
27.	Chapter Twenty-Seven	298
28.	Chapter Twenty-Eight	307
29.	Chapter Twenty-Nine	324
30.	Chapter Thirty	347
31.	Chapter Thirty-One	367
32.	Chapter Thirty-Two	379
33.	Chapter Thirty-Three	393

34.	Chapter Thirty-Four	404
35.	Chapter Thirty-Five	415
36.	Chapter Thirty-Six	421
37.	Chapter Thirty-Seven	425
38.	Chapter Thirty-Eight	442
39.	Chapter Thirty-Nine	455
40.	Chapter Forty	464
41.	Chapter Forty-One	472
42.	Chapter Forty-Two	485
43.	Chapter Forty-Three	492
44.	Chapter Forty-Four	507
45.	Chapter Forty-Five	514
46.	Chapter Forty-Six	534
	Epilogue	540
	Acknowledgements	545
	Afterword	547
	About the author	548

Hello friends

As this book was written in the UK, you might notice some *'foreign'* spellings (e.g., *colour* instead of *color*, *favourite* instead of *favorite*).

Rest assured; these are not mistakes — just the quirks of British English. Think of it as part of the charm, like crumpets instead of pancakes, or chips instead of fries.

Enjoy!

To the Army of fans who Stay true, who never Blink, live like NCTzens in Neverland, and believe in magic. Once MOA with feeling — this one's for you. Lightsticks up.

An Introduction

GVibes

- **Park Min-Jae** – The leader and oldest. Part of the vocal line. Height: 179cm. Age 26.

Nickname: Jae.
The wise negotiator. Often translates for the group. Speaks fluent Korean, Japanese and English.

- **Choi Woo-Jin** – Main rapper, second oldest. Height: 171cm. Age:25.

Nickname: Jin.
Known as the serious one, has a loyal following. Speaks Korean and decent English. Is learning Japanese.

- **Lee Sung-Min** – Second Rapper and the best dancer in the group. Height: 176cm. Age: 22.

Nickname: Lee.

The loveable clown. Terrible at English, but he's trying. Speaks Korean and some Japanese.

- **Baek Ji-Hoon** – The main vocalist and second-best dancer. Also known as the Visual. Height: 182cm. Age: 24.

Nickname: Joon.

The sexy one. A title he privately dislikes. Speaks Korean and fluent English, is learning Japanese.

- **Kim Seok-Min** – The youngest in the vocal line – The Maknae. Height:177cm. Age:19.

Nickname: Ace, but the members call him 'little brother.'

Known for being shy in person, but not on stage. Speaks Korean and is learning English.

Part One
제1부

Chapter 1

April. Tuesday

They say spring brings new beginnings, but for me, it meant navigating the absurdities of Los Angeles one chilly morning at a time.

As I stood in front of the mirror applying eyeliner while Becka bundled up in layers, I couldn't help but wonder if this was what adulthood felt like — an endless cycle of unexpected moments wrapped in laughter while simultaneously wondering what was for dinner.

"Seriously?" I laughed as I watched Becka wind a scarf around her neck.

"What?" She said defensively. It's cold!"

"It's..." I lifted my smart watch up to my face to briefly inspect the home face, "16 degrees," I teased, "it's a balmy spring day." I lifted my foot to rest it on the little bench by the front door so I could tie the laces of my Vans hi-tops.

"What's that in real-world temperature?" Becka had moved on to fluffing her mid-length blond hair in the mirror.

I put my leg down and raised the other one, taking a moment to think. "Um, like, 60ish?" I supplied.

"Kaiya, that's practically arctic for LA."

I laughed as I turned to unlatch the front door, but Becka stopped me with a hand on my arm.

"Hold on, you've got something tangled in your hair."

I turned back to look at myself in the mirror, running my hands through my long, chestnut toned hair, eventually finding and picking out a shred of paper.

"I swear, I'm going to be finding this stuff for days, with all the shredding Jeremy is making me do," I grumbled, discarding it. Life as an intern at Pisces recording studio was not the glamorous gig I had expected it to be.

"Count yourself lucky that's all you're doing." Becka groaned. "Trevor Kyle has been in and out of our office all week, having 'secret' chats with Celine." She put air-quotes around the word, but she might as well have just said 'bullshit', as her tone implied.

"Oh hey," Becka said suddenly, "I forgot to tell you. He asked about you yesterday."

"Me?" I'm baffled by the idea he would even deign to notice me.

"Yeah, he asked who the 'exotic' new hire was." The air-quotes got more airtime while I mimed throwing up.

"Oh, ew!"

As if to emphasise my point, I threw open our front door. We made our way down the short hallway, jogging down the stairs to the big front doors. "Are you even allowed to say that anymore?" I scoffed, pulling open the heavy doors.

As always, I'm struck by how bright and loud it is beyond the front door. It's like being hit by a cartoon-version of life. Everything is just so frantic, and this isn't even downtown.

"God, no, but he does what he wants and everyone's too scared to upset the money-maker to tell him when he's being a racially-insensitive, misogynist asshat."

I laughed, but he wouldn't be the first person to point out my half-Japanese appearance, and no doubt he wouldn't be the last.

"Gah, it's colder than a witch's tit out here."

"You're so soft," I scoffed.

"We can't all have developed the thick skin of the Brits," Becka paused a moment to tuck her scarf into her tan trench coat. "You're used to the cold and the wet. Some of us have evolved to thrive in more forgiving environments than 'jolly old *Lundun*'." Becka thought the way she pronounced 'London' was hilarious. I'm not actually sure I've heard her say it properly yet.

Truthfully, London and LA were strikingly similar in April. They shared similar temperatures and even rained about the same. Or, at least, so far as I'd been able to tell. I'd only been here about 3 weeks and so far, the only real differences were the accents, the colour of the taxis and the alarming number of skateboards.

When Becka had first raised the idea of me coming to LA, I have to confess my mental images were vastly different from the reality.

For starters, we were nowhere near any beaches. Becka had laughed when I'd pointed this out.

People were the same wherever you went – despite how insistent Americans are that they are far nicer than us Brits. They got cross at you for taking too long at a street crossing, but they held doors open for you if you were right behind them. They offered you a seat on the bus if you looked like you had too many bags. Or they pretended to ignore you. People are people.

"Speaking of thick skin," I said, "we are not getting an Uber. We're catching the bus." Becka groaned, throwing her head back dramatically.

"Whhyyyy?" She whined. "It's cold and the morning bus smells like gas."

"Oh, it does not," I laughed, reaching out a hand to grab her elbow and pull her along with me. "Besides, we've spent so much recently on Ubers. Food doesn't buy itself, you know."

Becka grumbled, but didn't argue. "It's your fault, anyway," she muttered darkly.

"Behave! How is it?" I asked, raising my eyebrows at her but not slowing down.

"Well, I can hardly show you around from the back of a bus, now can I?" Becka clearly thought this was a solid argument, but I only rolled my eyes.

"Alright then, now you've shown me around, I'd quite like to enjoy the benefits of food security for the rest of my time here."

"Yeah, yeah. Quit manhandling me, crumpet-muncher," Becka laughed as she pulled her arm free from my grasp, but continued to match my pace all the same.

I scoffed. That was one of her better ones.

"That would hit harder if it wasn't coming from someone who microwaves her tea."

"I've started taking the bag out first!" She protested.

I clutched my chest and pretended to keel over. "Y'know, you wouldn't be allowed to step foot in Yorkshire."

She looked at me with a frown. "The Shire?"

I sighed. "Never mind."

Suddenly, Becka pointed away from me and cried "Yo! That's our bus. Run!" And without waiting for me, Becka began to double-speed it down the road to where a bus was just now pulling up at our stop.

"Bollocks!" I muttered, earning a scandalised look from a middle-aged lady just coming out of the Seven-11 on my left.

Becka was already on the step of the bus by the time I caught up to her. She smirked at me as I fumbled for my pass.

"Not bad for someone who microwaves her tea." She laughed as we moved towards a couple of free seats in the middle of the bus.

She'd been right though; the morning bus did smell like petrol.

Just like every morning since I'd moved here, I looked out of the window as the city sped past and I smiled. Would the novelty ever wear off?

I'd come to LA on a whim, a vague, fuzzy sort of hopefulness for a bright future that wasn't yet fully formed in my mind. Isn't that why everyone moves to LA? To follow their dreams?

All I knew was that I wanted to be involved with music. From its inception to its creation. I loved everything about the journey it took from pen to record, and I wanted to be right there in the process.

Chapter 2

It's been three weeks since I started working at Pisces Studios and I was still not quite used to it.

Before I started working here, I'd had some big misconceptions about what a commercial recording studio was actually like. It made me laugh to think about how I used to picture it. I'd always envisioned it to be some tiny little building, niche and unspeakably cool where you just went in and magic came out.

I feel like such a tit even admitting that to myself. My imagination was based on the recording studios we had at university. They were small and purpose built, basically an office with an enclosed booth separated by a pane of glass. Professional, but small and identical to the half dozen others in the same building, a rabbit warren of aspiring musicians and technicians.

In reality, a commercial recording studio was a far more scaled-up affair. The front of the building was polished stone and looked like any other trendy-but-corporate offices. The inside was a little more like what I expected once you got to the 1st floor – or 2nd floor, as my American hosts called it. Once you were past the reception area and into the back of the building it became a collective of where music creation meets corporate. Reception and storage were on the 1st floor, along with a cavernous room used for orchestral and big band arrangements, the studios were on the 2nd and the business and meeting rooms were at the top on the 3rd. That was where Becka worked as head of the social media team.

She also managed client expectations as a secondary responsibility.

"Needs, wants, and wishes," she called it. These varied from things our guests absolutely needed, like a specific brand of mic, to their 'wants', like a specific brand of soft drink, to 'wishes', where they might demand to have a masseuse present for the whole booking to massage their throat with jasmine oil in between sets- to my knowledge, that's never happened, but with some celebrities, you really never know.

"Do they get everything they wish for?" I asked once.

"They can certainly ask." Was all she'd tell me.

Me? Nothing so glamorous. Broadly, my job role was 'intern'. What that actually meant was that I was technically under the general operations team, which covered social media, marketing, public relations and the bookings team. I, however, did none of that but it was the only team that Becka could get me a job in because the production team – musicians and technicians- didn't take on interns. I was a paid intern, but barely. I made enough to split utilities and food with Becka, but not the rent, which she covered on her own.

Then again, I wasn't here for the money. I was only here on a year-long Visa. When it expired I'd go back to the UK with 12 months of hands-on experience at a famous LA recording studio. Or at least, that's what I'd put on my resume. I'd probably gloss over the fact that I was pretty much just the person that you'd get to make the coffee for the meetings, but work was work and there were worse places to be a paid intern.

"Meet you for lunch?" I asked Becka as we rode the elevator up to the top floor.

"Natch," she replied as the doors slid open. "See ya later!" She called over her shoulder as she sauntered off down the corridor to her office. I took a more leisurely pace down the corridor directly in front of the bank of elevators to the general operations unit.

There were three corridors up here that went left, straight, or right. The one to the left has three meeting spaces: a casual lounge and two meeting rooms. Each one had a large table and enough chairs to seat a dozen people, complete with a total audio-visual set up for conference and video calls. The one that went straight on from the elevator led to general operations. The corridor that went to the right was social media, bookings, and PR. The first time I'd gone in one of the conference rooms during a meeting, the camera had followed me around the room as I carried in a tray of drinks. I was thoroughly creeped out, thinking some perv was focusing in on me and I said as much to my boss once I'd gotten out of there.

Jeremy had laughed as he explained it tracked movement and sound to make sure all speakers were always in the frame. Some random creeper was not remote controlling the camera to follow me around the room; I'd just been so noisy clattering around with the tray that the camera had automatically focused on me.

Jeremy was the head of Gen Ops and was my direct line. He was an alright guy and had a plaque on his desk that read *Jeremy Olsen - Gen Ops and Chief Cat Herder* which made me laugh every time I saw it.

He was sat at his desk when I knocked, the door slightly open as usual.

"Come in, Kaiya," he called.

"How'd you know it was me?" I asked pushing the door open. He didn't look up from where he was tapping away at his laptop; just pointed at the clock on the wall. It was 08:50.

"Same time every day." Half of his mouth quirked up in a smile.

"Only when we take the bus." I countered.

"You must be saving Rebecca a fortune," he mused, finally closing his laptop and turning to look at me.

"I consider it my great act of charity."

Jeremy scoffed and leaned back in his chair. I guessed that he was in his mid-40s with nondescript dark brown hair, a perpetually scruffy chin and kind eyes. He was exactly the kind of person you could imagine as running the Ops team of a studio.

"Remind me, who were you with yesterday?" He asked, running a finger over his chin.

"Foley." I answered at once, smiling. Jeremy returned the smile. "Ah, yes. Make anything interesting?" Foley artists were such a trip. Whenever you heard rain, footsteps on gravel, or even horse hooves on grass in a film or whatever, chances were you were hearing a Foley artist, sitting in a dark cupboard with a whole bunch of random crap around them making every sound you can imagine.

"A bar fight," I responded. Jeremy raised his eyes. "No shit? Who's that for?"

I opened my mouth to tell him, but Jeremy quickly interrupted me. "Forget I asked. It'll be 'That Pain In The Ass again.'"

I pursed my lips to hide my smile. It was, indeed, for the rap artist. Began with a D, ended with an E.

"Anyway," Jeremy continued, "nothing so exciting today, I'm afraid. Tech team just received a bunch of new guitars, for some reason." He rolled his eyes. "They've asked for someone to tune them. Why they can't do it themselves, fuck knows." He huffed. In the short time I'd been here, I'd noticed that the different departments were constantly at each other's throats for one thing or another.

"I don't mind," I replied gamely.

"That's what you spent three years at University for, right?" He glanced up at me, raising an eyebrow wryly. I didn't think he would appreciate me reminding him of the donkey-work he regularly had me doing that similarly had nothing to do with my degree either.

At least I'd get to play with some cool gear.

It was a good thing I was proficient at both bass and guitar because the tech team had indeed just shipped in a load and all of them needed tuning. I wasn't a particular enthusiast, but even I had to sigh in appreciation of some of them.

They were absolute works of art, no other way to describe them; perfectly curved bodies of ash and alder, so shiny the overhead lights were dazzling as they bounced off the varnish. There were also a lot of them. So many that it took me right up until lunch time to get it done. My fingers were throbbing by the time I put down the last electric guitar. My phone vibrated in my pocket and I pulled it out, sparing the screen a glance as I headed towards the elevators.

Becka

Meeting room 2. I got news x

[Sent 12:09]

13

I raised my eyebrows with interest and took the stairs up to the 3rd floor.

Pushing open the door to meeting room 2, I saw Becka sitting at the head of the conference table. Blessedly, the AV setup was quiet and still. Becka had our lunch spread out on the table in front of her, the meal prep containers I insisted on buying us when I moved in coming in clutch, yet again. Before I moved in, Becka lived off of take-out and Uber Eats. Even though I didn't pay rent, I liked to think I was saving her money.

"Yo," I said in greeting as I pulled out a chair and sat down, pulling a container of chicken salad towards me.

Becka waved her fork at me, her mouth already full.

"Good day?" she mumbled around a mouthful of leaves. I made a non-committal noise and then we sat in companionable silence while we ate.

Once I was done, I put the lid back on the glass container, slid it across the table, and picked up my water bottle. "What was your news?" I asked as I unscrewed the wide lid.

"Hmm? Oh, that." Her words were casual. Entirely too casual, which caught my attention. Warily, I eyed her.

"Remind me," she said, wiping her mouth on a napkin and twirling her fork around. "What's the name of the KPop group that did that collab with Haley a couple weeks ago?"

I narrowed my eyes at her. "You know full well that was GVibes – I've played the song enough times." And I had. Ever since it came out recently, I'd been playing it multiple times a day. That song slaps.

"Ah, yeah, you're right." She speared an olive with her fork and popped it into her mouth, chewing thoughtfully.

"And?" I prompted.

She finished chewing before she said, "There's like, a lot of them, right?"

"Five," I said through gritted teeth.

"Yeah." She took a sip from her straw.

"Which one is the tallest one?" She asked casually, like she was asking after the weather. For a moment, I was caught off-guard.

"Baek Jihoon," I said tentatively, the words more question than answer.

She tipped her Stanley cup towards me. "That's the one!" And then she put her cup on the table and rummaged around in her bag before pulling out her compact mirror and a tube of lipstick. Silence fell as she took her sweet time.

"Becka!" I almost shouted. She only laughed at me before opening her compact.

"Okay, okay," she chuckled, "I figured you might be interested to know that that one-" she waved her lipstick at me, vaguely.

"Jihoon," I finished.

"Yeah, that one." She nodded, before uncapping her Mac lipstick – shade *Retro* – "is booked in for Thursday."

Silence.

Becka slicked the lipstick across her bottom lip as I watched mutely before –

"FUCK OFF!" The words burst from my mouth in an exhalation of disbelief.

Becka flinched, smudging her perfect application at my almost-shout.

"I'm sorry?" She looked at me, affronted.

"Are you joking right now? Is this a joke?" I leaned towards her; drink forgotten. She was lucky I hadn't spat it at her.

"Ok, first of all," Becka started, giving me a side-eye as she took a napkin and delicately wiped at the smudged corner, "chill the fuck out. Secondly, no, absolutely serious." Seemingly satisfied with her repair, she began on her top lip. I waited until she had finished and blotted, but she held her hand up to stop me. She recapped and put the lipstick away before she swivelled in her chair and for the first time all lunch, gave me her full attention. The Rebecca Hanson take-down.

"Sorry," I muttered.

Gradually, her lips relaxed, and her eyebrows went back to their normal altitude.

"I'm glad you're excited, but it's actually kind of a total fuck-up." I watched as she almost went to bite her lip, before she remembered her recent application and relaxed her mouth. Despite my overwhelming need to squee, I put that aside for the moment and dug deep for my 'supportive friend' mode. It was an effort, but I got there.

"Why, what's occurred"? I asked, which made her smile. For some reason, that phrase in particular always amused her.

"In a nutshell, booking buggered it up." It was her time to amuse me with her phrasing; one she'd picked up from the year she'd spent studying in London. British curse words coming out of her all-American mouth was endlessly funny to me.

"They need to be letting us know weeks in advance for a booking for an SCC," she groused, referring to a 'special category client' – someone crazy famous.

"Two fucking days is not enough time!" Becka threw her hands up.

"Bugger." I sympathised. "Is there anything I can do?" I offered. She gave me a side-eye that had me holding up my hands. "Hey, I mean it," I pressed. "Can I help?"

She sighed. "Thanks babes, but no. There's no chance Celine will want an intern anywhere near him."

Disappointment gnawed at me, but I pushed it down.

"Who's working with him?" I asked, trying for casual.

Becka curled her lips, which would have been answer enough, but she said, "Trevor."

Ah. Trevor. I thinned my lips and nodded.

Trevor Kyle was the top producer at Pisces and had worked with basically every big name that walked through the door. He was also a total douchebag.

Bossy, arrogant, and kind of grabby – from what I'd heard. I'd never actually worked with him myself, of course. I'd only ever seen him in passing and he'd never deigned to glance in my direction, but

I'd heard enough about him to have firmed up my opinion of the guy.

"Isn't this something Booking should be handling?" I asked. Becka sighed again.

"I mean, yeah, to a point. They're handling transpo and the hotel. He's got his own management and security so we're hands-off with that, but everything he does or needs within this building falls on client relations, which is..." She pointed both thumbs at herself.

"I mean, to be fair," she began, glancing over to the wall of windows that overlooked the street, "his team hasn't laid out many demands. Mostly needs and wants, y'know? No wishes. So far anyway." She laughed.

"No cordoned-off toilets or bowls of rose-quartz crystals, then?" I laughed with her.

"Not yet! There's still time to be surprised."

Chapter 3

No one mentioned anything, but I had a feeling that I'd been pretty useless the whole rest of Tuesday. That night, back at Becka's apartment, I'd connected my laptop to the TV in the living room and forced her to watch GVibes' music videos.

We were mid-way through their newest song, 'Fall in Love', the collaboration with American singer Haley, when Becka finally shouted, "Alright!" Throwing her arms up in the air, she exclaimed, "I get it! They're God's gift to the modern music scene."

I laughed and disconnected my laptop. "So, you get why I'm hyped, then?"

"Sure, yeah," she'd conceded, "so, like, I knew you liked their songs, but are you in their fan group? Oh, what's it called?" She huffed, flopping back against the sofa cushions. "Celine told me about them to look into on social media, but I can't remember what they're called. Y'know how Gaga has her 'Little Monsters'?"

I smiled to myself before I answered. "Vibers."

"That's the one!" Becka snapped her fingers.

"And no, not really." I said hesitantly. "Apparently, I wouldn't qualify as a Viber because I've never seen them live, don't own any of their CD albums, don't own any merch..." I ticked off these gross offenses on my fingers.

Becka frowned at me. "Who says you don't qualify?" she asked, immediately outraged on my behalf, which made me chuckle.

"Other Vibers."

Becka made a 'pfft' sound and waved her hand dismissively. "Sounds like political bullshit to me."

She stood up and moved towards the kitchen. "I'm showing my age here, but I remember the Savage Garden fandom in the 90s had exactly the same elitist nonsense." She opened the fridge and rummaged around before saying, "If you identified as a 'light sider', you were a traitor. Bollocks and nonsense." She trailed off, muttering too quietly for me to hear.

Suddenly, she spun back around and, waving a slightly-wilted stick of celery in my direction, proclaimed, "You can be a vibe if you bloody well want!"

I laughed, loving her to my soul, not having the heart to correct her.

Later that evening, I sat on my bed, staring out the window as 'Broken Promise' played softly from the little portable speaker perched on my windowsill.

"Most people think this song is about heartbreak," I'd explained to Becka earlier, just before she'd made me turn GVibes off. "But it's really about life not living up to the expectations you set for it." Becka had hummed in half-hearted acknowledgment, already tired of my endless fawning.

'Broken Promise' had always been one of my favourites. It resonated with me — probably with anyone who'd ever been let down by something they'd counted on, only for it to fall through. It made me think of my mum. Of my... biological father.

It reminded me of the lengths I'd go to, the sacrifices I'd make, just to achieve the things I felt I needed in life. A purpose.

As the song ended, I sighed and started getting ready for bed. Just one more day to get through until *he* was here. A nervous flutter began in my belly, and it was some time before I could sleep,

Wednesday

All of Wednesday my patience was tested. I was mostly stuck with busy-work for admin. I photocopied so many copies of NDAs, contracts, and affiliate-use forms that, by midday, my hands were splotchy with ink and my thumb was indented from stapler over-use.

At lunch, I'd tried to meet up with Becka, but she'd been too busy to stop, sending me an apologetic text to say she couldn't leave her desk. I'd wandered aimlessly down to the market instead to grab a few things for dinner.

By the time the end of the day had rolled around, I'd had to practically drag Becka away from her desk.

"You would not believe how busy this dude is making our social calendar," she muttered darkly and sounding not-at-all enthusiastic.

"Aww, I'm so sorry that the international superstar is making your life difficult." I poked my tongue out the side of my mouth. She cracked a smile, but I could tell she was feeling the strain.

"It's not really him that's the problem. It's the press. You would not believe how fucking nosy they are." She ran a frustrated hand down her face – carefully though, she spent ages doing her makeup this morning.

I would absolutely believe that of the press.

"And obviously we're not allowed to confirm that he is actually coming here," she continued. "I honestly have no idea how they even know. We've only just found out, for fucks sake. She exclaimed, pushing open the front door to the street perhaps a little harder than necessary.

"I mean, it wasn't even this bad that one time we had 'you-know-who'," she said. We were on the street walking towards the bus stop, so no names.

"Voldemort?" I asked innocently. She gave me a droll look.

"All I'm saying is, this kid better be the nicest person to ever walk through those doors," she huffed out, seemingly running out of steam.

I said nothing. We both knew I was hyped to be in the same building as him, but that was no reason to rub it in. I only took her arm in companionable silence as we waited for the bus, which didn't smell half as bad this time of the day as it did in the morning.

Sometimes the patrons did though, but one problem at a time.

Thursday

Without even needing to discuss it, Becka and I had both decided we'd get into the studio early today.

She was at the kitchen counter filling both of our travel mugs when I emerged from my bedroom. She gave me an assessing look up and down and then nodded approvingly. I appreciated the support because lord knows I'd agonised over this outfit all bloody morning.

In my position, I did not have to wear anything resembling formal or office-attire, but I also couldn't just rock up looking like I'd just rolled out of bed and given that I'd only been here a scant month, my choices were distressingly slim.

I'd finally settled on a pair of black combat boots, black denim slim-fit jeans, a white t-shirt and a black and white plaid shirt that I could either put on over my t-shirt, or wear around my waist if I got too hot. I left my hair down, like I normally did, but I'd given it a bit of extra attention this morning when I'd blow-dried it. I normally don't bother, but I was damned if I was going to be in the same building as an artist I admired and not take an extra 10 minutes of effort. I wore the same amount of makeup as I usually did – mascara, brows, and a neutral colour lip crayon. I'd never hear the end of it if anyone at work thought I was trying to doll myself up.

"I've sorted us an Uber," I said, skipping over the whole 'good morning' thing.

"Spectacular." Becka said with a grin as she handed me my travel mug.

"Hmm," she hummed, "what perfume are you wearing?"

I unlocked our front door as I answered, "I'm wearing two."

Becka followed me out and locked the door behind her. "Two?"

"Thought I'd give it a go and I'm actually pretty happy with the result." I grinned at her as we walked towards the big door to the street.

"Which ones?" she asked, unlatching the door.

"Laura Mercier's Vanilla and Midnight Fantasy." I replied.

"That explains why you smell like a vanilla candy," she laughed.

"It's good though, right?" I said, quite convinced of my own genius.

"When you walk through the halls, it'll be like Hansel and Gretel following a trail of candies right to the witches house." She laughed.

"Ok, rude," I frowned, "am I not the witch in that scenario?"

"Always said you were a baddie, babes." She winked at me. I tutted and took a sip of my coffee.

Just then, a Honda Civic pulled up to the kerb in front of us and the driver lowered the window.

"Uber?" He asked.

"Right on time!" I smiled and opened the back door, but before I could slide in, Becka grabbed my arm. "Um, hello?" I said, looking at her in confusion.

"Don't be such a Bambi," she scolded me before leaning closer to the driver's window.

"What names do you have?" Becka asked primly. The driver, a young-looking guy wearing a Bears t-shirt, reached for his phone and reading off a message said, "Booked by Kaiya?"

I gave Becka a 'are you happy now?' look as she released my elbow, and I slid in to the backseat. It smelt like brand new air freshener trees.

Becka slid in next to me. "Safety first," she said in a tone that very much implied the 'duh,' she didn't say.

We made it to the studio at exactly 08:05. I tipped Kenneth (our driver) and we made our way inside.

At first glance, everything looked as normal as ever, but on closer inspection it was clear someone had been through here with copious amounts of polish. Everything gleamed and there was a faint smell of lemon on the air.

Becka and I exchanged smiles.

"But sure, yeah, no big deal," she said. I laughed.

It wasn't a surprise that pretty much the whole of the 3rd floor was already in or piled in shortly after we did. I didn't linger in their office, technically I wasn't supposed to be there and the minute

Becka put her bag on her desk, one of her colleagues came over to speak with her, so I made my way to Jeremy's office.

"Ah, good morning, Kaiya. Is it just me or is everyone acting weird this morning?" he asked, looking up at me from his laptop.

I shrugged, but answered, "I think it's probably something to do with the client coming in today."

Jeremy frowned. "Who?"

I blinked in surprise. "Baek Jihoon from GVibes?"

Jeremy leaned back in his chair and steepled his fingers together, leaning his elbows on the arm rests as he thought about it for a minute.

"Yeah, nah, I got nothing," he said finally. "Give me an equivalent from the 90s," he asked, raising an eyebrow at me. This was a game we'd played before. I wasn't completely convinced he wasn't having me on, but I played along all the same.

"Um, Justin Timberlake, N*SYNC," I replied confidently.

"Ahh, got it. Frosted tips, as well?"

I laughed. "Not yet."

"Give it time," he said darkly. "Anyway, pop stars aside, I've got a shit job for you today," he said apologetically, grimacing slightly. "Some absolute jobsworth in tech wants us to inventory the store room and move some stuff upstairs to the suites and move some other stuff back downstairs to storage."

"Well, thank God for elevators, eh?" I replied with a smile, even if it was a bit forced. Storage was... probably going to be featured on an episode of Hoarders any day.

Jeremy huffed out a laugh. "Heh, yeah. Come on, let me get you started and show you what I'm talking about." He pushed himself out of his chair and together we made our way down the stairs to the ground floor and to the storage room.

Twenty minutes later, and I had already taken off my plaid shirt and wrapped it around my waist. Yeah, it was going to be one of those days. Spectacular.

2 hours later

I was covered in dust. I was hot and my fingers ached from lifting boxes. I huffed out a breath to blow hair out of my face as I stood there in the middle of the room, assessing the situation and re-assessing my life choices. I looked at my watch. Just after 10:00. Surely, I can get away with having a quick break?

I'll just take up one more box and then I'll go get a drink, I reasoned with myself. It would also give me an excuse to scope out the suites. I didn't think he'd arrived yet, but you never know.

With a sigh, I picked up a clear, plastic box full of cables that had been designated to the recording suites on the second floor and awkwardly opened the door leading out to the lobby. Blessedly, it was cooler out here and I took a moment to breathe it in. It was also nice and bright, making me feel less of a cave troll living in my dark, cramped, hot, storage cupboard.

The elevators were on the other side of the large reception, and I headed towards it. Fuck, this box was heavy.

Just then, the front doors slid open, allowing in the noise of traffic and mid-morning chaos from the street. I slowed my steps as I immediately spotted Trevor Kyle, the producer with the golden touch and the grabby hands. He was with Celine, the Booking manager. There was a very tall man with them who was hard not to spot. He had close-cropped black hair and was wearing a black suit jacket and blue jeans. He was holding his arm out towards the door.

And that's when I saw him. *Him.*

"Ooft!" My vision blanked for a split second as pain radiated from my left hip and my body jolted, bending nearly double over the metal bollard I hadn't seen before crashing into it, knocking loose my grip on the box I was carrying. To my horror, it crashed to the ground with a noise not unlike a car crashing into a wall.

I froze. No. No, please God, no. I closed my eyes and took a deep breath in through my nose, trying to ignore the pain throbbing in my hip. I opened my eyes and saw, to my increasing mortification, that the entire group had paused and was facing in my direction.

Celine let out a high-pitched sort of laugh that sounded more like a horse whinnying than a normal, human laugh. "Whoops," I heard her say, even though they were still some distance from me.

I tried to bring myself to look towards the middle of the group. I just couldn't.

Mortified, I dropped to one knee and hurriedly began to scrape the fallen cables across the shiny, marble-effect floor towards me, grabbing at them and stuffing them back in the box in whatever order I was able to grab them.

So focused was I on the fallen piles of cables that I didn't notice *him* until *his* hand was mere inches from my own. Long, pale fingers with several rings began to reach for the same cables I was frantically trying to grab. Startled, I looked up and was immediately stunned, frozen mid-movement.

People say that all the time, don't they? That they were lost for words, or stunned into silence, and it always sounds like such nonsense. But it's true. I literally froze as a remarkably kind pair of dark eyes met my own. He'd been wearing a black face mask, so commonly worn in Asia, but a bit jarring in the US. He'd pulled it down under his chin. I could still see the faint pink lines on his cheeks where it had cut in slightly. I don't know how long we stayed like that. It can't have been more than a few seconds before another man dropped down to the floor beside us. The spell was broken.

"Gwaenchanhayo?" The tall man directed this at *him*, not me, brow furrowed.

He nodded and put the cable he'd been holding in the box. With a moment's hesitation, the tall man – the bodyguard, maybe – began grabbing fallen cables. Suddenly regaining my senses and my ability to move, I waved my hands and said, "Oh, no, please, you don't have-" I broke off in a hiss, placing a hand on my hip, the pain taking me by surprise.

He reached towards me and gently took the cable out of my hands.

"Are you okay?" His voice was accented and quiet. I could barely meet his eyes. I was painfully aware of how mortified I was, desperate not to embarrass myself further.

I nodded. "Yes, thank you. I'm so sorry." My voice was barely a whisper. I'm sure my face said it all. He waved it away and together, all three of us managed to put all the fallen cables back into the box. I pulled my knee off the floor and reached for the box to pick it up.

He gently pushed my hands away and picked up the box, standing up with it. The tall man – his bodyguard, I decided – made an unhappy noise and tried to pull it out of his hands.

"Naneun geugeos-eul gajigoissda," *he* muttered to the big man, straightening up.

"Please," *he* said to me, "I will help you."

Self-consciously, I pushed my hair out of my eyes and took a calming breath, internally trying my damnedest not to freak the fuck out.

"O-ok, thank you," I stammered. We crossed the room together and the group waiting by the front doors met us halfway. Trevor looked amused. Celine looked like she was chewing a bee. There was a new man there now; a shorter, dark-haired man wearing fashionably thick-framed glasses.

"Where does this go?" *He* turned to me and said.

I had to push past the brain fog to find an answer in an appropriate amount of time. "Oh, um, 2nd floor. I think we're going to the same place." I even managed a smile. God, I hope I didn't look too deranged.

He smiled and nodded but also looked over to the shorter man who said something to him in Korean. *He* nodded again, making a sound of understanding.

"Shall we?" said Trevor Kyle, holding out his arm and we all started moving towards the bank of elevators.

We all piled in. Blessedly, these elevators are big enough to accommodate large groups and heavy, bulky equipment, so we got on comfortably enough. I don't know how it happened, but I was somehow positioned against the far-right wall and *he* was stood next to me. He was several inches taller than me and was so close I could feel his body heat.

The doors closed and no one spoke. It was only one floor, but it felt twice the normal ride time. When the doors finally opened, *he* looked at me and motioned with his head that I should get off before him. I complied, following behind Trevor Kyle, who was now in conversation with the shorter man.

I stood to the side while *he* and the bodyguard got out of the elevator. He looked around from side to side and lifted the box in his arms.

"Where do I put this?" he asked, smiling at me slightly. I shook myself and reached forward to take it out of his arms, but he angled his body to stop me.

"No," he said firmly. "I have it. Where?" he asked again. He held my gaze, and I unconsciously bit my lip. I saw his eyes flick down briefly before meeting my eyes again.

"Um, r-room two" I forced out, holding my arm out and indicating the door to the left of the elevator two doors up the hallway. He walked towards the room I'd indicated and I had to take two steps to one of his long strides to catch up. I opened the door as he reached it and gestured to the floor where there were already several boxes piled up haphazardly.

"Anywhere is fine," I said. He complied, squatting to place it far more gently on the floor than I would have done.

I felt like I should look away when he put the box down. I absolutely did not. But I did make sure my eyes were at the ceiling when he rose to his full height again.

"Thank you," I said, my voice unusually breathy.

He waved his hand and said, "No problem." His voice was... it was unreal. It was so familiar and yet completely and utterly new.

His eyes were hypnotic. Part of me knew I should look away, leave, whatever, but I literally could not.

With a moment that felt like the air rushing back into the room, he took a half step forward and extended his hand. "Hello, I'm Baek Jihoon, nice to meet you." It sounded practiced; it rolled off his tongue far easier than anything else he'd said so far.

Thankfully, my muscle-memory seemed to be intact and on impulse, I wiped my hand on the back of my jeans before reaching forward to clasp his outstretched hand. His hand was warm, his rings hard against my skin, and I prayed to whoever was listening that my palm wasn't damp. He held my hand gently, but firmly. He smiled that famous smile and I couldn't help but mirror his expression, a contagious reaction. Hopefully it was a normal person smile and not a frantic, star-struck leer. Judging by his reaction, I guessed it was a normal smile.

"Kaiya," I breathed. He cocked his head to the side, his eyes assessing my face. I knew what he was noticing for the first time. People didn't tend to notice until I introduced myself.

He held my hand for what felt like a longer time than was strictly usual, but it could just be that my internal clock had stopped. Sooner than I'd have liked, he let go and took a half-step back.

"Thank you again, for the help, "I said, gesturing at the box.

He shrugged and smiled. "No problem."

"Jihoon, you good?" Trevor Kyle poked his head round the door and for the first time, I noticed that the tall, beefy-looking man was standing there. Had he been there the whole time? You'd have thought I'd have noticed – the man was not subtle.

"Yes," Jihoon said and walked towards the door, following Trevor out. He turned back once and held up a hand. "See you," he said. I waved back.

Fuck I hope so, I thought to myself as I slumped against the wall, equally terrified that I actually might.

Chapter 4

Not long later.

"Y ou're laughing at me," I accused, holding my injured hip with one hand and propping my fist on the other.

Becka arranged her face to look as contrite as possible, but then immediately ruined it, her face crumpling as she snorted like the undignified arsehole she is.

Crossly, I kicked her desk, rattling the aesthetically coloured cup of pens she had pleasingly arranged.

"I'm sorry, I'm sorry," she gasped, holding up a hand to wave me off. Huffing, I threw myself into the chair opposite her desk and immediately regretted it as it twinged my hip.

"Clean yourself up, you're a disgrace," I groused at her, chucking a packet of tissues at her that I pinched from on top of her desk. She plucked them out of the air easily enough before they hit her in the face.

She made several more 'hmm-hmm' sounds as she took a tissue and delicately wiped it under her eyes, her shoulders shaking every so often. Just as I think she's done; she looked over at me and started all over again.

"Literally, go jump out the window," I rolled my eyes at her at her, crossing my arms over my chest.

"I'm sorry," she gasped, wiping a tear off her cheek with the tissue, "It's just so *you*. You're such a fucking mess."

I held up my middle finger in response.

Eventually though, Becka settled. I wasn't actually mad. I mean; to be fair, I am an absolute mess. It really does go without saying, and had Becka righteously embarrassed herself in front of, say, Liam Hemsworth, I would be equally inconsolable.

"Okay, but in all seriousness," Becka said, clearing her throat, "are you actually alright? Those barriers are solid." I leaned backwards in the chair and pulled aside my clothes slightly to reveal where I'd smacked the crap out of my hip. Becka hissed and winced in sympathy. It was a reddish splotch right now, but it would bruise up nicely later.

"I'm fine, just mortally embarrassed."

Becka leaned back in her chair, lifting her steaming mug to her lips. It would be some herbal concoction that she swore didn't taste like compost, but totally did taste like compost. She only had one cup of coffee per day. I couldn't relate, I practically swam in coffee.

"Tell me what happened next," she prompted, "describe the entire scene. Was TK an absolute ass?" We abbreviated names when we were in semi-public like this, although there were only two other people in the vicinity and honestly, they'd probably agree that Trevor Kyle was an absolute ass.

I recounted the entire interaction, including Celine's face.

"That woman badly needs to get laid," Becka interrupted. I continued and ended with how sweet *he* had been to help me with the box into studio 2.

"We stan a respectful king," she said approvingly, and I nodded.

"So," Becka leaned forward conspiratorially, prompting me to copy her. Together we were basically leaning over the desk. I could smell her hot drink. Peppermint. Vile.

"How did he smell?" She leered at me, but I could only blink in confusion.

"I-I have no idea," I confessed sheepishly.

"You mean to tell me that you were that close – nay – you touched the idol you've been crushing on for decades-" I rolled my eyes at her gross exaggeration, "and you didn't take the opportunity to smell the guy?"

I raised my eyebrows at her. "Just what, exactly, did you guys talk about in those Savage Garden fan groups?"

Becka waved my question away. "Pssh, the 90s were a lawless time. Don't change the subject."

"You are the oldest young person I've ever met," I accused. She blew me a kiss.

"Oh, heads up," she said and nodded her head in the direction of the corridor behind us. Turning quickly in my seat, I saw Jeremy emerge from the Ops corridor and head towards the elevators.

"Oops, better dash," I hissed, getting up and out of the chair as discreetly as I could.

"Come back up here at lunch, I may have a job for you," Becka said, winking at me in such a way that my heart lurched uncomfortably. My mind couldn't help immediately wondering what Becka would 'need' me to do, but given the look on her face, it didn't take a huge leap to assume it was something to do with 'the idol'. But I couldn't allow myself the leisure of speculation, given the current urgency of beating Jeremy downstairs.

"I both love and hate you," I hissed, throwing a look over my shoulder.

"Quite right." She laughed quietly as I slipped out of the room and army-ran towards the stairs.

I managed to beat the lift down the stairs, nearly breaking my neck in the process, and met Jeremy in the lobby. He'd come to check up on me and point out some more tasks for me. It was mindless work, but I figured it counted towards my step goal for the day and so I didn't mind it too much.

I especially didn't mind that most of my trips took me past Studio 3, which is where *he* was.

On every pass, I walked extra slow – on account of the heavy box I was carrying, of course – so I could glimpse in the porthole-style window. No sound made its way out into the corridor, except for the occasional few bars of a beat or backing track. From what I'd been able to see, *he* wasn't in the booth yet. He seemed to be talking to the producer – Trevor Kyle.

Every time I walked past, I could only see the top of his head, he was sitting in a chair facing away from the window. The manager and tall man (gotta be a bodyguard, the man is built like a standing-up submarine) were sitting on one of the sofas against the far-left wall.

I may or may not have walked past studio 3 a good dozen times, but I'd down-play it if ever asked.

Lunchtime

As Becka had cryptically requested, I made my way back up to her office when lunchtime rolled around. I stood in front of her desk, arms crossed, tapping my foot on the floor, but it was more to do with nerves than annoyance.

"You rang?" I sassed. Becka scoffed.

"I need you to go down to reception and get the Uber Eats delivery that should be arriving in a few minutes," she said.

I frowned. "Can't you get one of the reception girls to bring it up?" That's normally what she did, when she ordered in.

"Trust me, babes, you want to get this order."

I unfolded my arms and instead put my hands on my hips.

"Ok, you've got my attention."

"And then I need you to deliver it to Studio 3". She grinned at me. She knew what she was doing.

"*His* studio?" I cleared my throat.

Becka laughed at me. "You haven't said his name even once, have you? I noticed it when you were telling me the story this morning." I narrowed my eyes at her and pursed my lips.

"*Jihoon.*" I forced out, but despite my best effort, I could feel my face and neck grow hot. That didn't stop Becka from laughing at me again.

"Yes well, *he*, his team, and TK need to eat, so..." she made a shooing gesture with her hand as she turned back to her laptop, "off you pop."

"I love and hate you in equal measure," I hissed, but grinned. She didn't look back up at me as she blew me a kiss.

I walked towards the elevator, but decided to take the stairs instead, to work off the nervous energy coursing through me. I had to play it cool, I decided. Aloof. Like it was no big deal. Only cool cucumbers here. I repeated this mantra the whole way down to the reception.

By the time I'd opened the door to the airy lobby, I had almost convinced myself that I was capable of being as cool as I told myself I was going to be.

The receptionist was sat at the imposing desk, but she was on the phone, talking into her headset and paying absolutely no attention to me.

"Um, I'm here to take this-" I gestured at the multiple bags and boxes stacked up on the counter, the tell-tale symbol of the restaurant stamped all over them, but she impatiently waved me off, not bothering to look at me.

I shrugged and began to artfully weave my arms through the bag handles and carefully balance the boxes within the cradle of my arms. I considered myself something of a master at this, from years of practice of refusing to make more than one trip from the car to the front door with all the shopping. Mama didn't raise no two-trip chump.

I'd just arranged myself to my satisfaction and was making my way over to the elevator when – "You, stop!" A voice stopped me in my tracks. Annoyed, I turned back to the reception desk, my arms aching with being so overburdened.

"You can't take it up like that!" The receptionist looked scandalised. She was a well-coiffed woman in her mid-40s and I'd seen her telling off a senior sound tech for stomping muddy boots across the lobby floor, so she clearly gave zero fucks about any kind of chain-of-command in this building. Not that I counted as anything higher than, say, plankton.

I just looked at her dumbly. "Um..." I trailed off. The receptionist... Rhonda? Shonda? Belinda? She tutted at me... Loudly.

"Come back here and take the hospitality cart. Were you planning on slapping an armload of take-out bags down in front of a client?" The look she gave me rather implied this was a grave offense, similar to, say, murder.

Quickly, I walked back over to the big desk and unceremoniously dumped the bags on the countertop, trying to ignore the look she gave me. She imperiously threw a thumb over her shoulder to where I could see a two-tier, wheeled cart pushed up against the wall. I rushed round to grab it and then unbagged the containers, bowls and boxes. Luckily, the take-out place had supplied utensils. I turned back to thank the receptionist and was able to see her name tag.

Donna. Damn, I wasn't even close.

"Thanks, Donna." I shot her a grin, which she did not return as she was already on another call.

A couple of minutes later, I was approaching the door to Studio 3 and I could feel all the blood had drained from my face. My hands as well, judging by how suddenly cold they were. I was really committing to this whole, 'cool as a cucumber', thing.

I looked in at the porthole window to make sure I wasn't about to interrupt anything ground-breaking. Trevor Kyle was fiddling with the soundboard and wearing headphones. I could see everyone else was seated around the room, either on their phones or chatting idly.

I took a deep breath. And knocked.

Fuck me, *he* looked up. We locked eyes and he smiled. Quickly, I ducked my head down and puffed out a breath before I forgot to breathe. Looking back up, I could see Trevor Kyle hadn't moved. I felt conflicted about if I should just go in, or not.

Just to be sure, I knocked again. Still nothing, he must not be able to hear me. I bit my lip, looking down at the cart, heart hammering with my unease.

Just then, the door opened, taking the decision out of my hands.

There he stood, framed in the doorway and so close to me that had he been anyone else, I would have instinctively taken a step back. As it was, it was the weirdest sensation – I felt a pull to step forward, like we were opposite magnets suspended in motion.

"Hi," he said, smiling down at me. He'd taken his mask and hat off and it was almost too much to have the full effect of his startling beauty mere inches from me.

Luckily, I remembered to act like a normal person. "Hi," I said, my voice breathy, "I hope I'm not interrupting. I have lunch," I said, gesturing down at the trolley. He looked down to where I was holding the trolley with one hand.

"Ah," he said and poked his head back into the room and said something in Korean. Not waiting for a response, he opened the door all the way and waved his arm, indicating I should come in. I was hyper aware of every part of my body as I walked past where he stretched out an arm to hold the door open. It honestly felt as though I was straining towards him, seeking out more of the body heat that radiated from him, even through his t-shirt and jacket. And when I moved past the immediate vicinity of his body, I still felt pulled towards where I just knew he stood behind me. It was the strangest sensation.

The manager stood up as I got to the large, dark wood table that went along the length of the back of the room. He bowed to me slightly and smiled and on instinct I copied the gesture, my hair falling in front of my face as my body dipped. God, I hope I did that right.

Hurriedly, I began to pile the dishes onto the table.

In a mirror-like move from that morning, I looked down at the table, focused on my task when a pair of pale, be-ringed hands came into view and started to help. I looked up briefly, only to meet *his* gaze. Now his whole face was exposed; the effect was off balancing. He looked so kind and open; it was almost like we were friends, or at least acquaintances, as opposed to the total strangers we actually were.

I tried to mentally rein myself in. It was probably just because his face was so familiar to me.

We both reached for the utensils at the same time, our fingers clashing, knocking the pot over. We laughed awkwardly, muttering apologies in a mix of Korean and English.

But eventually it was all on the table and there was no reason for me to still be there.

"Ok, well, um, enjoy!" I closed my eyes briefly, mortified at how ridiculous I sounded, and I scurried back across the room. My hand was on the handle of the door before he spoke. "Thank you, Kaiya."

I turned around and he smiled at me, inclining his head slightly. I mirrored the gesture and grinned, stupidly, probably like an idiot, but completely genuinely.

He said my name.

Chapter 5

He said my name. Baek Jihoon said my name.

I kept repeating this mantra over and over again in my head as I floated happily around the building.

And he was so *nice!* I mean, I hadn't thought he'd be horrible or anything, but having it confirmed that he was actually just a nice guy was... hell if it wasn't some kind of relief. It made him more of a real person and less of an 'idol'.

My pace eventually slowed back to a normal, less frantic speed and I began to wonder what he was doing here. I hadn't heard of any collaborations, normally they tease them weeks – if not months in advance. Maybe he was working on something solo.

For the rest of the day, I tried to carry on as normal, I really did. I caught up with Jeremy once I was done bringing all the boxes upstairs, I checked in with Becka to let them know Studio 3 had their food. She tried to press me for details, but I fobbed her off with the excuse that I had to get back to work – which was true, but didn't normally stop me. I hadn't wanted to gossip about this. It felt weird, somehow.

I wanted to keep the experience to myself, for as long as possible.

The last thing that Jeremy had me do that day was construct a drum set in Studio 1. I thought he was joking.

"I don't know how to do that," I told him flatly. We'd moved past the point of sugar-coating in our relationship. I'd learned early on with Jeremy that he had no time or patience for people to blow smoke up his ass.

So now, if I didn't know something, I didn't waste his time trying to botch my way through it, I just came out and told him.

Today he just sighed and handed me a manual.

"This should be Tech's job," he grumbled, "but it turns out their union is considering a strike." He looked more tired with every word he said.

"That explains why they've not been around much this week." I said, nodding my head in understanding.

"Yeah, hence why this is now our problem. It's not just drums either," he said darkly. "It's never just drums."

Honestly, he looked kind of murderous so I decided to just roll with it in the spirit of our good relationship and that despite the copious amount of donkey-work, I really did love working here.

"You can count on me, boss. Consider the snares snared, the drums mounted and the cymbals... whatever it is the cymbals do." I cheerfully saluted him, which earned me a ceiling-high eye roll and some under-the-breath mutterings as Jeremy walked away. Something about 'funny Brits'.

I wasn't nearly so cheerful about an hour later as I stood in the middle of Studio 1's booth surrounded by various bits of drum kit, including the screws and clamps. I'd tried to arrange all the parts on the floor in an order that would reflect their construction and instead ended up standing in the middle of what a drum kit would look like once it's gone through a wood chipper. I dragged my hand down my face.

"Well, fuck," I said to the empty room. "I wildly overestimated my ability to follow a manual."

In despair, I flopped down onto the ground. Bending my leg up, I leaned my elbow on my knee and rested my forehead into my hand. I sat there for a while, contemplating my life choices until I heard a door down the corridor open, followed by a stream of voices, laughing, and talking. The party passed by my room when I realised I'd left the door partially open.

A moment later there was a light tap at the door. I looked up in surprise and... there he was.

Because of course he was.

Baek Jihoon was standing in the doorway, witness to my complete failure at the IKEA of percussion.

"Are you okay, Kaiya?" I still could not believe he knew my name.

"Oh, hello." The words fell out of my mouth on blessed instinct as I mentally flailed for a second. "Yeah, just... you know. Trying to build a drum set." And then I laughed. Laughed! I might have gone mad for a second there. I rubbed a hand down my face tiredly.

"Can I help?" Snapping my eyes back to his face, I was surprised to see that he'd stepped fully into the room, and though he had his hands in his pockets, he looked genuine as he assessed the parts around me.

"Oh!" I puffed out a breath. "I'm not sure..." I trailed off as his manager appeared in the door. He said something to Jihoon in Korean. I had no idea what, but I did make out 'Hard Rock' in the mix, which, unless Jihoon was experimenting with music genres, I guessed meant they were going to the Hard Rock Café for dinner. I mean, when in LA...

Jihoon waved him off, replying in Korean and holding up both hands in the universal sign for '10 minutes'. The manager looked disapproving but left. I heard the group in the corridor start talking again before the elevator doors opened with a chime and then closed again, taking the sound of voices with it. I watched the whole interaction with interest, intrigued at Jihoon dismissing his manager. I'd always kind of assumed the power-dynamic in idol groups was the other way around, but then, GVibes had become wildly successful in recent years. Maybe that changed things.

And that's when he took off his coat. I felt my mouth drop open the same moment I wondered if I'd lost total control of my face.

Thankfully, I managed to snap my jaw closed just before his eyes landed back on me after he'd laid his coat on the back of a chair.

It's not that he was wearing anything particularly extraordinary, just an oversized, plain, white t-shirt and black jeans. Maybe it was seeing his arms in real life? They were very nice arms, I mused.

"Can I see?" he said quietly, holding his hand out for the manual I'd flung irreverently at my feet.

"Oh, sure!" I grabbed for it and passed it to him. His brow furrowed as he looked over it.

Huh. He was reading the manual. I kind of got the impression he'd just sort of dive in and figure it out. But when I'm wrong, I'm wrong.

He read those dog-eared pages with the kind of intensity reserved for life-or-death situations.

"Okay," he announced before stepping over the line of nuts and bolts and dropping down into a squat next to me in the centre of the anatomy of a would-be drum kit.

His immediate proximity made me lose my balance, my arm slipping off my knee and I veered comically to the side, fully prepared to accept my fate as I fell.

Until, I stopped.

Jihoon had a hand on each of my biceps, steadying me. He ducked his head down to look me in the eyes, a move straight out of every good K-drama.

"Are you okay?" He asked, and I could only nod. His hands were wrapped gently around the bare skin of my biceps, the sleeves of my white t-shirt rode high, almost to my shoulders. Immediately I felt my skin prickle with goosebumps. He was so close that I finally got to see what he smelt like. I mean, obviously I'd gone mad by this point, so hell, why not double down?

I leaned forward slightly, so slightly that it could be passed off as re-centring myself, but I was actually trying to see what he smelt like. It was nothing strong. He just smelled like laundry. Clean.

I wondered if my double-team of perfumes could still be smelt. To be honest, I'd just settle for not smelling like I'd spent the whole day humping boxes up and down the damn building.

Mentally, I gave myself a shake and leaned back slightly to be able to look him in the eyes. I forced a smile onto my face and said, "Thanks. I guess I'm a bit tired."

He smiled back at me and nodded before taking his hands off my arms. I immediately missed the gentle warmth of his hands wrapped around me.

"I don't know where to start," I admitted, waving a hand around.

He nodded again, frowning slightly. "Okay, let's try." He said, grabbing a long, metal pole and one of the clamps I'd so carefully laid out and grouped.

I just watched in wonder as he built the whole damn thing. Under his careful directions, I passed him parts and held things as he screwed things together, or threaded things on other things and when he finally set the biggest cymbals at the top of their respective stands and tightened the clamp that held them at the desired angle, I couldn't help but whistle in admiration.

He looked up at me and grinned shyly.

"Do you build a lot of drum kits?" I asked, laughing quietly.

He waved his hand from side to side. "One or two," he answered.

"Wow." I wasn't faking how impressed I was. "Do you play?"

He shook his head. "A little," he said.

"Uh huh," I said, as a mischievous notion occurred to me.

I picked up the sticks from where I'd left them on a chair and held them in front of him.

He looked up, first at the sticks in my outstretched hand and then to my face. I raised an eyebrow and smirked. He huffed out a little laugh, looking away for a moment before taking them from my hand.

He sat down on the little stool, adjusting a few things here and there. He raised the sticks, looking at me out of the corner of his eyes and smiled in an embarrassed sort of way. I giggled.

Giggled. For fuck's sake.

He played what I'm sure is a basic, scales-like rhythm, but to me it looked and sounded like proper playing.

His hair flew around his face slightly as his body moved with each hit, his knee bouncing as his foot worked the bass drum.

He finished with a flourish and looked down at his feet like he was embarrassed. I clapped enthusiastically, my reward that full beam smile that made my heart lurch.

"Bravo," I said softly, stuffing my hands in my pockets.

"Thank you," he said shyly as he got to his feet.

In the aftermath of the loud drums and clash of the cymbals, the air in the room felt like it was vibrating in the silence that followed and I suddenly became aware again of the magnetic pull that seemed to grow in the space between where we both stood. It felt like all the hairs on my arms were standing up, like the air before a thunderstorm. Charged.

I bit my bottom lip. I couldn't help it and even less so when I noticed his eyes flick down to my mouth. Oh, holy hell.

I watched the bob of his throat as he swallowed, which only brought my attention to the slight V of his shirt as it sat against his collar bones.

This didn't feel like fan-girling. I'd fan-girled before when I'd met other celebrities whilst working here. Those times had felt like the bubbles in a soft-drink, crackly and brief and enough sugar to make you giddy for a time. This felt like the burn you got from drinking whiskey; heavy and deep as it warmed you from the inside out.

I felt like I wanted to reach forward and only my deeply ingrained propriety stilled my hand.

The moment was broken when a door down the corridor slammed shut, the sound like a crack in the silence of the room. He jumped slightly and I laughed to hide my embarrassment.

"Well, I don't have any more drum kits to construct." And then I obviously blacked out for a second because I could have sworn I heard him mutter, "shame".

But, because the universe has a sense of humour, that was the moment that the (in)famous Trevor Kyle decided to stick his head round the door.

He jerked when he saw Jihoon, obviously surprised to see him in here. I unconsciously took a step back, studiously not seeing the way Jihoon tilted his head in my direction.

"Jihoon, you're still here?" Trevor asked, a smile plastered on his face like wallpaper.

"Come, let me escort you downstairs." He said all this with that smile, but the way he pushed the door open wider and held out his arm said very clearly this was not a suggestion.

Jihoon walked towards the door and grabbed his coat off the chair on his way. Trevor Kyle slid his eyes over to me and stared. The expression that passed over his face as his eyes skimmed over me made me uneasy. Like he was seeing me for the first time.

When Jihoon got to the door, he turned back to me and said, "Goodbye, Kaiya. That was fun."

And to my surprise, I realised it HAD been fun.

Chapter 6

Friday

"Another day, another groupie-fashion choice." Becka laughed at me as I met her at the kitchen counter.

"Oh hush," I countered, "I literally moved to America with one duffel bag, I'm doing the best I can." I said this defensively but knowing her jibe was in jest. I thought I looked cute today in my artfully ripped black jeans, hi-top black Vans, a dark grey t-shirt and my black leather jacket.

Cute, if a little monotone, I supposed.

"Yes, very student-chic," she joked, sliding her sunglasses on top of her wavy, blonde hair.

"I was literally a student less than a year ago. The transition has been a struggle," I said dramatically, picking up my travel mug and my rucksack.

"No more lecture-naps," Becka sighed.

"No more student discounts," I lamented.

"No more one-dollar shots." She held the door open for me.

"Or one-pound shots." I corrected, walking past her into the corridor.

"Which one is more expensive?"

I took a moment to think as we descended the stairs.

"British shots. You yanks get more bang for your buck."

"Depends how many shots you take," she said, wiggling her eyebrows at me before sliding her sunglasses down over her eyes as we pushed open the door to the street, emerging into the bright sunlight of a typical, spring morning in LA.

"No Uber this morning?" Becka asked, hopefully looking up and down the already congested streets.

"Not unless you got a raise I don't know about," I said as I began walking down the street.

"Hey!" she called, easily catching up to me. She had several inches on me since her legs were longer. "Some people might consider yesterday's lunchtime favour an incentive to reciprocate with comfortable travel." She grinned at me, but my only response was to sling my arm around her and begin propelling her down the street.

"I'm going to smell like a gas station," Becka whinged as I pushed her forcefully towards the bus stop.

"Better than surviving off crackers and twice-used tea-bags," I pointed out.

Becka groaned loud enough that the people already waiting at the bus stop turned to look.

08:50

Jeremy heaved a soul-deep sigh the moment I raised my hand to knock on his door.

"I could have been anyone, you know. I could have been Trevor Kyle, or Scarlett Johannson," I said, crossing my arms over my chest.

Jeremy didn't even look up; he just pointed his pen at the clock on the wall behind his desk.

"Punctuality is not a crime," I pointed out.

"Nope, but you and I must have fucked up in a past life to get the brunt of it this week." He said, throwing his pen down on his desk and dragging both hands down his face.

"Boss, it is way too early to be this cheerful, you need to calm down." I joked, earning me the drollest of droll looks.

"I got an email this morning at fucking 5 o'clock to say that Tech are striking and won't be in. Indefinitely."

"Oh, bugger," I stated. He huffed.

"Yeah, 'bugger'." His approximation of my British accent was poor, but given the givens, I'd allow it.

"So, what's the plan?" I asked.

"Let's just hope you really enjoyed your day fucking around with shit from storage yesterday." He dead-panned.

My fingers twitched in remembered pain at the memory.

Half an hour later and I was headed back up to the studios with another box. This one was filled with boxes and cases of microphones and their various heads and pop shields.

The second floor corridor was quiet and dark. There were no external windows on this level and with the lighting being sensor activated, it could be quite spooky wandering around here on your own.

The only light on in the corridor currently came from the small lamp that hung over the sound deck in Studio 2, where I was headed with this box of mics and where I'd already moved to the sides all the boxes I'd moved up here yesterday.

I pushed the partially-open door further open with my shoulder, humming happily to myself, already thinking about my next coffee.

I'd just dumped the box on the floor when the massive producer's chair swung around –

"Oh, fuck!" I exclaimed loudly, clutching my chest in fright.

"Sorry, sorry!" Insisted a voice I knew so well and yet was still brand new to me.

Jihoon jumped up out of the chair so quickly that it pushed back against the producer's sound deck, making the whole thing shudder.

He held out both hands in a placating manner and looked so contrite that I couldn't help but smile, even though my heart still thudded against my ribs like an Acme cartoon character's.

"It's cool, no worries." I tried to wave away his apologies, still rubbing my chest.

"You just took me by surprise. I didn't see you there." I ran a hand through my hair, pushing it out of my eyes.

"It is very dark in here," he agreed.

"Do you need anything?" I asked, poking my head out into the corridor. No sign of anyone.

"Ah, no," He admitted, fiddling with the phone in his hands. "It was quiet here. I was taking some time. It's very busy in the studio." He looked embarrassed, for some reason. I think I understood.

"Have you been recording all morning?" I asked, giving him what I hoped was a sympathetic look.

He grimaced and nodded. "Yes," he said.

'I should not do this' was the thought I immediately steamrolled as I then said, "Would you like to hide in here for a while? I mean, if you don't mind me working in here, but I won't get in your way or anything. I'll just be here, quietly, sorting a bunch of stuff out..." I trailed off, thoroughly self-conscious of my inability to filter my words on the journey from brain to mouth. I bit my lip as my face heated to fever levels. Thankfully, it was dark in here.

"Is it okay that I'm here?" he asked quietly, putting his phone in his trouser pocket.

I fiddled with the edge of my shirt. "It's okay with me," I said, shrugging. "Won't someone come to find you? Your manager, or...?-"

"No," he said firmly. "I said I needed time. He'll let me be alone." Jihoon looked down for a moment and huffed a little laugh, "For a while."

I guess even international superstars have a short leash.

Chapter 7

"Ok, cool. Well, don't mind me, I'll just crack on." I smiled as I indicated the boxes of stuff all around the room. He flashed me the universal hand gesture for 'okay'.

With as much grace as I had – scant – I sat down on the floor cross-legged and pulled the nearest box towards me. The cursed box of cables I sported a mottled blue bruise on my hip for, which I now had the arduous task of winding properly and tagging with the right colour zip tie so its purpose was immediately identifiable.

Certified donkey work.

I almost wasn't surprised when Jihoon sat down in front of me, on the other side of the plastic box, although he did so far more gracefully than I had, folding in on himself like origami.

"Can I help?" he asked, quietly.

I looked at him for a moment, cocking my head to the side. He was so different to all the media I'd ever seen of him. He was clearly bare-skinned. I could see the scars on his face and his eyes, while dark and earnest, were normal. No contacts, no liner. For some reason, it made me feel more at ease around him.

"You don't have to," I said, my voice making it quite clear – I hoped – that he didn't need to feel obligated to help just because he was sharing the same space as me.

"I know," he said, "I want to. It's... normal." And I think I got it.

"Alright then," I conceded, "we need to sort these cables by type." I grabbed a handful to show him.

"TRS cable," I laid it next to the green zip ties. "Speakon cables," went next to the red zip ties. "Banana plug-"

"Yellow?" he interrupted me, forcing me to look up at him in surprise. He was grinning and I laughed.

"Ha, yeah, exactly. Now you're getting it." We shared a companionable smile. He watched how I looped the cables around my elbow and hand to form a neat loop before I tied it off with the correct colour, before he picked up a speakon cable and copied the loop and tied it off with a red zip tie.

"Perfect," I said, nodding approvingly. He nodded back and that was that.

We went through the box, identifying, looping and tying the cables in silence, only broken by the occasional check-in from Jihoon; "This one?"

"RCA, pink."

And then we'd fall into silence again.

It was... nice. His presence was calming, now that I'd gotten used to it. He was a real person after all. I smiled as the thought crossed my mind. I saw his eyes flick up to my face, although he said nothing.

At about 9:30, his manager came by. He said something to Jihoon in Korean and Jihoon answered, barely looking up, before the manager went away again.

I looked at the door in confusion. I'd expected him to pull Jihoon away.

At my quizzical look, he said, "Ah, the producer, he is still working. I am not needed just now." I made an 'ah' sort of noise.

"Is that your manager?" I asked, nodding my head towards the door. Jihoon looked up at the door before looking back to me.

"Yes. Youngsoo."

"Youngsoo," I repeated, trying to make sure I got the inflection right.

"You're English?" he asked. I guess the accent gave me away.

"Yes." I reached for a green zip tie.

"Where from?" he asked.

"London now, but originally, I'm from the North of England. A place called the Lake District."

Jihoon shook his head. "I don't know it."

"It's beautiful," I said wistfully, "full of mountains and rolling hills." Impulsively, I pulled my phone out of my pocket. "Can I show you?" Blame it on my nostalgia, but for some reason, I wanted to show him where I hailed from.

At his nod, I unlocked my phone and pulled up some pictures from Google. I turned my phone to show him.

"Wow," he exclaimed, "so pretty." He looked up at me with that smile I was beginning to live for. I grinned back.

"You're from Seoul, right?" I asked as I looped and tied the last cable.

He nodded enthusiastically. "You know Seoul?"

I winced, "Ah, no, sorry." That was literally the extent of my knowledge of his background.

He didn't seem to mind though as he whipped out his own phone and pulled up some pictures.

"Whoa, that's so dope!" I exclaimed as he proudly showed me pictures of Seoul lit up at night.

"Do you miss it?" I asked, looking up at him. He shrugged and ran a hand through his hair. He leaned back on his other arm, the very picture of casual.

"Sometimes," he admitted, "but we travel so much, we do so much. There's not much time to get... homesick," he said, finding the words.

I nodded, mirroring his pose and leaning back on my hands. "I get that," I said. Since moving to LA, I hadn't had time to miss home. I think it kind of helped that my time here had an expiry date on it, though. My contract only ran for a year, and after that my Visa expired. I'd been playing around with the idea of finding another job after Pisces. LA was growing on me.

"Knock, knock" said a gruff voice at the door, followed by someone actually booting the door, by the sound of it. A moment later, the door opened all the way, albeit a bit forcefully, and in the doorway stood Jeremy, his arms full of one, two, no three soft guitar cases.

"Special deliv...ery..." He trailed off as his eyes went from where I sat on the floor, to where Jihoon sat.

He froze for a moment before his grip seemed to slip and one of the cases lurched alarmingly downward. "Oo fuck," grunted Jeremy, trying to re-balance and hold it all.

Immediately, both Jihoon and I jumped to our feet and rushed towards him, each of us grabbing a guitar and catching the slipping one until Jeremy stood there, eyeballing us, his eyebrows so far into his hairline they may never come all the way back down. I turned around quickly to hide my grin and caught Jihoon with the same expression, leaning a case carefully against the wall.

Jeremy hadn't moved, he still had the same pose as if he was still holding three guitar cases.

"You okay there, boss?" I asked.

"Yeeeeah," he answered, slowly. "Do I uh, do I wanna..." he waved an arm vaguely in the direction of Jihoon. "Nope. No, I do not." He proclaimed, evidently finishing his own thought. "Those just arrived, obviously a couple days late, but whatever, what do I know," Jeremy grumbled, running a finger over his chin.

"Do they need tuning, as well?" I asked, hands on my hips.

"I'm tempted to tell you to sack it off, but..." he sighed.

"It's not worth the trouble?" I offered.

Jeremy threw his hands in the air. "You said it, kid." He turned on his heel and walked back out of the room. I only had a split second to look at Jihoon, before Jeremy stomped back in.

"Someone knows he's here, yeah?" He frowned at me, his mouth an unhappy pinch.

Jihoon stepped forward and held out his hand to a surprised Jeremy. "Yes sir, my management is aware."

"Well, yeah, alright then." Jeremy shook Jihoon's hand but narrowed his eyes as he looked between the two of us. "Just..." he trailed off and released his hand. "Nope. Nope, not even gonna start. Nope. Not my monkey, not my circus." He turned around and left again. We could hear him muttering all the way down the corridor until his stream of mutterings was cut off by the sound of the stairwell door slamming shut.

I looked at Jihoon. He looked at me. I pinched my lips together.

And then I snorted.

Fucking. Snorted.

I slapped my hand over my mouth and looked at Jihoon, my eyes so wide my eyebrows strained.

He burst out laughing. At me, with me, who even knew. And then we were both laughing. I mean, doubled-up, holding our stomachs, howling.

"Poor Jeremy," I said weakly, wiping tears off my cheeks. Yet another reason to be grateful I never bothered with much make-up – besides the fact that I had zero skills at applying it.

"He seems very stressed," Jihoon commented, still grinning.

"He's a busy lad," I agreed, walking over to where I'd placed one of the guitars.

Unzipping the soft case, I ran my fingers lightly over the strings before making a face of disgust. Completely out of tune.

I gently lifted it out and flipped it over in my hands. It was a Gibson Hummingbird, an acoustic with fantastic harmonics. I hummed in approval, running my hands gently down the finished wood.

"You play?"

"A bit," I said distractedly as I crossed the room and sat in the big, padded chair. I crossed one leg over the other, balancing the 'Bird and began to carefully turn the pegs, making sure to keep my hand away from the neck, only strumming here and there to check the sound.

Out of the corner of my eye, I noticed Jihoon had unzipped another guitar from its case. He pulled up another chair, not far away from mine, and began to fiddle with the tuning pegs.

Surprised, I looked up from my task to observe.

"You play?" I asked, mirroring his earlier words.

He flashed me a small smile and replied, "a bit."

"These strings are factory fresh," I muttered as one slipped beneath my hand.

"Yes." He replied, frowning.

But a couple of minutes and some tentative strumming later, we were done.

I strummed a few chords, just to make sure. The sound out of this thing was honestly such a treat, I couldn't help myself.

Smiling slyly, I looked up at Jihoon from underneath my lashes, waiting to see his reaction. I was a handful of bars in before he noticed and laughed.

"Broken Promise?" he asked, raising his eyebrows.

I looked back down at my fingers, tapping my foot in time with the beat I could hear in my head. "It's your song — you tell me." I quirked the corner of my lips in a half-smile.

"You asked me before," he said, his gaze shifting to the instrument in his hands, "if I ever get homesick. I do, but not for Seoul. I grew up in Busan." He paused, his fingers brushing over the strings. "I miss Busan. I wrote this song about what I thought my life was going to be — back when I lived there. Before I moved to Seoul. Before GVibes."

I froze mid-strum. I hadn't known he'd written 'Broken Promise,' much less the reason behind it. Hearing him talk about why he wrote it struck a chord deep within me. It felt like a parallel to my own feelings — those quiet, bittersweet aches I sometimes felt, when I let myself think too deeply.

Something shifted inside me, an unseen string between us.

I was so distracted that I didn't realize I'd started playing the intro over again until Jihoon slid his fingers up the strings.

He counted himself in by tapping his fingers on the body of the 'Bird before picking up the tune with me. He strummed for a bit and then started to quietly sing along, taking over all of the other vocal line parts and turning the solo into an acoustic performance.

The smile on my face was so wide, it almost hurt.

It wasn't to last.

We played our way through 'Broken Promise', 'Basket Case' by Green Day, and were half-way through the introduction to Metallica's 'Enter Sandman' when his manager, Youngsoo, came looking for him.

Jihoon knelt in front of my chair as he carefully put away the guitar, looking up at me to smile as he zipped up the bag.

Holy hell. Everyone always talks about dimples being this amazing feature and I never really cared for them, but when this boy in front of me smiled at me and I saw those dimples... my breath literally caught in my chest. I bit my lip. I knew I was doing it, just like I knew my eyelids lowered slightly at the same time. I know what this look on my face felt like.

The sight of Jihoon on his knees in front of me sent me somewhere and by the assessing look on his face, he knew it too. I tried to rein it in, but it was an effort.

After an eternity, he rose to his considerable full height. He placed the guitar carefully on the table against the far wall and moved to the door, where Youngsoo stood waiting, hopefully oblivious to the exchange we'd just had. Or, at least I'd had.

Jihoon put one hand on the door frame and turned back to look at me.

"Thank you for the fun," he said, smiling at me. It wasn't a small, shy smile, nor was it that big, famous smile. This was a different one altogether; it was one that made me tuck my leg tighter over the other and made my fingers clench around the neck of the guitar I held.

Holy hell.

Chapter 8

I didn't see Jihoon again for the rest of Friday. Work kept me running around all day, I didn't even have time to troll past Studio 3, hoping for a sneaky glance in through the port window.

Except for the very end of the day.

Becka and I were both late leaving.
Me, because I'd gone practically blind trying to make out the tiny writing on packs of switches.
Becka because she was on the phone arguing with someone from *The LA Sun*.
It had been well after 6:00 by the time we made our way across the lobby. The glass doors to Pisces are polarised, which is why I hadn't

seen the black SUV parked up at the kerb outside until the doors slid open as we approached.

Which is about the same moment Jihoon looked over his shoulder, standing in the open door of the SUV, about to climb in.

His bodyguard – Eun, I'd learned – and Youngsoo were standing on either side of him, effectively blocking him from being seen on either side of the sidewalk, but it was a clear visual between where he stood and where I emerged from Pisces.

For a whole moment, we locked eyes. He grinned at me and I raised a hand to give him a little wave and a shy smile.

Eun put a hand on his back and moved to stand further in front of the car door, blocking our line of sight as the car door was closed after Jihoon got in. Youngsoo glanced over at me, bowing ever so slightly before jogging around the car to get in the other side while Eun slid into the front passenger side.

"I saw that," Becka hissed at me as the SUV pulled away.

I pulled at the collar of my jacket. "You're imagining things," I replied, finding other things to look at, rather than her face.

She was quiet the whole way home, but if looks could talk, she would have been saying a whole hell of a lot.

Saturday

"You need a new hobby," Becka said from my doorway. I looked up from where I was sat cross-legged on my bed, a note book open across my lap.

"Why?" I asked defensively, "What's wrong with this?" I held up the notebook. Admittedly, the page was currently mostly empty.

"Nothing, normally." She said, leaning against the door frame, mug in hand. "But you've been sat like this all morning. Have you even moved?" She gave me a look that very clearly told me she disapproved of whatever it is she thought I was doing – which was sat on my unmade bed in my crumpled jammies, pretending to write lyrics while forlornly looking out the window that faced the brick wall of the building next to ours. Not a lot of inspiration to be found in that view.

"I got up to brush my teeth." I shrugged.

Becka rolled her eyes and made a 'uh huh' sound. "You know," she started, "most people would be super psyched after meeting their celebrity crush. But you're acting weird." Becka cocked her head to the side, staring at me with entirely too much intensity for 10:00 on a Saturday.

"I can't put my finger on it," she said, uncertainly. "He seems like a nice boy," she said, tapping the rim of her mug against her lip like she was trying to puzzle something out.

"He IS a nice boy," I said. "A nice man. He's... nice." Not my finest work.

"Hmmm." Becka made an unhappy noise.

We fell into an awkward silence and I began to feel uncomfortable with the way she was staring at me. Becka had an uncanny ability to laser focus on a person or a problem and find a way to solve whatever mystery she found and I wasn't certain I wanted to be that mystery.

More out of awkwardness than an actual desire for coffee, I tossed my notebook into my rucksack and got off the bed and headed towards the kitchenette. I poured myself a cup from the already-made pot on the side. Becka followed me over.

"Why does this feel like a 'thing', though?" She asked, leaning against the kitchen island that separated the kitchen area from the living room.

"I don't know what you mean," I said, looking at her over the rim of my mug as I took a sip.

"Remember that time we went to go see Flaming Sunrise when they performed at the SU?" I nodded. It still blew my mind that all it cost me was £5 to get in.

"Yeah, well, remember when we got to do shots with the lead singer-"

"Tad Logan." I supplied helpfully.

"Yeah, him," Becka agreed dismissively, "I remember you wouldn't shut up about that for literally weeks afterwards. Weeks. I had to talk you out of getting a tattoo."

"Still think that would have been dope," I muttered.

"And now you've met a celebrity you are arguably far more invested in and... what?" Becka put her mug down on the kitchen island.

"What?" I reply.

"That's what I'm trying to figure out."

I rolled my eyes. "And in your opinion," I said, pointing at her with my mug, "how should I be acting?"

"That's just it," she said, shrugging her whole upper body, like she was mad at me, for some reason, "more!"

"More?"

"More!" She exclaimed loudly. "More excited, buying useless shit with his face on it, threatening to get a tattoo with his song lyrics. More!" She put her mug down on the counter. Not slammed, but harder than was strictly necessary.

"Help me out here, Becka," I said, laughing, "how am I acting, as opposed to 'more'?"

"You're acting like he's a normal person," she said, her eyes widening suddenly. "That's it! You're acting like he's a normal person you've met and you're *into him!*" Becka gasped and pointed at me, her eyes as wide as saucers. It felt like she was accusing me of having an affair with the President, such was the drama.

"You're **INTO** him!"

"Pssh, am not." I waved her accusation away as I turned to put my mug in the sink.

"No, no, I'm right, aren't I?" She said, coming around the counter to stand next to me, forcing me to actually look her in the eye.

I leaned my hip against the sink and folded my arms across my chest.

"So what if I am?" I said, trying not to sound like a kid caught with her hand in the biscuit jar. "I mean, me and millions of other fans, right?" I laughed.

Becka frowned. "I mean, suuure…" she trailed off, chewing on her lip. "I just think it's a bit weird. You've met him, you've spent time with him. You've gotten to know him, in, y'know, real-life. That makes him real to you."

"He was real before now," I scoffed.

"Not to you," she said, pointing her finger at me and narrowing her eyes, "he was Jihoon, the 'Visual' from GVibes. That's a character. I feel like that's not who he is when you've been around him," she said, running her hand over her neck, distractedly.

My smile faded, but my stomach felt fluttery. Well, when you put it that way…

I shook my head to knock those thoughts loose.

"Look, I'll level with you," I said, "he is different than I would have thought. He's really cool, actually." I smiled, thinking of all the different ways I came to this conclusion.

"But that doesn't change anything. He's still who he is and eventually, he's going to finish recording and he's going to leave."

Becka nodded along, slowly. I could see I was making sense to her again.

"And this will just be another story we laugh about in a handful of years." I smiled, but damn if my heart didn't squeeze just a little bit.

"Maybe I'll even get a tattoo," I joked, bumping my hip against hers as I moved away from the counter. She chuckled, and I knew we were done.

"Where are you going?" She asked.

"Shower." I answered.

73

"Good, because you smell like an old man's slipper," she said.

I turned around, my whole face scrunched up, "the fuck?!?" I threw my hands up.

Becka shrugged. "I say these things to help you."

I snorted a laugh as I walked towards the bathroom.

Chapter 9

Later, when I no longer smelt like an old man's slipper....

"Hey, hey, hey!" Becka called from where she was laying on the couch, "where the fuck are you going?" She paused the show she was watching on Netflix.

I pulled on my plaid scarf before answering. "I'm going to Pisces. I left my earbuds there. I need them to write music." Perfectly valid excuse.

"Bullshit!" Becka cried. "You're going there to see the idol!" She pointed the remote at me, accusingly.

"He's not even there today!" I protested, pulling on my black beanie.

"You know the fuck he is!" She looked outraged. I shrugged in response, grabbing my rucksack and slinging it over my shoulder.

"I'll be back later," I called, heading out the door. I heard her call something with the word 'ho' in it, but I was already half-way down the hall.

It doesn't take long to get to Pisces from our apartment by bus. Just long enough for me to change my mind back and forth, oh, half a dozen times by the time we got to my stop, a few minute's walk from the building.

Despite my inconstant thoughts, my legs kept propelling me onwards. Just like how my hand reached into my pocket and withdrew my keycard and then swiped it against the black pad next to the side entrance door.

"Earbuds," I muttered to myself as I pushed open the door and walked into the cool lobby and towards the elevators.

"He's not even here," I muttered as I got off on the third floor.

"See?" I said to myself as I opened my locker and grabbed my little earbud case.

As if on instinct, I looked down the corridor to where Becka's office was. Obviously though, she was still at home, presumably still on the sofa watching Netflix. There were a couple people in though; there always were. Pisces was a famous studio and we had clients all over the world in different time zones.

I pressed the call button for the elevator and waited. Slapping my keycard against my palm, tapping my foot on the floor, humming to myself.

This elevator was taking ages.

"Bollocks to it," I hissed and shoved open the door to the stairwell and stomped down the steps.

When I got to the door to the second floor, I stopped. I lingered and debated with myself. Me, myself, and I all knew he was probably here. Time is money, you never want to spend longer than needed on studio time.

My fingers lightly pressed against the metal plate of the door, hesitating.

I suppose I could briefly see if he's here. No harm in a quick look. And I'm here, after all. Sounded reasonable to me, so I pushed against the door and entered the second floor.

It was dark in the corridor. Only the low-level emergency lights, the green 'Exit' sign, and the red light above the door to Studio 3 were on. The light above the door indicated that not only was the studio occupied, but that it was currently in use.

The ceiling spotlights came on as I walked down the corridor, not that I needed the light to see where I was going. I couldn't hear anything the closer I got, but that could have been because of the excellent soundproofing in the rooms.

In this instance, it was because there was actually no sound being made. The producer's deck was empty, the big, padded chair turned around and empty.

My heart sank, the room was empty.

I looked up at the red light, puzzled, but then, why –

And that's when I saw Jihoon pushing open the door that led to the vocal booth. He stopped by the empty producer's chair and took a drink from the water bottle he was holding. In the process of tipping his head back, he looked over to the door, spotting me peeping in the porthole window, like some sort of creeper.

Quickly, I ducked back out of view, heart hammering.

A moment later, the door to the studio opened and Jihoon poked his head out. He smiled at me, a surprised, but pleased smile.

"Kaiya! I didn't think you'd be here today," he said, stepping out fully into the corridor, letting the studio door close behind him. It did not escape my attention that this brought us closer together. Close enough that I could just reach out my hand...

"Ah, I forgot these yesterday," I said, waving my earbuds case like it was evidence. "I just came in to get them."

He made an 'ah' sound and shoved his hands in his pockets. I wondered if it occurred to him that I probably could have retrieved my earbuds without the detour to his studio.

"Where's TK?" I asked to cover the burgeoning silence.

He frowned, cocking his head to the side. "TK?" And then his expression cleared. "Oh! Trevor Kyle, TK."

I giggled. Good grief. There was something about this man that reduced me to a simpering teenager.

"Yeah, sorry," I cringed, "bad habit."

He waved his hands. "No, no, I get it." A look passed his face that I couldn't decipher.

"You know," he started, looking down at the floor and toeing the carpet with his black boots, "you can call me Joon. If you want." he amended quickly. "Most people do. It's easier than saying my full name." It could have been the glow of the red light above us, but I could have sworn his face pinked up. Adorable.

I smiled, feeling fluttery.

"Because 'Jihoon' is so hard?" I teased. He looked back up at me and smiled, his eyes crinkling.

"You say it well. I don't mind; Joon, Jihoon, whatever you like."

Holy hell, the flutters engulfed my entire torso now, no longer content to be confined to my stomach. My chest felt light, giddy, as I took a deep breath in.

"In that case, you can call me Ky. That's what my friends call me." I grinned at him.

Just then, the ceiling lights went out, plunging us into darkness, the sensor not detecting enough movement to keep on.

"Oh!" I exclaimed. "The sensors," I said, uselessly. I went to raise my arm to wave it around to turn them back on, but just then Jihoon reached out a hand and took my wrist. Startled, I looked at him quizzically.

"It's better," he said. "Not so bright," he explained, flicking a finger in the vague direction of his eyes.

"Ok," I said quietly, the darkness made me feel like I should be quiet. But what followed was a silence that started to feel... heavy, the longer it went on. He still held my wrist. I licked my lips, suddenly nervous. I began to wonder if he could hear the thumping of my heart, like I could hear the breaths he took.

I don't know which of us began to move first, but as inevitable as rain fall in the spring, we began to move towards each other, a slight step here, a lean there, until I was close enough to see the way his eyes shone in the reflected light of the studio. He had such pretty eyes; irises so dark they could have matched his pupils. When he smiled, his eyes seemed to smile too, the corners crinkling ever-so-slightly. Fascinated, I watched as his eyes trailed down my face, eventually falling to my mouth. My lips parted on an inhale –

I jumped in surprise as the chime from the arriving elevator dinged loudly through the thick silence of the hallway. The ceiling spots came on as the elevator doors opened and two people stepped off.

I pulled back from Jihoon, his hand falling away from my wrist and I fiddled with my rucksack strap as I saw Trevor Kyle and Youngsoo heading towards us.

Jihoon's other hand, the one not facing the elevator, darted out and took my hand. I turned back to him, my brows furrowed.

"Eat lunch with me?" he asked quietly, quickly, almost urgently.

I nodded as I darted a look down the corridor; the two men had slowed their steps as they looked at us in plain confusion.

"Floor three, room one." I whispered, relieved when he nodded in understanding and let go of my hand just as Trevor and Youngsoo reached us.

Youngsoo's eyebrows were furrowed and his mouth pinched in a firm line, but he nodded his head at me, if a bit stiffly. I repeated the gesture far more magnanimously.

Trevor Kyle, well, there was no other word for it. He smirked at me and looked me up and down, but neither one said anything to me. Youngsoo put his hand on Jihoon's arm and seemed to push him – gently – into the studio.

I rushed off back down the corridor, not looking back.

Chapter 10

Not knowing what else to do, I headed straight upstairs to Room 1, which was the lounge next to the two larger meeting rooms.

The lounge was as the name suggested, a relaxed space with couches and smaller tables and chairs. This was technically a client relations room, but we rarely ever had clients in here, so it was the unofficial staff room.

There was a flat screen mounted on the wall that was currently tuned to a music channel, the volume turned low enough to serve as ambiance. The far wall was floor-to-ceiling windows that faced out on the busy streets of LA, but the glass was so thick that only the very loudest of noises made its way up here.

The other side of the room was hospitality focused. Counters ran the length of the room, home to a fancy coffee machine that I rarely bothered with – a kettle and freeze-dried instant was good enough for me – snack displays containing various treats, fruit bowls and all the utensils and containers you could need.

I didn't bother looking at all this, of course. Instead, I sat down on the thickly padded sofa. I stood back up, then moved to one of the little bistro tables before getting back up again. I stood for a while in front of the full-length windows, feeling restless. Finally, I circled back to the sofa, took out my phone, and pretended to check my social media.

I have no idea how long I stayed like that. Somewhere between five minutes and five days, approximately. Or at least, that's how it felt.

I was just taking off my beanie and scarf when the door to the lounge snicked open and in slipped Jihoon, pressing the door closed behind him like he was trying to make sure he wasn't seen coming in here. Perhaps that was the case.

He turned to look around the room, his eyes searching until they fell upon where I sat. He smiled, a wide smile that made his eyes crinkle at the sides. He made his way over to me, sitting down on the sofa a respectable distance away.

"Hi," I said, my voice taking on that weird, breathy quality again.

He smiled. "Hi."

"Have you managed to escape?" I asked, fiddling with the threads of a hole in my fashionably-ripped jeans – I think I actually did rip that bit though, caught on a cupboard door.

To my surprise, he tipped his head back against the sofa and let out a big puff of air.

"That bad, huh?" I asked, scrunching my nose. He looked tired, now that I noticed it. I mean, he was still crazy good looking, but there were shadows under his eyes and his hair had that fluffy look that was usually only achieved by copious amounts of time spent running your hands through it.

He was silent a moment, before he replied, "It's a lot. We have a lot of work to do before we have a vacation, so we're trying to do it all now before the comeback." He ran a hand down his face before he turned to me.

"Sorry to complain..." He sat up a little straighter, as if he thought I was going to judge him.

I held up my hands to wave him off. "No, please don't say sorry. You're human. I can't imagine how hard you must have to work. I'm amazed you even have a vacation." I admitted, pulling my leg up in front of me so I could angle my body to face him. I leaned my arm up on the back of the sofa and rested my head in my palm.

The small smile he offered damn near broke my heart.

"I am human. But I am also a performer. It can be..." he paused, took a breath and then said, "hard."

"I'm sorry," I said, putting as much empathy into the word as I could.

He closed his eyes and waved a hand. "Don't be. It's hard, but I am happy." And this time, when he smiled, I believed him.

We lapsed into silence for so long that I thought he might have fallen asleep. Not that I could have blamed him.

While I had the opportunity, I admit I creeped a little. My eyes ran over his face, greedily taking in every little detail. The fan of his dark eyelashes as they rested against his cheeks, the curve of his neck. The slight throb of his pulse was endlessly fascinating to me.

The silence was broken by the door opening and the two of us jumped as if we'd been caught doing something immoral.

Well, maybe I had been. My face flamed as I met the eyes of Youngsoo as he entered the lounge.

He said something to Jihoon, who had stood up. Youngsoo lifted a white paper bag and Jihoon pointed at one of the bistro tables, replying in Korean. Youngsoo made a 'hmm' noise and deposited the bag on the table and then turned and left. I watched this exchange in surprise, thinking for sure he was going to insist Jihoon leave, or at the very least that he was going to stay, as a sort of chaperon.

I very much got the impression from Youngsoo that he did not think I should be around Jihoon.

"I, ah, ordered food," Jihoon said, holding his arm out to the bag on the table. "I wasn't sure what you might like..." he looked so shy, I couldn't help but smile.

"Wow," I said, getting to my feet, "you didn't need to do that." I walked over to where he stood. "But thank you, that was really kind of you."

Jihoon ducked his head and began to unpack the bag. I recognised some things right away, whereas others not so much. Once we had it all laid out on the table, including the utensils and drinks, Jihoon surprised me by pulling out a chair and indicating that I should sit. For some reason this made me unspeakably shy, but I sat – as ladylike as I could manage – and he pushed in my chair before taking the chair opposite me and sitting down.

There were two dishes each of rice and a soup of some kind and a bunch of other, smaller containers filled with colourful, delicious looking things. I recognised the kimchi, which I am a big fan of. There was marinated tofu, mixed vegetables and… that's where I drew a blank.

Jihoon pushed one of the containers of rice towards me as he pulled the other towards him. He picked up his chopsticks, and I tried, I really did; to copy the way he held them in his hand, but I'm sure I embarrassed myself.

He picked up a bit of the kimchi and put it on top of my rice.

"Thank you," I said with a smile, my chest doing that silly, fluttering thing again.

He began to eat, picking at bits here and there and I did the same. Albeit, when I ate, it was with far more awkward hand gestures.

The second time I dropped the cube of tofu, Jihoon pursed his lips, having the courtesy to pretend he was not laughing at me.

"Hey!" I scolded, pretending to scowl, "I'm trying here."

He waved his hands and said, "I'm sorry, it's just…" his eyes darted away before coming back to mine, still crinkled at the sides with mirth, "You're so cute."

Holy hell. I almost slumped in my chair.

Instead, I played it off, by cupping my face in my hands in the universal symbol of aegyo – acting cute. I even poked my tongue out, which was absolutely worth the cringe when I saw his red ears.

"Here," he said, scooting his chair around the table until he was sat next to me, instead of opposite me. Gently, he picked up my hand holding the chopsticks and positioned my fingers around them until they felt more secure. Which is absolutely not what I was focused on.

What I was focused on was the way he leaned so close to me. So close that I could clearly see the little mole on the side of his nose. I saw the way his hair fell over his face; it was wavier than I'd seen it before and for some reason this surprised me. Which is obviously the reason I couldn't stop staring. Absolutely no other reason.

"Now try," he said, interrupting my reverie as he looked up at me.

The trouble with closely inspecting something is that you sometimes get closer to it than you mean to.

Which is why, when Jihoon lifted his head, my face was mere inches from his own. Certainly, close enough to see the way his eyes widened in surprise, close enough to see the way his mouth fell open slightly. Close enough to notice when his eyes dipped down to my lips, his pupils dilating.

Close enough to know I was dancing dangerously close to a boundary I wasn't sure I could cross.

With effort, I leaned back, dipping my chin to focus instead on the way my hand now held the chopsticks.

I cleared my throat and gave them a few experimental clacks.

"Hey! That's much better!" I exclaimed.

Jihoon blinked several times before he said, "Good."

It took real effort on my part to keep the disappointment off my face when he scooted his chair back to his side of the table

We made small talk as we ate. Safe subjects like foods we did or didn't like – he hated shellfish, I hate mushrooms – what song was his favourite to perform – a song from their second album, 'Earthquake' –, which was my favourite to listen to – it had been 'Stardust', but now it was 'Broken Promise' –, countries we'd been to, which ones we'd like to – both of us had too many mention on our list of ones we'd like to visit, although he thoroughly trumped me on countries he had been to. GVibes had toured all over the world, whereas I had seen but a small fraction.

There was an expectation that GVibes would announce a world tour soon; it had been a couple of years since their last one. When I asked Jihoon about it, he ducked his head.

"I'm not allowed to talk about anything that isn't public," he said softly, an apologetic smile tugging at his lips. The reminder of who sat across the table from me sent a flush to my cheeks, and I felt embarrassed for even asking.

"It must be so hard to travel around so much and do such big shows," I offered quickly, hoping to fill the awkwardness.

Jihoon lifted his head, chewing thoughtfully before responding.

"It is hard," he admitted. "We go to sleep in one country and wake up in another. Sometimes, we forget where we are when it's just show after show."

He paused, his gaze drifting momentarily before it locked back on me.

"But it's also fun," he continued, and I watched in wonder as a small, genuine smile tugged up the corner of his mouth.

"We get energy from our fans. When we're up there on stage, we want to do our very best for them. So, we forget about all the airports and how much our bodies hurt, because we have our fans – and they have us."

I studied his face carefully as he spoke, looking for any hint that his words were rehearsed, but he meant every word. His fans truly mattered to him, to the group. It made me pause, my admiration for him growing as I saw yet another layer of the man I was beginning to suspect he was, not just the idol.

I just couldn't imagine that life. The mind truly boggled at the amount of effort and dedication and talent that his every-day called for.

"Your life is crazy," I remarked, shaking my head in disbelief.

"Yes." He laughed.

We fell silent for a while, concentrating on our food, when Jihoon suddenly asked, "How old are you?" I blinked. While not a weird question, it was unusual to just come out and ask, but then I remembered that in Korea, age was an important factor.

"22," I replied.

He nodded. "I'm your elder, then," he said, matter-of-factly.

"How old are you?" I asked, putting down my utensils. He cocked his head to the side, a small smile pulling the corners of his lips up. "I'm used to people knowing such little things about me. It's... nice, to start fresh." His eyes crinkled at the side, and he fell silent again. I could only imagine how bizarre it must be to have so many people know so much about you and for you to know nothing about them, like you'd always be playing catch up.

"I'm 25 in Korean age." He finally said, glancing up at me as he wiped his mouth on a napkin.

"Is that different from the rest of the world?" I asked, frowning.

He nodded, a serious expression on his face, "We say that a child is age one from the day they are born. So, in Korea, I am 25 –"

"And you're 24 in western culture?" I finished for him, and he nodded.

"It must sound strange to you," he smiled and hunched his shoulders, like he was used to writing this off as an oddity, as opposed to what it was – a unique, cultural difference.

"Oh, that's nothing," I said, leaning back in my chair. "In England, we roll cheese down a hill and then chase after it."

Jihoon frowned, his mouth pinching slightly as if he was trying to figure out if I'd just started talking nonsense.

"And that's not all. A lot of the time, people get hurt. Badly. Broken arms, legs, noses. One time, a man even died."

"This is a... story?" He said slowly.

"Oh no." I waved my hand dismissively. "Totally true, they do it every year. Does Korea have any weird traditions?"

"Not like that," he said, raising his eyebrows. I laughed and took a sip of my drink.

After we'd eaten, we each cleared away the containers.

"Would you like a coffee?" I asked, moving towards the shiny, chrome machine. Normally I'd not bother, but, when in Rome…

"Something sweet?" he asked, hopefully.

"I can certainly try," I laughed.

For me, a simple white coffee with a pump of hazelnut syrup was perfection. For him, I looked at the menu card from the pocket taped to the machine before I tried my hand at 'something sweet.'

A couple minutes and a lot of hissing steam later, I walked over to where he was standing in front of the windows, watching the Saturday traffic.

"Jihoon?" I said, tentatively. He turned around and I handed him the mug with a flourish.

"Caramel macchiato. Or at least I hope so." I laughed.

He took it from me, his long fingers sliding against mine.

"I like the way you say my name," he said, his voice barely above a whisper, like he was telling me a secret he hadn't meant to say.

The breath in my chest seized and I knew I was biting my lip again, but this time it was less to do with feeling self-conscious and all to do with the way those words made me feel. Like I was too hot, but not because of the room temperature.

"Will you be here tomorrow?" he asked, taking a sip of his drink and then making a 'mmm' sound which would have sent me somewhere, had he not paired it with the cutest face. The duality of this man…

"No," I said, with genuine regret. "I don't think I could come up with a good reason for me to be here on a Sunday."

His mouth turned down at the corners and he frowned.

But naturally, our time was up.

Youngsoo at least had the courtesy to knock on the door before he opened it.

Jihoon looked... annoyed? Frustrated? Both. I heard him sigh under his breath before he turned to look at Youngsoo. He said something that had him backing out the door.

I looked at Jihoon, my brows furrowed.

"I asked him to give me five minutes."

"Oh," I said, puzzled. "To drink your coffee?"

"To ask for your number."

Holy hell.

Chapter 11

Sunday

B ecka was not pleased with me. I'd told her – briefly, and leaving a lot out – about the interaction I'd had with Jihoon on Saturday.

She'd made me sit at the kitchen island and listen to a lecture about crossing professional boundaries and how never once had it ended well when a famous musician had gotten involved with 'a normy'. Much less, an 'intern'. This last word seemed to make a big difference.

"The scandal practically writes itself!" She'd exclaimed as she paced back and forth in front of the fridge, fanning herself with a hand.

"Becka, open the fridge," I said calmly.

She halted in her tracks and turned to look at me, frowning as her hand hovered over the door handle. "Why?"

"Because you need to chill," I said, face perfectly straight.

Becka rolled her eyes and flipped me the bird as she continued with her pacing.

"This is not that big of a deal." I'd insisted.

Now, once more with feeling because even I didn't buy it when I said that.

"The idol gives you his phone number, and it's not a big deal?" Becka stopped pacing, but the alternative wasn't any better; instead she was leaning over the kitchen island, looking at me like my next words had better be the confession to a murder, or I was going away for a long time.

"You have the rapper's number!" I shot back, not using his real name because he'd been a nightmare. Again, begins with a D (for dickhead), ends with an E (Ego).

Becka waved this away, saying, "he gave it to any woman standing still long enough. Not the same thing!"

"So surely this is a better situation, then!" I insisted, "Seeing as how he respected me enough to ask?"

The look she gave me could have melted the ice in my glass of water. "It's even worse that the idol is nice!"

"He has a name." I had begun to bristle a bit, I admit.

"Maybe so, but he's not just 'Jihoon', though, is he? He is, 'the idol'." She softened her tone, "That's all he ever can be to you, babes." She came and sat on the stool next to me.

"Look, I'm not trying to be an asshole here, but you need to understand this. When he's done recording, he'll be gone, and where will you be? In exactly the same place. This isn't 'Pretty Woman', he isn't going to climb the fire escape for you. He is not for you, Ky." Becka tried putting her hand on my arm, but I stood up, trying to pass it off casually.

"Look, I hear you," I said. "I know all of that. I'm not trying to get myself a situationship. I'm not here to groupie. I know what this is and it's harmless! It's just a harmless flirtation, if it's that at all. Once he's gone, he's gone. I get it."

And I did. I did get it, and I'm pretty sure I did a good enough job of convincing Becka that I did, in fact, understand that this wasn't a thing, because she did drop it after that.

But, for the whole rest of Saturday and Sunday, I felt wrong. Off-balance and deeply conflicted.

Which is why – I told myself – that I didn't text him.

But, he didn't text me either, so...

I walked into Pisces on Monday in a foul mood.

No sleep, barely having eaten anything since Saturday, confused as all hell. Yeah, I was pissy.

It's didn't help that Jeremy had already texted me to tell me to carry on cataloguing the crap in storage. I didn't really mind the work, but damn if it wasn't mind-numbing. And dusty. Super dusty. Becka was coming in later, she'd taken the morning off for a 'dentist' appointment, (read: she was getting her nails done).

So, when I stopped in front of the elevator to wait for it to come down, my mood was not improved by Trevor Kyle stopping to stand next to me. Unnecessarily close, I observed.

"Well, if it isn't our newest intern," he said lightly.

It was not in my best interest to be anything less than polite and friendly, so I half-turned to him and said, "Good morning, Mr Kyle."

"Trevor, please." He waved his hand in a very good impression of magnanimous joviality. Like he was just like one of us peons.

When the door opened, he held his hand out in front of me, smiling, and taking my cue, I boarded the elevator, but before I could press the button, he put a hand on my arm.

"What floor?"

I was puzzled. I'd entered on the side closest to the button panel. It was literally six inches from my left elbow.

"Um, two," I said. And then, to my surprise, he leaned past me to press the '2' button. He was so close that I was momentarily engulfed in a cloud of his cologne. It wasn't that strong, blessedly, and I'm sure it was eye-wateringly expensive, but I had to force down a cough.

The moment the doors closed, I began to wish I'd taken the stairs. There was no reason why he needed to stand so close to me, it was a big elevator. He was so much taller than me, I felt crowded and I knew it was deliberate.

He didn't say a word to me, but when he put his hand on the small of my back, I got the message. My t-shirt skimmed the top of my jeans, so it really wasn't hard for him to brush his pinkie finger downward, hooking it slightly under the soft fabric of my shirt. He ran that finger lightly back and forth, tracing patterns into my back, branding me.

I froze in a kind of panic. My fingers started tingling and I had to really focus on keeping my face neutral. Pretending it wasn't happening.

Finally, the doors chimed and rolled open, but I felt frozen to the spot, my knees locked into place.

Which is around the same time I noticed Jihoon standing there. He was smiling as the doors opened, and when my eyes met his, I wanted so badly to feel the warmth I saw in them. I saw the moment his gaze dropped to where Trevor Kyle still had his hand on my back. He stood close to me, but there was a gap between our bodies, it must have been quite clear where his hand was.

I felt my face crumple at the same moment I regained control over my body. I took in a great gust of breath as I forced myself to step forward, returning the slight bow from Youngsoo and the habitual, but unsure one from Jihoon.

"Good morning, I mumbled." I rushed past the group, making a bee line for the studio I was working in that day.

"Our tech interns are always rushing off somewhere." Trevor Kyle laughed.

Arrogant dickhead. There are no tech interns. And I'm literally the only intern in the building. Fucker.

I rushed into Studio 2 and shut the door behind me, barely even noticing that it was pitch black in there as I leant back against the door, taking a tremulous breath in, trying to settle myself.

Chapter 12

I turned on the overhead lights and tossed my bag across the room. Angry. At Trevor Kyle. At myself. Just... angry.

When my phone beeped, I was ready to toss it, too.

But that's when I saw the name on the screen.

1 unread message from: Joon

I slid my finger up the screen to unlock it and tapped on the message, heart thumping slightly.

Joon

Are you ok?

[Sent 08:57]

I tapped the side of my phone, thinking how to answer.

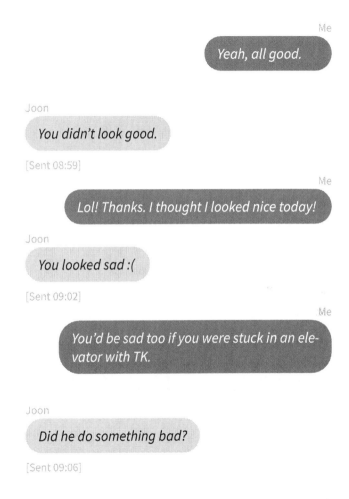

Me

Yeah, all good.

Joon

You didn't look good.

[Sent 08:59]

Me

Lol! Thanks. I thought I looked nice today!

Joon

You looked sad :(

[Sent 09:02]

Me

You'd be sad too if you were stuck in an elevator with TK.

Joon

Did he do something bad?

[Sent 09:06]

Apparently, he was not going for my 'play it off' tactic.

Me

No, Joon, it's cool. He's just a prick

He took so long to reply that I figured he must have had to put his phone away, but just as I'd stopped staring at my screen, it chimed.

Joon

You called me Joon. You never have before.

[Sent 09:12]

Me

Maybe not to you ;)

Joon

Ah, so you talk about me, I understand ;)

[Sent 09:14]

Me

Yeah, moaning about how badly you tuned that guitar.

Not my best work and took way too long to think of that come back. It would have been much faster had I not spent a solid two minutes biting my fist.

Joon

> *I made you moan?*

[Sent 09:19]

I had to quickly pick up my tossed rucksack so I could stifle my scream into the fabric.

Joon

> *Ah, sorry, my English is not so good.*

[Sent 09:20]

Me

> *Don't you – a super famous pop artist – have actual work to do right now?*

Joon

> *Always. Will I see you later?*

[Sent 09:23]

Me

> *I hope so.*

> *Go make another Billboard hit. I'll be around.*

Joon

I said something wrong before.

[Sent 09:26]

Me

?

Joon

You look really good today.

[Sent 09:30]

I put my phone back in my pocket and held my fist to my lips, pressing my smiling mouth against it, feeling that now-familiar fluttery feeling in my chest.

Oh boy, I was in trouble.

Chapter 13

Monday Lunchtime.

"That PIG!" Becka exploded, her chicken Caesar wrap taking the brunt of her anger as she slammed it back into the container, lettuce spewing from the tortilla in little surrendering slivers.

I nodded, stirring my drink with the straw.

"You're not the first girl he's done this to," Becka said darkly, "there's always rumours about him."

I didn't reply, still feeling the ghost of his finger running along the waistband of my jeans. I shuddered and let go of my straw in disgust.

"You should go to HR," Becka said matter-of-factly, picking up her wrap and taking a savage bite out of it.

"Oh yeah?" I huffed, "and how did that turn out for the other girls? Where are they now? Cos TK is downstairs, making millions for Pisces."

"Ky, he sexually assaulted you," Becka hissed. "Did he?" I leant back in my chair. "He touched my back –" I held up my hand to stop her when I saw her open her mouth to argue with me, "and while it was gross and inappropriate, I'm just an intern and he's who he is.

"I'm only here for the year. I don't want to get tied up in a game of reputation and ruin it for myself over something so minor." Becka looked unhappy, but by the way she clenched her jaw and nodded, I knew she agreed with me, even if she hated it.

"I just want to forget about it and go back to being the invisible intern he doesn't deign to notice." I took a deep breath and puffed it out, picking at the skin around my thumb.

"I was going to ask you to deliver lunch to Studio 2 again," Becka groused, "but I'll get reception to take it up instead."

"No," I said quickly, "I'll do it."

"Babes, you don't have to-"

"I want to," I interrupted, "I don't give a fuck about TK, but I would quite like to see the idol again," I said, a shy smile creeping its way across my face.

"I thought it was 'Jihoon,'" Becka crooned. I gently kicked her under the table and she laughed at me, the air between us light and easy again.

Becka's phone chimed, the screen lighting up with a message. She leant over to read it.

"Speak of the devil," she said, still looking down, "food's been delivered. It's downstairs now."

"That's my cue." I stood up and started to pack away my things.

"Are you going to be okay?" Becka asked, wiping her hands on a napkin.

"Yes," I said firmly. "Fuck him, he doesn't get to ruin this for me."

"Your internship, or your time with the idol?" Becka asked. She said it in a casual tone, but by the intense way she held my eyes, it was quite clear she was asking a real question.

I don't even stop to think. "Both," I said, firmly, slinging my rucksack over my shoulder and pushing my chair in. "See you later?"

"As always," she nodded, and I walked out of the lounge with my head held higher than it was when I walked in earlier.

I was absolutely clear on one thing: I wouldn't let that fucker ruin my time here in LA, this job, or my time with Jihoon. The fact was, he was a big money player for the studio, and I was... an intern. He held all the power, and if it came down to a he-said-she-said, there was no doubt in my mind that I'd come out worse.

So, I had two options: ignore it and try to stay out of his way, or stick my neck out and see where that got me. It made me so mad that I was even in the position where I had to weigh those choices. Why was this being made *my* problem? All I'd ever wanted was to work in the music industry, to learn from people like him, and he had to go and ruin it by being a fucking creep.

At the lockers, I dropped off my rucksack, grabbed my earbuds, and slid them into my pocket before locking up. I took the stairs down to reception, using the time to try and calm down. Getting mad wasn't helping anything. As I swung open the door from the stairwell, I blew out a breath and tried to shake it off.

Donna was standing behind the desk again, talking quickly into her headset in a tone that was both polite and annoyed at the same time. She had her hands on her hips as she turned to look at me, not pausing her conversation.

I waved and pointed at the food bags, miming taking them upstairs. Donna rolled her eyes and pointed one manicured finger at the hospitality tray behind the desk.

Dutifully, I wheeled it over and decanted all the food containers onto the trolley in a more aesthetically pleasing display, grabbing a couple of chilled water bottles out of the mini fridge behind the desk and filling up the water jug.

Donna watched my every move with an impressive amount of diligence, considering she never once halted her conversation and only once she had given a begrudging nod and turned away, did I wheel the trolley towards the elevator. From Donna, that nod might as well have been a standing ovation and a clap on the back.

As the doors closed behind me and I'd reached for the button, I remembered this morning in this same elevator. I resolved to take the stairs from now on.

The ascent up to the second floor was really too short for me to work myself up into any big feelings and this was probably a blessing, as I didn't have the luxury of spiralling about either Jihoon, or Trevor Kyle and seeing them.

Once the doors opened on the second floor, I pushed the trolley down the corridor to Studio 3, that by-now familiar red light beckoning me forward.

This time, I was far less anxious as I stopped outside the door and looked in through the porthole window, although I'd be lying to myself if I tried to deny the very real existence of the fluttering in my belly. It was a tentative, hopeful sort of fluttering though, as if the butterflies weren't sure if they were supposed to be there, or not.

But that's when I saw Jihoon and the butterflies decided that yes, they were most certainly in the right place. My breath hitched as he looked up and met my eyes through the glass. He smiled and even from here I could see the way his eyes crinkled slightly at the sides. That he was smiling like that for me... It made me want to cry and I didn't know why.

I knocked lightly on the door to announce myself, but knowing that Jihoon had seen me, I pushed down the handle and turning my back to the door, pushed it open, backing into the room. Before I'd hardly crossed the threshold, Jihoon was there, holding the door open and standing so close to me that I could smell that clean, laundry scent of his. Unthinking, my head angled to the side and lifted slightly until I was almost touching his chest with my nose. I looked up, a little bit startled and embarrassed. Jihoon met my gaze, his eyes warm, a playful light in them. I felt the way my whole face beamed back at him, I didn't even try or want to tone it down.

When Youngsoo cleared his throat, I remembered we were not alone, and I hurried to pull the trolley all the way into the room and wheel it over to the long desk.

Just like last time, Jihoon helped me to offload all the food containers. We kept sneaking peeks at each other, trying not to smile, like two little kids hiding a secret.

Just as we finished, his phone rang. He pulled it out of his pocket and looked at the screen, moving away to the sound booth before answering with a cheerful "yeoboseyo?"

I'd inadvertently tracked his movements with my body and as I spun around, I knocked over one of the sealed water bottles and it rolled under the desk.

Apologising to Youngsoo, who didn't seem to be paying me the slightest attention, I dropped to my knees and crawled slightly under the desk to reach for it.

"Well, hello, what do we have here?" I jumped, my head hitting the underside of the table at the sudden and unwelcome voice behind me. I craned my neck around to see Trevor Kyle standing behind me, leaning slightly to the side and making absolutely no effort whatsoever to disguise the fact that he was staring at my backside. I turned back around and scooted quickly to get out from under the table, feeling the way the hair on my arms raised as I shuddered, revulsion tasting sour on my tongue.

Still on my knees, I raised to one knee, now out from under the table, and looked up at him. He'd crowded me, standing so close I couldn't stand back up without effectively body rolling him.

"Thats a good look for you," he said so quietly it took me a moment for my brain to actually understand what he'd said.

Stunned, I momentarily froze, still on one knee and looking up at one of the industry's biggest producers as he openly leered at me. Distantly, an alarm was sounding in my brain, but it was like I'd short circuited. All except for the trickle of apprehension that rolled down my spine like a droplet of ice water.

Just then, the door to the sound booth swung open, the sound proofing bristles along the frame making a loud 'hissing' noise. I looked over to see Jihoon, phone-in-hand. He looked over at me and his smile died on his face. God only knows what expression he saw on mine.

"Is everything okay?" he asked, looking between me and Trevor Kyle. The question prompted Youngsoo to look up from his phone and bless him, he immediately stood up from where he'd been leaning against the table and offered me his hand. Gratefully, I took it. Not because I needed the assistance getting to my feet, but because his physical presence made Trevor Kyle take several steps back.

He shrugged as he moved back to the production desk and said, "Interns," with a tone that seemed to imply I'd somehow done something wrong or was somehow inept.

And damn me, but it worked. I felt shame creeping up from my stomach to my face, bringing with it a flush of redness I'm sure was already burning my cheeks. I just wanted to leave.

I thanked Youngsoo with a grateful bow and hurried towards the door. I opened it and glanced up as I turned around to close it behind me, and just before the door swung closed, I saw Jihoon, but he wasn't looking at me, he was looking at Trevor Kyle, who was openly staring at me.

I wondered what Jihoon was thinking.

I closed the door and practically ran down the corridor and didn't slow down until I was upstairs.

Chapter 14

4:35pm

My feet were dragging as I headed into Jeremy's office. As usual, he didn't look up from where he was tapping away at his laptop.

"Tired?" He asked, gruffly but not unkindly.

"It's just been a day," I answered, puffing out a breath as I leaned against his open door.

"Any problems today?" He asked, angrily hitting a key several times in a row.

"Not a one. The boxes have all been arranged in a very Tetris-like way, the hard-drives are all downstairs and Donna has the call list you gave me. Oh, and she told me to tell you to 'call your own damn covers, next time'." I said, ticking off my tasks on my fingers. Jeremy huffed a small laugh at the last one.

"She's a real hard-ass, that one," he muttered.

"She's always been a peach to me," I said, earning me a quick look up from Jeremy, his eyebrows raised in disbelief before he saw my wry grin.

"We should send her to negotiate with these union punks," he grumbled, "the lot from tech would be back at work within the day."

Deciding not to comment on that one, I instead asked if he wanted a coffee as I was going that way.

"Only if it's laced with cyanide," he groaned, dragging his hands down his face. I flashed him a look of sympathy, even if I was secretly on the side of the 'union punks.'

"Sorry, boss, we're all out of cyanide."

Just then, the elevator down the corridor chimed and I instinctively looked over my shoulder to see who it was. To my surprise, Youngsoo stepped out, followed by Jihoon and another man I'd never seen before. They turned right to go down the corridor that led to the conference room and the lounge, where Jihoon and I had had lunch together on Saturday.

Only once they'd gone out of sight did I go a few further steps down the corridor to sneak a peek around the corner. All three men went into the conference room at the end of the corridor.

I stood there for a few moments, looking in through the narrow window in the door, catching glimpses here and there of the men getting settled into the seats around the table.

Behind me, the elevator chimed again, and the doors clunked open, and then closed.

A hand suddenly ran down my arm from shoulder to elbow, squeezing me slightly and scaring me half to death. I jumped and pulled away before even looking around. When I saw Trevor Kyle standing there, smiling down at me, I had the strongest urge to press myself against the wall. I held myself still, however, trying to control the expression on my face. I could still feel the heat of his hand on my skin. It burned like shame.

"Get us some drinks, would you, sweetheart?" he asked and winked at me, luckily turning around and walking down the corridor towards the conference room before seeing the gag I'd only just suppressed when he'd winked at me. I couldn't, however, suppress the sinking feeling I had at understanding that I was now on Trevor Kyle's radar. If I'd had any doubt before, it was gone now.

"Everything alright, Kaiya?" grumbled the far more welcome voice of Jeremy as he walked to where I still stood, next to the elevator.

"Yeah," I answered on an exhale, pushing myself away from the wall, "TK asked me to get some drinks for the conference room, but there's not many of them so I won't be long."

"Don't worry about it. Sort them out and then you might as well take off, there's no point you starting anything else today," Jeremy said.

"Alright, thanks, boss," I said, knowing full well that I'd only be hanging out with Becka until she finished anyway.

With that, I hustled to the lounge to get started on some refreshments. Becka had showed me how this went on my first day, just in case I was ever asked to do it. Normally, it would be someone from her office, but you never knew and it wasn't complicated. I brewed a fresh pot of coffee and piled everything I needed onto a large tray; mugs, spoons, one container of milk, individual sachets of sugar and some napkins. I also grabbed some water bottles out of the fridge and waited for the pot to finish brewing. Once it was done, I grabbed one of the mugs and poured coffee into it, topping it up with frothy milk and a shot of caramel syrup.

Once done, I picked up the tray and carefully made my way to the conference room. I had to push the door open with my back and I tried my best not to clatter the tray too loudly. From the screen on the wall and the mounted speakers, I could hear other people speaking, the meeting having obviously already begun. I didn't look up, but I could hear the other party speaking very fast Korean.

As I walked around the room to the other side where there was a table to set out hospitality items, I could hear someone in the room speaking quietly, it sounded like there was someone translating into English.

Once I slid the tray onto the table, I chanced a look round and saw the man I wasn't familiar with leaning in closely to Trevor Kyle, presumably translating. Looking back round, my eyes naturally snagged on the big screen. I inhaled sharply and looked away immediately, my hands tightening on the tray. There, on the big screen in full, sharp definition were the other four members of GVibes: Park Minjae, the eldest of the group and the leader, part of the vocal line with Jihoon, Kim Seokmin, the third vocalist and also the youngest of the group, Choi Woojin, the group's best rapper and lastly, Lee Sungmin, second rapper and also the best dancer of GVibes, except for maybe Jihoon.

I listened to Minjae speaking, the voice so familiar to me, feeling so surreal I had to really fight to keep from giggling at the absurdity of my life right now.

I took a deep breath and resolved to focus on my task. I grabbed the water bottles and ducking my head down, hurried round the table, putting them to the right-hand side of each person sitting there, not lingering before heading back to the table, where I grabbed the coffee I'd specially made for Jihoon, and two little packets of sugar. I carefully placed the mug and the sugar packets on his left.

"Thank you," he whispered, lifting his eyes to smile ever-so-slightly at me. I returned it with a small smile of my own, before turning to Youngsoo and quietly asking if he'd like a coffee. I repeated this with everyone else and bustled away to pour coffee into mugs, adding milk when it was wanted and adding spoons, napkins and sugar packets to each person in turn before I was done.

I'd done a very commendable job of pretending my favourite band in the world weren't live on a screen just a couple of meters away, weren't able to see me as the camera captured the full width and breadth of this room.

I also did an amazing job of drawing absolutely no attention to myself, and as I silently slipped out of the room, I mentally high-fived myself on not falling over, not spilling coffee on anyone, not knocking anything over or otherwise similarly making a spectacle of myself.

"Ohmygodohmygodohmygodohmygod," I panted, practically galloping down the corridor and hot stepping into the office space Becka shared, earning me several looks.

"Babes, what?" Becka said, looking up at me in surprise, pushing aside her laptop.

I low-key loved it when she dropped everything for me, and even in the midst of my fan-girl-freakout, I felt a warm glow of love for her.

"I just saw GVibes! All of them!" I dramatically flung myself into the chair opposite her desk like it was a fainting couch, earning me a couple of laughs from the other people on her team.

"What?" Becka said, frowning, "Are they here? We didn't know about that, did we?" She directed this to Celine, a couple desks away, who looked up like a meerkat scenting danger.

"Here? No!" Immediately she shoved her glasses up her nose and started squinting at her computer.

"No, no!" I say quickly, waving my hands around for emphasis. "They're on the video conferencing screen, they're in the conference room right now. TK made me make drinks for the room."

"Oh God, don't do that to me," Celine slumped back into her chair, heaving a sigh of relief.

"Sorry Celine," Becka and I chorused, and then giggled.

"Holy hell, that was so wild!" The grin stretching across my face felt manic.

"While that is very cool, and I am happy for you," Becka began, "I'm confused as to why this seems like a much bigger deal to you, when you've been in physical contact with the idol for days."

Celine sharply looked up, the laser focus of her glare was almost a tactile feeling and Becka quickly looked over to reassure her.

"Stand down, Celine, figure-of-speech, I just mean that he's been here, in the building and we've seen him walking around. She has not, I repeat, not touched the idol."

Mostly true, I thought to myself, a small smile teasing the corners of my lips.

"She better not have," Celine muttered darkly, pushing her glasses higher up her nose and narrowing her eyes at me. I held my hands up in silent surrender, and she turned back to her laptop.

Becka and I shared a grin. "You done for the day?" she asked.

"Yeah, Jeremy said I might as well finish early, so here I am, riding high and fancy free." She rolled her eyes at me but smiled.

"Alright, I'm nearly done and then we'll head out, okay?" Understanding that she needed some time to concentrate on her task, I got up and said, "I'll go and get my stuff out of my locker and meet you by the lifts?"

"Sure," Becka said, waving a hand at me but having already gone back to staring at her laptop.

I left the office and wandered slowly down the corridor, turning into the Ops hallway toward the lockers. I took my sweet time, letting the quiet stretch as I reflected on how bizarre my life had become.

Not so long ago, I'd been sitting cross-legged on my single bed in a cramped flat that would be generous to call a 'studio,' watching GVibes' practice videos on YouTube. Now, I'd just served coffee to one of them, while the other members chatted casually on a video call.

This was not normal life.

And as fun as it was, the thought nagged at me: how long did I really want this life? A life where I play-pretended to have a career in the music industry but mostly fetched, carried, and occasionally brushed shoulders with celebrities. Sure, it made for a great story, but... did I want my life to be just that – a story to tell?

I had just gotten my jacket out when I heard the distant thud of a door closing, followed by a procession of people walking down the corridor. A few moments later and the group from the conference room filed past the Ops corridor and stopped at the elevator, still talking amongst themselves.

Except for Jihoon. He was staring down at the phone in his hand. A moment later, my own phone chimed in my pocket and Jihoon looked up and saw me standing a few meters away. He grinned, holding his phone up in greeting. I glanced at my phone screen and saw his name in the notification box. I grinned back at him, holding my own phone back up in silent acknowledgment.

Just then, the doors to the elevator opened and everyone started piling on, but Jihoon held back, saying something to Youngsoo and waving him on. Only once Youngsoo had boarded the elevator did Jihoon turn back to me and walk towards me. Over his shoulder I spied Youngsoo's face. His eyebrows were pinched together; his lips a thin line. Worried, if I had to guess. I deliberately did not look at Trevor Kyle.

"Hi!" Jihoon breathed, as if he'd jogged to me.

"Hi," I replied, ducking my head, suddenly shy.

"I wanted to talk to you," he said, "I'm glad I got to see you."

"Oh?" I looked back up at him and I was surprised to see he was frowning down at me, the expression making the scar through his eyebrow more pronounced than it usually was.

"I wanted to know if you were okay." Jihoon began fiddling with the ring on his thumb, sliding it up and down, his eyes darting away like he found the question difficult. "When you came at lunch, I saw the way the producer looked at you. It was not appropriate, and you looked upset."

Whatever I had expected Jihoon to say, this wasn't it. His words hit me like hailstones, and I flinched, looking down at the buttons on his shirt.

I licked my lips before I answered, "It's not a big deal. He's a pig, everyone knows it."

"Should I do-" he began, but I interrupted before he could say more.

"No, please. It's not a big deal. He didn't even know I existed before last week. I just need to avoid him." I forced a smile onto my face and looked up to meet his eyes. His mouth was pinched, but he nodded.

"I wanted to talk to you about something else, as well," he said, shuffling his feet and looking down the corridor, but it was still empty. I nodded to show I was listening.

"Tomorrow is the last day I will be here. We're nearly done with recording, and I fly home on Thursday." His eyes dropped before flicking back up to meet mine.

"Oh," I exhaled. I'd known it was coming; I'd even known it would be soon, but hearing it made it real and put an end-date on this strange, fairytale bubble that the past week had been. I suddenly felt as though my hands had lead weights attached to them and it was an effort to not slump.

"Everyone is going to a celebration dinner tomorrow, after we're done. Will you come?"

His question took me by surprise. Maybe it shouldn't have, but it did and for a moment, all I could do was blink up at him. Finally, I spoke.

"Um, I'm not sure I'd be allowed to go..." I trailed off, a bit embarrassed.

"You will be allowed because I invited you," he said firmly, smiling now, finally. Seeing that look on his face, my breath caught in my throat and the butterflies were let loose anew in my stomach. The weights around my wrists suddenly disappearing and I grinned at him, broadly and without restraint.

"Is that a yes?" he asked, his own smile widening. I nodded enthusiastically and he stepped towards me, just a slight movement, but enough to bring him close enough that I could pick out the flecks of amber in his eyes.

I suddenly became very aware of my breathing; the way my chest expanded with each breath, the way the air felt on my moistened lips as they parted on an inhale, and as I looked up into his eyes, I drew my bottom lip into my mouth, tugging on it lightly with my teeth, feeling some type of way.

Fascinated, I watched the way his eyes darkened. It made me feel loose-limbed, fluid in a way and as my head tilted slightly to the side, his lips parted, ever so slightly.

"Ky?" The voice calling from the end of the corridor snapped me out of whatever daze I'd just fallen into and my head turned in that direction to see Becka standing there, bag over her shoulder and eyes narrowed, mouth pinched unhappily. Uh oh.

Jihoon followed my gaze and cleared his throat. "I should go," he said quietly, but before he turned, he brushed his hand against mine, so slightly and so briefly that you could have played it off as an accident. But he met my eyes as he did so, and I knew it was no accident. My heart skipped a beat as tingles ran over my hand. I had to pinch my lips together to suppress the silly grin I knew would spread across my face. Oh yeah. I was crushing, hard.

Once he'd walked a few steps away, I turned back around to face Jeremy's office – blessedly vacant – and took a few moments to compose myself. Behind me, I heard him mutter a greeting to Becka and then the tell-tale sound of the staircase door opening, and then closing.

I'd just turned back around when Becka marched up to me, grabbing me firmly by the same hand that Jihoon had just touched. She was not as gentle.

"What the fuck was that, and don't say 'nothing'," she warned, eyes flashing as I'd opened my mouth to do just that.

"Can we at least wait until we get home?" I hissed, as several people from her office strolled by, chatting noisily and oblivious to the drama mere meters away.

Becka looked over to where they now stood, waiting for the elevator and gave me a terse nod in reply.

She barely spoke to me the whole way home. The silence gave me time and space in my own head that I hadn't necessarily welcomed. I knew what Becka would say and if I was really honest with myself... I didn't think I disagreed. I mean, what the hell was I doing? It's one thing to flirt with a handsome celebrity – when you're around them so often, these things happen. Pretty much everyone at Pisces had 'a story,' that was practically a rite of passage in this job.

This felt different; like I was toeing the line of something I wasn't supposed to. Something reckless.

I just couldn't seem to help myself. The more I saw of him – the person he was behind the choreographed image of stages, and cameras – the more I wanted to know him. It was a dangerous game I played; I knew that. But... I think I would regret it more if I didn't at least see where this might lead, even if all I came out of it with was a good memory.

Chapter 15

Later, at home.

The atmosphere between Becka and I as we walked from the bus stop to our building was frosty. Becka had barely looked at me the whole way home, and when she did, it was with a scowl I'd rarely seen on her delicate features.

I hadn't even tried to break the silence, opting instead for following her dutifully, hoping my obsequence would soften her slightly, but as we walked up the staircase to our shared apartment, I didn't think I'd been successful, judging by how hard she was stomping the wooden floorboards.

I braced myself as the apartment door closed behind me, but she just unwound the scarf from around her neck, hung it and her coat up and moved into the living room.

I divulged myself of my coat and hat and toed my shoes off, following after her.

"Becka?" I tried, tentatively.

She looked back at me and held up a hand to stop me. "I need a drink for this," she said, moving into the kitchenette and reaching into the top cupboard where we kept bottles of wine and spirits. To my relief, she opted for a bottle of Rosé, and not the scotch, although how she could stand the taste of scotch, I'll never know. I was partial to a crisp gin and tonic, myself.

I watched for a few moments as she opened the wine bottle and poured herself a small measure, my nervousness fading to a dull twinge, impatience taking its place.

I leant my hip against the counter and waited for her to be done.

"Ready?" I asked as she re-capped the bottle and put it in the fridge. Finally, she turned to look at me, wine glass in hand like some 90's housewife trope. I felt my lips twitch.

"Well?" she prompted me, like I'd been the hold-up here.

"Okay first of all," I began, "this does not need to be this dramatic."

"Okay, first of all," she snapped, "this IS dramatic. Don't you get that?

I sighed. "Look, I know what you're going to say. You've said it all already and I *agree* with you. I just..." I looked away.

"You what?" Becka pressed when I didn't continue.

"I know all the reasons why getting involved with him – an idol – is a bad idea. I just can't seem to help myself," I admitted.

Becka huffed and took a gulp of her wine. "Well, at least you aren't trying to deny it anymore."

"Is there any point?"

"Not really. How long has it been like that?" She looked up at me as she swirled the wine in her glass.

"Like what?"

Becka gave me a droll stare before replying, "like pressing you up against the wall and staring at you like you're the last glass of water in the desert."

The blush that flamed my face and neck was immediate, and not the only thing that made me burn. "A bit dramatic, don't you think?"

"You tell me, you're the one staring in a k-drama." Becka took another sip of wine, leaning her hip against the counter in a mirror of my own stance.

"Oh, behave!" I cried, a laugh bubbling up my throat, despite the look I was still getting from Becka. "Yes, ok, there have be en... looks and even some flirting, but no one's pressing anyone up against the walls." More's the pity, I silently added.

Becka moved away from the counter and walked towards the sofa. "Okay fine, so let's cut the bullshit and you tell me exactly what's going on, so I can get started on telling you exactly how much of an idiot you are, and we can continue on with our lives." She sat down far more gracefully than I could possibly hope for whilst holding a glass of wine.

In contrast, I moved to sit on the other side of the sofa and flopped down. Becka lifted her arm holding the glass to keep it steady as she bounced slightly in my wake. She gave me a stern look.

"What do you want to know?" I sighed.

"Literally everything," she replied. "Tell me how it started, when you've met, what's been said, everything." Her tone implied this was non-negotiable, and in the interest of our long and cherished relationship, I did tell her. Mostly everything.

I started with what she already knew, how we'd met in the lobby after I'd dropped the box of cables, to when I'd first taken them lunch, except I now filled in with more detail about how our interactions had always seemed more... intense.

She was scandalised when I described our lunch together and almost choked on her wine when I told her that we'd exchanged telephone numbers.

But her eyes grew soft when I described how I'd started to feel, and I knew she was remembering her recent break-up with the man she described as her 'first and most incompatible love'.

"Oh Ky," she breathed. "You're really feeling this, aren't you?"

Wordlessly, I nodded. Becka reached for my hand and squeezed.

"You know how this will end though, don't you?"

I swallowed past the sudden lump in my throat and, looking down, I said, "I know. I've known from the start this wouldn't go anywhere. I've considered it, y'know," I lifted my eyes to meet Becka's sad, blue ones.

"I've thought about how it could work; video calls and the like, but every time I find a logistical work around, I keep coming back to the obvious." My voice hitched and I took a moment to compose myself. Becka kept rubbing soothing circles on the back of my hand.

"K-Pop idols are a whole different thing. If he was in an American boy band," I huffed a small laugh, "it wouldn't be so bad. But his fandom, his company, the whole idol culture..."

"There's a million different, very valid reasons why a relationship would not work."

It felt like I'd thought of every single reason – quite apart from the fact that I hardly knew him.

Then there was the distance, the necessary secrecy, and, of course, the undeniable imbalance of power between us. Those reasons alone should've been enough to make me slam the brakes, but the truth was, they weren't what scared me the most.

What made me hesitate the most was the overwhelming way in which I felt myself falling further down this rabbit hole. It scared me because my feelings felt disproportionate to the scope of our actual interactions, how much time we'd spent together, talked with each other. What I felt was... too big, for how little time we'd known each other.

And what if I was alone in that? What if all these moments I'd turned over in my head, replayed countless times, what if they'd been something to me, that they hadn't been to him?

Because surely there was no way Jihoon could feel the same way. It was so inconceivable when he was who he was, living the life he did, and I was... just me. What if all this was for nothing?

Becka watched me with sad eyes. "I wish I had something I could say that would make this a little less shitty for you, babes," she said softly. "If it was just a fling, it would be so much easier to let it go and just have the fun memories. But I think you understand that this can't be anything more than memories, and maybe one day they'll be fun to look back on."

She sniffed suddenly and looked away, before taking a fortifying gulp of her wine. I knew intuitively she must have been thinking of her ex – Ben. The reason why she'd had a spare room in her apartment this year. The reason why she was refusing to date at the moment. The reason why I sometimes found photos, or trinkets hidden in drawers, or under the sofa. Things and memories tucked away so as not to be reminders, but also things she couldn't bear to throw away.

My eyes pinched in shared pain for my best friend.

Turning back to me she said, "There's nothing you can do about the way you feel. What you can do is decide how to deal with it. If you decide to stay in contact with him, you need to be very realistic with yourself about what this can only ever be."

Becka puffed out a breath. "It would probably be easier to go with a clean break. Delete his number and admire him from afar, just like you were doing before. But," she sighed, a sound so full of unresolved feelings of her own, "you need to decide if you can do that."

"Can't you tell me what to do?" I half-joked, attempting a smile that felt almost painful.

"Oh babes, I can't even tell myself what to do," Becka chuckled wryly. "I can tell you what I think you should do, but I'm not in your feelings, only you are."

Becka's eyes suddenly flashed, as if she'd only just thought of something. "Ky, do you know how he feels about you?"

"How does anyone ever really know?" I countered. Becka nodded in agreement.

"But, I think..." I worried at my lip, "I think he likes me." And lord help me, I couldn't help the way those words made my heart flutter.

"Oh babes," Becka sighed again.

"I know," I agreed, shaking my head, sadly.

We sat like that, in companionable silence, for several more minutes, the sound of traffic from the street outside filtering up to provide a constant background hum, reminding me that the world outside goes on.

Tuesday

"Hello?" I said into my mobile phone, bemused that the caller was from Pisces. I was just downstairs in the storage cupboard, sorting through some music sheets.

"Food's here," snapped a brusque voice before the line dropped.

I stared at the now blank screen like it would provide any further context, but only the smiling faces of me and Becka on a trip to Camden last year stared back at me.

Reasoning it could only really have been one person; I stood up from where I was sitting on the floor and made my way over to the door. Poking my head out, I looked over to the reception desk where Donna stood.

"Did you call me?" I called over. Donna looked over at me with a scowl and pointed one sharp fingernail at the side of her head where I could now see her headset. She said something into it, presumably on a call. She then pointed that sharp fingernail at the reception desk. Following her nail, I saw a collection of white, plastic bags.

Ah. Lunch was here.

This had become my accepted task, and although Becka had floated the idea of me not doing it today, in the spirit of distancing myself, I assured her I could handle it. I was also not sure if I wanted to do as she suggested and distance myself.

I closed the door behind me and walked over to the reception desk and as had become my habit, I grabbed the hospitality trolley and began unloading the food containers from the plastic bags. I rearranged the contents as aesthetically as I could, fully aware that it would all just be spread out on the table in Studio 3. I half-smiled at the futility of my actions, but didn't stop.

I heard Donna hang up her call, so I looked over to her and said, "You knew where I was, you could have come to get me, you didn't need to call me." I meant it as a friendly barb, but Donna looked so affronted I might as well have suggested she start day drinking.

"I can't leave this desk," she sniffed.

"Are you chained by the ankles? Need me to bust you out?" I meant this as a joke, I really did, but by the withering look she gave me, you'd think I'd called her incompetent.

"Okay then," I muttered, wheeling the trolley round and heading for the lift.

The whole way to the studio, I kept telling myself to be cool, but all that had been running through my mind all morning – and most of last night – was how this was the last day I was going to see Jihoon. It made me antsy, feeling like every moment I wasn't up here was a moment wasted. If I was never going to see him again, I didn't want to waste any time.

I got to the studio and looked in through the porthole window. The producer's chair was spun around so that I could see it was empty, so no Trevor Kyle. From my vantage, however, I could clearly see that Jihoon was in the vocal booth and he was singing. For a few moments, I just watched, but then Youngsoo walked past the door and not wanting to get caught peeping, I knocked lightly. Youngsoo turned around and, seeing me, opened the door to allow me entry.

"Good afternoon," I said, bowing slightly, still self-conscious I wasn't doing it properly. He returned the gesture but said nothing. He did help me lay out the food on the table, however. Jihoon hadn't seen me yet, the vocal booth was directly in front of the production deck, and the table I was setting the food on was on the far side of the wall, not in direct line of sight so as not to be disruptive.

Just then, Youngsoo's phone rang. He looked at it briefly before hurrying out of the studio to pick it up. I was now alone in the studio, besides Jihoon in the booth. I couldn't hear him though; the volume must be going through the headset that I could see resting on the producer's chair.

Feeling slightly voyeuristic, I just stood there, watching Jihoon sing. I watched the sway of his body as he moved with the song, leaning into it, the way his eyes scrunched closed, the way his nimble fingers pressed against his headset. The way he licked his lips.

I moved towards the deck, unconsciously hovering my fingers over the sound bar that would move the output from headset to room speaker and allow me to hear what he was singing, but I hesitated. I knew from experience how personal a draft track was. I didn't have the right to intrude like that. I let my hand drop back to my side and instead allowed myself to admire the man behind the glass, in silence.

And as I watched, I knew absolutely and without reservation that GVibes was not what I was attracted to. It was this man right here. It was the way he looked at me so intently. It was the kindness and respect he gave without hesitation. And yes, it was also that he was wildly handsome.

When he was in full performance mode with the outfits, the makeup, the faces he pulled...it was almost hard to look at him directly. But here, when he was just in a sound booth, not performing for anyone but the microphone... there was even now something so perfect about him. I couldn't describe it, but I could feel how my

133

body felt pulled towards him, a force so persuasive I almost took a step forward.

Without warning, Jihoon opened his eyes, almost immediately seeing me. He jerked, grabbing at his chest before laughing and I gave a little wave. He pointed at his ears, a questioning raise of his eyebrow. I shook my head and lifted the headphone on the chair, pointing to them. He looked relieved, which I thought was adorable. One of the world's most in-demand performers was shy.

He moved towards the door to exit the booth, and I walked to meet him, but just then, Youngsoo re-entered the room, looking surprised to see me still there. He pointed at the food on the table and said, "All okay?"

I nodded and said, "Yes, sorry, I'll be on my way." Youngsoo bowed and held out his hand to hold the door open for me, the hint clear as day.

I spared a look back at the booth to see Jihoon standing there, watching us. He lifted a hand in goodbye and I smiled back at him before leaving the studio.

I allowed myself one deep inhale as the door closed behind me, one last glance in the porthole window, before moving back off down the corridor and back to my task in the storage cupboard. I would keep these moments, these snippets in my memories of the time I met the popstar.

4:45

I huffed, blowing a strand of hair out of my face as I shook out my arms, tired from lifting the boxes of sheet music.

Just then, my phone chimed with a new message. I pulled it out of my pocket to see the screen illuminated, the name there making me smile as I swiped to open the message.

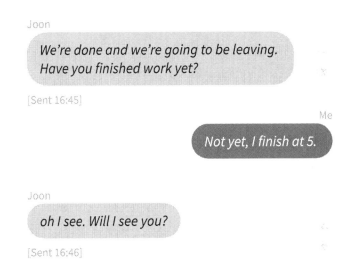

Joon

We're done and we're going to be leaving. Have you finished work yet?

[Sent 16:45]

Me

Not yet, I finish at 5.

Joon

oh I see. Will I see you?

[Sent 16:46]

I didn't try to suppress the smile that pulled across my lips, knowing full well it was goofy, but there was no one here to see.

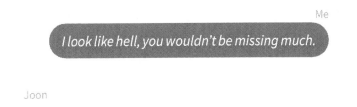

Me

I look like hell, you wouldn't be missing much.

Joon

both of those things are wrong.

[Sent 16:48]

I grinned and then took a moment to try brushing the dust off, it was everywhere. After some fruitless slapping at my arms and hair, I gave it up as a bad job and tapped out a brief reply.

Me

I'm done here, I'm going upstairs to get my stuff. Maybe I'll see you on the stairs.

I quickly stuffed the last box under the shelves, giving it a firm nudge with my boot to make it fit and hustled towards the door, closing it carefully behind me and walking quickly across the lobby.

I waved at Donna, but she only frowned at me. I wondered who — if anyone — she was actually friendly to, because it certainly wasn't me.

I pushed open the door to the stairwell and made my way up, the air in there blessedly cooler, a balm to my warm face.

I was just turning the corner on the first flight when the second-floor door opened above and then closed, the sound reverberating in the enclosed space. A head popped over the railings, a familiar grin under a halo of wavy, black hair.

I took the stairs two at a time until I was level with him, breathing slightly harder from the effort.

"Hello," I panted slightly.

"Hello," he greeted me with a smile, but his expression shifted as his gaze caught on the side of my head. He frowned slightly, lifting a hand as if to reach out, then hesitated. His eyes met mine, silently asking for permission. I didn't say anything, just stared up at him, and whatever he saw in my eyes was all the encouragement he needed.

His long fingers reached for my hair, gently lifting a strand. As he pulled it slightly forward, I noticed a curl of shredded paper tangled in there pretty good.

Patiently, and with the dexterity of a skilled guitarist, he gently untangled the paper from my hair and let it float down the stairwell.

"Thank you," I murmured, very aware that his fingers still lingered in my hair. I watched as he rubbed the strand between his fingers. My nerve endings were stretched so tight I swore I almost felt it. When his eyes flicked back to mine, I felt it almost as a physical force, the piercing intensity wiping away the light-hearted moment and making the air between us feel as charged as a thunderstorm.

"Kaiya," he said my name softly, as if testing how it felt on his tongue. "Do you have a boyfriend?"

I inhaled, "a bit late to ask that, isn't it?" I tried to make a joke, but I could see it landed flat the moment he frowned and dropped my hair.

"Too late?" He repeated.

"Oh, no!" I said, catching on to what he thought I must have meant. I waved my hands in emphasis, "no, I don't have a boyfriend." I tried to laugh, but I was too breathless from my heart jumping into my throat to pull it off.

"Oh!" He smiled and sounded relieved.

"Baek Jihoon!" The sudden shout made us jump apart as if there was a fire between us. I looked over the railings to see Youngsoo and Eun, his bodyguard, standing at the bottom of the stairwell. Youngsoo looked cross and didn't seem to care about hiding it, while Eun just stood there, quietly assessing, face indecipherable.

"Whoops," Jihoon said, "they were waiting for me downstairs. I better go." He smiled a crooked smile. "Will I see you tonight?" he asked hopefully.

I nodded. "Yes." And then he surprised me again by raising his hand, the metal bands on his wrist clanking gently against his watch as he tucked the strand of hair back behind my ear.

"See you later." He smiled at me before he practically ran down the stairs. I waited until I heard the door slam shut, taking the sound of footsteps and voices with it, before I leaned against the wall, puffing out a breath as I tried to calm my hammering heart.

Chapter 16

Later

"What do you wear to a 'casual' wrap-up party for a recording celebrity?!" I flung the only dressy dress I'd brought with me to LA across the room, narrowly missing knocking over the lamp Becka and I had bought from IKEA when I moved in.

"What was wrong with that one?" Becka asked, casually leaning against the door frame watching me.

"Too much."

Becka rolled her eyes at me as she took a sip of her hot, compost-tasting drink and then said, "I really feel like the more of a big deal you make this, the more stressed you're gonna get, babes."

"And I really feel you should get in the bin, but here we are!" I threw a pair of trousers across the room to join the dress and groaned in frustration.

"Do you have any clothes left?" Becka calmly asked.

"No!" I slumped to the floor and looked around at the piles of discarded clothes. Why had I never foreseen the possibility of being asked to a dinner being thrown for a famous person? "Because I'm an intern!" I cried, answering the other half of my own question out loud.

Becka pushed herself off the door frame and took one step into my tiny bedroom. "Okay, crazy lady, up you get," she said, extending a hand to me to help pull me off the floor. "Let's go have a look in my closet, I'm sure I've got something you can wear."

I allowed myself to be led to Becka's marginally bigger bedroom to where she had a built-in wardrobe.

"Sit." She pointed at the bed, and still holding onto her mug, she began to rifle through her clothes, muttering to herself as she did, "No, too small, too slutty, not slutty enough..." and on it went until we had a small pile of contenders piled up on the bed next to where I was sitting.

Suddenly, Becka pulled a hanger out and cried, "Bingo, baby!"

I frowned down at the pool of fabric. "Are you sure?"

"Fuck yes," she exclaimed in triumph, "this is the one!"

"I don't know, it doesn't scream 'casual' to me."

"Babes, trust me. I spoke to Celine about this dinner and it is not casual, she's booked it at Emporia. It's chill, but not casual."

I stood up and took the hanger from her. "Do you think my black stilettos will go with this?"

"Definitely." Becka nodded enthusiastically.

"Okay then," I said with a sigh, "I bow to your superior knowledge."

One hour later

"Becka, come on!" I yelled at her closed bedroom door from where I was standing in the kitchenette, popping rolled up chunks of bread into my mouth. Mama didn't raise an idiot; always line your stomach before going out and drinking.

My heels clinked softly as I walked across the small apartment to Becka's bedroom door and knocked. "Are you coming, or not?" I called.

"Jesus Christ, give me a minute!" She called back. I rolled my eyes and walked back over to the full-length mirror by the door to once again make sure I hadn't somehow smeared my eyeliner, or some other such fashion disaster.

Critically eying my image, I had to concede the win to Becka on this one. I looked kind of fire. I was wearing a black playsuit that flowed loosely around my mid-thighs, so it looked like it could be a skirt, but I had the confidence of not being able to accidentally flash anyone. It had butterfly sleeves that covered my arms to mid-bicep and a neckline that only went down to show a hint of cleavage. From the front it looked playful, yet modest. But when I turned around, it was a different story. The back was almost entirely open all the way down to my tailbone. There was a strap across my shoulders and that was about it. I didn't have any jewellery on except for one simple silver bangle and my shoes were pretty, but nondescript black stilettos with a silver chain across my ankles.

I couldn't do makeup for crap, so I'd stayed basic with some eyeliner and mascara, giving my eyes a smoky, but understated smoulder. I'd brushed some highlighter across my cheekbones and lightly applied a shimmery pink lip balm. I'd left my chestnut brown hair down, it was so long that unless I moved it to the side, my exposed back would be less... exposed.

"If you're gonna leave him with any last images of you, let it be this one," Becka smiled at me in the reflection, sneaking up on me.

"Holy hell!" The words burst out of me as I saw what she was wearing. "Have they always been that big?" I couldn't take my eyes off her chest, and she laughed.

"The magic of a body-con wrap dress, babes," she winked at me.

She looked stunning. She was wearing an emerald green wrap dress that hugged every contour of her body, and invented a couple new ones, by the looks of it. With her blonde hair ruffling around her shoulders in artfully created waves, she looked like a sexy forest nymph.

"There was no part of this evening that was going to be 'casual', was there?" I asked sceptically.

Becka laughed, "No, babes. Wait till you see what half the office is wearing. It's ho season."

I barked out a laugh that had Becka grinning at me.

"Come on, we better go. I'll call an Uber."

Half an hour later we pulled up outside Emporia and it was immediately evident from the outside that this was not a place you came to 'casually'. An imposing stone façade lit up by art-fully concealed lighting gave the impression of a fashion show, including the roll of red carpet extending from the massive front doors to the kerb.

I gave a low whistle as the Uber pulled away, leaving us stand-ing there, looking up at the restaurant.

"How did Celine manage to get a last-minute booking here?" I asked, wonder in my tone.

"Pfft, she name-dropped, obviously." Becka scoffed, although even I could see the look of admiration in her eyes. "From what she told me, they practically rolled over when they heard who she was booking for. Your boy has pull," she said, with an ap-provingly nod of her head.

"Y'know," I said conversationally, deciding to ignore the 'your boy' comment, "if we were in a film in the 80's, this is the moment where we'd take one last drag of our cigarettes, before dropping them on the pavement and stamping them out."

Becka looked at me, her nose scrunched. "You're so weird."

"But am I wrong though?"

"Come on, Molly Ringwald," Becka huffed and grabbed my arm to wind it with her own and together, we walked up the red carpet to the front doors.

There was no bouncer on the door, but there was a very pretty, professional looking woman standing at a maître d' podium inside the foyer.

"Good evening," she said in a pleasant tone, "may I take the name on your reservation, please?"

Becka gave Celine's name and confirmed it was a VIP booking. The woman's face immediately changed from pleasant disinterest to something resembling reverence.

"Of course," she said, "please wait one moment." She turned and flagged down a young man dressed uniformly in black suit trousers and a black shirt. "Jake will take you to the lounge where the rest of your party is gathering. I hope you have an enjoyable night." She smiled widely at us as we followed the young server.

Becka and I tried not to gape as we were led through the restaurant, the dark aesthetic and discreet background club music confirming Becka had been right about the dress code. All the guests we saw were dressed in much the same way we were.

The server, Jake, led us all the way through the restaurant and then up a staircase to the second floor, which had a much more relaxed vibe. It was a similar palette of black, dark grey and silver accents, but the lighting was more wall sconce, instead of pointy chandelier, like it had been downstairs. The music was also more relaxed, less club, more Ibiza chillout. It was a vibe.

It was clear that our party had booked out the entirety of the upstairs. There were other tables laid out, but all were empty. Our party was spread out over four or five large circular tables in the centre of the large room. It looked like most of the building had been invited, although at a glance there were plenty of people there I didn't know, so perhaps it wouldn't be quite so obvious an intern had somehow snagged an invitation.

The server stopped a respectful distance away from the party and asked us if we'd like any drinks. We both ordered a glass of wine, and he nodded and disappeared back to wherever the wine was.

Becka and I lingered awkwardly, each of us not knowing where to slot in when, blessedly, Celine walked past and stopped when she saw us. She was clearly already a wine or two deep as she was far friendlier to me than normal.

"Guys! You look great, mwah!" She actually said the word as she air-kissed us in turn. I shared a look with Becka.

"Why are you just standing here? Come, sit down!" Celine waved her arm magnanimously and pulled us over to a table that still had a few empty seats. Becka and I sat down, and I was relieved to be seated next to a person from Becka's team that I actually knew enough to make small talk with. Bonus points that Celine seemed either too drunk, or too merry to not remember I hadn't been on the official guest list.

I was just rearranging my hair over my shoulders when I looked up across the table to see Jihoon. He was sitting at another table across the way from ours, several people in between us, but as the tables were round, I had a completely unobstructed view of him, although he hadn't seen me yet.

I took the time to check him out, completely unabashedly. Jihoon was easily the least dressed up of anyone there, wearing an oversized black t-shirt and a silver chain – similar to mine, I realized – and several glinting earrings in his ears. He was laughing at something someone opposite him said, and as his eyes darted around, I saw them snag on me. His grin widened further. I didn't dare wave, but I smiled back.

About half-way through the dinner, I was more and more pleased with the wisdom of lining my stomach before coming out. Not only were the portions artistically small (we were apparently eating a taster menu of half a dozen dishes), but they also refreshed our wine more often than our plates. Looking around at our table, I could tell at least half of them would be calling off work tomorrow. Rookie mistake. I shook my head wryly.

Jihoon and I had snuck glances at each other all evening and instead of being frustrating, it felt playful, like we were sharing a secret. He'd look at me, then over at someone clearly three sheets to the wind and waggle his eyebrows, making me laugh, which I'd have to then either cover as a cough or pretend to be in response to something someone at our table said. I'm sure I had left quite the impression on some of these people, but I didn't care.

After my third attempt – and failure – at catching the passing waiter's attention to ask for some water, I decided to take matters into my own hands.

"I'm going to the bar to get some water. Do you want some?" I asked Becka next to me, who was so deep in conversation with the person to her right that she just waved her hand at me. I got to my feet and, looking about, spotting the bar way on the other side of the floor. I made my way over to it, realising as I balanced in my heels that I was slightly more buzzed than I intended to be, but I didn't stumble once. Which I was quite proud of.

I reached the bar and leaned my hip into it. There was no one manning the bar just then, but I was happy to wait. It was quite nice to stretch my legs after sitting for so long.

Just then, I became aware of a presence behind me. I don't know if it was the body heat I felt, or the way that the world seemed to fall just a little silent around him, but when I looked over my shoulder, Jihoon was there, standing a handful of feet away from me, hands in his pockets.

"Hello," he smiled at me.

"Hello," I replied, suddenly shy.

"Can I get you a drink?" he said, gesturing at the bar.

"Oh, um, I'm just waiting for someone to come back so I can get some water," I said, looking back at the bar and without thinking, I pulled my hair around over my shoulder, the sudden breeze at my back suddenly reminding me what I was wearing, and what it was not covering.

Jihoon said something in Korean so low I barely heard him, and when I looked back over my shoulder, his eyes were glued to my bare back. I quickly looked back around to hide my smile and suddenly, feeling a bit daring, I moved my forearms up to lean against the bar, flexing my back, hyper aware of every air current, nerves alight for every sensation, including the imaginary one I could feel from his gaze.

Then without warning, Jihoon was up against me, pressing me into the bar, the unexpected contact making me gasp.

"Excuse me, coming through," a server bustled behind us, carrying a tray so laden with drinks I was surprised he could carry it. "I'll be right with you," he called over his shoulder.

But even as the server passed us, Jihoon did not move. He was pressed so closely to me that I felt it every time he breathed. His arms were braced on the bar on either side of me, so instead of pushing against me, he was caging me in, almost protectively.

Slowly, I turned in the circle of his arms, rubbing my bare back against him like a cat, delighting in the feel of his hard, muscular chest hidden under the soft fabric of his baggy t-shirt.

Once I was fully turned to him, our faces were only inches apart. I drew my bottom lip into my mouth as I watched his eyes roving over my face and further down my neck before snapping back up to meet my own inquiring gaze.

As if suddenly remembering where, and perhaps who he was, Jihoon stepped away from me, arms dropping to his sides, sliding one hand into his pocket, the very image of aloofness.

"There's a roof garden. Do you want to see it with me?" he asked, his tone light and not at all matching the intense darkness of his eyes.

Wordlessly, I nodded and followed him, forgetting all about getting a drink.

Chapter 17

I smelt the rosemary and mint before I saw the many bushes of both lining the far wall, trellised by thousands of tiny, twinkling lights.

"Wow," I breathed, "pretty."

"Yes," Jihoon replied, but he wasn't looking at the patio arrangements. I blushed under his stare.

I sniffed suddenly, smelling cigarette smoke. Looking to my right I saw a couple sitting under a patio warmer, their clouds of smoke puffing into the air. They talked too low for me to hear, and I didn't think they'd seen us yet. I also couldn't tell if they were from our party or not.

"Over here," I whispered, and without thinking I clenched my fingers in his t-shirt and directed us both to a spot along the wall farther away from the door and the couple.

There was a lone padded rattan sofa here, but no further furniture. It was clear this was not part of the patio's main area, which suited me fine, even though it was dark.

Once I was sure we hadn't been spotted, I looked back around to see Jihoon looking down at where my hand was still fisted in his t-shirt. Embarrassed, I dropped my hand.

"Sorry," I mumbled.

He looked down at me, dark eyes shining in the lights reflected off the glass buildings all around us, expression unfathomable.

"Should we sit?" I motioned to the sofa beside us. He gestured that I sit first, so I sat down and crossed my legs. Jihoon sat beside me and folded his hands in his lap. He didn't look at me, his eyes were focused on the view spread out in front of us.

"You must be tired," I commented, "it's been a long week."

He pursed his lips as he cocked his head to the side, "Yes, but I'm used to it so it's not been bad."

"Have you been able to do anything fun while you've been here?"

At this, he looks at me. "I got to meet you." My blush could have acted as one of the patio heaters, but I wasn't sure he could see it, tucked away as we were.

"I'm not sure I count," I mumbled, fiddling with my bangle.

"I think you do." He nodded as he said this and I beamed at him.

"Can I ask you something?" The frown on his face made me pause, even though I thought I knew what he was going to ask.

"Anything," I said quietly.

"Are you a fan?" So straightforward, but then what would be the point of beating around the bush?

I inhaled deeply. "Would it matter?"

Jihoon tugged on his earlobe and looked back over towards the street, his earrings glinting. "I want to say no, but I think it does."

I nodded, looking down at my fingers

"I've been a fan for a couple years, although I'm not sure I'm at 'Viber' level," I chuckled quietly, remembering the conversation Becka and I had had about this very subject.

Jihoon hummed. "Have you been to a concert?"

"No," I answered honestly, "last time you toured the UK, I couldn't get tickets."

He tutted at me, "Next time, I'll get you tickets, don't worry."

My heart stuttered in a way that reminded me who I was sitting next to. The giddy little flutter made me feel guilty, which in turn reassured me that his idolness was not the reason my breath caught in my throat to see the way he looked up at me from under his eyelashes.

I laughed, the tension rolling up my throat to bubble out in a burst of laughter that had me slapping my hand over my mouth. Jihoon smirked at me, and I leaned my head back against the wall as relief made my whole-body tingle. I was also woman enough to acknowledge I was buzzed from all the times the efficient servers had re-filled my wine glass.

"I was so afraid you were going to tell me to get lost," I admitted.

He frowned and I quickly explained, "I thought you'd tell me you didn't want to see me anymore."

His eyes widened and his lips made a silent 'o' before he nodded, "Normally, it is hard to be friends with fans, they want you to perform all the time, to be the stage person, but you don't make me feel like that."

Before I could stop myself, hell before the thought even crossed my mind, my mouth opened and out fell, "Friends?"

Jihoon's eyes shot to mine before quickly flicking away. He huffed a quiet laugh. "More?" he said, so quietly I leaned forward, but he still didn't look at me, just fiddled with his thumb ring.

I felt like we were teetering on the edge of some precipice, still dancing around each other. There were so many reasons to hold back. A clean break, like Becka had said. I should stay away from him; I shouldn't even entertain the idea of him. He was off limits and so far out of my league...

I opened my mouth to say something – what I don't know because at that moment, my phone chimed with several insistent chirps.

Frowning, I pulled it out of my pocket and slid my finger up the screen to unlock it.

"Ah shhii..." I hissed quietly, reading the multiple messages from Becka.

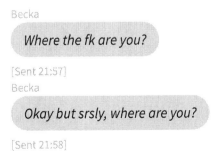

Becka

Where the fk are you?

[Sent 21:57]

Becka

Okay but srsly, where are you?

[Sent 21:58]

Becka

> *you're not in the bathroom, where R U?*

[Sent 22:01]

Becka

> *C says JH isn't here either R U WITH THE IDOL?*

[Sent 22:02]

Becka

> *Babes, people are starting to look for him, so if you're with him, SCATTER!*

[Sent 22:03]

"Fuck," I muttered, looking around to see if people were indeed starting a search party.

"What's wrong?" Jihoon asked, following my gaze.

"Becka says people are looking for you."

"Fuck," he sighed, and I burst out laughing.

"What?" he asked, frowning at me as I tried to stifle my giggles, my happy buzz not dampened by the thought of the drunk staff of Pisces searching for the man sitting next to me.

"You're not supposed to say, 'fuck'," I giggled.

"You said 'fuck'," he protested.

"I'm not an idol," I stage-whispered, holding a hand to my mouth.

To my delight, he just rolled his eyes and stood up. "Come," he said, and he held out a hand to me. Without hesitation, I put my hand in his larger one and allowed him to pull me to my feet. I wobbled slightly in my heels, but his firm grip on my hand held me steady as we stood face to face once more.

Not laughing anymore, I said, "We better go back in." He nodded, and I turned to walk away towards the door.

I'd taken one single step past the bench when Jihoon grabbed my wrist, turning me around so fast that I stumbled back into his chest. His other hand found my waist as he firmly guided me backward until my back hit the wall. He released my hand to put his above my head, holding me gently as he caged me in.

Panting suddenly, I looked up at him, his eyes dark but his face gentle.

"Tell me 'no'," he whispered. I said nothing, my chest heaving above my pounding heart.

His head lowered until his hair tickled the side of my face. "Tell me to stop," his voice was almost a whine as he ran his nose softly down my cheek.

"No." My voice was barely a breath, my thoughts scattered.

"No?" He pressed his mouth to the sensitive spot just under my ear and I shuddered, heat coiling low in my belly, tension thrumming through me like a struck chord.

"Don't stop," I said firmer this time, then gasping as his hand moved upwards from my waist, tracing the contour of my side and feathering up to my shoulder.

"Yes?" he whispered against my cheek, the heat of his body burning me through the thin fabric of my clothes.

"Yes." The word was barely out of my mouth before his hand trailed up my neck, his thumb tipping my chin up to meet his mouth as he pressed his lips to mine.

I groaned into his mouth as the touch ignited something inside me. His lips were soft as they moved against mine, insistent and hungry and I met him with my own insistence, parting my lips slightly. He tilted my head back further, deepening the kiss, pushing me more firmly into the wall. His body was hard against me, all the firmness of his body pushing into the softness of mine.

He tasted of whiskey and warmth, his tongue teasing along my bottom lip. It was like I was falling into him. My head swam with the intensity of the need I felt, and I had to physically restrain myself from pawing at him.

When he finally pulled back, he was panting as he leaned his forehead against mine and I realised I was tightly clutching the front of his t-shirt in my fists. I let go, embarrassed and he grinned. He gently tucked a strand of hair behind my ear as I looked up at him, still breathing heavily.

"I have a free day tomorrow and I want to spend it with you. Will you come?" he said softly, not making any effort to move away from me, seemingly quite comfortable with his hand still resting on the wall above my head.

Not even taking the time to think it through, I nodded and said, "yes."

Jihoon smiled and kissed the tip of my nose, the action so sweet and unexpected that I felt my eyes prick but I blinked away the sensation as I looked over his shoulder towards the door that led back into the restaurant.

"We should go before someone comes looking for you."

Jihoon sighed, but didn't refute the idea. His hand fell away from the wall, and he took a step back. I immediately missed the warmth of his body as a chill breezed over my skin, making me shudder and I unconsciously swayed towards him. I wished he could put his arm around my shoulder, but heading back into the party like that would be ill advised.

I silently sighed to myself, feeling a confusing mix of elation and melancholy.

We decided it would be best if we went in separately, so Jihoon went in first, the idea being that everyone would be focused on him so that when I went back to my table, no one would notice.

While waiting a couple of minutes to give Jihoon time, I went over to the balcony to look out over the block. Emporia was in a trendy, downtown spot surrounded by other bustling nightlife, but across the street was a small park that seemed out of place surrounded by concrete, thumping music and neon lights. It wasn't big, just a handful of trees in a grassy square with a meandering path lit by quaint streetlights. I watched for a few minutes, seeing a couple strolling through, hand-in-hand, completely unaffected by the idea that someone might see them.

I sighed and turned away, heading back inside.

The rest of the night was a blur of noise, loud talking and stolen glances and before long, the restaurant was closing, and we were being herded out.

Looking down at my phone I saw it was just past 2;00am. It was amazing we hadn't been kicked out hours ago, but then I imagine that's what being a VIP got you.

Most of Pisces was amassed on the sidewalk, laughing raucously and calling rides and so almost no one noticed when a black SUV pulled up to the kerbside and Jihoon and his team piled in. I was watching though, I saw him scan the crowd once, twice before his eyes found mine. He smiled and I waved back.

Becka was quiet next to me, practically falling asleep standing up and when our Uber turned up, the driver got out and shouted our names over the hubbub of the crowd, I had to pull her along and shove her in the backseat where she proceeded to lean her head back on the seat and fall asleep.

"Good night?" The driver asked amiably.

"The best," I replied, looking out of the window as the lights sped past, smiling the whole way home.

Chapter 18

Wednesday 06:15

My alarm went off, almost unnecessarily, as I'd barely slept. *Dozing,* my mum would have called it. I knew the second we got home, and I got ready for bed that I wouldn't be able to sleep. My mind had raced, replaying our kiss countless times, and I'd wavered between joy and anxiety, making sleep impossible.

I sighed as I got up, knowing I'd probably catch grief for calling off work, but I didn't care enough to reconsider. I 'pffed' to myself just thinking about it, *as if.*

I shuffled from my bedroom into the lounge as I dialled Jeremy's mobile number, knowing full well he wouldn't pick up at this time in the morning.

"Hi Jeremy, I'm really sorry to do this to you, but I'm not feeling well enough to come in today. I've got a banging migraine, and I need to take the day to rest up. I'll see you tomorrow."

I hung up and turned to see Becka standing in her bedroom doorway, black makeup smeared across her eyes.

"You look fresh," I quipped.

"You're playing hooky?" she yawned, running a hand down her face and smearing last night's makeup even further down her cheeks.

"Yes." I walked over to the coffee pot and began to prepare a fresh pot. "Want one?" I asked over my shoulder.

"Desperately," she croaked, "but after my shower. Why are my toes muddy?"

"You refused to wear your shoes when we got home and said you wanted to feel the grass on your feet." I rummaged through the cupboard for a coffee filter.

"They're still in the bag on the counter," Becka said, "what grass?"

I turned around and looked through the unpacked grocery bag, finding the pack of filters. "Thanks. The grass outside on the sidewalk, the bit with the tree."

"That's where Jose takes Milo to do his business!" Becka wailed, and I cackled. Jose was our downstairs neighbour, and Milo was his very sweet, very geriatric chihuahua.

Becka ran to the shower, hot-stepping like she was jumping on stones, and I laughed as I prepared the coffee.

By the time Becka was out of the shower, wrapped in a towel and drying her hair on another, I was sat at the counter, drinking a coffee and eating buttered toast.

"If you're staying home today, you can clean these floors," she grumbled, pouring herself a coffee.

"Can't. I won't be here."

Becka slowly spun around like a turnstile mannequin to face me. "Whhyyy..." she said, drawing out the word, eyes narrowing in suspicion.

I finished my bite of toast before I answered her, deciding honesty was best. "Because I'm spending the day with Jihoon before he flies home tomorrow."

I watched Becka's face as it slackened, her mouth falling open. She put her coffee down and took the seat next to me.

"Babes, are you sure this is a good idea?"

"No," I said honestly, "but it's what I want."

Becka regarded me plainly for so long I felt the need to fill the silence with something other than the sound of crunching toast.

"Okay," she finally said, taking a sip of coffee.

"Okay?"

"Okay," she repeated. "Ky, you're a grown-ass adult and I'm not your mother-"

"Thank God," we chimed in unison and shared a grin at the years-old joke.

"If this is what you want, who the hell am I to tell you not to?"

I finished my toast and wiped my hands down my pyjama bottoms. "I appreciate that, thank you."

"But I reserve the right to tell you 'I told you so' when you come home crying about it!" She waggled her finger at me, but there was no ice in her tone.

Becka stood up and took a few gulps of her coffee before dumping it in the sink and walking back to her bedroom.

"What are you both going to do today, anyway?" she threw over her shoulder.

I thought for a few moments before realising I had absolutely no idea. We hadn't spoken about it.

"I have no idea," I laughed.

"I'm rolling my eyes at you," Becka called from her room.

"Yeah, me too," I said to myself as I pulled out my phone. There was one new message, sent about half an hour ago.

Joon

Good morning

[Sent 06:23]

Me

Good morning. Sleep well?

Joon

no, lol. You?

[Sent 06:51]

Me

Not even slightly.

While I waited for a reply, I pottered around the kitchen, tidying things away, running possible outfits choices through my head.

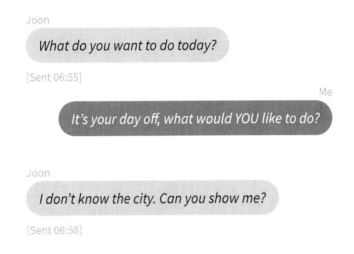

Joon

What do you want to do today?

[Sent 06:55]

Me

It's your day off, what would YOU like to do?

Joon

I don't know the city. Can you show me?

[Sent 06:58]

I put my phone down as I undressed and turned the shower on.

Me

I'll think about what we can do together.

I'd just put my phone down when it dinged with a new message and unable to resist the urge, I opened the message before getting into the shower, feeling a sudden heat that had nothing to do with the steam pouring out of the cubicle.

Joon

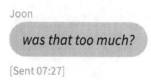

I think about that a lot.

[Sent 07:01]

I groaned and put my phone face down, stepping under the pouring water and immediately adjusting the heat to cool it down.

The pounding water gave me the clarity I needed to run through our options for the day. I immediately discounted actually strolling through downtown LA because while GVibes was still relatively unknown in the eyes of American media, they had a very large and loyal fan following, and all it took was one person recognising him and posting it on-line. And then, boom. Disaster.

One 'nearly-everything' shower later, I was just drying my hair, the plan beginning to formulate in my head when my phone chimed. I draped the towel around my neck and picked it up to see one new message notification.

Joon

was that too much?

[Sent 07:27]

I frowned and opened the bathroom door, the steam wafting out into the hallway as I padded to my room.

Me

too much?

Joon

did I come on too strong? You didn't answer.

[Sent 07:30]

Sudden realisation had me crooning, 'aww', out loud.

"What, 'aww'?" Becka popped her head around my door, making me squeal and grab for my fallen towel.

"Babes, I've seen it all before," she waved my modesty away, "what's so cute?"

Fixing my towel back around myself, I thrust the phone at her, and then immediately felt weird for sharing a personal text exchange. Which was weird in itself, as Becka and I always compared notes.

"Awww," she crooned, passing me back the phone, "he thinks he's being sexually aggressive," she pressed a hand to her heart.

"I know, right? I think they're just a lot more reserved in Korea. That probably is sexually aggressive to him," I pondered aloud.

"You could really freak him out and tell him you're a virgin, really make him feel like a corrupting influence," she laughed.

I snorted and waved her back out of my room so I could get dressed without an audience.

I still hadn't told her about the kiss last night. I wanted to keep it to myself for a while longer, at least until after he was gone. Dissecting it felt too much like making the illusion a reality and right now, I wanted to live in the dream.

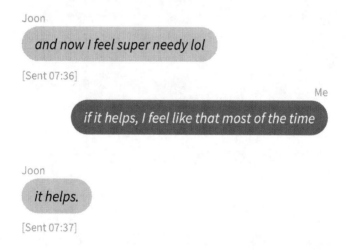

Me

sorry, I was in the shower, that's why I didn't reply.

I had started to really appreciate how upfront he was. There was no ambiguity, no game play. It was... unexpected.

Joon

and now I feel super needy lol

[Sent 07:36]

Me

if it helps, I feel like that most of the time

Joon

it helps.

[Sent 07:37]

I pulled on a pair of denim shorts and a white shirt, the outfit I'd decided on during my shower that would work best for what I was thinking we could do.

I had just finished blow-drying my hair when Becka shouted through my closed door that she was going to work. I shouted back that I'd see her later and started on my makeup, my usual blend of very minimal products.

Ten minutes later, I was ready.

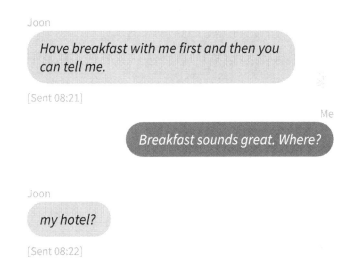

Me

I think I know what we can do today.

His reply was nearly instant.

Joon

Have breakfast with me first and then you can tell me.

[Sent 08:21]

Me

Breakfast sounds great. Where?

Joon

my hotel?

[Sent 08:22]

I knew it was a sensible, no fuss suggestion, and it made sense. Hell, the location was probably as private as it got, but it still made my stomach flip to think about meeting him in his hotel.

Me

Send me the address.

Forty-five minutes later, my Uber pulled up in front of a sky-scraper, the towering 'I' symbol of the Intercontinental Hotel prominently displayed high above, visible from miles away.

"Intercontinental Hotel, Wilshire Boulevard," the driver announced.

"Thanks," I murmured, sliding out of the car while craning my neck to take in the imposing structure. As I walked toward the entrance, I couldn't help but feel under-dressed – an impression that the doorman seemed to share, though he was polite enough not to say anything as he held the door open.

The ground floor was nothing short of palatial. It was vast – so expansive that a few laps around it might get a person well on their way to reaching that golden 10,000 daily steps.

"Miss Kaiya," a voice politely halted me in my tracks, and I looked around for the speaker. Eun, Jihoon's body-guard walked towards me from where he seemed to have been stationed close to the doors and I breathed a sigh of relief that I wouldn't have to try to navigate this place by myself.

"Good morning," I nodded at him politely, which he returned with a brief smile.

"Good morning. Baek Jihoon-nim has asked me to take you to his room for breakfast." Eun's voice was heavily accented, but his language was excellent, like Jihoon's. I think this was the first time I'd actually heard him speak.

"Okay," I smiled, but he just turned around and walked away, presumably thinking I'd follow. I hurried to catch up, the man's legs were like stilts.

The elevator we rode ascended so quickly that my ears popped, the numbers on the little screen racing past so fast that when the doors opened, I had no idea what floor we were on, but I followed Eun like the obedient puppy I felt like.

It felt like several minutes had passed before we finally turned down a quiet, plushly-padded corridor. About halfway down, Eun reached a door and knocked brusquely. He had just raised his fist to knock again, when the door swung open and there stood Jihoon, smiling broadly at me and giving Eun a brisk bow.

"Kaiya, I'm so happy to see you." His face was like sunshine, his expression so genuine, so open that it tugged on my heartstrings.

"Hi, Jihoon," I said shyly, tucking my hands into my pockets.

169

"Please, come in," he said, gesturing for me to enter. I chanced a brief look up at Eun, and though his face was stony, it didn't seem unkind. Just... disapproving. Jihoon didn't seem to care and closed the door behind me as I stepped over the threshold.

"Wow," I murmured, looking around the well-appointed room, but I was really looking straight past it all to the floor-to-ceiling windows that ran along the whole back wall, looking out over downtown LA and as far reaching as the distant mountain range.

The suite itself was really two rooms: a bedroom, visible through a door to my left, and the main room we were standing in. In front of the windows was a seating area with a plush sofa and two padded chairs arranged under a hanging lamp, and further along the back wall, a small dining area clearly positioned to take advantage of the view. The main living area was as big as our entire apartment, I thought wryly to myself.

"I wasn't sure what you'd like, so I got a bit of everything," Jihoon said. He led me over to the dining area, where the table – set for two – was indeed laden with different dishes of pastries; toast and assorted butter, jams and preserves; and bowls of brightly coloured fruits, yogurts and even some small, individual boxes of cereal.

"This looks great, thank you," I said, my stomach rumbling at seeing all the food. Just as he'd done when we ate lunch on Saturday, Jihoon pulled out a chair and motioned for me to sit, pushing it in for me as I did so. It was such a little gesture, but it made me feel warm.

Jihoon sat in the chair opposite me and offered me a plate filled with pastries. "Please, eat," he encouraged. I took a Raspberry Danish and, together, we began to eat.

It was all delicious, the pastry in particular making my eyes flutter closed in pleasure, which made Jihoon laugh. Then he tried one and his laughter silenced in favour of quiet enjoyment.

We'd made a pretty big dent into the pile of food when I pushed my plate of toast and jam away and leaned back in my chair, declaring, "I can't eat another thing, or you'll have to roll me out of here." That made Jihoon laugh again.

"Like Violet from 'Willy Wonka'", he said, surprising me.

"Exactly like that," I moaned, rubbing my belly, accidentally moving the fabric of my shirt when it caught on my navel piercing, the metal bar and gemstone glinting in the light pouring in through the plate-glass windows and drawing Jihoon's gaze.

"You have a piercing," he said, sounding surprised.

I pulled down my shirt, self-consciously. "Yeah, the product of a drunken night out when I was eighteen."

Jihoon looked back at the door to his suite, and then back to me, his eyebrows lowered and a playful smirk on his face. He held a finger to his lips and said, "Ssh, don't tell anyone." And then, to my surprise, he lifted his top up. Once I'd taken a second to get over the shock, I noticed what he must have intended me to see, which was a black lined feather drawn around his side right over his ribs.

"Oh, wow," I breathed, leaning forward in my chair, taking a closer look. "It's so well drawn," I commented, "it almost looks real."

He nodded. "I went to Japan for the artist, he's the best."

I let out a self-derisory little huff and said, "I just went into town for mine."

"You have a tattoo?" He looked surprised.

In answer, I lifted my leg, unlaced my converses, and pulled off my sock. I held out my foot to show him the cluster of vines and flowers I had trailing over the top of my foot and around my ankle.

"Cool," he said, eyes focused on my foot as he scooted his chair to get closer. Gently, he grasped my foot in his hand and pulled it forward so it rested on his jeans-clad knee. My breath caught in my throat as he gently began to trace the meandering vines. I don't think he meant it to be anything more than innocent appreciation of good ink, but the more he ran his fingers over my ankle, the more uncomfortable I got. In the good way.

When I squirmed, he looked up at me and must have seen something in my eyes because he grinned at me, the expression proprietary. He did not remove his fingers, but instead traced patterns over my foot that had nothing to do with the inky flowers.

A sudden knock at the door had us springing apart like errant teenagers, but when no one burst in, I let out a strained giggle. Jihoon got up to open the door and I hastily pulled my sock and shoe back on.

I looked over to the door and could see the tall outline of Eun stood there, but he and Jihoon conversed in low tones and even if it was in English and not Korean, I wouldn't have been able to make it out.

Finished talking, Jihoon headed back to me, leaving Eun stood in the doorway, watching us.

"The car is ready," he said, holding out a hand to me, which was about the same moment I realised that obviously we wouldn't be taking the metro or a bus around the city. I mentally face-palmed that it hadn't occurred to me earlier. I took Jihoon's outstretched hand and allowed him to pull me to my feet, but he held onto my hand as we crossed the room, the warmth of his palm a correlating heat to the expanding warmth in my chest.

Once we reached the door, however, he let it go but flashed me a brief smile so it didn't hit so hard.

Just as before, Eun guided us back through the halls of the hotel and down to the ground floor to the street, where not far away, a black SUV was waiting at the kerb.

We were hustled into the car quickly, Jihoon sliding in first and only once we were settled did I see that Youngsoo was sat in the front seat. He was turned around to watch us, his face unreadable.

"Miss Thompson," he nodded at me, surprising me that he knew my last name and I had a sneaky suspicion that he'd looked me up.

"Hi Youngsoo," I said, waving awkwardly.

"Jihoon said you'd made plans for the day. Where would you like us to take you?" I'd had no idea he spoke such fluent English. I was beginning to feel like the odd one out, with only my rudimentary command of GCSE French.

"Um, I thought we could go to Santa Monica. The beach there is really pretty, and they have a fairground on a pier." I said this to Jihoon, who nodded enthusiastically at me. Youngsoo looked over at the driver and said, "Take us there." I saw the back of the driver's head nod, and off we went, merging seamlessly into the mid-morning LA traffic.

It wasn't a long way, but the traffic at this time in the morning made it slower. It didn't seem to bother Jihoon, who stared out of the windows the whole time with interest.

We made small talk about how different it was to Seoul, how different to the UK, how many times he'd visited, how long I'd been here. Surface level conversation, constantly aware of Youngsoo, Eun and the driver also being in the car with us.

It felt just like that time I went on a date with Leighton Myers in year 10 and his parents had chaperoned us. Same vibes.

Finally, we pulled up to the short-stay car park on the ocean front-walk. It was still early, so there weren't many people milling about yet.

"It opens at 10:00am," I said, looking down at my watch. "It looks like we got here right on time."

Looking up, I saw Youngsoo hand Jihoon a cap and a pair of dark sunglasses, which he promptly put on. I cocked my head to the side, trying to see past the accessories. I mean, I knew it was Jihoon so I could tell it was him, but if I didn't know, or I wasn't looking for him, I wouldn't be able to tell. He was just a guy wearing Ray-Bans, a Cubs cap and nondescript baggy clothes. He looked like any other 20-something you might find hanging out in Santa Monica.

"What do you think?" he said.

I nodded my approval., "You'll do." He smirked and opened his door, the bright sunlight making me raise my hand up to cover my eyes.

"Miss Thompson," Youngsoo pulled my attention back to him, and away from the way the sun framed Jihoon like some sort of religious idol. Youngsoo held out a pair of mirrored shades to me.

"For me?" I said, surprised at the gesture.

He shrugged, as if embarrassed. "Just in case," he said, not elaborating on what the 'case' might be.

I gratefully accepted the sunglasses and opened my side door, stepping out into the bright sunshine of LA in April.

Chapter 19

"Waaa," Jihoon exclaimed drawing out the sound as we walked up the steps leading us to the pier. From here we could see the Ferris wheel and the yellow coaster about half-way down the pier.

I'd come here with Becka when I'd first moved to LA and I'd had a similar reaction.

The UK doesn't really have anything quite like this. There's Blackpool Pleasure Beach but I'm not sure the Wild Mouse compares to an actual roller-coaster on a pier.

All the way up the pier to the Pacific Park there are food stalls, games stalls and arcades. I watched with pleasure as Jihoon's eyes darted from side-to-side, trying to take it all in.

"What do you want to do first?" I asked, looking up at him, enjoying the way he seemed so excited.

"Everything!" he grinned and grabbed my hand, guiding us towards the arcade.

It seemed like we played on every single machine in that arcade at least once. Jihoon absolutely destroyed me on the basketball hoops game, but I got him back when we went head-to-head in Commando Shooter.

He poured an absolute fortune in quarters into those coin-pusher machines, and didn't seem even remotely bothered when his only reward was a keyring and a couple dollars in change.

We were both giddy as we stepped out of the arcade and back onto the pier, squinting in the bright light of the morning sun.

It was still early enough that there weren't too many people milling about, but I did notice how Jihoon hastily put his mirrored sunglasses back on and gave his cap a slight tug. He flashed a smile at me before asking, "Roller-coasters?"

"Heck yeah!" I agreed happily, and together we began walking down the pier again. Our pace was unhurried, and we often paused to look at this or that. Jihoon stood, mouth agape in front of a sugared doughnut vendor. The smell wafting from the fryer could probably have coaxed Snow White out of her glass coffin. I handed over a couple bucks in exchange for a paper bag dotted with fresh grease spots, the heat from the sugary treats inside almost burning my fingers. Gingerly, I tore off a chunk, steam coiling into the air.

"Want some?" I asked, playfully. I expected him to take it from me, but to my surprise – and some illicit delight – he leaned forward and bit the morsel from my fingers, his lips brushing my fingertips. Straightening up, his mouth quirked in a smile even as he chewed. I couldn't see his eyes, but I knew he was watching me, so I feigned indifference as I tore off my own bite sized chunk and popped it into my mouth, before running a fingertip around my lips to catch any sugar there and then licking my finger... slowly.

Jihoon coughed and then turned away, hitting his chest with his fist as if his bite had gone down the wrong way.

"Okay?" I asked, coming up behind him and putting my hand lightly on his back, not failing to notice the way his muscles flexed under my hand.

"Hot," he gasped, clearing his throat again.

I turned away to hide my smile.

Eventually, we made it up the pier to Pacific Park, where we both 'oohed, and ahhed' over the rides. Luckily, the queues were so short we managed to get on pretty much everything we wanted at least once. I almost puked from laughing so hard when we went on Shark Frenzy. Jihoon insisted we ride in the great white shark, of course, but we were both completely unprepared for how much we were going to get thrown around as we rotated around the track. We kept sliding into each other, apologising profusely and then it would keep happening until we just stuck together and slid side-to-side. Eventually Jihoon put his arm around me and held me so tightly I forgot to feel self-conscious.

It was mid-afternoon by the time we finally got round to queuing for the Ferris wheel, after I'd said no to going on the Plunge ride again. I'm not sure my stomach could take another go, and besides, the crowds were getting thicker by now, pressing in on us as we moved throughout the compact park.

Jihoon had been quiet as we stood in line and as we finally stepped into our own pod, I turned to him and asked if he was okay.

"I saw some girls," he said, looking out over the crowd. "I think they might have recognised me." His jaw was clenched tight, and he was fiddling with the hem of his shirt, practically radiating worry.

"Did they take pictures?" I discreetly looked out over the crowd – now some feet below us, trying to see if anyone was pointing in our direction, but I couldn't see anything.

"I don't think so." He sighed. "I just wanted one day."

I took his hand and pulled it into my lap, holding it gently. He turned to look at me and I swear I could feel the intensity of his gaze, even through the sunglasses.

"It must be exhausting, constantly having to look over your shoulder." He didn't respond for so long that I thought he would just breeze past the comment, so when he did talk, I was surprised

"In the beginning," he said, gazing out over the ocean, "it was like a fun game. We'd go somewhere – a store, a café – and see if anyone recognised us." He grinned at some distant memory. "But at some point, it stopped being a game and started being... inconvenient. If we went to the shop, someone would see us and post on Instagram."

He paused, the grin fading. "I didn't mind that so much, but once, someone took a picture of Ace – Seokmin – buying snacks, and it turned into this big thing about his diet." Jihoon shook his head, his jaw tightening.

"As we got bigger, more well-known, we stopped being able to do normal things, like going to get coffee or meeting up with friends." He shrugged, like it didn't matter, but the tightness around his eyes told me it did.

"Sometimes, I just wish I could be normal. And then I feel guilty for not being more grateful for how lucky we are." He shook his head again, a wry smile tugging at his lips. "I just wanted one day to be Jihoon."

What could I say to any of that? So instead of trying to say anything, I just squeezed his hand in silent support as we watched the crowds below us getting smaller

It had gotten quieter the higher up we'd gone, until finally all we could really hear was the whistle of the wind and the distant sounds of the crowd and the passage of the other rides as they whizzed along on their tracks. For a brief period, all there was, was a boy and a girl, sitting in a Ferris wheel, looking out over the sweeping view of Santa Monica Beach all the way to the mountains.

"I think you were right," I said quietly, but urgently, as we exited the Ferris wheel. A handful of young girls were turned in our direction, scanning the crowd of people as we all came off the ride. Jihoon ducked his head and we both quickened our pace as we rejoined the main thoroughfare, the groupings of people now so thick we had to push through in some places.

Just as we were making our way to the exit, someone shouted, "Jihoon-oppa!" I startled, almost shocked still, but Jihoon didn't falter. He pressed his hand into my back and urged me forwards, pushing us both into the bottleneck of tourists exiting the park at the same time.

Finally, we were out. "Go," I hissed, "I'll meet you at the end of the pier." He turned to look down at me, indecision clear on his face. "Go," I pushed him gently, "you can't be seen with anyone and they're not looking for me, I'll be fine." He looked unhappy but nodded before he turned around and took off down the pier, going behind the buildings and out of sight while I followed, but at a walking pace, just merging with the crowd.

Not long after, four young girls scrambled out of the park some ways behind me, making enough of a scene that I distinctly heard a few shouts of 'Hey!' in response. I didn't turn around, instead pulling out my phone and pretending to look down at the dark screen. "I know it was him!" I heard one girl whine.

"He's definitely in LA, I saw it on Weverse," another said, matter-of-factly.

"I don't see him!" The first girl whined again, closer now, their combined pursuit sounding like a pack of horses on the wooden boards.

"Are you even sure it was him?" said another voice, fed-up and sceptical.

"Yes!" one insisted, earning a loud scoffing sound, presumably from the sceptic.

"I'm going back in the park, this is bullshit, it wasn't him. Megan, are you coming?"

"Yeah, I don't wanna waste my ticket. I'm coming."

The herd split up, and now only two of them were walking quickly past me, with the others heading back into the park. I glanced up from my phone to track the progress of the remaining two, but it was clear they had no idea where to look. They just kept power-ing onwards, swinging their heads from side-to-side.

I smiled indulgently and with the grace of one who does not have to worry about being chased by random young fans. What must that life be like?

Then, the more I thought about it, the more the smile slipped from my face. This was a novelty to me, but to Jihoon, this was his every day. He'd told me they all felt real love for their fans – and I believed that – but it must be hard to reconcile the two sides of being so famous; millions of adoring fans propelling your career into the stratosphere, but never being able to simply walk to the shop, or go on a date, without risking the wrath of the few fans who took it too far. It was a trade-off I wasn't sure I'd be willing to take.

Me

There are 2 girls heading down the pier looking for you.

I kept walking down the pier, but when he hadn't replied for several minutes, I began to get worried, especially as I could now see the stairs and not Jihoon.

Me

I'm at the bottom of the pier. Are you ok?

183

Now at the bottom of the stairs and overlooking the busy street, I began to feel a bit nervous, but then I saw the SUV with the blacked-out windows parked in the short-stay car park, right where we'd left it some hours ago. Had they been there all this time? I guess I should have expected them to hang around.

As I stared at the car, the back door opened, and Jihoon stepped out. Closing the door behind him, he jogged over to me, and I noticed he was wearing a different shirt and a bucket hat now.

"You're like a spy, changing outfits in the back of cars," I smiled and gestured to his shirt. He rubbed a hand down it and shrugged.

"Seemed like a good idea."

Silence fell between us. I wanted to say something about what had happened back there, but I didn't know how to articulate what I was feeling. I must have opened and closed my mouth half a dozen times without actually saying anything.

"I'm sorry about that," Jihoon said, breaking the silence. I looked up at him in surprise.

"What do you have to be sorry about?"

He scuffed his foot back and forth along the pavement as he stared back at the pier behind me, the noise of the fairground distant, but the memory of the girls chasing him still close by.

"I didn't want to run," he admitted, his voice low. "But you were right. We can't be photographed together."

It was true, I knew it was. Hell, I'd even said as much. So why did it sting when he said it? It was just another reminder of all those good reasons to not take this – whatever this was – any further.

He shoved his hands into his pockets, his gaze darting anywhere but at me. With his face hidden by the shade of his hat and sunglasses, I couldn't tell what he was thinking, but there was a palpable tension in the air between us.

"Do you need to leave?" My voice wavered at the end, barely audible over the sounds of people chattering and laughing around us.

Jihoon looked up at me, tilting his head as if weighing his next words carefully. "Do you want to leave?"

"No," I said quickly. "I mean, not unless you want to."

"I don't want to."

I smiled. Just a quick, giddy sort of smile, but it lifted my mood immeasurably and, perhaps less obviously, it brought an unexpected burst of relief. The kind of relief you get when you pass a test you expected to fail.

"Do you want to walk? The beach isn't too busy." I hooked a thumb over my shoulder and he nodded, so almost in unison, we both turned and started walking towards the beach.

It was a sunny afternoon, but too cold for most LA natives. I almost laughed out loud when we walked past one guy wearing a scarf.

Jihoon looked down at me and smiled, "What's funny?"

Instead of answering directly, I asked, "Do you think it's cold today?"

"Cold?" He seemed to think about it for a moment. "No. Are you cold? We can go somewhere inside…" he swung his head around, presumably looking for indoor locations. I laughed, holding my hand over my face to hide how cute I thought he was.

"No," I said, waving my hand. "I was laughing because everyone else seems to think this is a cold day. Back home, this is a mild day."

"Ah," he nodded. "Seoul is the same."

"Really?" I was surprised.

Jihoon nodded again. "In summer it gets really hot, much hotter than this, but spring is mild."

"I'd love to see it, someday," I said, without really thinking.

"I hope you do," he said, ducking his head down and for some reason, I feel my cheeks heating.

We walked like that for a while, making small talk. The sound of the waves our constant companion, even though the sea was still quite far out. The beach wasn't full – only a few dedicated surfers and families with young kids. Runners and cyclists created a steady flow of traffic along the path bordering the beach, but no one looked twice at us. We were just another faceless couple strolling along the Santa Monica Beach.

We'd just passed Palisades Park when my stomach gave a very insistent growl. I laughed and put a hand over it, embarrassed. "I guess breakfast and doughnuts were a long time ago."

Jihoon grinned and nodded, "I'm hungry too." He glanced around for a moment before looking back at me. "Wait here, I'll be right back" He jogged away before I could say anything. Stunned,

I watched as he ran over to a small beach-side eatery a little further up.

"Well, alright then," I muttered to myself before I sat my happy ass down in the sand.

There were fewer people out here now. Perhaps they're all heading home for their dinner, I mused as I looked out at the waves. Not so distant now, the tide was definitely coming in.

Jihoon didn't keep me waiting long. He sat down beside me, pulling off his hat and sunglasses. With a triumphant flourish, he unpacked the brown paper bag. I moaned in appreciation as I saw the thickly stacked burgers, chips and sachets of sauces.

"And I have beer," he crowed happily, pulling out two green, glass bottles from his pockets.

"Truly, a feast for kings," I said appreciatively, giving him a little clap. He laughed and handed me one of the paper-wrapped burgers.

We were silent for a time as we ate, only murmuring in appreciation here and there. Then we were fighting over the hot sauce, each trying to dip a chip in at the same time and laughing when neither of us managed to get any, only bruising our chips in the endeavour.

Eventually, stomachs full, we scrunched up our wrappers and leant back on the sand, content. Jihoon twisted the caps off the beers and handed one to me.

"I'm not actually sure we're allowed to drink on the beach," I admitted, taking a swig.

Jihoon shrugged. "They're non-alcoholic," he said, taking a deep pull from his own bottle. I coughed, surprised, and had to swallow quickly to avoid choking before looking down at my bottle and seeing that indeed, they were non-alcoholic. I burst out laughing, giggles that had my shoulders heaving and I looked over at Jihoon to see that he was chuckling, but far more demurely than I was currently capable of.

As my giggles subsided, I said "I didn't know you'd be so funny." I meant it as an off-hand comment, but Jihoon looked over at me in a way that made me think I'd said something wrong. He pulled his legs up to his chest and draped his arms over his knees, facing forward once more.

"Did you know much about me, before?" he asked, taking a sip from his bottle.

Sensing my misstep, I thought about my reply. "Not really," I admitted, pulling off my shades and sliding them into my pocket. "I mean, obviously I knew who you were, but not the details, y'know?" I finally caught his eye and I could see he was listening to me. "I don't know when your birthday is, I don't know what your favourite food is, I don't know your secret fears, and I don't know what made you want to be an idol." I dropped my head, smiling a little.

"I'm sure that makes me a bad fan. I just like the music." I shrugged and turned back away to look at the sea. The waves really were getting closer now.

Jihoon was silent for a moment. "Sometimes it's hard to know who wants to know you and who wants to know the idol. Most people want to know the group version of me.

"When I was a trainee, there was a girl I knew from school," he paused, taking a sip from his bottle. "I really liked her, and I thought she liked me too."

When he didn't continue, I said, "What happened?"

"She kept asking to meet the other members, my hyungs. But we were always so busy training. When I told her I couldn't, she got mad and threatened to sell pictures to Dispatch."

I gasped, "She was going to sell you out like that?" At his nod, I exclaimed loudly, "What a rat!"

Jihoon barked out a laugh. "Yes."

"I'm so sorry that happened. Making real friends is hard enough in real life. I can only imagine how hard it must be as an idol." He nodded again.

"Tell me how you met your friend – Becka." He surprised me with the question, but then it's as good a segue as any from a subject that's clearly a little sore, although I couldn't help the curiosity about how he made any 'normal' friends. But perhaps that was a conversation for another day.

If we ever got another day, I reminded myself, the pang of regret hitting me deep in my chest.

I distracted myself from that acute pain by sharing the story of Kaiya and Becka. I told him how we'd met in London at University when she'd done a year in the UK. I told him all about Becka's messy breakup, which had led to her having a spare room in her apartment and seeing as how I was freshly graduated and jobless, I'd taken her up on the offer to come to LA and work for Pisces.

"But I only have a Visa until next March. One year," I sighed, "after that I have to go home."

"The studio can't keep you?"

I scoffed. "They barely hire me as it is. Becka's dad knows my boss, Jeremy, and managed to get him to take me on as a paid intern because of all the strikes. Normally Pisces doesn't hire interns, so my Visa is only temporary."

"But it's ok, it's always nice to go home. I miss my folks." I mused, kicking my feet in the sand.

"Your parents, they live in England?"

"Yep. Married for nearly 20 years."

"What are their names?"

"Valerie and Ernest." I took a drink, but not before I saw the way his brows creased. I smiled, understanding his expression.

"My mum met my dad, Ernest, when I was two."

I saw him struggling to think of the words to say before he said them. "He's not your..."

"My biological dad?" I supplied. "No."

I took a deep breath, deciding on how to put it.

"Before I was born, my mum travelled the world. She went to so many countries, honestly, I'm jealous," I laughed softly, "and then she ended up in Japan. She loved it so much she tried to get a Visa to stay, but the only way she could do that was if she was working and had a sponsor."

"She eventually found work as a foreign language teacher way out in the country. Nowhere near any cities, just this rural little town. She got to stay in Japan for a couple of years."

"Eventually, she met a boy and, well, you can probably guess what happened." I laughed again, embarrassed.

"But then she fell pregnant." I sighed, feeling that odd and familiar pang that always accompanied this story.

"The boy didn't want to be a father, and his family didn't want to acknowledge her – or me, I suppose," I shrugged. "The school she'd been working in didn't want an unmarried, pregnant foreigner working for them, and without a sponsor, her Visa wasn't valid. So, she had to leave. She moved back to England and had me."

"When I was two, she met my dad and the rest is history. They got married, Ernest adopted me, and they lived happily ever after."

I smiled. I always ended this story with the same words because, honestly, it's true. My parents were so in love that sometimes it was hard to be in the same room as them. It wasn't uncommon to come down to the kitchen for breakfast and find them slow dancing in front of the fridge. My dad built my mum a porch in the garden, just so she could sit outside on autumn mornings with a coffee and greet the day.

Theirs was a love I could only dream of.

Shaking my head, I brought myself back into the present.

"You love them very much." Jihoon nodded, the statement a fact, not a question.

"Yes," I said.

"They must miss you."

I pulled my legs up to my chest and lay my head on my knees, so I was facing him. "I'm sure they do, but they have each other." I let the silence fall into place between us as I watched him, watching the waves make their slow creep up the sand, ever closer but still plenty far enough away. For now.

"Is it weird for your parents?" I asked, and the question seemed to take him by surprise because he looked at me, a light crease forming between his brows before his face relaxed into an easy grin.

"I think they're used to it now. I've lived away from home since I was eleven."

"Eleven!" I exclaimed, lifting my head from my knees.

Jihoon nodded, letting his legs fall as he gracefully folded himself into a cross-legged seating position facing me. I mirrored his movements until we were facing each other, knees nearly touching.

"I lived with my imo and imobu – my aunt and uncle – in New York when I was eleven. I went to middle school there for three years while my parents travelled for work, and then when I was fourteen, I auditioned for ENT." He was so matter of fact. I didn't know how to feel about it. I couldn't imagine moving away from my parents at such a young age. That must have been so hard.

"You didn't move back home?"

He shrugged. "I didn't have a home. My parents sold our house in Busan when my dad accepted the job abroad. I flew back to Korea in the summer I auditioned and moved into the trainee dorm. I started school in Seoul in August."

"So fast," I murmured. "That must have been so weird."

Jihoon huffed and smiled. "It was, but we were so busy that we didn't have time to think about it."

"I've heard that idol training is intense," I offered. It was well known how brutal training was for K-Pop idols. There were so many documentaries and accounts of idols being starved and worked so hard that they'd pass out.

Jihoon was silent for a moment, staring down at the empty bottle in his hands as he absentmindedly picked at the label.

"When you're in school, it's not so bad. You wake up, exercise, go to school. Then you train for a few hours. But you get that time off during the day to just be a kid, y'know?" He looked up at me, and I wanted to agree, but honestly, I couldn't imagine his life.

"English lessons were the best though," he cocked his head to the side, a small smile playing across his lips.

"Why?"

"Because I had three years of practice from living in New York. It was the one class I was better at than my hyungs." He grinned. "My teachers were not so happy though; they had to spend a lot of time correcting the New York accent I'd picked up." He said 'New York' in a way that reminded me of Joey from 'Friends', and I giggled.

"But because I spent so much of my day in school, I had to work extra hard after classes to make sure I wasn't letting my trainers down.

"We'd practice for so many hours that I hurt all the time," he chuckled. "Every muscle was sore, all the time, there was never enough rest time. But you get used to it, so when I sometimes wasn't in pain, I would train harder because I thought I had been lazy."

"That's insane," I breathed.

He shook his head, but it wasn't quite a disagreement. "It's necessary."

"Did you ever think about quitting?"

"No." His immediate response surprised me, but then it didn't, when I considered that the man sitting in front of me was considered to be one of the most talented idols in the industry right now.

"It was hard," he admitted, "but it was…" he fumbled, his fingers waving in the air as if trying to snatch a word out of it.

"Purpose," he settled on, meeting my gaze finally. "It was my purpose."

I nodded. I could understand that. I wasn't sure what mine was yet, but I understood the desire to fulfil it when a person does find it. He was lucky.

"I wish I knew what I wanted to be when I grow up," I joked.

"You don't want to work in music?" he asked, sounding surprised.

"Yes. No. Maybe?" I laughed. "I don't know anymore. I always thought I wanted to be a music producer. It's what I studied at university. But now… I'm not sure if being behind the sound deck is what I want anymore." I shrugged, trying to play it off, but the truth gnawed at me. After three years of certainty, studying toward that goal, realizing I might not want it anymore was… terrifying.

"I thought working at Pisces would be a fun sidestep into the career I've always wanted, but now I think maybe it's shown me it wasn't what I thought it was."

Jihoon nodded thoughtfully. "You'll find what you're meant to do."

"You think so?"

He held my gaze and smiled – a wide, confident smile, the kind of confidence I could only aspire to.

"Of course. You're smart, you work hard, and you're brave."

"I'm brave?" I asked uncertainly.

"You moved across the world on just the idea that you might find your purpose. That's brave."

"So did you, and you were far younger."

He waved his hand dismissively. "That's how I know you'll find what you're meant to do. Where you're meant to be."

We fell into a comfortable silence, watching the waves make their steady climb up the beach as the sun began to bleed across the horizon.

"It's getting dark," he said, looking around as if suddenly becoming aware of the dusk that was rapidly falling, turning the clear blue sky to a softer shade of pink and orange.

"We should probably start heading back," I said, but I didn't make a move to stand. Jihoon nodded, holding my gaze. "We fly back in the morning," he said, quietly.

"I know."

Neither of us moved and neither of us dropped our gaze. I didn't blink for so long that I began to feel tears threatening in the corners of my eyes. Even when I did blink, I could still feel them there, a constant reminder of how this evening would end.

"We should probably head back," I said again.

Jihoon sighed, but rose to his feet with a fluid, effortless grace that I could only aspire to.

He looked down at me and held out his hands, his long, graceful fingers reaching towards me. I reached up to take them, gasping only slightly at the way my skin slid against his, cool at first, but then so warm. His firm grip enclosed mine, calluses grazing my skin, the contradictory feeling of softness and roughness making this moment somehow more real.

He pulled me up, and suddenly he seemed to tower over me, his eyes holding mine with such intensity that my fingers tightened around his.

Slowly, he drew me closer until our chests were almost touching, the air between us charged with an almost tangible feeling. The world around us faded, leaving only the gentle sound of waves lapping at the sand, the ocean's rhythm the backdrop to whatever this was.

His lips parted and his soulful brown eyes roamed over my face in a slow caress, until they purposefully flicked back up to meet my own. A giddy, thrumming sort of need vibrated within my chest; a pull I could no more deny than the need to keep breathing.

I tilted my head up slightly, my head falling to the side. He didn't make me wait long. Jihoon lowered his head, his nose brushing softly against my own before his lips found mine. He pressed gently at first, as if mapping my lips with his own, but then he pressed against me more firmly, his lips moving mine, the urgency increasing as my lips parted on a sigh. He let go of my hands to wrap his arms tightly around my waist, pulling me against him so close I had to wind my own arms around his neck. My fingers ran up from the base of his spine to tangle lightly in his hair, finding it was as soft as it looked. He groaned against my mouth, the sound reverberating through me and making me press closer still. There was no gentleness now, only a wild sort of desperation to feel everything all at once.

When he lightly traced his tongue along my top lip, I bit down softly on his full bottom lip and honestly, if he'd lain me down in the sand, right then, I would have let him.

Instead, he pulled back with a pained groan that had nothing to do with my light nibble of his lip. He pressed his forehead against mine as we both stood there, panting. It took me a moment to understand why he had pulled away; his phone was ringing in his pocket, the sound breaking through our bubble and killing the moment.

He cupped my cheek, holding my gaze for a moment, before pulling away and taking out his phone to answer it. I immediately felt the cold of the oncoming night, a chill to replace the heat of only a moment ago.

I rubbed my arms as I heard Jihoon speaking. I couldn't understand his words, but his tone was clear enough. Resigned. Before long, he hung up and turned back to me, his expression sad.

"We have to go," was all he said. All he needed to say. Our time was up. I nodded and bent to pick up our rubbish. Jihoon grabbed the bottles and together we walked over to a mixed recycling bin. The clink of the bottles as they fell into the glass-receptacle was loud in the still air.

We opted to walk along the path instead of the beach, heading back towards the beaconing lights of the pier and its fairground.

Jihoon had pulled his hat back on, and I shoved my hands in my pockets, but just as I did, Jihoon surprised me.

"No," he said, pulling my hand out of my pocket and firmly taking it in his, his fingers gripping me in a gentle, but possessive hold that made my heart stutter.

"Is this okay?" I asked quietly, conscious of the few people that still milled around.

"Tonight, I don't care." His tone was as firm as his hand and so I chose to enjoy the moment, trying to preserve it in my mind.

Even as far as we'd walked, the pier still came close too soon, the lights getting brighter, the shouts and music louder, every step feeling more leaden, and before I was ready – if I'd ever be so – the SUV with the blacked-out windows came into view, still in the same place.

"They must have gotten so many tickets today," I muttered. Jihoon snorted.

As we approached the car, the passenger door opened and out stepped Youngsoo.

"All done?" he asked, and the phrasing was so bizarre that I could have put it down to his English, but I couldn't help but think he was asking if Jihoon had gotten it out of his system. Gotten me out of his system.

Instead of answering the question, he said, "We'll take Kaiya home first." Youngsoo's mouth pinched, but he nodded and opened the rear door for us. Jihoon helped me into the car and then slid in beside me.

"Hello," I said politely, bowing my head to the other occupants, who I'm sure must have had a pretty miserable day, sitting all day in a hot car. I spied some crumpled paper bags littering the door pockets though, so it looked like they at least availed themselves of the delicious stall food on the pier.

Eun politely returned my nod, while the driver muttered a quiet, "Hello".

I told them my address and the driver plugged it into the car's satnav and then we pulled away, the lights from the pier following us down the street, visible long after we'd turned away.

We were well into the evening now, so traffic was as quiet as it ever got in LA, and we slipped through it silently, with not even the radio to break the silence.

The tension from Youngsoo was clear, but Jihoon didn't seem to care. He hadn't let go of my hand yet, his thumb sweeping softly across my skin in a way that constantly radiated tingles that danced up my wrist.

The car was silent as we bumped along the sometimes-patch-work streets, the flash of the streetlights only increased the feeling of disapproval that seemed to pour off Youngsoo in waves.

Yet, with how firmly Jihoon was holding my hand, it somehow felt as though we were grounded in this moment together, the dark gaps of time between the halos of street lights a bubble of time that contained only us.

Too soon, we were turning down my street. My hand unconsciously tightened on Jihoon's, a tether to hold me to him for that much longer, and this time I knew I felt tears prickling in the corners of my eyes. We pulled up in front of my building, and out of habit, I looked out the window and up at our apartment and wasn't completely surprised to see a curtain twitch. I smiled a wry smile at the thought that Becka was looking out for me.

I almost couldn't look at Jihoon because I was afraid his face would mirror what I was feeling, but even though it hurt, I also couldn't stop looking at him, so desperate to hold onto any image of him that I could keep.

I wanted to ask him what this was. I wanted some reassurance of tomorrow. I wanted so many things I didn't have any way to articulate. I also knew I had never been guaranteed any kind of promise. I needed to make peace with what had been.

"I don't know what to say." My words were soft, but the meaning was clear. I had too much to say in a car full of people, and nothing to say that would even suffice.

"I understand." He didn't smile and I could have sworn I saw the sad pinch of his beautiful eyes.

"Will you text me when you land?" I asked impulsively, but immediately regretted it. "You don't have to. I know you'll be tired and busy and..." I tapered off, feeling foolish, pulling my gaze from his, but he only angled his head down to keep my gaze.

"Yes," he said firmly. "Yes."

I smiled, but it wavered. I tried again, and this time, I managed to keep it there, a testament to my willpower.

"Thank you for today. It was... it was the best." I didn't have the words, so I didn't even try.

Out of the corner of my eye, I saw the front door to the building open, a figure stepping out. Becka. Stood there with her arms folded across her chest, I couldn't tell if she was cross, or worried. Knowing her it could have been both.

"Looks like I better go," I nodded my head to Becka. Jihoon briefly glanced out the window before looking back at me. I could see the indecision warring across his face and so, to spare him from this moment becoming something it couldn't be, I leant forward and kissed him on the cheek, so quickly it was barely there, just a fluttering of lips on skin, before I spun around and opened the car door, sliding out all in one fluid move, a rare moment of grace for me, but right when it counted.

I turned around just once, a fleeting glimpse of his face as the door closed, me outside and him a world apart. I stood there for a moment, watching as the car pulled away, dragging a piece of me with it.

"Are you ok?" Becka asked from behind me. The question surprised me. Shouldn't she be asking if I'd had a good day, or what did we do? But something in the way I held myself must have told her the thing to say.

Because no. I was not ok. I heard her walk the few steps towards me before I turned and fell against her, the dam breaking as I sobbed into her shoulder.

End Of Part One.

Part Two

제2부

Chapter 20

Thursday

I considered calling in sick again, but the thought of lying in bed and having to face my feelings was more distasteful to me than the idea of going into work and having to pretend to be okay. So, I picked work and threw the covers off.

My alarm hadn't even gone off yet, so I took a moment to open the blinds and look outside, trying to muster up the energy to feel excited about another day in LA.

When that failed, I reached back and grabbed my phone, sliding my finger up the screen to wake it. When I saw the message from Jihoon, a lump immediately formed in my throat, but I opened it all the same.

Joon

> Good morning sleepyhead. We're taking off in a little bit. I just wanted to tell you I miss you already. Is that weird? Probably, but I don't care. I'm so glad I met you. Talk soon.

[Sent 06:23]

I looked at the time at the top of the screen. It was just after 7:30am. I'd missed his message by an hour. He was officially gone, out of the country. I wanted to berate myself a little for feeling so morose, but I just couldn't muster up the energy. I honestly wasn't even sure how to feel.

Last night, once Becka had gotten me back inside, I'd cried myself hoarse. I suspected I'd even scared Becka a little bit. At first, she'd tried to comfort me, then she'd tried to feed me wine, but I'd just... cried. Eventually she'd just pushed me into the shower and put me to bed, where I'd cried myself to sleep.

No matter how many times I'd told myself that his leaving was inevitable – a done deal, a known eventuality – it hadn't mattered. And now, even in the cold light of day, I felt... bereft, confused, and frustrated. We'd never had a conversation about what happens next, or if anything even would happen next. It was entirely reasonable to assume this had just been a wonderful few days.

Mostly, I was frustrated because I didn't understand myself right now. Sure, Jihoon was wonderful, so much more than I ever expected him to be—on the rare occasions I'd even considered him as a real-life person—but it's not like he and I ever had a chance of being anything more than acquaintances. I should just feel grateful for the opportunity to have met someone I greatly admired.

But damn me, I wasn't feeling grateful right now. I was a mess of emotions and confusion. I barely knew him. I *should not* be this deep in my feels. And that was the worst part: knowing that my emotions for him were entirely disproportionate, yet still being unable to rein them in. It was like I *knew* I was being an idiot, but I just... couldn't... fucking *stop* being one.

I groaned and threw myself face-first into my pillows.

Fuck, maybe I should take the day off.

Before I could spiral any further into my funk, I fumbled around the pillow pressed into my face and typed out a quick message to Jihoon.

Me

> *Good morning – or whatever time it ends up being when you read this! :D I hope you got some rest on the plane. It's gonna be so weird to be at Pisces without you. Come back soon!*

"Good morning, sleepyhead." Becka's voice from my door startled me so much I dropped my phone, which was about the same moment I realised her greeting mirrored his.

"Oh fuck, are you crying again?" Becka's forehead creased as she wrung her hands.

"No," I wheezed.

"Oh god, oh Ky, oh no, oh don't do that." Becka was flapping her hands, coming at me as I bent over the bed, unprepared tears squeezing out through thoroughly exhausted ducts.

"I don't want to!" I wailed, "but I can't fucking stop!"

Becka sighed and sat next to me on the bed.

"Look, there's nothing I can say that would help. I think... I think you've just gotta go through this, you know? I think you need to be okay with feeling this for a while."

I snivelled, trying to take big gulps of air in-between heaving sobs.

"When Ben and I broke up," Becka began, and for her sake, I tried to calm enough to really hear her. She so rarely even mentioned him. "I wasn't okay for the longest time. I was so angry all the time, and when I wasn't pissed, I was crying. And pissed I was crying!" She huffed a laugh. "I was a mess. And I think you're gonna be one too, for a while." She ran her hand up and down my back and my cries finally softened.

"But, then one day, you don't cry, and you start to get a little better. One day at a time."

"I'm sorry you're going through this. I don't think either of us thought this would happen, huh?" She smiled at me, and I found I was able to smile back, because no, this was not supposed to happen. But here we were.

"I'm here for you, babes. Whatever you need, when you need it."

"I'm sorry I wasn't here when Ben left," I murmured.

"Ach," she waved my apology aside. "How could you have been? And besides, you're here now. Paying his half of... well, paying some of his half, anyway."

We both laughed, my pitiful intern salary a well-trodden joke between us.

"When does he land, anyway?" She segued neatly away from Ben, still a subject best left alone.

"Hey Google," I sniffed, "how long is the flight from LAX to Seoul?" My screen flashed with an answer. "Apparently, thirteen hours."

Becka whistled. "I hope they at least give him slippers and the good snacks. That is a long-ass flight."

I didn't disagree. I also didn't bother to mention Jihoon and his team were flying privately. The snacks were bound to be good.

"It'll be well after 7:00pm California time before he lands, which..." I quickly did the maths in my head, "will be 11:00am on Friday in Seoul."

"Is he flying TARDIS-Airlines?" Becka joked and I attempted a half-smile for the effort she made at making a Dr Who joke before 8:00 in the morning.

"South Korea is sixteen hours ahead of us." I sighed. "A whole world away."

Becka gave me a sympathetic smile and grabbed my knee. "Come on babes, it's time to get up."

And, not having a good enough argument to disagree, I did.

The rest of the day was a blur; the first day I'd had at Pisces where I just went through the motions in order to get the day over with. If someone had asked me at the end of the day what tasks I'd completed, I wouldn't have been able to tell them. Maybe humped some boxes around. Possibly set out some music stands in the big hall. Honestly, I'd have been guessing.

But then, when 7:00pm rolled around, I was glued to my phone, willing it to buzz but, nothing. And then 8:00pm still nothing. 9:00pm, I turned it off and back on again and called Becka to check my line was working. Still nothing.

When 10:00pm came and passed, I went to bed.

Friday

Friday felt like a copy-paste of Thursday, except with the added bonus of dodging Trevor Kyle in the stairwells. I knew he had followed me in there because A. He never takes the stairs, and B. I saw him looking up the middle of them before going back out into the lobby. I don't know how he didn't spot me, but I was relieved all the same. It was like creeper hide-and-seek.

It felt like I was on his radar now. Once upon a time, I might have welcomed someone like Trevor Kyle knowing who I was. I'd openly admired his work on more than one occasion, but now that I'd actually met him—even through our brief and unpleasant interactions—I couldn't even bring myself to talk about him. He made me feel... uneasy.

This morning, he'd sent a message to Jeremy, asking if I'd be interested in shadowing him on his next project.

The opportunity to learn from someone so influential in the industry had been tempting, but the blaring of my red-flag radar was impossible to ignore. Even Jeremy had read the email out loud with a face more pinched than usual, his relief obvious when I told him I still had too much to do.

So, I spent the rest of the day making myself scarce.

Not thinking I could top that level of excitement; I was just gearing up to cozy up on the sofa and binge watch Supernatural when

Becka suggested going out. I scoffed at the suggestion and started combing my hair back from my face.

"Not the scrunchie!" Becka begged, pulling it away from me and holding it behind her back. Silently, I stared her down and held out my hand.

"No, babes, if you put this in your hair, I'm never getting it out again tonight and I want to go dancing!"

"Go then," I urged, "I'm not stopping you. Give!"

"I can't dance on my own, I need the divine beauty of two babes in order to tempt the men-folk." She had a point. Every time two women danced together, it was like moths to a flame. Law of nature, I guessed.

I shook my head. "I'm having a moment, I don't want to go out."

"That's precisely why you should!" she insisted, "you can't mope all the time, it won't make anything better, it'll just make things worse. Believe me, I know."

And she did, I knew that, just like I knew she was right. Sighing, I said, "Fine, but I really don't want to be out until all hours, ok?"

Becka held up her hands, making a small effort to not gloat. "Scout's honour."

Barely an hour later, we were in the back of an Uber and heading downtown to a club where Becka knew a promoter who who had sworn up and down he could get us a free round of shots.

Becka texted him to secure our spot and I was just staring into space. I was resolutely ignoring my phone, knowing there was nothing on there I wanted to see. I stared out the window at the bright lights of LA in the evening, a cacophony of noise and bustle so much like London that I very briefly, but still deeply, got homesick. I supposed it was about time that I would start to long for home, I had been here nearly two months, the novelty was wearing a bit thin. The past week had made me forget, but the phone call I had earlier this evening with my mum and dad had only settled me further in to the melancholy I had been feeling all day.

Finally, we pulled up outside the club and Becka's friend was true to his word. He was waiting for us at the curb and ushered us through the doors to the club, completely bypassing the line that was already half-way up the street. I didn't react to the calls of protests, but internally, I grinned and felt my spirits lift, just a little.

Immediately I was hit by a wall of sound as we went further into the club, past the foyer. The lights strobed just above head height, a kaleidoscope of acidic greens, razor-sharp reds and effervescent purple cutting through the haze from the heat of hundreds of dancing bodies, all pulsing to a beat that vibrated up from the soles of my feet to my chest, pulling me into the throng as though by a tether.

"I'm going to get our drinks," Becka shouted, leaning closer to me to be heard over the music. I gave her a thumbs up and then moved forward to stand against the railing of the raised platform we were on that overlooked the dancefloor below.

Bodies pressed firmly against each other, all moving to the pulse of the music, and I let it in to block out the noise of my phone and its deafening silence.

Becka returned with not just two drinks, but a whole tray of shooters and a grin on her face that suggested mischief.

"Whoa, what happened to one drink each?" I had to shout to make myself heard.

"Carlos is trying really hard to get in my good books." She put the tray down on a tall table on my other side.

"Your good books, or your pants?" I eyed the tray of drinks sceptically.

Becka laughed, but I didn't hear the sound. "He's not interested in my pants!" She waved a hand at me, as if this suggestion were completely outrageous.

"He wants me to put in a good word for him with his ex-boyfriend."

Ah. "What did he do?"

"You don't want to know." Becka shouted, shaking her head, eyes wide.

Becka arranged our drinks on the tray, half on the side closest to me, half on the other, the almost-luminous colour of the artificially flavoured drinks visible even in the dim light.

"Ready?" She grinned at me as she held the little cup of bright green liquid out to me. I took a fortifying breath. To hell with it all. I took the shot from her and together, we downed our first drink.

"Blech," I stuck my tongue out as Becka visibly shuddered.

"Again!" she shouted picking up another and handing it to me before the taste of the last one had even fully registered on my tongue. Together, we threw the drinks back.

And so, it continued until the whole tray was gone and I've counted six shots, all in various colours and all now decidedly mixing in my stomach. It's at that moment I realised I had forgotten to properly line my stomach before coming out, my last meal some hours ago.

"Oh, fuck me," I groaned, holding a hand up to my forehead.

"What's wrong?" Becka shouted close to my ear, "Are you feeling sick?"

"Not yet," I shouted back, and then giggled at her confused expression. "Let's go fucking dance!" We might as well, I thought to myself.

The night passed in a pleasurable buzz of lights and thumping beats that were so loud they almost sounded muffled, but that might have been the buzz dulling my senses. We danced, mostly together but sometimes with others, especially a group of girls we met in the bathroom who were on a work trip from Sacramento. Our group expanded when, inevitably, a group of men wound their way in-between our number, posturing like exotic birds, with their gelled-up hair and patterned shirts. I laughed so loud and so long that somewhere along the way, I forgot to be sad and confused and instead, I just had fun.

When Becka dragged me off the dance floor, I protested, only stopping my whining when she shouted, very loudly, that she didn't want to, "queue with all the other peasants," when the club closed in an hour. So, I followed her out, grabbing my bag from the bag check in the foyer on the way out and together, we stood outside while she ordered an Uber.

I swayed on my feet, still feeling the music whizzing through my veins, along with the copious amount of alcohol. The chill night air felt nice on my over-heated skin, and I tipped back my head, enjoying the sensation of feeling so light and so at peace with the world.

Becka was grumpy, I could tell by the way she just stood there, head down and arms crossed, but then she always was a morose drunk, whilst I – I was prone to joy and joyous things, like chips and ice cream.

"Can we get a takeaway?" I sing-songed at Becka, who only frowned at me like I'd said something really weird. "Take out? Now? Ky, it's like, late."

"Yeah, yeah I get you, but like, I'm super hungry. It was all the dancing," I said, patting my tummy, like this proved my point.

"It was all the beer, more like," she muttered, and I nodded sagely in agreement. There had been beer.

"Do we have crisps at home? Oh, oh and dip. Do we have crisps and dip?"

"Babes, it's nearly 1:00am. You can't eat chips and salsa at 1:00am."

"Why not?" I demanded, outraged.

Becka just sighed, but then a silver Honda with an Uber sticker in the window pulled up to the kerbside, a middle-aged woman leant out of the window, "Rebecca?" After confirming the name of the driver, we piled into the back.

Becka was quiet the whole way home, but I didn't mind the silence because my brain was still so nice and fuzzy, my skin tingling in that good way it did after a lot of dancing and drinks. The bad times were still there, underneath my cozy buzz blanket, but I was not so inclined to lift it up and inspect it. I was, however, very interested in snacks, and all I could think about the whole drive home was what was left in the cupboard.

Not too long later, I was rummaging through the cupboards when, with triumph, I pulled out a box of Ritz crackers.

"Ah-ha!" I cried out with joy, doing a happy hop from one foot to the other. It felt really nice to flex my feet, newly freed from their stiletto prisons.

Becka was still very grumpy, but as I spun around to share my spoils, I also saw her putting my phone back on the counter. Catching my eye, she looked guilty, but defiant.

"What are you doing with my phone?" I asked, putting down my box of crackers.

"Texting the idol." She raised her chin.

"I – you-WHAT?" I spluttered. "Why?"

"Because someone had to remind him you exist!" She bit out sharply. I didn't know how to respond, because I knew she wasn't taking this out on me, not really. She never talked about Ben, or what went down, but it didn't take a genius to figure out she was still hurting and whatever she'd just sent to Jihoon was a reaction to that.

"Forget it, you're right. I'm going to bed." Becka sighed and got to her feet, heading towards her bedroom. I watched her, mouth agape as she shut the door quietly behind herself.

"But, I didn't even say anything," I said to myself. The cracker triumph of a few minutes ago didn't seem so... triumphant now. I sighed as I put them back in the cupboard and instead, pulled my phone towards me. Becka had left it open on the message app, my green, little text bubble almost glowing with accusation.

Me

If ur going 2 brush Ky off, at least have the decency 2 tell her. Ghosts r 4 movies.

Not her most eloquent work, but succinct, all the same. Quietly, I groaned, dropping my head into my hands. I was way too buzzed to deal with this and it was stealing my joy.

I shuffled over to my room and tossed my phone onto my bed, opting to kick the can down the road in favour of a shower.

I took my time, as well, even chucking a shower fizz in for good measure. The eucalyptus scent worked wonders on my brain, and by the time I was done, wrapped in a fluffy towel and hair wrap, my head was much clearer. I did note, however, that Jihoon still hadn't replied by the time I closed my bedroom door behind me. I had debated sending a follow-up message to assure him of... what, I wasn't sure but decided against it. My own curiosity demanded some sort of yes or no confirmation and, as clear as my head felt, my stomach felt clenched in knots.

I knew I wouldn't be able to sleep like this, so instead I settled on going through a proper skincare routine – the kind I'd seen on TikTok so often but never had the time or energy to properly emulate.

And because fate is a funny thing, my phone buzzed with an incoming call just as I was running leave-in conditioner through the ends of my hair.

I picked up my phone to see an incoming video call from Jihoon. In a burst of anxious energy, I tried to arrange myself to look as casual, but put-together as possible before nervously accepting the call.

Immediately, his almost-painfully handsome face filled the screen, like so many videos I had seen of him doing Lives and Insta Stories, that for just a second, I forgot where I was. He was leaning back on what looked like a sofa, so I guessed that he was at home, maybe.

"Hi," his clear, accented voice now so familiar to me filled the space of my tiny room, only adding to the surreal feeling.

"Hi," I breathed, finally able to respond.

"Are you ok? I know it's very late there now," he said, his eyes seeming to dart around his screen, taking in my surroundings. I chanced a look at the smaller image from my camera in the bottom of the screen and took in the details he must be seeing; curtains closed, bedside lamp on, me sitting on my bed wearing a robe with wet hair.

"It's fine," I said quickly, "Becka and I went out, we only got back an hour ago."

Jihoon made a noise of understanding before we both lapsed into silence again. I glanced up at the top of my phone screen where I have two time zones displayed. I saw that for him, it was just after 6:00pm.

"Are you done for the day?" I asked, trying to sound as casual as I was trying to look, even though my back was starting to hurt from the position I was holding.

He frowned and then puffed out his lips in a weary sigh, a hand rising up to run through his hair. That's when I noticed how tired he looks.

"We had a lot of meetings; scheduling meetings, and project meetings, just meetings and meetings," he grumbled, and I suddenly felt bad for thinking he was ghosting me, when he'd probably not had a moment to himself after being on a plane for half a day.

"Kaiya," he said, snapping my attention back to him, "I'm sorry I didn't call you."

I tried to wave it away, but he continued. "I fell asleep on the plane, and I didn't know my battery had died. We drove straight to the company. I didn't have a chance to charge my phone."

"Honestly, it's fine," I tried again to wave his explanation away, but he ploughed on, talking over me.

"And then I fell asleep at the company until it was too late to even call you, and today I've been –"

"In meetings, I know." I cut him off this time, and he fell silent. "Jihoon, it's fine, really."

He chewed on his lip for a moment, his expression unreadable. "Was it your friend who sent that message?"

I sighed, loudly. "Yes. I didn't know she was going to do that, I'm sorry."

Jihoon nodded. "But you were worried it was true?"

I wanted to brush it aside, but I was too tired to put up a front. I was too tired, full stop. I fell back on pillows, finally comfortable, but as my head settled down against the soft pillows, I was reminded of how inebriated I still was, as the pleasant tingles swept over my face and down my arms.

"Worry isn't the word," I said, my mouth involuntarily smiling at the buzz, "I was just kind of expecting the brush off, and preparing myself for it." Definitely still buzzed. Sober people are not this honest.

"Why would I brush you off?" His face grew larger in the screen, as if he had pulled it closer towards him.

I giggled. "Because you're... you and I'm-" I gestured at myself.

"Are you drunk, Kaiya?" He smiled and I couldn't help but smile back. God he's pretty.

"Yes," I sighed, "many drinks were drunk, and now, so am I."

"I see. Perhaps we should talk about this later, once you've had some rest."

Absurdly, I didn't want our call to end, I just wanted to look at him and hear him speak, but my inner people-pleaser was also desperate to not 'be that girl,' which made inner-me cringe in outrage at the female stereotyping I was doing.

"Look," I said, in what I thought was a perfectly reasonable tone, "you don't have to. We don't have to do this."

"Do what?" Uh oh, he's frowning again, and even though it is absurdly sexy, the way that his dark hair falls across his furrowed brow, I feel I might not have made myself clear. It seemed the momentary clarity from the shower has ebbed away.

"You don't have to call me. You must have so many more important people to talk to than me."

He was silent for so long, I thought the phone might have frozen, but then when he did speak, I had to strain to hear him, because his voice sounded weirdly distorted.

"You don't want me to call you?"

"No, I'm just saying you don't have to. Don't feel obligated to, y'know?"

But he didn't know, because this time the phone really had frozen, which I only figured out because Jihoon took so long to reply that I squinted at the screen long enough to see the frozen pixels. At least I got to look at his beautiful face for a moment longer. Until the whole app shut down.

"Oh, for fucks sake," I muttered, before angrily mashing the combination of buttons to shut my phone down for a restart.

Except, I had fallen asleep before I remembered to power it back on.

Chapter 21

Saturday, mid-morning.

R olling over in bed, I groaned as my brains sloshed around inside my skull, and debated how urgently I needed to go pee, versus the need to stay in bed and not move for a good, long while.

But the urge to go won out, and so I reluctantly rolled myself out of bed and took the two steps it took to get to my door.

"Morning, champ!" Becka called from the kitchen, waving a spatula at me. I grunted a response and headed on my way, while Becka laughed merrily. It wasn't fair, she drank more than me, she should be heaving, but no, she's probably making pancakes. At the thought of food, my stomach perked up with interest but I had to shelve that in favour of more pressing needs.

On my way back from the bathroom, I paused on the threshold of the living area and leaned against the wall to watch as Becka artfully flipped fluffy pancakes at the oven top.

"You wouldn't happen to be making enough for two, would you?" I croaked.

"It just so happens that I am," she replied, cheerfully. Truly, she was the saddest drunk you'd ever met, and the chirpiest hungover person known to man. The duality of this woman was enough to give a girl whiplash.

Becka shook the now-cooked mini pancakes onto a warming plate before pouring more batter into the pan, each a perfect circle.

"So, about last night," she began, glancing at me once and then quickly looking away.

I mentally ran through the night in my head in a series of snap-shots, going round in my head like film on a projector, trying to find the cause for her apparent embarrassment.

"I know I shouldn't have sent that message, and I'm sorry. I just got so mad at the thought he was ghosting you," and as if to emphasise the point, she slammed her mix jug on the counter harder than necessary.

And just like that, the memory came flooding back in; us here in the kitchen, me rummaging for crackers like a crazed seagull, and Becka... Becka sending Jihoon a message accusing him of ghosting me.

"Oh fuck," I groaned, grabbing my forehead.

"You didn't remember?" she said, incredulously. "I thought I heard you talking to him-"

"Oh fuck!" I darted back to my bedroom, flinging myself on my bed to grab my phone off the nightstand. I tried to wake it, but it was fully powered off.

"Oh, fuck," I drew out the word in a groan as I grabbed my power cable and plugged it in before holding down the power button and watching anxiously as it powered on.

It took a hot minute to load up my home screen and connect to the Wi-Fi, despite me silently promising it a violent end.

Eventually though, my apps loaded and my screen flashed with multiple, time-stamped notifications.

"Oh fuck," I murmured. I had four missed calls and two messages from Jihoon, all around 2:00am. I opened the messages, bracing for the worst, but instead, they just made me feel guilty.

Joon

> *What did you mean? You said no.*

[sent 02:14]

Joon

> *Please call me. I don't mind what time. I just want to know you're not mad at me.*

[sent 02:20]

I groaned and pushed my head into the pillows, but then almost immediately looked back up and checked the time on my phone. It was after 3:00am for him now, I couldn't be the asshole that messes him around and then wakes him up at 3 in the morning.

"Everything ok?" Becka stood at the threshold to my room, holding a steaming cup of coffee that I could smell from over here.

"Not really," I grumbled. "I think Jihoon thinks I broke up with him."

"Is it really breaking up if you're not technically together?"

"Yes, thank you for that, Becka," I snapped, scowling at her.

"Sorry," she muttered, face screwing up, "I didn't mean that."

I sighed and rolled over onto my back, staring up the ceiling fan. "I know." And I did. But that didn't mean she wasn't right; it just wasn't the issue right now.

"Can't you call him to straighten things out?" she asked, not unkindly.

"Can't, it's past 3:00am in Seoul right now."

"Ah, shit." She's silent for a moment, shuffling her feet in a way that tells me she's feeling awkward. "Might as well come have some breakfast first. Y'know, re-group, re-nourish, get yourself ready to call him later."

She had a point, and by the way my stomach grumbled, my body agreed. I rolled off the bed and followed her into the kitchen. We both sat at the counter, where Becka had laid out a platter of pancakes, jars of honey, syrup and a can of whipped cream. I eyed her over the feast and she shrugged.

"I really do feel bad."

"I can see that. I didn't know we even had half of this stuff." I pulled the platter towards me and started forking mini pancakes onto my plate until I had a small stack.

Becka snorted. "That's because I went to the store this morning to buy it."

"It's not natural that you're this perky after a night out and a grumpy, baby bear on a work day." I opted for maple syrup and liberally poured it over my stack.

"That's not the same thing," she protested. "I'm still on a high in the morning after a night out. I'm not high on a work day."

"I should hope not," I replied dryly, "they test for that."

She laughed as she drowned her pancakes in whipped cream.

"Sprinkles?" she asked innocently, holding out the little tub of brightly coloured bits.

"Stop it, now you're just showing off."

She laughed again, and then we both lapsed into silence as we devoured our stacks, each of us lost in our own thoughts.

Later

We'd alternated between sitting on the couch and binging Netflix shows and doing chores all day, until we'd finally moved into a zone where it was time-appropriate for me to call. But I kept putting it off, feeling nervous bouts of anxiety that weren't helped by Becka asking me every ten minutes whether I was going to call now.

After the fifth such time, I finally snapped, "For fuck's sake, get off my ass, I'm going!" I stormed into my bedroom, slamming the door behind me.

"I'm rooting for you!" Becka called from the other side of the door, and though she couldn't see, I flipped my finger up at her, the effect somewhat broken by my reluctant smile. She may be annoying, but she was still kind of wonderful.

It was just past 8:00am now in Seoul. Early for a Sunday and I almost used this as an excuse to chicken out, but at the last second, before my screen blanked, I hit the 'call' button and waited for it to connect. Anxious energy surged through me, turning my fingers to ice.

I almost dropped the phone when I heard it connect, the familiar blipping-ring of the app twisting my stomach into roiling knots.

It rang for what felt like minutes and I nearly lost my nerve again and hung up, but then—

"Kaiya," his voice breathed, so close in my ear it was almost like he was there with me.

Chapter 22

"Hi," I said, trying for neutral, but fearing I missed and hit 'weird' instead.

"How are you feeling?" he asked.

"Oh, you know how it is," going now for light and carefree, "hungry, and trying to forget all the embarrassing parts."

"Sure, I get that."

"How are you? I hope it's not too early to call," I said, lying back down on my bed.

"No, not at all. I'm usually up early anyway. I'm glad you called, because I wanted to make sure you were okay after last night." His voice had an edge to it that I didn't know him well enough to identify.

"What did you mean when you said, 'no?'" he asked, bluntly.

"No?" I repeated, confused. "No what?"

"Ky, you said, 'no,' when I asked if you wanted to keep talking, and then you hung up."

For a moment, I just lay there. My brain stalled as I tried to reconcile my memories with what he was saying. Trying to recall the conversation was a physical effort, like trying to wake up hamsters to get them to run around the wheel. Until—

"You don't want me to call you?"

"No, I'm just saying you don't have to. Don't feel obligated to, y'know?"

"Oh, oh," and then, horrified, "oh, no! That's not what happened!"

"It's not? Look, can we switch to video?"

"Hmm? Oh, yeah sure." I'm quick to agree, forgetting my appearance until our screens are on and I see myself in the little window.

"Oh god," I moan, slapping a hand over my face.

"Kaiya, what?" He sounded impatient, which is totally fair, considering.

"Nothing, never mind," I sighed, "I just forgot I looked like this today." I took my hand from my face, which was thankfully, at least free of the facemask and eye patches that Becka and I had been using while binging Supernatural.

"There's nothing wrong with how you look. You look great." His smile is indulgent, and I tentatively return it.

"No, you," I mumbled as heat ran up my neck to warm my cheeks.

He laughed before turning serious again. "So, to be clear; you didn't hang up, last night?"

"No!" I shook my head vigorously. "I swear, what I actually said was that you didn't need to call me, if you didn't want to, and then my app crashed, and then I went to restart my phone, but I must have fallen asleep before turning it back on." I sounded ridiculous, but it was the God's honest truth.

"Why would I not want to?" Boy, he was really stuck on that, huh?

"Well, you know..." I was beginning to feel increasingly more foolish the longer I looked at his earnest face.

"No, I don't know," he huffed out a laugh and shrugged his shoulders.

Jihoon was proving more and more that he wasn't here to play games.

It was unfamiliar but refreshing. In almost every one of my previous relationships, we would have danced around the hard stuff, but Jihoon just said what he meant. His openness gave me nowhere to hide, and while that felt a little confronting, it was also strangely reassuring. It made me feel like he took this – whatever *this* was – as seriously as I did.

I sighed and took a moment to think my reply through. "I just thought it would be easier to give you an out, in case you were being too nice to say so."

Jihoon tilted his head to the side. "What's an 'out'?"

"You know, the opportunity to... walk away—" I couldn't say 'end things' when, as Becka pointed out, there was no 'thing,' technically, "—without anyone getting hurt feelings."

He frowned at me. I was so garbage at explaining this.

"Do you want an 'out'?" He said the word like it was offensive and I knew I'd mucked this up.

"No," I said emphatically. How do I fix this?

"Look, Jihoon...." My brain raced, trying to find the words. I settled on just saying what I felt. "I really like you. I liked spending time with you so much." I dropped my head, shaking it slightly, like I couldn't believe I was saying these words out loud. "It was the best time I've had in so long." My lips tugged up as I remembered that kiss on the beach.

"But?" he prompted when I didn't immediately continue.

"But you're an idol, you live in Korea and I... don't. Your life is so different to mine."

"And you're not okay with that?" I could see in his eyes that I was losing him. His face was as remote as I'd ever seen it, so far removed from the open, smiling Jihoon I'd come to know. My heart sank at the knowledge that I was the reason.

"It's not that," I said tentatively. "But I worry it'll be a problem for you. I worry that *I* will be a problem for you."

"You?" His tone is disbelieving, but I thought I saw a hint of a smile twitch at the corner of his mouth.

I groaned and closed my eyes and, without looking at him, I said, "I don't want you to feel obligated to keep in touch with me just because we had fun together. It's okay, I'd understand."

"Kaiya."

I didn't open my eyes.

"Ky? Look at me, please." And damn me, but who could resist that voice? So, I cracked open my eyes as if anticipating a physical blow. But, to my surprise, he was smiling at me.

"So, to be clear," he said, "you want to keep talking to me, but you're scared I don't want to talk to you, because our lives are too different, and I'm just being polite?"

Damn, I should have gotten him to summarise my point earlier.

"I mean... yes?"

"Is that a question?"

"No," I said, more confidently this time.

"Okay then, let me be clear. I like you, Kaiya. I want to keep talking to you."

"You do?" I could hardly believe it.

"Yes." He nodded, his face unexpectedly serious. "We..." He took a breath and looked away for a moment, before looking back at me. "It's not easy to meet people, especially someone that isn't a part of this world." He gestured as if to encompass his surroundings. "And when we do, sometimes that person just wants the Idol part of us. The persona we are on stage. You don't make me feel like I need to perform for you."

I tucked my hair behind my ear, trying to act causal, even though internally I was anything but. "I'm glad you don't feel like that with me. That's what friends are for"

"It's not just that." He cut in quickly, like he needed to have this be said. "I have friends, I don't need more."

I looked up at him, tilting my head to the side.

"I don't feel friendly with you," he admitted, dipping his head down as a blush crept across his cheeks. "I want to be more than your friend."

The grin that split my face apart would have hurt if my heart hadn't felt so light. I had to physically resist the urge to roll around my bed and squee, and I would have if I hadn't been holding the phone.

"Okay?" he asked. "Are we good?"

I nodded vigorously, giddy that I hadn't tossed this – whatever 'this' was – down the drain.

"Yes, we're good. I'm sorry."

"I'm just relieved," he said, "I really thought you were telling me to, uh, 'kick rocks'."

I laughed at his phrasing, an Americanism I'd only heard recently myself.

"As if!" I waved his concern away, but to my surprise, he pressed on.

"No, really. I really thought you never wanted to speak to me again. I couldn't sleep. I kept trying to think of what I'd done!" He held a hand to his heart, scrunching up his face as if he was in agony and I laughed again.

"I'm sorry, I'll never do that again." I held my hand up like I was making a vow, and Jihoon nodded earnestly.

"Good, that's a promise!"

Just as we were laughing at each other's silliness, Jihoon's head snapped around to stare at something out of view. He said something I didn't understand and nodded his head a few times before he turned back to me.

"I have to go," he said, looking regretful. "We're working on something." He held a finger up to his lips, making a 'ssh' face and I grinned.

"I can't wait to hear it."

"I'll message you." And with a final wave, he'd gone.

It was only after the call had ended, and after I'd pushed my head into the pillow and screeched with glee, and happiness, and all the emotions that bubbled up over, that I realised:

"He called me Ky."

And I grinned all over again. Nicknames felt that much more... More.

The next day, a massive bouquet of spring flowers arrived, complete with a beautiful cut-glass vase.

"I was just thinking we needed a massive vase for all the flower arrangements we get," Becka said, bumping my hip with hers as we both stared at the colourful mound of blooms dominating our small kitchenette.

"Extravagant idol, isn't he?" she added, pretending to sidestep around the spray of flowers to reach the kettle. I couldn't reply – I was too busy smiling so hard my cheeks hurt.

Chapter 23

May

The phone rang softly, waking me from a dream I forgot the moment my eyes opened. I looked over to my phone and, seeing the incoming video call, I reached out a hand and slid my finger up the screen.

"Good morning, sleepyhead." Jihoon's voice had become my favourite way to wake up. His smooth, accented voice never failed to bring a smile to my face. If I'd ever thought that regularly hearing his voice would become normal, I'd yet to experience that. Each time he said my name elicited a thrill like nothing else.

I smiled, sleepily, and rolled over so that I was more fully facing the phone that was docked on my bedside table, Jihoon's face filling the screen. He was dressed in an over-size, dark blue t-shirt and his hair was rumpled.

"You going to bed?" I asked, stifling a yawn.

"Yes, it was a busy day." He nodded and copied my yawn, which only made me yawn again.

"Can you tell me anything about it?" I asked, although he couldn't always say. He had been clear that if he could, he would discuss the group's schedule, but his contract was absolutely airtight. He could only discuss what was publicly known, or at least what had been released to the press, and I didn't want to push him. Even if I was wildly curious. I was still a fan, after all.

Jihoon looked thoughtful. It had been speculated about online whether the group would release a new album this year. The expectation was that they would – they released at least one a year – but with the expected tour next year, no one was certain.

"I can't say much, but we've just finalised our schedules for the year. It's going to be busy." He looked tired, but happy, so I supposed that was a good thing.

"I hope you get to rest though." They were always doing something, with so few periods of real rest. I hated the thought of him being tired all the time.

"I will, I promise. You're so cute." He grinned at me and I pulled my duvet up to my chin, acting as shyly as I really did feel. It still felt strange to be complimented by someone who looked like he did. I'd forget about it one moment, and then he'd change his expression, and all over again I'd be knocked on my ass by how good looking he was. I was really out of my league.

"No, you," I said, and he smiled, a stupid little joke that had become a kind of thing we did now.

I held my arm up to wake my watch and, seeing the time, I bolted upright.

"I gotta get up and get dressed!"

"Don't let me stop you." He smirked at me and I resisted the urge to fan my face with my hand. I loved the way that he made me feel so desirable, even first thing in the morning, when I probably had dried drool stuck to my cheek.

"Stop distracting me." I pointed at him, throwing off the bed covers, careful to make sure my long shirt was covering me appropriately, but I didn't miss the way his eyes flicked down, or the look of interest that passed his face. And nor did I really make much effort to make sure my shirt covered a lot of my thighs.

"Call me later?" he asked, innocently.

"If you like," I replied, nonchalantly.

"I always like."

Later that month

I fluffed my hair up in the mirror reflection of my screen, waiting for the video call to pick up. I was sat at the kitchen counter alone, Becka having already gone to bed.

Jihoon and I had started using KakaoTalk to call and message after the first month we'd started long-distance communicating. It only took one phone bill for me to figure out I did not want to play that game with my phone provider.

"Hey Ky," Jihoon smiled as he picked up, but I noticed he was in a car, his headphones in.

"Oh, are you busy? I can call you back tomorrow, if you are." I tried to hide my disappointment. We only got to actually speak in either the early mornings or the late evenings, and sometimes not even then, depending on his schedule. Even though we usually called every day, the time we actually got to speak was mere minutes. It always felt just a little bit rushed.

"I'm always busy," he laughed, not realising he'd voiced my thoughts. "But we're actually done for the day now, just going home."

"I hope you got to do something fun today."

We did! We just finished taping a variety show. It'll air later." His eyes crinkled in that way I had come to recognise when he was really amused by something. It made me smile to see it.

"Oh, awesome! What show was it? I can stay up to watch it."

"No," he said quickly, "don't do that. It won't be until 8:00pm KST. You need to sleep."

I did the quick maths in my head. "That'll be 4:00am here. Yeah, perhaps I'll catch up on it tomorrow," I laughed. "Can you send me the show details so I can find it?"

"You really don't have to watch it. It won't be captioned." He smiled, pleased but still embarrassed, which just made me want to watch it more.

"Well now I'm even more interested," I tease. "Plus, some clever i-Viber will have probably translated it by the time I get to see it, so you might as well give me a hint."

Jihoon groaned and held a hand over his eyes, which just made me laugh.

"It can't have been that bad if you had fun!"

"It was a cooking show," he finally admitted, "we had to try to make jjajangmyeon."

"That doesn't sound so bad."

"Whilst memorising girl group dances. They rang a bell randomly and we had to drop what we were doing to do the dance."

I burst into laughter and had to slap a hand over my mouth to make sure I wouldn't disturb Becka. Jihoon rolled his eyes, but he was clearly trying not to smile.

"And did you manage it?"

"The jjajangmyeon or the dancing?"

"Either."

He snorted, which on him was far sexier than it had any right to be.

"Sungmin and Jae were the only two who got the dance right, Seokmin and Woojin just ate all the banchan and I... tripped."

My eyes widened at the description of the chaos, and through the ensuing silence, I know I heard laughter in the background. Jihoon's eyes kept darting away, so I guessed his members were sharing in on the joke.

"Well, that certainly does sound like a variety. Are you ok?"

He waved my concern away. "Yes, only my pride hurts."

"Poor Jihoon," I crooned, and he rolled his eyes at me.

Just then, I had to stifle a yawn.

"You should go to bed, it's late for you." And though I wanted to argue the point, I was tired.

"Ok, speak later?"

"Yes. Goodnight, Kaiya."

June

Jihoon yawned and I frowned but kept my comments to myself. He'd asked me to call him later than normal today because they were still in the dance studio. So, while it was only 09:00am for me, for him it was one in the morning. But he said they had today – Sunday, for him – off, so he didn't mind staying up a little bit.

"Did you get the choreo nailed down, at least?" I asked, noticing the way his eyes were drooping slightly.

"Yes. We know the moves, we just need to perfect it so we can film the practices."

Due to a "leak," it was now widely known that GVibes were working on a new single for their comeback. Jihoon had explained that leaking information to the media was a common tactic to build hype – it required little effort or expense, and both sides benefited.

"When are you recording the song?"

"Next week," Jihoon sighed. He never complained, but I knew from what I'd read online the comebacks were a busy period of time, and they occurred often enough that I wondered when they ever rested for longer than one day in seven.

"Will it take you long? You were only in the studio a week when you came over in April." I folded my legs underneath me in bed.

"That was just some solo projects," he said. "This will take a little longer because we are going to record the remix tracks at the same time."

"Wow, that sounds like some long days."

"Yes, but then we'll have a few days before we start to do the music video."

"Well, if your studio ever needs someone to rearrange their cables and tune their guitars, you know who to ask." I pointed both thumbs at myself and flashed my best, winning smile.

Jihoon chuckled, "I wish."

It was my turn to sigh as I said, "Yeah, me too."

"Hi, Mum!" I waved at the screen, grinning.

"Hi, baby! Golly, you look so tanned. Doesn't she look tanned, Ernie?" The phone jostled as she handed it to my dad. He held it at arm's length, peering down his nose at me through the screen.

"Your glasses are on top of your head, Dad," I said, laughing.

"Oh yeah, that's where they went." He chuckled, pulling his glasses down from his forehead and bringing the phone closer. "Oh, you're right, Val," he nodded, looking off-screen. "She does look tanned."

The phone jostled again until my mum came back into view. "Have you been sunbathing, love?"

"No, Mum, it's just really sunny over here."

"Yeah, alright, just you mind that skin of yours. I didn't spend nine months making it just for you to get skin cancer."

"I rolled my eyes but murmured a, "Yes, Mum," all the same.

"How're you getting on, love? Your last email made it sound like that studio isn't all it's cracked up to be. You doing alright?" Her forehead creased as she peered at me through the screen.

I sighed. "I'm alright, Mum. The studio is great. It's just... because I'm only an intern, I don't get to do anything exciting." Telling my parents I was no longer sure I wanted to work in music production felt a little too much like making it real. Too much like manifesting the end of a career I'd thought I wanted. I didn't want to worry them, and, if I was honest, I wasn't ready to face a future that felt more uncertain than ever.

"Hmm." My mum pursed her lips, clearly gearing up for a whole speech, so I went in with a derailment.

"Did you get your hair done?"

"What?" She frowned. "Oh, well, no, but I am trying a new mousse."

"It looks nice! Very chic, very trendy." I might have been piling it on a bit thick, but she looked pleased.

"Thank you, love. Anyway, sorry to cut our call short, but I must dash. I've got an appointment, and your dad's driving me."

"What appointment?" Since moving away from home, I'd become weirdly nosy about my parents' comings and goings.

"Oh, never you mind," she said cryptically.

As my mum moved from the kitchen through the hallway to the front door, flashes of my childhood home appeared in the background, stirring a strange sense of nostalgia.

"Love, have you got your referral letter?" my dad's voice called in the background.

"What referral?" I said loudly, trying to get my mum's attention. She waved a hand at me impatiently.

"I'll call you later, love. Kisses!"

She was still blowing kisses as the line dropped, leaving me staring at her WhatsApp profile picture.

Jihoon and I barely talked at all over the week GVibes was recording. They were so busy between vocal training and the actual studio time that our schedules rarely aligned, but we sent messages to each other through the day. Jihoon was especially guilty of sending multiple selfies a day, which never failed to cheer me up, or make me laugh, or more often, make me swoon, especially that one he sent from the makeup chair when GVibes was having a style consultation for the music video. He'd clearly been bare from the neck down, and while the photo he'd sent was a head shot, there had been enough revealed that sent my pulse skyrocketing.

K-pop companies had such a tight leash on their idols that even when they filmed content of the groups in pools, or beaches, they almost always covered them up entirely. This photo was a reminder that Jihoon wasn't just an idol, he was a man. Not that I had needed the reminder, but I had needed to sit down afterwards.

One afternoon, a week after they'd wrapped recording, I was lying in bed, sick as a dog and having taken the day off. I was feeling a little miserable, when my phone buzzed with a text message from Jihoon.

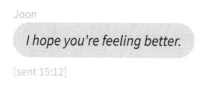

Joon

I hope you're feeling better.

[sent 15:12]

He must have just woken up. I'd texted him early this morning, when he would have been asleep.

Me

Not dead yet

Joon

Please don't die. Watch this.

[sent 15:14]

The next thing he sent was a link, which I saw was a link to VLive. I'd watched the group's lives before, but they normally filmed them in the evening, Korea time, so I'd watched the playbacks, once some clever iViber had put captions on, but it was still difficult to keep up with.

I clicked on the link, and it took me to a page that said, 'loading,' until a few moments later, Jihoon's face appeared on the screen. He was sat at his studio desk, by the looks of the surroundings, with all his carefully-chosen anime figurines and the different coloured light strips along the back wall.

"Annyeonghaseyo!" he cheerfully greeted, waving a hand. Already the chat was filling up as people joined, having received the notification that Jihoon was going live.

"Annyeonghaseyo, good morning, everyone. I thought it would be nice to come on early to see you all before work or school. I hope you don't mind!"

I smiled. Would it be big headed of me to assume this live was timed for my convenience?

Comments on the live were pouring in, the diversity of the languages being typed was immense, I recognised Korean, English, Spanish, French, and so many others I didn't know. People from all over the world were tuning in to watch, even if they couldn't speak the same languages. It blew my mind.

"What have you guys been curious about recently? Let me see..." Jihoon peered closer at the screen. I guessed he was reading through some of the comments.

He said something in Korean, and then in English. "We have just finished the new song, so please look forward to it, it'll be out soon."

Again, he peered at the screen, it was so cute the way he squinted, although I had no idea how he could read anything when the text flew by so fast. Maybe he had a way of pausing it?

"I promise I'm getting enough sleep!" He laughed, and then spoke again in Korean. I guessed that he was repeating what he was saying in Korean and English. His comments were flooded with people saying how good he was at English, and demands for him to speak in other languages, and bizarrely, several people claiming to be his wife. I laughed at those ones.

The rest of the Live followed in the same pattern, he'd pick up on some comment in the chat and answer the question in both languages. Watching him speak Korean was oddly soothing, his manner of speaking was very different. He used his face more, his expressions conveying much of his words, in a way he didn't when he spoke English.

I was tempted to comment in the chat, but something held me back. Even the thought felt weird, somehow. Like it would break some kind of barrier between being a fan and being... whatever it was we were.

So, I just watched in peace, enjoying the sound of his voice as he described his plans for the day, that he was eating well, thanking the fans for all the support and wrapping up by reminding us all that the new song is coming soon and to please support it.

Barely a minute after the Live ended, my phone buzzed with a message.

Joon

Did you watch?

[sent 15:42]

Me

Watch what? I was in the shower.

Joon

...

[sent 15:43]

Me

Kidding! Hahaha

Joon

Ky! I was about to put my head on the desk!

[sent 15:45]

Me

Aww, I'm sorry. Ofc I watched it! I loved it, thank you for including me. I think you blew everyone's minds with your epic English.

Joon

I have a very good reason to keep practicing ;)

[sent 15:47]

Me

Appearing on American talk shows?

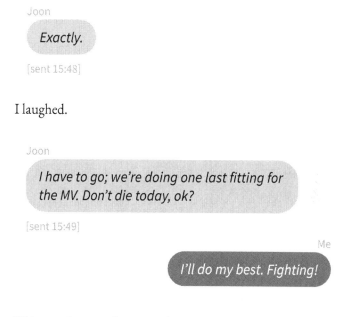

Joon

Exactly.

[sent 15:48]

I laughed.

Joon

I have to go; we're doing one last fitting for the MV. Don't die today, ok?

[sent 15:49]

Me

I'll do my best. Fighting!

I'd learnt that one from watching K-dramas.

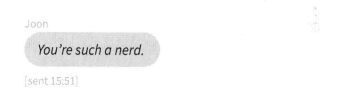

Joon

You're such a nerd.

[sent 15:51]

Later that afternoon, a delivery arrived that I had to go downstairs to collect. I wasn't too happy about getting out of bed, but I trudged to the front door, assuming it was something for Becka since I never ordered anything online.

Back upstairs, I placed the package on the counter and only then noticed the name on the brown paper bag—mine. Curiously, I peered inside and found a couple of takeaway containers, a small jar, and two drink bottles. Pulling them out one by one, I lined them up on the counter for inspection.

The drink bottles had labels in both Hangul and English, announcing themselves as Ginger and Cinnamon Tea and Ginseng Tea.

I picked up the small jar to read its label. "Yuja Cha," I croaked, spinning it around. Apparently, I was supposed to mix a spoonful into hot water.

Raising my eyebrows, I realized I'd been sent a very specific bag of groceries.

Next, I examined the food containers. The first one, labelled rice porridge, caught my attention – it was something I'd heard of in K-dramas but had never seen in real life. Tentatively, I lifted the lid and inhaled. The warm steam managed to cut through my blocked nose, and the smell was surprisingly delicious.

The second container made me a bit more cautious after reading it was fermented soybean soup, but even that smelled appetizing.

Smiling, I snapped a picture of my haul and sent it to Jihoon with a single question mark.

He responded almost immediately:

Joon

I'm happy it arrived so quickly! Eat the soup before it gets cold! And drink the Yuja cha first, it'll help.

[Sent 17:12]

I choked on a sip of Ginseng tea.

When the music video and the song dropped for 'Work Harder,' it seemed like the whole world flipped out, or at least, the online sphere I was plugged into.

It was edgy, it was catchy, and once I'd looked up a translation of the lyrics, it was as meaningful as any of the other songs.

A song about never giving up, always reaching further, always working harder for the thing you want.

The music video concept was visually striking, featuring solo work and dances from each member, as well as ensemble. The way they moved didn't seem human, especially from Sungmin, the group's best dancer.

Where Sungmin was the dancer and Woojin was the best rapper, Jihoon was the main vocalist and also known as 'the visual,' which he had told me he still found strange. In the music video, they'd dressed the members in all black – money-men suits and slicked back hair, heavy emphasis on their eyes. I could see why he was called the visual, because damn, I couldn't take my eyes off him.

The group were in full promo-mode now, Jihoon had said. So, at the end of the month, they were flying to Japan for three days to attend the TMA awards show. It was a star-studded, annual show where they, along with a host of other groups and soloists would perform and potentially bring home yet more awards to add to the stockpile they'd been collecting since their debut.

Jihoon had already told me he probably wouldn't be able to speak with me during the trip, even if only because they were being filmed the whole time by their staff for content. They also had to be at the actual awards venue nearly the entire day, from blocking rehearsals in the morning, going back to the hotel for food and to change, back to the venue for the red carpet and interviews, and then the ceremony itself would take hours. It sounded exhausting, and not at all the fun, glamorous event it seemed on tv.

I also wouldn't be able to live stream it because it wasn't available in the US, so I'd have to be content with watching whatever footage was published after the event, which bummed me out a bit.

GVibes flew out early on the Wednesday morning, which was Tuesday afternoon for me. I'd snuck into the ladies' room to take his call as he was heading to the airport, which earned me a couple of disapproving looks from the people who'd come in to actually use the bathroom. The flight was only a couple of hours from Seoul to Tokyo, so he'd called again as the group shuttled from the airport to their hotel, since I was at home by that time.

He'd shown me the view from their hotel; it seemed like they were staying in the clouds, they were up so high. I didn't mention it, but it felt weird that he was there – in Japan – where my mum had spent so much time and where she'd met my father. I didn't even know if he was still alive.

Normally the thought of my biological father didn't even cross my mind, but I supposed it was a normal reaction to Jihoon being there.

But it did put me in a weird funk for the rest of the day.

I tried to talk to Becka about it later, and while she sympathised, I could tell she hadn't really known what to say to me.

I'd been getting a bit testy recently, my temper fraying a little more easily than normal, though I couldn't put my finger on why. Becka seemed to think it was the combination of having such a high-profile 'situationship,' but it felt like a bit of a cop out to put it down to that. I'd been feeling... restless.

Work had continued to stagnate. I hadn't minded doing the grunt work at first, but now I'd finished everything Jeremy needed me to do. I think I'd outlasted my usefulness, and it was becoming increasingly clear that my employment had always been more of a favour for a family friend than a real opportunity. While I appreciated the work experience, the situation had started to feel awkward. I enjoyed my time with the different departments, but lately, there just hadn't been much demand for an apprentice or helpful intern. It left me feeling useless. A feeling I did not enjoy.

It didn't help that while I was stuck in this rut, Jihoon was off having the time of his life.

Japan was on the same time as South Korea, so I woke up to plenty of cute selfies. Photos of Jihoon eating a circular cake with a hole in the middle, kind of like a bundt cake, Jihoon posing in front of the view from his room, Jihoon buying a can of hot coffee from a vending machine, Jihoon posing in front of a red building with the SEGA logo on it.

I laughed at the one he'd sent where he was wearing a fluffy, yellow hat with a cutesy creature face on it. He was grinning so wide that his nose was scrunched, and he didn't look like an idol – he just looked like a young guy having fun.

I was happy for him, but if I was honest with myself, I was jealous – jealous of the time he was having, and jealous that I wasn't there to share it with him.

I didn't know what to do with this snarl of negative emotions, it was starting to get exhausting.

Chapter 24

The awards show in Japan took place at around 1:00am Friday, LA time and it only took until Friday afternoon for the footage from the awards show to make its way onto streaming platforms, but I'd had to anxiously wade through the day at work first before I could watch it.

"I brought snacks!" Becka said proudly, dumping a string bag full of rustling wrappers onto the kitchen island.

"My hero," I called, appreciatively, from my seat on the sofa as I tried to find the specific video of the show that had been captioned.

"Do we even know what the group has been nominated for?" Becka asked as she sat down next to me, putting a tray of assorted snacks onto the little coffee table in front of the sofa.

"No idea," I admitted, "and the videos I found are strictly no spoilers."

"Very considerate," Becka nodded.

"Vibers," I said, as if this was answer enough. "There were online voting options, but they were geo-locked, I couldn't even see which categories GVibes were up for."

"Rude."

"Right? Oh, here it is!" Excitedly, I selected the captioned video – it was only two hours long. "They must have cut all the ads out."

"Very considerate," Becka said again, nodding her appreciation.

"Vibers." I grinned.

Together, we watched the show, carefully looking out for when the cameras panned to the talent section, which they did frequently. GVibes certainly got their fair share of air time.

"Handsome SOB's," Becka muttered, sipping a glass of wine.

I just nodded, because there was no denying it. All five members were dressed in a manner similar to that of the music video for 'Work Harder,' black suits cut in various styles that suited each member perfectly. Their hair and makeup was flawless. Their eyes were shadowed and lined, giving them mysterious, moody vibes. Thirstily, I took a gulp of my wine.

Finally, "Here they are!" I pointed at the TV as the first few bars of 'Work Harder' were played to an immediate and thunderous roar from the crowd, the lights in the auditorium dimming as the stage lighting flared. Silhouettes artfully played against a white back-drop as lights strobed across the stage, drumming up the excitement to a near fever-pitch that the other performers just hadn't managed.

Then, just as the beats from the extended song's intro began to pound through the speakers, all sound cut off and five figures shot up into the middle of the stage from hidden trapdoors and a camera raced forward to focus solely on Jihoon, now undeniably Baek Ji-Hoon, main vocalist and 'the visual' of GVibes.

He began to sing a cappella, no backing-track, just the clear, confident opening lines of the song, turning his head side-on as he tilted his head back. The view of the muscles in his neck flexing as he sang was undeniably sexy.

And then the music flooded back in and GVibes burst into motion – in perfect sync, a single, living entity. Their movements were graceful yet edgy. Impossible to look away from.

The cameras swooped around them, each vying for the best angle and yet still capturing the whole.

When the song transitioned into 'Make Some Noise,' the crowd near exploded with screams and chants. My feet were tapping away of their own volition and I found I was somehow anxious for Becka to also admire the skill, the catchiness of the song, the outfits and overall performance. Like I was anxious for her approval, which was ridiculous.

I tried to put it aside, and when the performance finally ended, I tried to pretend I wasn't as hyped as I really felt – like my heart wasn't fit to bursting.

As the house-lights raised, replacing the strobing stage lights, the cameras panned in close as the five of them clustered together, raising their hands and bowing to the audience, all of them smiling widely and shouting words of thanks. I could see the sheen of sweat glistening on their faces; they'd worked hard. I hoped they had gotten some rest and good food before the show.

Not long after GVibes left the stage, a podium was carried on, followed by the two hosts. It was time for the awards ceremony.

GVibes wasn't nominated for the first handful of categories: things like Best Male and Female Acts, Best Solo, Best Newcomer and Best International Tour, but when the MC called out – and Becka and I read the caption for – Listener's Choice, GVibes were one of four groups nominated. I clasped Becka's hand and together we waited until...

"GVibes!" The camera panned to where GVibes was sitting in the performers area, capturing the moment where their faces changed from polite blankness to surprised and then delighted, clapping each other on the shoulders.

Minjae, the leader, got up first and lead the group back to the main stage as various other idols and groups watched them pass, some standing to cheer them on.

Minjae accepted the award graciously and they all huddled around the microphone grinning. They thanked their fans first and foremost, their management and their friends and family for their unwavering support. Or, at least that's what I gathered from the captions. I began to feel the first twinges of annoyance at not being able to understand even a single word– more so when Jihoon spoke, again reinforcing how grateful they were for their fans.

They went on to win three other awards: Best Music Video for 'Make Some Noise', Best Collaboration for 'Fall in Love', which they'd collab'd with Haley for and Fan's Choice, which I think was one of the online polls.

By the end of the show, I was weirdly exhausted, my emotions feeling so strung out that I felt the need for a relaxing bath.

"You know where the nice oils are," Becka just said in response, already flicking through episodes of Supernatural.

Even though the bathroom was fairly compact, Becka and I had made the effort to make it as spa-like as we could. Ben, her ex, had kept promising to re-grout the tiles, but he never had, so when I moved in, one of the first things we did was go to a Lowe's and pick out some rental-friendly peel-and-stick floor tiles, a new shower curtain and one of those fancy, slatted, bamboo floor mats. We couldn't do anything about the small bath/shower, but with the addition of a few scented candles, the room felt 'more yuppy, less guppy' – as Becka had put it.

Still feeling a bit off-kilter, I lit a couple candles, turned only the over-mirror light on and liberally dosed the bath with essence of ylang ylang. I slid down into the bath as far as I could, bubbles and warm, scented water tickling my collar bones as I tilted my head back and sighed. Bliss.

That was exactly when my phone vibrated in the bath caddy, the noise echoing around the small room.

It took me a moment to get to it though, as I had to dry my hands off on a hand towel first, and then when I saw Jihoon's face on the screen with an incoming video call, I nearly dropped it.

For a hot second, my finger hovered above the 'voice call' button, but then a wild, impulsive and somewhat devilish side of me nudged my finger to the side and hit 'video' instead.

I held the phone quite close to my face as Jihoon lit up the screen, greeting me with that smile of his that crinkled his eyes, and made my heart squeeze in my chest.

"Hi," I said, shy again now.

"Hi!" His voice was bright and happy, and I supposed winning several awards would do that to a person.

"Where are you? It's so dark," he said, moving his head around as if that would grant him a clearer view of my background.

There was that devilish impulse again. I tried to repress a small grin as I pulled the phone back, only slightly, to now include a view of my neck and shoulders, the candle on my right illuminating the view more fully, reflecting off the bubbles that skimmed the bare skin of my clavicle.

"Wah..." he trailed off, his jaw falling slack. I watched as he leaned back in his chair, misjudged whatever was behind him and promptly dropped the phone, the loud bang startling me so that I almost dropped my own phone. I laughed, holding a hand over my mouth as I watched fingers scrabble for the phone, scrapping noises and darkness, before Jihoon's slightly reddened face reappeared on the screen.

"Everything alright?" I asked, not trying to hide my laughter.

"Dropped my phone," he said, sheepishly. I knew I wasn't imagining the trajectory of his gaze. I also knew that I was fully covered, but it was a fine line, and one I was currently quite interested in teasing him with. That devilish side making me reckless and perhaps something a little more... interested.

I pressed my thighs together, the motion of the water lapping up and down my chest, revealing a little more in the waves as they crested and ebbed away.

"I watched the show," I said.

Jihoon's eyes snapped back up to mine, a small crease forming in between his brows.

"Oh!" he exclaimed, if a little late, "did you like the performance?"

I found it adorable that he would ask if I liked watching them perform, before asking if I'd seen them win.

"Very much!" I enthused, "I loved the staging, it was so cool!"

Jihoon ducked his head, grinning. "We had to practice it so many times, the trapdoors were so fast, Seokmin-ah kept falling over."

I laughed, the image of Seokmin, the youngest member of the group at just nineteen, springing up so coolly, only to ruin the effect by falling. It was very on-brand for the group's maknae – who was famous for being able pull off the most challenging dance moves, only to then trip over his own feet.

"You looked so cool." I was gushing just a bit, but it was hard not to.

Jihoon smiled, embarrassed but clearly pleased. "Thank you, we all worked hard to make sure we gave a good performance."

"Were you surprised you won so many awards?"

He shrugged, looking off to the side. "It's always nice, we never expect to win. There are so many talented performers. We work really hard for our fans, so the awards we cherish the most are the fan-vote ones, because it's them that motivate us to be the best we can be."

I nodded, this made perfect sense, given how vocal GVibes had always been about their fandom, always crediting them with being the reason they had the success they had, dedicating all their accolades to them and being remarkably tolerant – even when things got a bit intense.

Last year, a fan had somehow found out what hotel they were staying in on a trip to Singapore and broke into Woojin's room. She had been taking a shower when Woojin came back. Woojin had called his management to the room, but had made them wait in the other room as he'd calmly talked to her through the closed door. He had waited for her to get dressed before asking his management to escort her out. ENT had wanted to press charges, but Woojin told them not to and instead offered to pay for her to attend therapy.

The public wouldn't have even known about half of it, had the fan – a saesang; someone who takes being a fan to extremes, often to the detriment of the idols – not spoken about it to Dispatch. ENT had verified the story but offered no further comments. It was a huge deal for months. Last I'd heard, the girl had actually taken up the offer of therapy though, so I guess that was a net win.

"Judging by the reaction of the crowd, I'd say the appreciation is mutual." I smiled, remembering the roar of the crowd, how the light sticks had illuminated the waves of cheering fans.

Jihoon nodded and then yawned widely.

"Are you back in Korea?"

"Yes, we flew back this morning." That explained why he looked so tired. It wasn't a long flight, but the show was last night and they'd flown back this morning. Not a lot of down time in their schedule.

"Did you even get to sleep?"

He made a face and a 'so-so' gesture with his hand. "We have a free day today and tomorrow, so I'll get plenty of sleep and eat well, don't worry." He smiled at me, such a smile that warmed my chest, and I grinned back at him.

"So, you're in the bath?" He waggled his eyebrows at me in a way I was not aware he could do, and my cheeks flamed.

"It's been a hard week," I said, trying not to sound defensive. Seemed like my little devil had fallen off my shoulder.

"You should get a massage."

"I can't."

"Why not?" He frowned.

"There's no one here to give me one." Ah, the devil had climbed back up. I flashed him a smile that I'm sure wasn't hard to interpret.

Jihoon groaned and theatrically grabbed his chest, throwing his head back. Then he stood up suddenly and started walking, a determined look on his handsome face.

"Jihoon, where are you going?" I laughed.

"I'm going to the airport."

263

I laughed harder, splashing water everywhere.

"Mwo hae?" A voice in the background asked and I didn't need to know Korean to understand from the tone that someone was asking what the hell Jihoon was doing.

"Don't interrupt me, hyung," Jihoon shouted back, "I'm going to the airport."

"Jihoon, stop!" I cried through my giggles.

Another face very briefly came into view on the screen before it went blank and I heard a muffled, "Wahh!" I could have been wrong, but I would have sworn that was Minjae.

I heard scuffling through the phone, but the screen remained blank, like it was being held to his chest.

"Jihoon!" I called, growing more mortified by the moment. Several heartbeats later, the screen brightened as it was lifted further away. I saw Jihoon leaning back against a wooden door, grinning.

"Did you win?" I asked with a wry smile.

"No," he laughed. "I am not allowed to come to LA."

"Probably for the best," I grumbled, inexplicably and irrationally disappointed.

"Soon," he promised, slyly grinning at me.

"Really?" I leaned forward, surprise momentarily making me forget that only a generous layer of bubbles was covering me.

"Oops!" I hastily ducked back under as Jihoon smacked a hand over his eyes and I laughed, pretty certain I hadn't actually flashed him. Well, not much, anyway.

"Jihoon, it's fine, I'm decent," I covered my embarrassment with a little laugh. "You were about to tell me when you're coming here."

"Oh, um, I'm not sure, we do a lot tof USA shows, so I'm sure it'll be soon." He cleared his throat and looked back up at me with an expression that heated the water that had been starting to cool down.

He opened his mouth to say something, but just then, someone pounded on the door he was leaning against. "Jihoon-ah!" the person called. Jihoon rocked his head back against the door, looking pained and sighed.

"I have to go," he said with such a sad puppy expression I wanted to laugh again.

Instead, I just said, "I understand. I hope you have a good day."

He shook his head sadly. "It won't be as good as this."

I laughed and blew him a kiss, my hand covered in bubbles. He groaned again and closed his eyes.

"Bye Jihoon." I pressed 'end' and put my phone back on the caddy before covering my face with my bubbly hands to muffle the shriek.

Chapter 25

July

"What in the world is a 'chicken message?'" Becka said, looking over my shoulder to watch as I translated the Hangul characters into English.

"I have no idea," I sighed, "but apparently the app developers thought it was important for me to learn."

I was on a nine-day streak for the language app I'd finally gotten around to downloading and I had now moved onto section three: Basic Phrases, which included such cultural treats as 'the baby's cucumber,' 'chicken message' and 'the fox's newspaper'.

"Will you ever find out what the message is?" Becka asked, feigning a serious expression.

"You know, I really don't think I will." I sighed, putting my phone down on the counter.

"That's one mysterious bird," she said, nodding in sympathy. "How's it going otherwise?"

"I'm recognising more of the alphabet now and can pair up the letters, but my pronunciation is... quite literally garbage," I admitted.

"You can't be that bad," Becka protested on my behalf. "You're pretty decent at French."

I stared at her. I stared at her for so long she began to squirm. "In what world are the two comparable?"

"I don't know," Becka exploded, impotent outrage spilling everywhere. "I was being supportive!"

I huffed out a laugh and rubbed a hand down my face. "In French, the letters don't switch sounds."

"It could be worse," Becka said sagely. "You could be Korean and having to learn English. It's a way harder language. We spell 'knife'—"

"With a k, yeah I know."

"So, stick at it, champ." Becka clapped me on the arm gamely while I contemplated reaching for a Tylenol for my headache.

I wasn't sure how much of the language I was actually absorbing, but the app seemed to think I was making marvellous linguistic strides. I was determined to be at least able to introduce myself without making a fool of myself. I was a little embarrassed I hadn't thought to do it earlier.

Later that month

"When do you leave?" I asked, trying not to stare. Jihoon had called me this morning wearing full stage makeup and the effect was nothing short of devastating. The group had just finished a day of shooting a full ad campaign for a Korean fashion house. He'd already shown me the full effect when he'd put his phone down and walked across the room – strutted, really – wearing black leather trousers and a gauzy black shirt that I was sure the post-production team would have to airbrush certain features out of, because it was basically see-through. I'd had to forcibly shut my mouth to stop myself from panting.

Jihoon ran a hand through his already artfully-mussed hair and said, "In two days. We'll fly to the camp in Jeju and stay there for ten days and then we have a week off to spend with our families."

It was the annual group vacation. They'd announced it last month. The whole group went camping, did fun activities, cooked food together, and just generally hung out.

It sounded idyllic – were it not for the whole host of cameras and crew members accompanying them to film everything for the never-ending stream of content.

"Is it weird being on vacation, but still being filmed all the time?" I crossed my legs and grabbed a pillow to hug to myself.

Jihoon looked contemplative for a moment. "Yes, but also no because we're so used to cameras being around. It used to be weird and all our managers would keep saying, "Just relax, be yourself," but it was hard. Now, it's not so bad because we know Vibers like it and that makes it easier for us."

"We want to share parts of our lives with Vibers because..." Jihoon paused, twirling his be-ringed fingers in the air as he searched for the words, "they give so much of themselves to us."

I nodded. I couldn't imagine ever feeling at peace with being filmed every day.

"What about when you visit your family, will you be filmed then?" What a crazy notion, I could just imagine how un-chill my mum would be with that.

"No," Jihoon held up his hands in a cross, "they don't come home with us, that's our private lives and the company respects that."

That was something, I supposed. My mum wouldn't let them in the house, although my dad would definitely play up to the cameras.

"When was the last time you saw them?"

Jihoon thought for a moment. "Uh, Seollal," he said after a moment. He must have seen my blank face as he clarified, "It's Korean New Year festival, we go home to our families and honour our ancestors. And eat a lot." He laughed.

"Sounds awesome," I said honestly, although all I could picture was Chinese New Year and I made a mental note to look more into Korean national holidays.

Just then, Jihoon's watch vibrated loudly. He held it up to read the screen and tutted. "I have to go," he said, "we have a meeting."

"Okay," I said easily. "Will I get to speak to you before you leave for Jeju?"

"I don't think so," he said, frowning, "it's going to be busy. The crew will be here to film us packing, and then we travel there in the morning..."

"I get it, it's okay." I tried to sound reassuring, or at least not whiny.

"I don't know if I'll be able to speak to you when we're in Jeju," he admitted. "Even when they're not filming, there's crew everywhere. Minjae-hyung got a lot of online comments last year about being on his cell all the time, the managers weren't pleased."

I resisted the urge to roll my eyes; of all the things to get pissy about. I supposed it was the question of who he might have been contacting that had gotten the fans riled up, although I hadn't known about that particular scandal. I was rarely on top of K-Pop scandals and salacious gossip as a lot of it went over my head, I just didn't understand why half of it was such a big deal.

"It's okay, I understand," I said again. "We'll talk when you're home. I just hope you have a good time and get to do fun things!" Jihoon smiled, but then frowned when his watch vibrated again.

"You need to go," I said.

"Yes." Jihoon sighed. "I'll message you when I can."

Okay. Have the best time!"

He smiled. "Bye, Kaiya."

The Next Week

"So, I was thinking," Becka began, spreading cream cheese across a toasted bagel as we enjoyed a lazy Sunday morning together.

"Dangerous, but go on," I joked, taking a sip of coffee.

"Is it weird? You and Jihoon? Now that you're kinda... a thing?"

"Which part?" I huffed, "the fact that he's a best-selling artist with millions of fans and I'm a complete nobody? Or that I'm a complete secret, and will always have to be? Or that he's in Korea and I'm in LA, or that he is literally brain-meltingly handsome and I'm cute on a good day?"

Becka held up a finger and pointed it at me with a dangerous glint in her eyes.

"That's my best friend you're talking about, you better put some respect on her name."

I rolled my eyes but couldn't deny the quiet warmth her loyalty sparked in me. "Or is it that we're not technically together? We're in a..." I couldn't think of the word.

"Situationship," Becka supplied, nodding sagely.

"Yes," I clapped, "exactly. So, yeah, which part of that do you think is weird?"

"Okay, yeah, sure, all'a that," she said, waving her hand in a circle, "but more specifically, I meant the part where you're in a..."

"'Situationship?'" I supplied helpfully.

"Yeah, that. Is it weird dating someone this way? I mean, it's been more than three months, you guys talk more regularly than most couples I know, your camera reel is stuffed with photos you have to either delete or encrypt, and you don't even know when you'll see each other again."

"Yeah, thanks for the reminder of that," I said, sipping my coffee.

"I didn't mean that!" Becka protested around a mouthful of bagel.

"Animal," I muttered and Becka rolled her eyes at me, but took the time it took to chew and swallow before saying, "I guess I mean more like... do you *feel* like you're in a relationship? Like, are you unofficially exclusive? Mark asked you out and you fobbed him off with some excuse about having a guy back in London, so like, are you dating, or...?"

I took another sip as I contemplated my answer.

"Okay, well first of all, Mark wouldn't stop looking at my boobs the whole time we talked, so really, he asked my boobs out, not me."

Becka choked on a bagel bite, slapping her chest while I tried not to laugh. Politely, I waited for her to get her breath back before I continued.

"And secondly... yeah, I don't know," I admitted. "I don't know what we are, I don't know if we're exclusive, although I get the impression we are." I frowned. "I really don't know."

"God," Becka exclaimed, doesn't that chafe the hell out of you?"

"Little bit," I quipped. "Just a smidge. A tiny fraction."

"A wee bit," Becka supplied.

"Tis but a flesh wound." I grasped my chest for dramatic effect and Becka laughed.

"But in all seriousness," I said, "I don't even know how we'd reconcile being in an actual relationship right now.

"I mean, we can't exactly date. We're not in close proximity and it would have to be in secret anyway."

"Does his contract have a dating ban?" She asked, surprising me.

"You've been looking into KPop!" I accused, laughing.

"Do you blame me? My roommate and best friend is dating Korean Usher!"

"Okay, I'm not mad about that comparison," I laughed, "but no, not anymore. The group did have a dating ban in their original contracts, but since they re-signed last year, they don't anymore."

"Ooh, any special reason?" Becka waggled her eyebrows at me.

"I think it was more to do with how established they are as a group now," I said, "they're so successful that they have a bit more bargaining power. And they're all older now, not teenagers anymore. Well, all but one of them," I said, thinking of Seokmin, who was still only nineteen.

"Oh, okay, sure, that makes sense," Becka nodded, taking another bite, "although it's still batshit," she mumbled around the mouthful. I couldn't disagree.

Just then, my phone buzzed with an incoming video call on WhatsApp. My dad's cheerful face filled the screen, taken from a photo this past Christmas.

"Hi, Pops," I said as I accepted the call, a smile already tugging at my lips.

"Hi, Mr. Thompson!" Becka called, pushing in next to me.

"Hi, girls!" Dad waved, peering down his nose at the screen.

"Dad, your glasses are on top of your head."

"Ah, so they are." He chuckled, sliding them down onto his nose. "Thanks, kiddo. That's better – I can see your beautiful faces now."

"Aww, Mr. Thompson, you're too cute!" Becka gushed, putting her hands under her chin.

"Am I?" Dad laughed. "Val, I'm cute!" he called off-screen. From somewhere in the house, Mum's voice rang out, "Cute bum!"

"Argh, Dad, can you two like, not, while I'm on the phone?" I groaned, while Becka just cackled and retreated to the sofa.

"My work here is done," she said, waving over her shoulder.

I rolled my eyes at her before turning back to my dad.

"You alright dad?" I asked. Normally I called them, it was unusual for my parents to call, especially my dad.

"Well," he started, leaning in a bit like he was sharing a secret. "You know your mum's birthday is coming up. I was wondering if you could come home for it."

I immediately felt a burst of guilt, because not only had I forgotten my mum's birthday was soon, but I also knew I wouldn't be able to get the time off. Not because I was busy, I thought with a twinge of frustration. Just that I seemed to recall my temporary contract did not allow for leave.

My dad must have seen the answer on my face because he sighed.

"That's okay love, we know how busy you are. And it's only for the year." He shrugged.

"Dad, is everything okay?" I'd begun to feel uneasy. Call me paranoid, but I had a niggle...

"Of course it is!" He grinned at me, a wide smile that on any other occasion would have been reassuring. "No biggie," he continued. "We were only thinking it would be nice to go somewhere fancy, but that's it. No need to fuss."

"If you're sure...."

"Course I am! We just miss you, love."

"I miss you too," I said thickly. "Hey pops?"

"Hmm?"

"You'd tell me if anything was wrong, yeah?"

"Don't be so soft," he scoffed. "Anyway, must dash, it's nearly time for Strictly Come Dancing, and I promised your mum I'd make her a cheese platter."

"I want a cheese platter!" I whined.

"Better marry a man like me then." He winked, and I laughed.

"I should be so lucky."

"I'm the lucky one," he said softly. "Talk to you later, love."

As the screen went blank, I couldn't shake the unease that had crept in during the call.

"Your folks alright?" Becka called from the couch, her mouth full of bagel.

"I hope so," I said quietly.

Labour Day weekend

"Where were you?" I whined. "I came up to the office and you weren't there! I had to eat lunch on my own."

Becka waved away my pout with one perfectly manicured hand. "I had to go back to the apartment to get something."

"You went all the way home on lunch to get something?" I asked sceptically. "It's Labour Day weekend. We won't be back in the office until Tuesday, what was so urgent?"

"I left something there," she said evasively, immediately piquing my interest. I wasn't going to press it before, but I would now.

"Oh yeah? What?" I crowded her, narrowing my eyes at her. She'd crack, she always did.

"Tampons!" She squeaked.

I frowned. "Tampons?"

"Yeah, geez, give a girl a break, Inspector Ratchet." She pushed me away gently.

"Hey, is that my bag?" I asked in confusion as Becka pulled my spare backpack out from under her desk. It was pretty obviously mine because it was covered in dinosaurs wearing party hats. I'd bought it 'ironically,' but I low-key loved it. It was also pretty obviously full.

"Er, yeah. Yeah, it is. I needed to go shopping on the way back to the office for...."

"For...?" I prompted.

"Snacks!"

"Snacks?" I said, propping my fists on my hips. "Uh huh. Why?"

"Oh, good grief, can we just go now, please? If I'd known you would make such a fuss about me borrowing your bag, I would have torn the apartment apart for the one I think I have in there somewhere, and left a whole load of mess. Is that what you want?" Becka turned the full force of girl-rage on me, her eyes wide, cheeks flushed.

"Whoa, chill out Regan, it's cool, use the bag."

"Who-the-fuck-is-Regan?" she hissed.

"Regan, the little girl from the Exorcist... you know what? Never mind, let's get you home." I made to gently shuffle her away from the office, but she stomped ahead of me. I followed her, shrugging.

"Did you get some Tylenol and chocolate along with those Tampons?" I called after her.

Becka threw a glare over her shoulder but kept walking.

We rode the elevator down to the lobby in silence, and when the doors opened, she strode purposefully across the marble floor to the outside door, where an Uber was parked up at the pavement.

To my surprise, Becka walked straight over to it, where she had a brief conversation with the driver through the window.

"Come on," she called to me.

"Aw Becka, not again, we can't keep getting Ubers," I protested.

"Just get in," she groused and obediently, I slid in beside her.

But it soon became apparent we were not driving home, as the driver completely ignored the signs for Glendale and kept going.

"Hey," I said in alarm, "we're going in the wrong direction."

"No, we're fine," Becka said and turned to the driver, "I gave you the right address, West Hollywood."

"Hollywood?" I echoed in confusion. "Why the fuck are we going to Hollywood?"

"*West* Hollywood," she corrected, distracted as she looked down at her phone.

"Fine," I gritted my teeth, "why are we going to *West* Hollywood? I swear, if you're dragging me to another Dildo Party—"

"Sweet baby Jesus, can you not?!" Becka cried, glancing briefly at the driver, who to his credit, had no reaction whatsoever. "That was one time!"

"One time was enough," I shuddered, the memories flashing through me. So much lube.

"You're such a prude," Becka muttered. "But no. It was meant to be a surprise, but we're meeting a friend there, they've swung back into town and wanted to meet up. It's no big deal." She shrugged.

"I feel like you could have just told me that," I said, slumping back in my seat. "Is that what the bag of snacks is for?"

"Yes!" Becka said with far more enthusiasm than I would have expected.

"Right, okay. Do I know them?"

"No. It's brand-new people."

"That you know in West Hollywood?" I was beginning to feel suspicious. Becka was a horrible actress. "Becka," I began, "it's not Ben, is it?

"What?" The look of alarm on her face convinced me I'd guessed right.

"It's okay," I said as gently as I could. "If you want some backup, I'm here for you, okay?"

"Yeah, okay," she said with such a weird expression. I decided to drop it, she was obviously feeling very conflicted about meeting up with Ben, no wonder she was acting so weird.

We rode the rest of the way in silence. Rush hour in LA meant it took about half an hour to make the relatively short journey. As we pulled up into a more secluded residential street, my mouth fell open. These were nice houses. Not mansions, but nice. Private driveways, privet hedges, security signs in front gardens, kind of nice.

I was about to ask what Ben did for a living, when Becka swung her legs out of the car and grabbed my dino rucksack.

"Hey, can you wait here for a second?" She turned round to the driver.

He shrugged. "That's what the ride said." I frowned, but before I could ask, Becka was telling me to hurry up, so I slid out and followed her up the driveway. There was no car parked there.

"Hey, are you sure this is the right place?" I asked, looking around.

"I'm sure," she said before entering in a combination on a number pad she'd revealed by sliding up a discreet panel on the door.

"Oh," I said, dumbly, as the door audibly clicked and Becka pushed down on the handle and stepped through.

"Come on," she beckoned, and I followed, my head on a swivel as I tried to take in the sumptuous, yet not bougie foyer. It was obviously fancy, but not obnoxious. The owners had nice taste. I slipped my bag off my shoulders and left it neatly by the front door.

"We're here!" Becka called, making me jump.

"Becka, what..." I trailed off, trying to make sense of her face. She wasn't looking at me, she was looking straight ahead, a smile stretching her face so wide I could count her teeth.

I turned my head to follow where she was looking, but it was like I was moving in slow motion, because when I saw him, I felt the breath halt in my throat.

"Jihoon."

Chapter 26

He moved towards me, fluid grace in every movement of his body, mesmerizing on a stage, devastating in real life.

When he was mere inches from me, he stopped, looking down at me with a smile that restarted my stalled heart.

"Kaiya," he murmured, reaching forward and taking my wrist in his warm hand. I felt myself being tugged forward. Powerless to resist, I allowed myself to be pulled into him. I curled my arms around his waist and buried my face into his chest, the warm smell of him, that clean laundry and soap smell making my head spin. I inhaled, shuddering slightly, pushing against the sense of being completely overwhelmed. I could hear his heartbeat, the warmth of his skin heating my suddenly cold fingertips as I grasped at him, a drowning person clinging onto a life raft.

"Jihoon," I rasped, too overcome to say anything else.

"It's me," his voice rumbled through his chest as I remained pressed so close, and I took a shuddering breath, trying very hard to pull myself together.

"You got her?" I faintly heard Becka say from somewhere behind me.

"I have her," he rumbled against me.

I hadn't realised until this moment how much I felt for Jihoon. It was a staggering realisation and one I hadn't known I'd needed to process.

I took several deep, calming breaths and tried to re-centre myself, and all the while Jihoon was rubbing soothing circles on my back.

It could have been minutes or hours by the time I had worked up the mental fortitude to straighten my back and take a half-step away, just enough that I could tip my chin up to look at Jihoon. He smiled down at me, his eyes shining, the natural mahogany colour of his irises deep enough to fall into, if I wasn't careful.

"Hello." My voice came out barely louder than a whisper.

He smiled broadly. "Hello."

"How are you here?"

"Well, I got on a plane, and then took a taxi from the airport–"

I lightly slapped at his broad chest.

"So feisty," he grinned. "We had a last-minute cancellation after our vacation, so we had the weekend free."

"The whole weekend?" I gaped at him. "Where's Youngsoo?" I looked around, as if the manager might just pop out from under the foyer table.

"In Korea."

"You're here alone? Do they know?"

Jihoon huffed a little laugh. "Yes, they know, I didn't run away. I just told them I was coming to have some alone time."

"Alone time," I said sceptically.

"We are allowed to travel solo," he said, and then amended with a tilt of his head, "sometimes."

"And this is where you're staying?" I asked, stepping back and looking around for the first time since my eyes had found him. Looking at the foyer now, I could see it was missing the personal touches of a lived-in home. It looked welcoming, but ambiguous, somehow.

"Yes, my stylist, Junsu, he booked this Airbnb under his name, for privacy." Jihoon shrugged as if this was a totally normal thing. I supposed in his world, it was.

"Why didn't you tell me you were coming?" I turned back to him. He held out his arms.

"Surprise." He winked at me and I laughed.

"So, you're staying here for the whole weekend, no babysitters, no bodyguards, no one?"

"Well..." he ran his hand along the back of his neck, looking up at me from underneath his eyelashes.

"I hoped you might want to stay with me."

I froze, staring at him, seeing the flush on his cheeks as he held my stare.

"You want me to stay here... with you?" Disbelief made my words come out a whole octave higher than my normal tone.

Jihoon's mouth lifted in a shy smile.

"If you want to. There's a pool…" he trailed off as pink splotches coloured his cheekbones.

"Oh, well, if there's a pool count me in!"

He laughed and held out his hand to me, which I took with no hesitation. His warm handed wrapped around mine firmly, making my heart flutter at the possessiveness in that one, small action.

Jihoon led me through the house on an impromptu mini tour. The foyer opened up into an airy living room, where a sectional sofa dominated the space. There was a massive TV on the wall, bigger than any TV I'd ever seen. The kitchen was to the left, through an archway and straight ahead, through an open set of French windows was a perfect, secluded oasis of a garden. The doors opened out underneath a pagoda, draped with flowering vines that swayed gently in a soft breeze. The terracotta tiles transitioned to lush, green grass with stepping stones leading the way across the lawn to a pool area. Around the pool was a tiled area with sun loungers underneath a sun sail and the pool itself, though not large, was a perfect proportion. There was a a separate area at the far end that I guessed was a–

"Hot tub?" I asked, looking up at Jihoon. He nodded and grinned.

"For the cold, LA nights."

I laughed, the mercury hadn't gone a degree below 25 C in weeks.

I looked around the garden, so oddly quiet and peaceful, it was hard to believe we were still in central LA.

"I could get used to living in a place like this," I said wistfully. Jihoon squeezed my hand, gently.

"Do you want to swim?"

"I don't have anything to wear, I'll have to go home to get some things."

"Ah," he said, chuckling quietly, "I think Becka packed you a bag."

I turned to look at him sharply, then, as realisation dawned, my mouth popped open.

"My dino bag! That lying snake!"

Jihoon, bless him, frowned in what I assumed was both confusion and concern. I waved a hand and said, "Yeah, I think you're right. Did she leave it in the foyer?" I turned back around to head back into the house, towing Jihoon behind me, neither of us keen to break the connection of our hands.

Unsurprisingly, my dino backpack was placed on the table in the foyer in plain sight. Unzipping it, I briefly rifled through, seeing a toiletries bag, socks, hair brush, just random things tossed in.

"I think I need to go through this to actually find anything," I laughed.

"Let me show you where you can change," Jihoon said, and together we ascended the staircase to the second floor. The landing was a hallway that seemed to run the length of the house, a large window at the end looking out over the garden. Doors led off the hallway on either side. We passed two open doors. One looked to be a bathroom with a massive walk-in shower. The other open doorway led to a mid-sized bedroom, decorated in all neutral colours.

Jihoon led me to a doorway at the end of the hallway on the right. He pushed open the door to reveal a large, well-appointed bedroom. The bed was huge, covered in plush-looking covers and piles of pillows that kind of made me want to jump in and see if I'd get swallowed right up.

To the left was a pair of sliding glass doors leading out onto a balcony that overlooked the garden, and to the right was a partially open door leading to an ensuite bathroom.

"The master bedroom?" I turned to Jihoon who nodded.

"Where's your stuff?"

He ducked his head and stuffed his hands into his pockets. "I put them in the small bedroom. I thought you could stay in here, if you wanted to."

"That's not fair. This is your rental, not mine. If anything, I should be in the smallest," I said, choosing to breeze over the 'stay' part – for now.

"We don't have to decide now," he said quietly. "I'll leave you to change and meet you at the pool, ok?"

"Sure, ok." I said easily, not knowing what to do with the suddenly-weird air between us.

Jihoon left the room, quietly closing the door behind him as I wondered what I had said wrong.

Sighing, I tossed my backpack onto the bed and began to pick through it, but after a few moments of fruitless searching, I opted to just up-end it onto the sheets.

What spilled out was a cacophony of random items of clothing and accessories, or so it seemed, but then I began to notice things I was sure weren't mine.

"Is this Becka's?" I muttered to myself, holding up a scrap of lace I knew I didn't own. Holding it by the straps to look at it more closely, I almost dropped it.

"Snacks, my ass, Rebecca Hanson!" I hissed at the offending item, the sales tag clearly visible. It was a black, lace 'baby-doll'—according to the tag. Eying it critically, I had to admit it wasn't as bad as I'd first thought. Nothing peeped, nothing opened indecently. The top part was a plunging lace front, but the lace was pretty and not sheer. The bottom, skirt bit was sheer by comparison, but nothing a pair of underwear wouldn't solve.

A far cry from the ratty shorts and t-shirt I normally slept in. I spotted a second one that was similar in style, but in a pretty blush pink colour. It had a large, satin bow under the bust and, on further inspection, it seemed to be holding the whole thing together.

Refusing to look at the offending items any longer than necessary, I tossed them to the side and continued hunting for a swim suit. I found undies, a sundress, shorts, bralette, and... ah-ha! A two piece that also had the tags on. It was a black, halter neck bikini and tie-string bottoms, but they seemed to blessedly be made with enough fabric that nothing would fall out. At least Becka had had the good judgment to know what wouldn't push my boundaries too far.

I laughed when I saw the tube of suncream nestled in amongst the clothes. Being a fair skinned Brit, suncream was really a non-negotiable for me, especially in this weather.

Trying not to think too hard about anything, I changed into the swimsuit and applied the suncream liberally. Ten minutes later I opened the bedroom door, wrapped in a towel from the generously sized ensuite and padded down the hallway and down the stairs. Jihoon was nowhere to be seen, so I continued on through the house until I reached the French windows leading out to the garden.

That's where I found him. Jihoon was stood on the grass and looking up into the trees surrounding the pool. His back was too me and he hadn't noticed me yet, which allowed for shameless voyeurism for me. He was wearing a pair of long board shorts, but he was topless, displaying his strong, muscled back which tapered down to a narrow waist.

My mouth went dry as I stood there, looking my fill, until I must have made a noise and he turned round to face me. The full force of seeing him half-dressed made my knees feel weak. Every time I thought I was past the constant shock of how attracted I was to him, I'd see him in a whole new light. Butterflies swooped and dived in my belly and I didn't try to fight the smile that inched up my face as we stood, looking at one another. His own gaze lingered as they traveled up my body, despite the towel I had wrapped around me, and for the first time, I felt a sort of... equality in our relationship dynamic.

After a moment, he held out his hand to me. I walked out and past the stepping stones towards him, sliding my hand into his once he was close enough to touch. He rubbed his thumb back and forth over the back of my hand.

"Do you want to get in?" he asked.

"Yes, absolutely," I said. The heat of the day, while well past its zenith, still lingered in the air, and honestly, the thought of sliding into that clear pool of water was irresistible.

Jihoon squeezed my hand before letting it go. He sat down on the ledge before sliding into the pool in one graceful movement. It wasn't too deep this end, enough that when he stood, the water came up to his ribs, and I was momentarily again distracted by his bare chest, the water sliding down it in a way I almost envied.

Jihoon ran a hand through his wet hair, bringing my attention back to his face, a smirk tugging up his lips, letting me know he'd caught me looking.

I flushed and hastily knelt down and then swung my legs round so they were dangling in the water over the edge of the pool. He held my gaze as my hands loosened their hold on the towel I still clung to and, heart pounding, I lowered the thick fabric to the sides and let it fall to the grass.

Jihoon waded closer until his chest was nearly brushing against my legs. His gaze was locked onto mine, unwavering, as he placed his hands on my knees, slowly guiding them apart. He slipped between them, his palms gliding up my bare thighs until he was pressed against the edge, his face level with my chest, which rose and fell with each unsteady breath. His hands left a trail of fire up my thighs, the burn settling into my hips as he grasped them firmly. His fingers tightened, drawing a gasp from me, my mouth parting slightly. I held his gaze, feeling the desire in his eyes and knowing it was mirrored in my own.

My hands trembled as I brought them up to cup his face, tilting it just so as I lowered to brush my lips over his.

Each of the times before when we'd kissed, it had been Jihoon who'd kissed me, now it was me kissing him and oh, how I'd missed him.

He opened his mouth without hesitation and I pressed against him more firmly, needy energy pulsing through me in a way I fought to satisfy. I ran my tongue against his full lower lip, and he groaned into my mouth, which only made me more greedy. There was too much space between our bodies, I tried to lessen it by pressing myself against him, but I couldn't manage it with this angle. Jihoon seemed to sense what I needed, as he tugged on my hips, which tore my lips from his, but tilted my pelvis as I slid further off the ledge. Jihoon was right there, a physical wall of muscle and warm skin and as I slid into the pool, I wrapped my arms around his neck, sliding down his body in a way that made my abdomen clench in desire.

Fully in now, I held tight to his neck, our bodies pressed close, no room even for the water to lap between us. I felt each rise of his chest against mine, each shaky exhale stirring my hair.

This time, when he kissed me, it was with a different kind of fire that set ablaze the need in my chest. It was sweeter, less all-consuming but deeper, as if the embers were burning through my skin and into my heart, rather than setting me ablaze.

His hands roamed gently over my back, soothing me. My own hands smoothed up his neck, fingers twisting into the damp strands of his hair, long enough for a gentle tug. I gave a playful nip to his lip before pulling away.

The look he gave me as he held his fingers to his lip froze the giggle that had been bubbling up my throat. The dangerous way he looked up at me from under his eyelashes had me backing away, pulse pounding in my throat.

"Oh, no, you don't," he growled as he followed my retreat, backing me up against the edge of the pool, caging me in with an arm on either side of me. He leaned in close, his mouth skimming my ear as he whispered something I didn't understand, before running his tongue up the length of my neck.

I gasped in shock, arching my back, pushing my breasts into his hard chest.

He groaned against my skin, peppering little kisses in the wake of his tongue.

His arm fell from the wall and ran down my side before settling onto my hip, pulling me against him so hard I could feel the evidence of his arousal pressing into my belly.

I went loose and taut at the same time, a sigh slipping from between my parted lips, so lost in delirium that I barely noticed when his lips fastened around the sensitive skin of my neck, his tongue lapping softly until he sucked harder, the sharp nip making me squirm. His fingers dug in tighter before his mouth released my neck. He met my eyes with an expression I could only describe as smug, while all I could do was pant.

In direct contradiction to the dangerous mood he'd just set, Ji-hoon leaned in and placed a sweet kiss to the tip of my nose and rubbed my hip gently.

I lifted a hand to where my neck tingled.

"Did you just give me a hickey?" I accused.

He smirked, that taunting tilt of his lips that did dangerous things to me.

"You bit me."

I bluescreened for a hot second, torn between disbelief and wanting to laugh.

Laughing won out in the end, a peal of giggles I could no more contain than the cloud can hold in its rain.

We splashed and floated around in the pool until the sun began to set in earnest, the sky streaking with shades of pink and orange before the solar lights strung around the garden winked on in unison, casting a golden glow over the pool.

"Wah," Jihoon sighed, "so pretty."

"Why, thank you," I quipped, flicking water at him.

"Not you," he scoffed, "the sky is pretty."

Just as my pride was taking a tumble down a steep hill, he added, "You're beautiful." He met my eyes with that searing look of his that made me melt and squirm all at once.

I drifted over to the ladder and put my hand on the rung, about to climb up when I felt Jihoon press up against my back, the heat of him like a warm blanket.

"Let me help," he murmured against my ear, sending shivers dancing up and down my spine like a line of lit fireworks.

I took my hand off the ladder and twisted around to face him. The smile he gave me... I could stare at it all day and consider it a day well spent.

Gently, he pushed my back up against the wall, instantly bringing to mind the events of only a couple hours ago. The way we'd played chase and shark since then had not erased the desire I felt for this man in front of me.

When he put his hands firmly around my waist, I saw from the way he moistened his lips and the dark look in his eyes that he was remembering it too.

But all he did was lift me, effortlessly it seemed, out of the water to sit me on the edge of the pool. I scooted back until my butt was on the grass, and not a second too soon, because Jihoon pushed himself out immediately after, and... good God, if I'd thought seeing him in the pool was something – seeing the way he pushed himself out of it, water dripping down his arms, muscles so clearly defined in the fading light of the day, that was a whole different kind of something.

I bit my lip as I shamelessly watched. He put one knee on the edge, and then the other, his arms casually caging me in as he all-but-crawled over me. I leant back further on my elbows as I helplessly watched him crawl up me until his face hovered above my own. There's no way he wasn't acutely aware of the effect he had on me, the way he smiled down at me; he knew.

"Are you hungry?" His words implied a completely different question to the one his tone asked.

"Starving," I whimpered, and honestly it was a valid answer to both questions.

He grinned and leaned back on his heels before rising to his feet. I will never get used to how graceful he is. If I tried doing that, I would fall ass-backwards into the pool.

Jihoon reached down both hands for me and I reached up immediately, his large hands gripping mine firmly as he pulled me to my feet.

"Come on, let's get changed and order something to eat."

The dangerous duality of this man...

I could only nod as we walked, hand-in-hand back into the house.

He led me back upstairs to the master bedroom before turning around and leaving me, like we'd just finished a date and he'd walked me to my front door.

My head spun as I walked through the bedroom to the bathroom and turned on the shower. How could someone so chivalrous be so skilled at seduction? Because I was absolutely certain I had been thoroughly seduced, and just like that evening we'd spent on the beach, I knew completely that if he'd laid me down in the grass, I would have let him.

As I stripped and then stood under the spray – perfect temperature and pressure – I examined my feelings on this.

Did I want to sleep with Jihoon? Judging by the lingerie Becka had stuffed in my bag, she was betting I would, but when I thought about it, I wasn't sure how I felt. I was unarguably, inexcusably attracted to Jihoon, I mean, who wouldn't be? But past just being nice to look at, the attraction went far deeper, I knew that. I wanted him and I wanted to know him. I wasn't sure I could skip that step, and while I felt like I was getting there, I wasn't sure if I felt secure enough in our 'whatever-this-was-ship' yet.

Half of me felt conflicted by my own resistance. Intellectually, I knew and agreed with the idea that 'virginity' was a social construct... patriarchy... yada, yada, yada. But the other part of me did see it as a big deal.

I sighed. I wasn't going to solve this in the span of one shower.

Not long later, I was clean and smelling like sea moss and citrus – according to the fancy bottles I'd found in the shower. Wrapped in a fluffy robe, I was just rifling through my bag for something comfortable to lounge in, when a knock at the door sounded.

"Come in," I called, without thinking. Jihoon opened the door and stepped into the room before he stopped abruptly and turned back around to face the door. I looked at him in confusion.

"What's wrong?" I asked.

"You're not dressed." He rasped.

Hastily, I glanced down at myself in case my robe had parted, but it was tightly tied.

"Jihoon, I'm wearing a robe, I'm not naked." I fought the self-conscious laugh brewing in my chest.

He glanced over his shoulder but turned back around just as fast. I put my hands on my hips.

"Jihoon, I was wearing less in the pool," I said, reasonably. "Turn around, please."

He did, but kept his eyes pointed at the floor. I walked towards him, adding in a little sway, just because. I stood in front of him and looked up until I caught his eyes.

"You can look at me," I said gently. He lifted his head, but kept his eyes on mine. I wanted to reach out, but I didn't want to overstep. I didn't know where the boundaries where.

I took a breath and decided to be mature and actually ask him.

"I don't understand why this–" I motioned to myself, "is worse than me in a bikini. I need you to tell me so I don't do something wrong." My voice wavered at the end, the events of the day, the emotional roller-coaster of it all catching up with me.

Jihoon frowned, his mouth an unhappy line.

"You've done nothing wrong, it's not bad." He sighed and reached for my face, cupping me gently, as if he was scared of hurting me. Then a look passed across his face, a subtle change that had me swaying towards him ever so slightly.

"It's different, because I know that if I were to pull this–" he moved one hand to the tie that fastened the robe around my waist and pulled on it lightly, but enough that my robe loosened just a tiny bit.

I swallowed, my heart hammering a frantic pulse.

"And if I put my hand just here−" he moved his hand from the tie to slightly further up, where the robe was folded over my chest, placing it flat against my ribs. "I could slide my hand inside." To illustrate his point, he pressed slightly. I gasped when I felt his finger tip lightly graze my skin. He softly ran it up and down, barely even touching me, not really, but in that moment, I was hyper fixated on every centimetre of skin he grazed.

I willed him to kiss me, to slide his hand all the way in, but instead he caressed my cheek with his other hand and then took a respectable step back. I almost went with him, that irresistible magnetism I felt nearly taking me with it. Instead, I drew a steadying breath into my lungs and was gratified to see he was scarcely more composed than I was.

"I'll get dressed and meet you downstairs." I croaked. He ran a hand through his damp hair, nodding as he turned around and left.

I huffed out a long breath, turning back around to consider my clothing options, trying my damnedest to ignore my pounding heart and mounting desire, something I'd done a half-assed job of ignoring up until this point, but there it was.

"Holy hell," I breathed.

Chapter 27

It took me longer than necessary to dress in the pair of shorts and t-shirt I'd found in my bag, owing to the extra few minutes I'd needed to come back down from the dangerous ledge Jihoon had placed me on.

I walked back downstairs, stopping at my work backpack, still by the front door, where I'd dropped it hours ago. I pulled my phone out and shoved it in my pocket before continuing on to the living room, where I found Jihoon. He was sprawled out on the massive sofa, flipping through channels. There was something oddly sexy about the way he was spread out. That, or my hormones were in a constant state of arousal. Honestly, probably both of those things were true.

"Hi," I said shyly, padding over to him when he smiled and patted the seat next to him.

I settled, tucking my feet under me and watched as he fiddled with the TV remote.

"What are we watching?" I asked, eventually.

"I don't mind," he admitted with a shrug, and handed me the remote. "You pick."

"Alright." I took the remote from him and, seeing it was a smart TV, pressed the button for Netflix and signed myself in.

"But you have to pick what type of movie," I countered. "Funny, romance, horror, or action?"

Jihoon thought about it for a moment, frowning in a way that made me want to run a finger between his brows.

"Horror. Then you can hold me when you get scared." He grinned at me lasciviously, making me laugh.

"Alright, but I warn you, I have a strong disposition, I'm not easily scared." I began to flick through the available scary movies, stopping every now and then to ask his opinion until we settled on Train to Busan. I knew of it, but I'd not gotten round to watching it.

We'd only just finished the opening credits when a loud knock at the front door startled me so badly that Jihoon's prediction came true, as I practically threw myself at him.

He laughed, and said, "I ordered pizza, I forgot to say."

I grumbled and peeled myself off him as he rose to his feet and headed for the door. I paused the film and pulled out my phone. I immediately saw several messages from Becka, so I swiped up to read them.

Becka

Have u let go of him yet? lol

[Sent 18:14pm]

Becka

Have u found the new clothes I bought 4 u yet, or don't u need them? heehee

[Sent 20:38pm]

Becka

Helllloooooooo

[Sent 20:09pm]

Becka

SIS!!! I WILL call the idol if I have 2!

[Sent 21:02pm]

That last text was sent just ten minutes ago, but before I could tap out a reply, I heard a burst of music from the foyer. Jihoon walked back into the room holding a flat pizza box and two smaller box containers. He hurriedly set the load on the wide coffee table in front of the sofa before pulling his phone out of his pocket. I had a feeling I knew who it was, based on the way his eyebrows rose as he looked at the screen before holding the phone up to his ear.

"Hello?"

He was quiet for a second, listening to the other person, his eyebrows getting progressively higher and higher up his forehead, until he looked at me with an expression that was almost... alarmed?

"It's for you," he said, holding the phone out to me.

My suspicions were confirmed when I saw the name on the screen and, trying not to giggle, I held the phone to my ear as Jihoon discreetly backed out of the room.

"BISH YOU BETTER BE DEAD, IT'S BEEN HOURS!"

"Hello to you too," I pinched my lips together to ensure absolutely no mirth escaped.

"Excuse me! I've been literally messaging you for hours! I drop you to a strange house to see a guy you BARELY know, against my best judgment, I might add, and I can't even get a reply? I was worried, ho!"

"In my defence, I left my bag downstairs."

There was silence on the line for so long that I pulled the phone away from my ear to look at the screen to make sure the call hadn't dropped.

"Um, hello?" I said, tentatively.

I heard Becka take in a big breath and then puff it out, obviously searching for the strength to calm down.

"So, you're not dead."

"No."

"You've not been treated badly?"

"No."

"Have you at least been ravished yet?"

I choked on my spit, unable to answer as I coughed and spluttered.

"Becka, Jesus Christ," I wheezed out, eventually.

Becka laughed, and I knew the storm had passed.

"It was a valid question," she protested, "did you see the things I got you today?"

"Yes," I hissed, keeping my voice to just above a whisper as I said, "are you serious about those negligees?"

Becka was giggling madly, her words coming out in a gasp. "I thought you might need a little encouragement!" I mean, what do you even say to that?

Out of the corner of my eye, I saw Jihoon walking back into the room, so I said as quietly and quickly as I could, "I've got everything under control and I gotta go, bye!"

"The condoms are in the front zipper pocke—" I cut her off, her shouted words seemed to echo in the quiet room. I couldn't tell if Jihoon had heard them or not though.

"Everything okay?" He asked as he put down a tray with plates and two bottles of beer on the table alongside the food boxes.

"Oh yeah, sure," I waved the question away with as much cheerful indifference as possible. "She was just worried when I didn't text her back."

"She thought I might have lured you here to murder you?" he chuckled, folding his legs underneath him to sit cross legged on the floor alongside the coffee table.

I scooted off the sofa to sit on the floor next to him, the plush, navy-blue rug as good a cushion as any.

"Something like that," I evaded.

He nodded easily and opened the boxes in front of us, releasing hot wafts of steam that immediately tickled my nose and reminded me just how hungry I was.

"I hope you don't mind," he said, ducking his head, "I ordered for us."

The pizza box contained a large, cheesy pizza with a variety of toppings; pepperoni, peppers, sweetcorn, Italian sausage and olives. My mouth watered. The other box, however, was even better.

"Dough balls!" I exclaimed, grinning wildly.

Seeing my reaction, Jihoon's face lit up. "Good choice?"

"The best!" I nodded enthusiastically, the little golden balls topped with a sheen of garlic butter, so unassuming in their plain box. The only other box was filled with a variety of dips.

"Honey mustard, ketchup, BBQ sauce, ranch and hot sauce," Jihoon read the little labels.

I re-started the movie while Jihoon filled our plates with a selection of everything, passing me my plate first.

I groaned as I bite into my first dough ball, the inside had a little pocket of garlic butter and I happily jiggled from side-to-side, doing what my mum called, my 'happy food dance'. I opened my eyes and found Jihoon staring at me so unabashedly that I immediately felt self-conscious.

"What?" I mumbled, swallowing my bite.

"You're just so cute." His expression confused me; he wasn't smiling, he looked dazed – it was the only word I could think of. He'd said it like... like he'd just figured something out.

Abruptly, he turned back to the movie and shoved a pizza slice into his mouth. I watched him for a while longer, but the moment seemed to have passed. I shrugged, grabbed another dough ball and settled in to watch the movie.

"So, tell me," I said after taking a sip of my second beer. We'd finished the first bottles pretty quickly. "Is Busan the place to go to escape the zombie apocalypse?"

Jihoon tilted his head to the side and made a 'mm' noise as he thought about it.

"Seoul has more military, but Busan isn't as populated and it's on the sea, so you could take a boat and just –" he made a sailing motion with the hand holding his bottle.

"Where would you go?" He turned to me, as the screams of the characters on screen were cut off and replaced by the sounds of zombies chowing down.

"Probably Jersey," I said after a moment's consideration.

"The city?" he said, with some consternation, and I giggled.

"No, the island." Seeing his frown, I went on; "there's an island, called Jersey, in the English Channel. It's not very big, and it doesn't have very many people, but it does have lots of farms and some castles.

"I'd sit my happy butt in a castle, pull up the draw bridge and wait it out." Pleased with myself, I took another swig and happily jiggled my feet, enjoying the warm buzz I was beginning to feel as a result of the salty, cheesy pizza and cold beers.

"If you lived in a castle, wouldn't that make you the queen?" He grinned at me and I laughed.

"Wanna be my king?" I waggled my eyebrows at him.

"God, yes," he exclaimed. I hid my delight with another swig from my bottle.

To my surprise, Jihoon grabbed first one of my feet, and then the other one, pulling them into his lap and possessively laying his large, warm hands on my ankles.

The mirth faded, replaced by something warmer, something that pricked the corners of my eyes and tightened my throat. I cleared it softly, turning my attention back to the film, where the main characters were, once again, running for their lives.

It was nearly midnight by the time the credits rolled on the film, and I was stiff from sitting on the floor. I stretched, arching my back over the sofa behind me.

"Time to sleep," Jihoon announced. I swear, this man was made of elastic, judging by the way he folded his legs underneath himself and pushed up to his feet with about as much effort as I expended in breathing.

He held out his hands to me and pulled me to my feet.

"Alright, let's clear this away first" I gestured to the food boxes and beer bottles.

Together, we cleared away our mess before heading upstairs.

Though Jihoon had said he'd slept on the plane over, I couldn't believe he wasn't exhausted, but he hadn't complained once and only yawned a couple of times.

The upstairs was dark as we headed up, lit only by soft runner lights illuminating the stairs. The darkness highlighted how quiet it was in the house, an experience I'd forgotten existed whilst living in the city.

We stopped outside the smaller bedroom, where Jihoon had put his things, and again I felt guilty that he was staying here, instead of in the master. The bedroom was nice enough, but it still seemed wrong.

I remembered how weird he'd gotten when I'd brought it up earlier, so I held my tongue, instead saying, "I'm really glad you're here. I had the best day." I leaned up on my tiptoes to press a kiss to his cheek. At the last moment, he turned his face and caught my lips with his own, placing his hands around my waist. The kiss was brief, but it left me breathless when he pulled back. I stared up at him, the moonlight shining in from the large window reflecting in his eyes, making him seem ethereal, like something I might have dreamed up. He seemed to be searching my face as I searched his eyes.

It was on the tip of my tongue to ask him to join me, but I... I just couldn't find the courage to push past that barrier. So instead, I told him goodnight and retreated back down the corridor to my large, empty room and shut the door quietly behind me.

Chapter 28

I brushed my teeth and washed my face with practiced efficiency, all the while staring at the girl in the mirror, asking her what the hell her problem was.

Once done in the bathroom, I stripped off my clothes and shoved them back into the dino rucksack, clearing off the bed at the same time, until I was then confronted with the dilemma of pink or black. I stared at the two scraps of lace after having mentally discarded the idea of sleeping in my t-shirt when it now smelt vaguely of beer and pizza.

Closing my eyes, I waved my finger around and then stopped, opening my eyes to see where I had pointed to. Pink it was.

It was a good fit, I thought at least. It was snug under my breasts, giving more support than I'd have thought it would. I did keep on my underwear though. The top may be enough to not wear my bra, but I wasn't prepared to go bare-ass.

I turned off the light and slid into the massive bed, the sheets cool and comfortable against my flushed body, the buzz from the beer still tingling gently under my skin. I closed my eyes and tried to relax, my mind processing the events of the day. It was so quiet that it felt like my thoughts were shouting inside my head. I tossed, and I turned and when I huffed in frustration and looked at my phone, only half an hour had passed. I turned on the bedside lamp, the soft glow barely illuminating the room; a reading light, at best.

I flipped onto my back and stared up at the ceiling, the fan spinning gently and with quiet efficiency. With more determination than I felt, I threw the covers off and rolled out of bed, striding towards the door before I could talk myself out of it. I pulled open the door, ready to stride down the corridor, but instead nearly crashed into Jihoon, silently standing outside my door, a hand raised as if he were about to knock.

"Whoa," he gasped, catching me about my arms to stop me from falling forward.

"Jihoon," I panted, adrenaline pounding through me from both the shock and my loss of balance. "What are you doing?"

He released my arms and ducked his head, rubbing a hand down his neck.

"I, ah, I was coming to see if you were okay."

Silence stretched between us in the darkness.

"Wait," he said, looking back up at me, although I could barely make out his face, "what were you doing?"

I felt the familiar flush crawling up my neck, but a sudden reck-lessness squashed it back down and I said, "Coming to see you."

"Is everything okay?"

I actually hadn't thought this far ahead, hadn't thought what I would say. So, I went with the truth.

"Stay with me tonight. I want you to." I swallowed, my toes digging into the plush carpet under my feet, feeling the weight of his gaze on me.

"Are you sure?" he asked.

"Yes," I answered, firmly.

"Okay."

I moved back a step and held the door open wider for him to step through, and then closed it behind him. I watched him approach the bed to stand by the side I had just vacated, and in the light of the dim lamp, I saw he was again shirtless, wearing only a pair of loose-fitting shorts. The light turned his skin into gold and for a moment, I was frozen to the spot where I stood.

Until he turned to me, his face so unassuming, so normal, even in the unbelievably attractive sense.

I took the handful of steps towards him that it took to reach the bed and, as I stepped into the small ring of light, Jihoon's eyes met mine, and then travelled down the length of my body. His dark eyes widened as they slowly made their way back up, meeting my own.

"You're so beautiful," he murmured, reaching for me and pulling me closer towards him. I went willingly, but he didn't try to kiss me. Instead, he lay his forehead against my own and together we stood there, just breathing in each other's presence, the glow of the lamp like a bubble in which only we existed, if only for this moment. I lay my hands against his forearms, feeling the strength just under the skin, the firm but gentle way he held me. It was everything.

Eventually, Jihoon pulled back and looked down at me, his expression unreadable.

"It's late," he said. I nodded, and he pulled back the covers and moved aside so I could slide in. He pulled the covers up to my shoulders and turned off the lamp, and it was only from the weak light of the moon coming in through the windows that I saw as he moved around the bed to get in the other side.

I felt the bed dip as he slid in, but he was far enough away from me that I couldn't reach him, even as I extended my arm out. Then I felt his fingers on mine as he reached for me and there, in the dark, in a bed that didn't belong to either of us, we held onto each other. My eyes closed and sleep claimed me soon after.

I woke up in the still-dark room, and for a moment I didn't know where I was. The almost-silent hum of the over-head fan as it spun softly was the first thing I heard, grounding me enough to wake up a little. I then became aware of a warm, firmness underneath me and I tentatively moved my fingers. Instantly I knew I was lying on top of Jihoon. I must have shimmied over here in my sleep, because I was now lying over half of his body, my head and torso sprawled over his chest like he was a body pillow and – I moved my leg slightly – yup, my leg was thrown over his hip and rested in between his legs, the little hairs on his thighs tickling my calf when I'd moved.

I knew I should move, I just really didn't want to. I listened to him breathe; deep, soft inhales that gently rocked me up and then down, a calming motion I couldn't bear to disturb. The warmth of his skin against mine was like a balm. It seemed to go deeper than surface level touch, I felt it sink into me in a way it never had before.

He was like the first, perfect sip of hot chocolate on a cold, winter's day, the heat chasing the chill away as it spreads through your whole body. For some inexplicable reason, I felt my eyes prickling as waves of emotion crested over me in ways I was unprepared for.

I didn't consciously move, but I wound my arm around his chest tighter and took a deep breath, inhaling the way he smelt of soap and clean skin.

I must have woken him when I'd moved, because he reached across his body to run his fingers up my arm. I tilted my head up just as he tilted his head down and we met each other's gaze.

"Why are you crying?" he said softly, his voice deep from sleep, his accent more pronounced.

I ran a thumb underneath my eye and it came away wet. "I don't know," I confessed.

Gently, he lifted his hand and wiped away the tear that had run down my cheek. I stared at him, eyes accustomed enough to the dark to make out his face, before I remembered how I was sprawled over him like a blanket. I made to shift, mumbling a weak apology, but instead of letting me rise, he firmly held me to him.

"Don't move, I like you here." He ran a hand up and down my spine in a way that must have been meant to soothe, but instead ignited something inside me, a fire I'd been teetering on the edge of all day, and when his fingertips grazed the base of my spine, my back arched involuntarily, pressing my breasts more firmly against his chest and throwing my head back.

I looked at Jihoon's face through eyes half lidded, my mouth parted on a sigh and silently begged him to close the distance between us.

Whatever expression he saw on my face was encouragement enough, it seemed, as Jihoon's other hand trailed up my arm to my neck, his thumb tracing circles in the hollow of my throat before moving up more firmly to cup my jaw. He paused a moment, gaze locked with mine, before he closed the distance and pressed his lips against mine.

I groaned against him, my fingers curling on his chest, a delicious slow-burn coiling deep in my belly. His lips moved against mine, softly at first, but I needed more. I wound my arms up and around his neck, pulling him towards me and pressing our bodies firmly together until I could feel the contours of his muscled arms and chest against me.

Jihoon deepened the kiss, rolling over so that he was now lying on his side, facing me, his tongue teasing my bottom lip. It still wasn't enough. I rolled onto my back, pulling him with me until he lay partially on top of me, his legs to the side so he wasn't pressing me into the mattress with his weight. I sighed in contented pleasure as I bent my knee up to cage him in on one side. Though I had no prior experience, everything felt so natural. I wanted to feel the way his body pressed against mine, wanted it with a need that I'd never felt before.

Jihoon pulled back and I almost whimpered. His face hovered some inches above mine as he locked eyes with me, panting softly. In silence, we watched each other, for what I wasn't sure, until I felt his hand pressing softly to my chest, just above the lace that cupped my breasts. I took a shuddering inhale as his hand moved, oh so softly downward, until his hand rested gently on my breast, cupping me.

"Is this okay?" he asked softly and without hesitation I nodded, silently urging him on.

He ran that hand down from my breast and down my ribs, his fingers dancing lightly over the thin fabric that still covered me, sending shivers that radiated outward to the far reaches of my body like tiny, exploding fireworks. As his fingertips travelled further down, tracing a map of my body in undulating, delicious little waves, I began to ache in a way I never had before. A tense pressure of clenched muscles, straining in anticipation.

Jihoon stopped when he reached the line of my underwear, his fingers playing lightly, back and forth, back and forth. Without meaning to, my hips lifted, trying to aid my body in getting him to where it wanted him to go.

"Slowly," he chuckled, "there's no rush."

I whined. There felt like a rush to me. I was rewarded a moment later though, when Jihoon shifted his weight so that he was lying more fully on his side, draping one leg between my legs. He propped his head up on the hand not currently spinning fire and ice several inches south of my navel.

He looked down at me and said, "Can I touch you?"

"You already are," I quipped, still riding that edge of frustration, and he chuckled again, mirth with a twinge of something a bit darker; a smokier vibration to his voice that wove into the feeling of anticipation that hadn't stopped building since the first moment he'd touched me.

Jihoon began to trail his fingers upwards, effortlessly pushing aside the gauzy fabric of my nightgown, grazing my skin so softly it sent shivers coursing through me. When he reached my bellybutton, my skin jumped and I giggled, slightly breathlessly. Jihoon looked at me, his lips curved in a slight smirk.

"Ticklish," I said, by way of explanation.

"That is interesting to know," he murmured, dancing his fingers further up my belly, dipping into the contours of my waist like he was taking a stroll along my skin. Impatient, I ran my hand over his forearm, feeling the way his muscles contracted beneath his skin as he moved his arm.

Jihoon paused as he got to the bow underneath my breasts.

"What's this?" He rubbed the satin between his fingers and I swore, it felt as if that bow held me together, as well as the night-gown. He gave the ribbon an experimental tug, just like he'd tugged the tie holding my robe together earlier this evening.

Jihoon lifted his eyes from the ribbon and held my gaze. After a heart-beats hesitation, he gently, but firmly began to pull on the delicate material. More and more I felt the fabric give way around me, parting like the scraps of fabric it had only ever been, held together by a well-placed bow. The last few inches slipped through and the lace parted down the middle, a clear line of my skin exposed between my breasts, running down my abdomen all the way down to my thighs. Somehow this felt more exposing than when he'd had his hand beneath the material.

Jihoon's eyes left mine, following the path of skin that had been revealed, like a runway. Softly, he ran one fingertip from my sternum, down to my navel, and back up again. My chest heaved as I shuddered and he raised his eyes back to mine.

"Is this okay?" he asked, and I knew if I said no, he'd cover me with the duvet and that would be the end of it.

I was okay, I was more than okay. I ached, and I needed for him to touch me.

Wordlessly, I wrapped my hand around his wrist and brought his hand back up to where the fabric gaped between my breasts, and I lay it there, over my heart. His palm was warm, the sensation soaking through my skin and deeper as I took a breath that seemed to still leave me breathless.

He swallowed as his fingers twitched, but he held my gaze as he ran his hand back over my breast, moving the fabric of the lace top aside as he did so, revealing me. My nipple peaked as the delicate fabric ran over it, a soft friction that made me gasp. As the lace lay to one side, Jihoon moved to my other breast and slid the lace aside there as well. I now lay under him, completely bare from the waist up, but rather than feel exposed, all I felt was... cherished. Jihoon looked me over, and when his eyes rose to meet mine, he had such an expression that made my breath catch in my throat. It was possessive, hungry. Triumphant, almost.

His fingers barely touched me though, hovering as if he was still unsure if I would allow this, or not.

"Touch me," I rasped, chest heaving. Jihoon ran his thumb over my peaked nipple, cupping me fully in his hand, lightly squeezing me. His head dipped, and I cried out wordlessly as he pressed soft kisses to my other breast, tonguing my nipple. The sensation seemed to stretch down my body to a deeper place, like a guitar string that is too tight being plucked.

What had started as soft and gentle soon became a thing more urgent, more firm. My back arched off the bed to meet his insistent touches as I moaned.

Without warning, Jihoon tore his mouth from my breast and crashed his lips down upon mine, pushing his tongue into my mouth in a frantic, desperate sort of kiss. He groaned into my mouth as I met his fervour with my own, raising my hand to his face, holding him to me.

The hand holding my breast began to trail down my body again, not quite so gentle or slow this time, a more determined press of fingers seeking downward until he once again paused at the barrier of my cotton underwear. He slipped just his fingertips underneath the elastic and stopped.

"Is this okay?" he rasped, his voice a deep and dark thing that echoed through me, intensifying the ache and, unbidden, my hips tilted, silently encouraging his downward pursuit with words I didn't have, so instead I nodded, trying not to draw blood as I bit my lip.

And then, finally, as his fingers skimmed underneath the thin scrap of fabric, I arched against him, almost dislodging him, but for his muscled chest so steady above me.

Almost lazily, my bent leg fell to the side in silent surrender and anxious anticipation. I gasped the moment his fingers trailed down the centre of me, gently exploratory and yet possessive. I felt that in the way his palm firmly pressed down on me, eliciting a small, choked cry.

Jihoon ran his mouth softly up my neck, leaving a trail of small, sweet kisses until he reached my mouth again.

"Is this okay?" he murmured into my lips as he gently pressed a finger against me.

"Yes," I gasped, the sound swallowed as he kissed me, a claiming and absolute kiss that almost distracted me from the moment he pushed that finger inside of me.

The feeling was so foreign and so all-consuming that I tore my lips from his as my spine arched and my breath caught in my throat. My entire focus shifted to that one finger and the way I pulsed around it, a strange feeling I had no basis for comparison for.

I was panting and yet breathless as Jihoon gently worked his finger in and out, maddeningly slowly. I didn't want him to stop, couldn't conceive of it, and yet I knew we were on a precipice I wasn't sure I could fall over.

"Jihoon," I gasped as he kissed the corner of my mouth, a sweet, almost reverent touch that nearly sent my thoughts scattering.

"Mmhm?" he murmured, not pausing his soft kisses, or his finger.

"I have to tell you something." The words tumbled from my lips, forced out on breathy exhales.

"Mmm?" He nibbled delicately on the sensitive skin just below my ear.

Needing him, but needing him to hear me more, I clasped his face between my palms and brought his gaze to mine.

"I... I've never... I don't know-"

"Ssh," he turned his face and placed a kiss upon my palm, "I know."

"How?" I frowned, calming slightly as his finger slowed its movement.

He smiled and ducked his head, hair falling over his forehead in tousled waves.

"I can tell." His voice was so quiet in the stillness of the room, but it felt like a declaration. I squirmed and tried to tilt my hips to dislodge him. Jihoon withdrew his finger and lifted his head to meet my eyes.

"It's okay," he insisted. "I didn't come here expecting that." With his words, he lay his hand over me, cupping me, that possessive gesture warming me more than the heat from his body that lay so firmly against mine.

"I didn't expect *you,* but here you are," he placed a soft kiss on the tip of my nose, before he pulled back to hold my gaze.

"Whatever you want, is fine. If you want to stop, it's fine. If you want me to go," he swallowed, but carried on, "it's okay. But I need you to tell me."

The heat from his palm seared me, and though the ache had faded during our conversation, it was only banked. The weight and mere presence of his hand being where it was, where no one but I had touched before was enough to start that climb again, that steady ascent that scattered my thoughts.

"I want to," I admitted shakily, "but I'm not ready to."

He nodded, "I understand, and that's okay. Do you want me to stop?"

I shook my head immediately, "No."

"Do you like it when I touch you?" His voice was deeper than normal, a timbre I felt as well as heard.

"Yes," I whispered.

"Like this?" His hand began a slow, undulating motion between my thighs, a firm press of his palm that hit in just the right spot while his fingers danced lightly downwards, almost tickling me. The combination brought a gasp to my lips and I sighed, "Yes."

He kissed me, harder this time, as if he couldn't hold himself back. He groaned into my mouth, his fingers more insistent, parting me and stroking up and down with ever-increasing pressure. I grabbed his wrist, causing him to pause, until I urged him on. I felt him smile against my lips and I giggled breathlessly. Until I wasn't laughing anymore.

Jihoon dipped his finger inside of me and gently pressed upwards. It was a kind of pressure that I couldn't describe but made me reflexively shift my hips seeking... something. I inhaled sharply as he withdrew, but he didn't go far, trailing his fingers back up to that spot that made me squirm. At first, he only lightly traced around it, but as my pants turned into gasps, he pressed down more firmly, alternating from circles to sweeps until my hips began to buck underneath him. He watched me carefully all the while, his eyes never leaving mine. And when I finally cried out and juddered under his hand, he grinned and pressed his forehead to mine. I clamped my hand around his bicep, curling my body into his, while his hand was still tucked between my thighs. I couldn't catch my breath enough to speak, and even if I had, what would I say? All rational thought had scattered like dandelion seeds in a breeze. I could only lay there vibrating as the waves slowly gentled from the epicentre of sensation and I reeled myself back in.

I pulled my leg over and rolled onto my side, dislodging him. He ran his palm up my belly and to my waist, pulling me closer to him.

Absurdly, I felt my cheeks reddening and I burrowed my face in his chest, the scent of him calming my racing heart. Jihoon chuckled, the sound vibrating through me.

"Where have you gone?" he said softly, reaching his hand up to tilt my jaw so that I was facing him. He was smiling down at me, a soft smile that crinkled the corners of his eyes.

"I feel shy," I admitted, "which I appreciate is silly, but it is what it is." I don't know how people are supposed to react after something like that.

"I mean, do I say thank you, tell you 'good job?'"

"Because, yes, to all of that." I rambled, then forcibly closed my mouth to keep my tumbled thoughts inside.

Jihoon chuckled and pressed a kiss to my forehead. "You don't need to feel that way with me, and you do not need to thank me," he huffed a laugh, "but you're welcome."

I was silent a moment, but internally I was doing mental gymnastics, practically falling over myself to think what the proper etiquette here was. I was so woefully unprepared from all my previous relationships, and it hadn't occurred to me that this might occur tonight, not that I'd had the benefit of prior preparation, being that the whole visit was a last-minute surprise.

A yawn took me by surprise and I tried to cover it, only being partially successful.

"I can see you thinking hard about something," Jihoon interrupted my spiralling thoughts with another kiss to my forehead, "you should sleep, it's been a long day."

I didn't reply, instead I lay my hand flat upon his bare chest, feeling the way his heartbeat pounded against his warm skin. I trailed my fingers across the expanse of him, delighting in the way he felt against my palm, and he sighed above me, his breath tickling my eyelashes.

My fingertips seemed to walk themselves downwards, towards his abdominals, those firm ridges of muscle so obvious even now, lying on his side. I lightly ran my hand over his stomach, hesitating when his muscles twitched, and I looked up at his face enquiringly.

"Ticklish," he mirrored my previous explanation with a quirk to his lips that seemed to rekindle a low-burning fire in my belly, a fire that nudged my mind towards a reciprocation, of sorts.

Now that the thought occurred to me, I felt a twinge of embarrassment. Swallowing, I tentatively swept my fingertips further down, following the line of soft hairs from his navel to where his shorts hung low on his hips.

Just as I reached the small knot holding his shorts up, Jihoon reached for my exploratory hand and, clasping it gently, brought it up to his mouth, where he placed soft kisses to each of my fingertips in turn.

"But what about you?" I asked, frowning, trying to stifle another yawn.

Jihoon smiled, holding my hand and pressing it back against his chest.

"That's not how it works. It's not an exchange.

"I wanted to make you feel good. I didn't touch you so you'd need to touch me."

I blushed, tucking my head down and staring instead at our joined hands against his bare chest.

"What if I want to?" I muttered, a little petulantly.

Jihoon laughed softly, the still night air seeming to snatch the sound and muffle it.

"Another time and you can touch me all you want. Right now, go to sleep, jagiya."

He nestled me into him more solidly, his arms wrapped around me, pulling me into him so absolutely our breathing synchronized.

I'd never slept beside someone like this before, and now that I had, I wondered how I'd ever sleep without it again.

Chapter 29

Light poured in through the open blinds of the double windows, casting long puddles of sunlight across the sheets and reflecting off all the polished surfaces of the bathroom through the open door opposite me, little solar flares that stung my eyes as they flickered open.

I scrunched my nose in disgust and tried to curl back into the thick, comforting duvet, but my progress was hampered by the heavy arm thrown over my waist and the firm body behind me.

The night before came back to me in a slow, leisurely narrative that had me curling my toes in delicious delight. Rather than feel embarrassed or shy, I surprised myself by feeling a little like the cat who got the cream.

I stretched, reaching my arms up and tensing my legs in a full body stretch that pulled at my sleep-relaxed muscles in a way that almost felt erotic.

The arm around my waist tightened, pulling me harder against the wall of skin and muscle behind me. I pressed my butt back against him, unthinking, and my mind momentarily blanked when I felt him poking into my behind. Jihoon's hand that lay flat against my belly began to trace a slow, leisurely path upwards over my ribs and then settled onto one of my breasts, palming it intimately. Goosebumps followed his fingers and I had to bite back a gasp as his warm fingers grazed over my sensitive nipple.

He nuzzled my neck, his breath tickling my skin. I sighed, leaning my head further to the side to grant him access. He pressed a light kiss to my pulse point as he lightly squeezed my naked breast, the nightgown still hanging open from last night.

I rolled onto my back and met Jihoon's gaze, his eyes a rich bronze in the morning light, framed by such dark lashes it seemed like his irises were casting shadows.

He smiled at me and said, "Good morning, sleepyhead."

"Good morning," I giggled, shy now under the scrutiny of the most beautiful man I had ever seen.

He lifted his hand from my chest and ran it up my neck to cradle my jaw, his thumb rubbing softly over my cheekbone. He made me feel so delicate, so treasured, that my heart stuttered. I knew I would be in trouble if things carried on as they had been, but all I saw in his eyes was unguarded contentment, so in that moment I made the decision to do this thing whole-heartedly. No more second guessing.

I reached up my arms to wind them around his neck and pulled him in towards me, kissing him soundly. I felt him smile against my lips, it was a feeling I would never take for granted.

It was the kind of kiss that had no rush or frenzy to it, just two people so into each other that kissing was a necessary thing. Our hands roamed up and down freely, exploring and caressing in equal measure. It felt like freedom. The freedom to touch him, and to kiss him after months of separation. The freedom to be here in this moment with him without concern of anyone seeing us together. The freedom to be unabashedly, with absolute conviction, in this together.

I was so into what was happening right at that moment, that I almost missed the niggling thought, the lingering uncertainty. The question mark that hovered in my head over the word, 'relationship.'

There had been no conversation, no declaration, no thought of it really. Except for now. I'd call it the 'harsh light of day,' but to be fair, though it was bright, the light streaming in the windows was quite lovely.

But still, now I'd thought about it, I couldn't unthink it. Jihoon must have sensed my hesitation because he pulled back from where he'd been nibbling on my lower lip to meet my gaze.

"You okay?" he asked, his voice so low and slightly breathless, I couldn't help smile.

"Yeah," I curled my fingers in his hair at the nape of his neck, "just thinking too hard."

"Mmm," he hummed, "don't do that." He lowered his lips to my throat, swirling patterns into my skin so successfully that it scattered every thought in my brain.

A little while later, we were lying in each other's arms, listening to the birds in the garden, when Jihoon tilted his head down to look at me.

"Can I ask you something?"

Languidly, I stretched, so relaxed my body felt like a pool of melted butter in the warmth of his arms.

"Sure," I said easily.

"How is it that you've never..."

I waited a moment for him to continue his thought, but when his cheeks pinked up, I understood what he was asking.

"Oh! Um." I chuckled nervously. "I guess I just never found someone I wanted to sleep with."

"No boyfriends?"

"I've had boyfriends," I said, keeping my tone even so I didn't sound as defensive as I felt. "Before I went to University, I was with my boyfriend for two years, but we were so young. Then he broke up with me." I shrugged.

"Why?" He asked, and I had to fight a smile at the confusion in his tone. It was very flattering.

"We went to different universities, and he didn't want to have a long-distance relationship," I said. "He didn't want to miss out on all the relationships he could have at uni." I scoffed. Last I'd heard, he was single.

"The next boyfriend I had cheated on me before we'd gotten serious enough to do anything. Although, maybe that's why he cheated," I added, contemplatively.

"After that, I just got too busy with uni and work. Dating wasn't a priority for me." I shrugged.

Jihoon was quiet for a while, his hand moving in a steady rhythm as he rubbed my back.

"And none of them ever touched you?" he asked, sounding so puzzled, like he couldn't wrap his head around it.

I giggled. "I mean, my long-term boyfriend was very fond of grabbing my boobs whenever the opportunity arose."

Jihoon grumbled and dragged his hand down to my waist, pulling me harder against him.

"But what about you?" I tilted my head up to look at him.

"I've never had a boyfriend."

I laughed, and lightly smacked his chest, enjoying the way his dimples appeared when he smiled down at me.

"Funny man. I meant, when did you ever find the time to have girlfriends?" I kept my tone light, but the words stung my throat on the way up, tasting bitter.

"No girlfriends," he answered, his mouth still quirked in a smile, before he gave me a brief peck on my forehead.

"None? But..."

"There were girls," he admitted with a sigh, saying the words slowly, like he was making sure they were the right ones. "Other trainees. But always brief, and always secret. Nothing real."

I let the words sink in for a moment, hating the sharp spike of jealousy that twisted in my gut, before asking, "Did you never want a relationship with any of them?"

"Once." He looked down at me, holding my gaze when I might have looked away. "But if we'd have been found out, we would have been kicked out of the company."

"She's at ENT as well?" I didn't mean to ask the question – it just kind of fell out.

Jihoon nodded, but didn't offer up her name, or if she debuted, and I didn't ask.

"Do you mind?" Jihoon asked quietly. The question surprised me because his expression told me my answer mattered to him.

I frowned, "Why would I mind?"

"Some people do." His mouth turned down, even as his hand tightened around my waist.

"Jihoon, you're a grown man. Frankly, out of the two us and our combined sexual history, I'm the weirdo."

He laughed, his breath warm as he pressed another kiss to my forehead, as I lay there contemplating all that we could be.

Some time later, my body decided we were done lying around when it loudly gurgled its disapproval at not being fed. I froze, trying to decide if I could ignore it or not.

Jihoon chuckled, mid-way down my sternum, where he had been laying a trail of kisses from my throat downwards.

"Hungry?" He looked up at me from underneath those shadowy eyelashes, his lips tickling against my skin. It would be so easy to make a femme-fatale joke here, seductively bite my lip... were it not for my insistent, apparently empty stomach making its displeasure known with another unhappy gurgle.

"Hey," Jihoon said, directing this at my stomach, "we're going, you must be patient." He kissed just above my belly button, and I laughed, both from the tickle and the tummy pep-talk.

He raised up onto his arms and crawled up my body.

"You're not making it easier to get out of bed," I murmured as he towered over me.

He grinned and leaned down to press a soft kiss to my nose before he rolled off me and the bed, rising to his feet in one, fluid movement. I would have complained, but it afforded me a front row seat to the way his muscles flexed, the way his back tapered to his narrow waist and, let's be real, the way his shorts hung off those hips was a treat for the eyes.

I rolled onto my back and sighed. "I do not know what I did to deserve this," I muttered under my breath, "but I must have been very, very good."

Not long later.

We opened the fridge to inspect the contents.

"Not a lot going on in there," I let out a huff, putting a fist on my hip and letting the door close. Milk and basic condiments did not a breakfast make.

Jihoon shrugged, rubbing a hand down his neck. "I thought they'd leave food here."

I hummed and pulled out my phone, pulling up nearby food delivery places and scrolled for a moment.

"We can order in." I looked up at Jihoon to see he was also scrutinising his phone. He tilted his head to the side and pursed his lips, which had no right to be such an attractive expression. I watched him for a few moments, just enjoying the quiet peace of the kitchen, sunlight glinting off the marble counter tops as bird song drifted in through the open window. Hard to believe we were still in central LA. The birds we had in London were downright scrappy, certainly not cheerful songbirds like were currently in the garden outside.

When I'd lived in Clapham, south-west London, I'd lived in a dingy little bedsit above a corner shop owned by the sweetest old couple in the world, but the old man had kept pigeons on the roof, as a kind of hobby. So not only could I never open the window because of the smell, but seagulls would regularly fly down to harass the sweet, fat old pigeons. London seagulls are something else. You could see it in their eyes; they'd seen some things.

"Kaiya?" Jihoon repeated, shaking me out of my mental tangent.

"Sorry, what did you say?"

"I said, let's go out." He put his phone on the counter and came to stand in front of me, pinching the fabric of the sundress I was wearing and pulled me towards him.

I put my arms around his neck, basking in his easy smile as his hands wound around my waist.

"Out?" I smiled up at him, an easy smile that came unbidden as his eyes roamed over my face.

"Yes," he nodded, "there's a market I want to see."

"A market?" I frowned, images of fruit and vegetable stalls coming to mind.

"Yes, a flea market, it's not far away."

I thought for a moment, trying to reconcile the words. I'd been to a flea market in France once; it was more like an antiques fair though. In England, we had jumble sales and open-air markets. I kind of think flea markets are a mix between the two.

"Yeah, okay, sure." I agreed easily, shrugging in the circle of his arms, but then frowned as I thought of something. "Won't you need to wear, like, a mask, or something?" I thought back to when we'd almost been cornered visiting Pacific Park, so many months ago.

Jihoon laughed a small, self-deprecating sort of laugh and ducked his head before answering me.

"My hyungs said wearing disguises is what makes people look." Jihoon brought his gaze back up to mine, his eyes twinkling in the light of the morning sun.

"They said—" he said something in Korean I didn't understand. Turns out two months of a language app won't make you fluent. At my blank look, Jihoon said in English, "hiding in plain sight."

"Ah," I got it. It was like when Henry Cavil went to New York and stood under a Superman billboard for like, an hour, and no one even looked at him. He'd even filmed the whole thing. People don't look for what they don't expect to see.

"So, no wigs?" I pretended to pout, earning me a smirk from Jihoon.

"Only if you want to wear one."

"Oh damn, I left all of mine at home." I poked my tongue out at him and he laughed, a sound so rich and deep it was almost a surprise. I felt myself go a little slack and knew I probably had a dazed look on my face.

"What?" He stopped laughing and frowned at me.

"You're just so..." I sighed.

"What?" He rubbed at his face, then looked at his hand as if he expected to see the answer there.

Words went round in my head on a carousel; wonderful, dreamy, sexy, gorgeous.

But to spare both of us, I settled on a more sedate, "cute."

"Aegyo?" he repeated the word in Korean sceptically. "Like this?" He cupped his face in his hands and made an exaggerated bubble-gum-pop pout, and then screwed his finger theatrically into the dimple on his cheek, winking at me.

I laughed and blushed, it was such a weird combination of sexy and cute and it was kind of doing it for me. Impulsively, I went to pinch his cheek, but he grabbed my wrist and pulled me towards him, all traces of aegyo gone, replaced by a smoulder I almost collapsed under the weight of.

"Is this, aegyo?" he rumbled, the duality enough to give a person whiplash. I just gaped at him, my pulse speeding up under his hand. With his other, he ran his fingertips down my face before tucking a strand of hair behind my ear, before he leaned in and ran his mouth gently along my jawline, stopping at my ear to whisper, "Is this aegyo?" He pressed a soft kiss to that sensitive spot where my pulse thundered and I felt the tremor that coursed through me at the soft exhale that skittered against my skin.

Jihoon pulled back from me and broke character by grinning so widely there were dimples proudly on display in both cheeks. I pulled in a ragged breath and put a hand on the counter to re-balance myself.

"Holy hell," I gasped. Jihoon laughed, a loud and joyous sound.

I moaned, completely unabashed, my mouth full as I swiped a finger along the corner of my lips

"You like it?" Jihoon grinned at me, but with my mouth stuffed, all I could do was nod vigorously.

Jihoon took a slow, deliberate bite of his Danish – cream cheese raspberry –, his gaze lingering on me as he lifted it in a teasing toast to my cinnamon bun. I finally managed to swallow the mouthful I'd probably taken too much of and licked the sweet icing from my finger. I watched with pleasure as Jihoon's head lolled back from his first bite. He hummed loudly in satisfaction and I laughed.

The sweet treats had been the first stall we'd stopped at when we'd arrived at the market, which turned out to be a long, pedestrianised street crammed with an eclectic mix of stalls, musical performers and craft displays. There seemed to be everything here, from mum and pop stalls selling home-baked goods, like the ones we were gleefully devouring now, vintage clothing, artists painting caricatures of tourists, antiques and anything else you could think of. There was even a mime having an imaginary fight with – I think – a dog.

It looked like his hyungs – the older members of GVibes – had been right about his non-disguise. No one had looked twice in our direction, and I had been discreetly looking for it. Jihoon just looked like any other insanely attractive guy today in his denim shorts, plain white t-shirt and slides. He was wearing a mirrored pair of sunglasses, but he'd left off the hat, leaving his glossy black hair to curl about his ears and the nape of his neck. I kept having to force myself to not stare at him, but it was challenging. Occasionally, I failed, and he always seemed to catch me looking. Judging by his grins, though, he didn't seem to mind.

We strolled down the street, contentedly chewing our pastries, just soaking in the vibes. We didn't hold hands though. I hadn't asked, didn't want to presume, but Jihoon had told me that if someone did take photos, we could at least avoid a dating scandal. He'd sounded guilty when he said this, like it was somehow his fault, but I'd reassured him that I understood. The fan culture surrounding idols was well-known to be intense, with some fans believing they had a type of emotional ownership over their idols.

It was a lot to think about, but not something I wanted to unpack today, our last day together.

We hadn't spoken about it much, but it was another looming thing over this weekend. We had tonight, but Jihoon had an early flight in the morning – Sunday – in order to be back in Seoul on Monday morning in order to prepare for the group's international leg of the comeback promotion. I was determined not to get too deep in my feels about that, I was just grateful for the time we had now, this unexpected pocket of time where it was just us, getting to know each other more.

I turned to look at Jihoon, who was licking a raspberry off his Danish. It was a weirdly sensual, yet cute image. He had frosting on his bottom lip and, feeling impulsive, I swiped my thumb across his mouth, but before I could move away, he proved he'd been paying attention after all and he grabbed my wrist, bringing my thumb to his mouth, where he intentionally wrapped his tongue around my thumb, his eyes never leaving mine. I felt breathless when he released me, flushed like I was catching the sun and I knew I was biting my lip again by the way his eyes darted down to my mouth. I released it with a deep inhale and mentally gave myself a shake. Would it always be like this?

We kept walking, occasionally stopping to admire – or raise an eyebrow at – the things we saw. If creation was a box filled with ideas, someone had chucked a grenade into it and this street is where it exploded.

Pottery, jewellery, sculpture, smears of paint across taxidermy animals, photographs of every kind of piercing mankind has conceived of... It was really quite extraordinary.

About half-way up the street, Jihoon paused at a pop-up stall for a tattoo artist. There was one person manning it, a surly looking biker-dude with more ink on him than the Oxford English Dictionary. But that tracked, given the type of stall he was running.

"Sup," he growled from underneath a proud, bushy moustache.

"Hi," I said cheerfully back, finding his gruff demeanour oddly charming.

I'd worked in a pub during my last year at uni. It had been a complete dive and most of the clientèle had looked like this guy, but they had all been so sweet and absolutely not shy about defending the bar staff when the football crowd came in after a game and got rowdy.

"You kids thinking about getting each other's names tattooed? Cos that's an A1 bad idea," he grumbled, or perhaps that's just how his voice sounded when filtered through such a thick layer of face fuzz.

Jihoon barked out a laugh and covered his mouth with his hand. I grinned and turned back to the stall guy.

"Maybe another day. I was just admiring the flash work," I said, pointing to the images taped up to the sides of the awning. The man turned to briefly look at them before turning back.

"Yup, that's all hand drawn by me. Don't even need a stencil for those anymore." I could have sworn that superb 'stache twitched up at the sides.

"That's so dope!" I crowed, "I'd love to see some of your bigger pieces."

He squinted at me, and it could have either been because of the bright day, or he was trying to figure out if I was taking the piss, but I had a real fondness for ink. I always planned on getting more, I even booked an appointment for the summer after I graduated, but then LA happened and well, I never got round to it.

"Oh, I'm Kaiya, by the way," I held out my hand, smiling just as brightly as the mid-morning sun.

"Albert." He took my hand with surprising gentleness and lightly squeezed it.

"I'm pleased to meet you, Albert." I nodded at him, still smiling.

Albert looked over at Jihoon, who had been casually flicking through the folders of custom and flash work on the table. Jihoon, sensing eyes on him, didn't miss a beat and held out his hand.

"Joon," he offered, "nice to meet you, sir."

Some folks who looked like Albert might have looked for the hidden insult at being addressed as 'sir,' but given Jihoon's utterly earnest delivery, it was clear it was sincere. Albert eyed us both speculatively.

"Y'know, we do this thing these days, where we can print custom, temporary tattoos so you can see how you feel about it on your skin before you have to live with it for life. You interested? I got a few minutes spare."

I turned to Jihoon to see what he thought. He raised his eyebrows at me, an interested gleam in his eye. He cocked his head to the side in a half-shrug, his mouth pursed as if to say, 'why not?'

I turned back around to Albert and said, "That would be awesome!"

"Yeah, well alright then," he groused, "why don't you kids let me get something drawn up for you, and you head back here in a little bit and we'll see how you like it."

"You'll pick something for us?" I asked, surprised.

"Sweetheart, that's what I do." Albert raised one bushy eyebrow, the northern neighbour to that majestic mouth canopy.

"Albert," I said very seriously. "I trust you."

He hacked out a laugh and waved us away.

"What do you think he's going to draw for you?" Jihoon asked when we were far enough away not to be overheard.

I pretended to give the question some real thought, before suggesting, "The Union Flag." For a moment, Jihoon stared at me, and even through his mirrored sunglasses, I could tell he was trying not to react, which just made me laugh.

"Yeah, I have no idea. I guess we'll take what he wants to give us."
I shrugged, feeling as carefree today as I'd ever felt.

"What about you?"

"By your guess, probably the Korean flag," he said dryly, making
me laugh again, and I automatically reached for his hand only for
him to pull away at the last second. He tried to cover it up by
reaching up to run his hand through his hair.

My laughter dried in my throat, and I turned away, trying to
pretend not to have noticed. I knew no handholding was a rule and
I was even completely on board with the why of it.

So why did that sting so bad?

I tried hard to push down the intrusive thoughts, the ones that
reminded me this was what our future looked like – always pretending we weren't a thing. The pretence was so convincing that even I
wasn't sure anymore: were we something real or was I just a good
time?

I hated the rule, but even more, I hated that I understood it.

But most of all, I hated not knowing what we were.

I cleared my throat to cover the sudden cloud of awkwardness that
had settled between us.

"Look," Jihoon suddenly pointed to a porta-cabin style pop-up
that was decorated in hand-drawn portraits in various different
styles, from Picasso to Renaissance. The words 'Photo Booths' were
lit up in neon tubes, even though the day was bright.

"You want to go in?" I nodded my head to indicate the small,
boxy building just as a smiling couple walked out, hand-in-hand,

clutching a long roll of photos. My stomach clenched, just ever so slightly at the sight of the happy pair.

"Yes, come on." He headed over and I followed.

Inside the doors, the cabin was small – about the same size as the apartment I shared with Becka – with several, differently coloured and themed photobooths. One was very obviously occupied, if the giggles and scuffling feet under the burgundy curtain across the door was anything to go by. We gave that one a wide berth and looked over the other machines as we passed. Musical booths, black and white portraits, old timey booths, one that I think made you look like cartoons, and then finally the last one – a normal yellow and black Kodak machine.

Jihoon pulled me inside, and it didn't escape my attention that he looked over my shoulder beforehand.

The booth was predictably small with only one small, flat disc passing itself off as a seat. Jihoon sat and then, with his hands securely wrapped around my hips, he pulled me down so that I was perched on him, and in that moment, all thoughts of hand-holding, or not, were erased to make room for the way he felt so close to me, surrounding me in every possible way. The booth was lit only by the screen, cheerfully asking us to make a selection, but all I saw was his eyes, his sunglasses pushed up onto his head. His eyes seemed to glow in the dim light, pupils so dark and wide they almost swallowed his irises.

"Hello!" chirped a mechanical voice, startling us both, "please make your selection."

Jihoon chuckled, his eyes crinkling slightly.

"Allow me," I offered, pulling some change out of my pocket and feeding the machine, selecting a standard 4-frame.

"Get ready!" the mechanical voice warned, the screen flashing a countdown from 5.

Jihoon and I turned to the camera and smiled before the flash went off.

"Holy hell," I muttered, "that is hella bright."

Jihoon chuckled but then the countdown started again and in that near-panic of indecision, we both ended up sticking our tongues out, half-laughing when we realised we'd done the same thing. I was a little more prepared for the flash this time and didn't look directly at it.

When the countdown began again, I impulsively turned to face Jihoon and pressed my lips against his cheek. The flash went off, but my eyes were closed. Jihoon turned his face so that my lips traced the contour of his cheek before finding his mouth. I sighed as his lips parted. I reached a hand up to cup his face, lost in the feel of his skin, stubble rough against my palm. Jihoon's hands tightened around my hips, pulling me harder against him as he deepened the kiss.

"Please collect your photographs and have a great day!" the mechanical voice politely telling us to leave was somehow hilarious to me in that moment, and I broke away from him, giggling, the opposite to Jihoon, who was grumbling.

Carefully, I eased myself off of Jihoon's lap and opened the curtain to exit the booth. The photos were waiting in the tray and I picked them up, scanning the images.

I grinned at seeing the silly faces we had attempted to pull after our first, slightly awkward photo. The third and fourth photos made my cheeks heat, and I wordlessly handed the strip to Jihoon as he exited.

He took them from me and looked them over, his mouth curling up as his eyes darted across the photos before he put them in his back pocket.

The sunlight outside the small cabin of photobooths seemed brighter as we pushed aside the bead curtain, and I hastily pulled my sunglasses back down, noting Jihoon had already done the same.

We wandered further up the market, looking but not stopping. I did pause at one woman's stall, though. She was selling hand-made jewellery that she and her husband made. He metal-worked and she designed, and it was clear they were in it for the love, both theirs and of the process.

Though she talked to me, she never lost contact with her husband, they were always either sweeping a carefree hand across each other, or looking at each other. It was kind of nice. I know some people don't like public displays of affection, but having grown up around my parents constantly proving how much they loved each other, I found it peaceful to be surrounded by reciprocated love.

I cooed over the delicate pieces of silver and onyx, the bands of hammered metal and stones, but I guess I gave off that air of 'young and broke,' so the couple hadn't seriously tried to sell me anything and had just been content to make small talk with me, until an older woman had paused to look, and they'd moved away to see to her.

We next stopped at a food truck to get a couple of coffees and a soft, doughy pretzel; which we shared.

I think we were both just content to walk and look around until we seemed to be approaching the end of the market where fewer and fewer actual stalls were and more vans were parked with the names of various businesses on their sides, so without needing to say it, we each turned back around and began to head the way we'd come.

About an hour had passed since we'd first come upon Albert's tattoo stall, and I was surprised to see another man there now, equally as inked up but far less follicly-blessed than Albert. The man was sat on a stool in the back, hunched over the back of another man, in the process of tattooing him, although I could not see the design.

"I'll be right back; I wanted to see something," Jihoon muttered to me, before darting off and back into the crowd, slightly busier now that the morning was turning into afternoon.

Just then, Albert emerged from somewhere behind a dusty curtain at the back of the stall, holding an A4 sized envelope.

"Just in time," he groused, heading towards me. He handed me the envelope, but then put his hand on the opening just as I'd been about to open it to look.

"Open it when you get home, that way I don't have to hear you bitchin' about it, if you don't like it."

I snorted, but closed the flap all the same. "Alright, Albert, keep your secrets. What do I owe you?"

"Call it an even $20 and promise not to post about it on your social media bull crap."

"Goddamnit, Al," moaned the heavily tattooed artist, lifting the needle from the prone man's back. "This is the opposite of publicity; we've talked about this."

"I don't give a good goddamn," Albert intoned, "it's my shop, I'll advertise how I want, and I don't want some pasty-skinned punks seeing some of my work on the Internet and getting the idea to come see me.

"If folks want a tattoo, they'd look me up in the yellow pages, or come find me here, like normal people."

I hid my smile at the outburst of this curmudgeonly, hairy, walking canvas of ink.

"See? The kid agrees with me," Albert said, pointing one thick finger at me. I held my hands up in mock surrender.

"Don't bring me into this, I'm just an innocent bystander."

"Al, I swear to God..." the other tattoo artist trailed off into incoherent, dark mutterings as he resumed his work on the man lying face-down.

"Look, there's instructions in the packet, it's easy, you can't go wrong. And if anyone asks where you got 'em, just tell 'em the old-fashioned way. We ain't got no website–"

"Yes, the fuck we do!" interrupted the other artist. This was the most bizarre exchange I think I'd ever been privy to. Just then, I saw Jihoon heading back towards me, weaving his way through the stream of people heading in the opposite direction.

"I'll be sure to give them your name and street address," I reassured Albert, who nodded his thanks at me.

"You do that, kid. Enjoy the ink."

I thanked him as Jihoon reached my side, but Albert just waved us off and disappeared back round that dusty curtain, like some sort of magician that only came out to begrudgingly read peoples fortunes.

"Everything ok?" I turned to Jihoon, who just nodded.

"Shall we head back?" he asked, and I agreed and together we walked the few streets back to our temporary home for the weekend.

No, I mentally corrected myself, for the next 18 hours.

Chapter 30

We'd stopped at a little corner mart to pick up a few provisions for this evening and now we were in the kitchen, putting away the few items of food we'd bought.

Jihoon had been particularly excited about the tub of ice cream we'd bought. For such a small store, they'd had a pretty impressive selection, so I'd let him pick the flavour while I picked actual food. We'd also bought a six pack of beer because the idea of a cold beer in a hot tub sounded like actual paradise on a day like today.

I'd just put the chicken away in the fridge when I turned round to see Jihoon with the envelope with our mystery temporary tattoos inside.

"Let's open this," he said, grinning as excitedly as a kid on Christmas.

"Sure," I said, walking towards him as he flipped open the envelope and pulled out two sheaves of paper. I leaned on the kitchen island next to him as he inspected the first one.

"I think this is mine," he said, tilting his head to the side. The words 'pretty boy' were written at the top of the page. I barked out a laugh; Albert had been right about that, I thought, but I kept the comment to myself. The design was of a swallow, the tail was so distinctive that it was unmistakable. The bird was in mid-flight, powering upwards and so detailed, down to the tiny talons on its feet.

"Waah," Jihoon exclaimed appreciatively. I gently pried the second sheet of paper out from under Jihoon's one and pulled it towards me, looking down at the page that had 'the redcoat' written at the top. I chuckled at that before focusing on the small design, no bigger than a credit card.

"Wow," I breathed in awe, the design similar to Jihoon's. It was a swallow in flight, like his, but softer, the lines more shaded, less harsh and where Jihoon's bird had taloned feet, mine were tucked around the stem of a dandelion in full seed puff.

"Matching tattoos," Jihoon said, holding his page next to mine and something about the way they were side-by-side made my throat tight. Swallows were a symbol of resilience and known for flying thousands of miles each year.

"I love it," I swallowed past the lump in my throat and said, "shall we apply them now?"

"Yes," Jihoon nodded and pulled his t-shirt off over his head in one smooth pull that had me gaping at him, somehow forgetting how we'd curled around each other the whole night, wearing far less.

He caught me staring and grinned at me, and I'm fairly sure he flexed.

"Where should we put them?" I wondered aloud, mentally placing the images on various body parts, dismissing some and filing others away for consideration.

"I have to hide mine," Jihoon said, bringing me back to the conversation. "I can't show it or it could be bad for the group." His mouth tightened into a firm line and I remembered reading about negative press some idols had gotten after getting tattoos, the way they had to cover them up with either makeup or even bandages. The one he had on his ribs was so high up that you would never know, even in the most risqué of wardrobe malfunctions.

"We'll put it somewhere no one will see it," I tried to sound neutral, but I'm not sure my face cooperated.

"It's probably the same as how you put kids tattoos on. Hold on, Albert did say there were instructions. One sec," I opened the envelope, looking inside for any other bits of paper. There was a card at the bottom and I reached a hand in to pull it out. It was a business card with the name and address of the parlour, and on the back were some hand-written instructions.

My eyes misted as I read Albert's words, so much more than the instructions I was looking for.

"Kaiya?" I shoved the card back into the envelope and tossed it onto the counter, spinning back around to see Jihoon holding his page, a frown pulling his eyebrows down.

"Okay?" he asked.

"Yeah," I said quickly, "it's as I thought, exactly the same as kids' tattoos. Let's do it!"

We decided Jihoon would go first – for science reasons. He'd decided to have his on his shoulder blade, it was one of the few places that would never be revealed, even accidentally, and still allow him to wear sleeveless tops. We joked about putting it on his thigh, but apparently his trainers back home took body measurements every week, so that was out.

Boy, if I'd ever entertained the notion that it was only women in the entertainment industry that were held to such unrealistic body standards, I was quickly becoming educated. When we'd shared that pretzel this morning, he'd told me that when he was a trainee, he hadn't been allowed near refined carbohydrates for months, not until he'd gone to visit family with one of his hyungs for Chuseok – kind of like the Korean equivalent of Thanksgiving, he'd said.

They were allowed a lot more freedoms now, but they still routinely monitored their weight, which seemed bonkers to me, considering how much physical exercise they all did.

I held the transfer paper to Jihoon's sculpted back, making sure it was firmly placed, before I pressed the wet cloth on top of it, making sure to thoroughly wet the whole area. Water dripped down his back, following the curves and dips and drawing my eye so inevitably that I had to remind myself to watch what I was doing. As if I couldn't resist, I ran my other hand down his broad back, skimming my fingertips over the contours of his muscles. He shivered under my hand and looked at me over his shoulder, a smirk pulling the corner of his mouth up as he raised an eyebrow at me. I blushed and refocused on the task at hand.

After the prescribed thirty seconds of holding pressure against the tattoo, I swiped the cloth downwards to remove the now-slick paper, leaving behind the transfer of the swallow.

"Is it ok?" Jihoon asked, flexing his shoulders, giving the appearance of a swallow in flight.

"It looks good," I admitted, putting my hands on my hips, admiring the image.

"I want to see," he whined, trying to stretch his neck over his shoulder and half-spinning around in the process, like a puppy trying to chase its tail. I doubled up, holding onto the counter for support as I belly laughed. The duality of this man, I swear. One minute he is pant-meltingly seductive, the next he is a complete clown.

Jihoon stopped spinning and pinned me with a heart-stopping smoulder, crowding into my space until I was backed up against the kitchen island.

I gulped as I looked up at him.

"Something funny, jagiya?" he rumbled, pressing his hips into mine as he caged me in with his arms on either side of my body.

I could only shake my head. His eyes seemed to hold me as firmly as his body, and we just stood there, unmoving for several moments until a smile broke across his face, erasing all the smouldering embers of just a moment ago, and I knew I'd been played like a fiddle at a country wedding.

"You..." I trailed off in exasperation, lightly smacking his chest, which only seemed to make him laugh harder as he moved to dodge me.

"I like having this effect on you. I just hope you like my brain as much as you like my body."

I rolled my eyes, but then turned away from him to hide my grin before I pulled my t-shirt off over my head. I turned back around, looking up at him from underneath my lashes.

Jihoon stopped laughing. He raked his eyes up and down my bared skin, his face growing more flushed with each passing second.

"Do me." I all-but purred at him.

He choked; literally choked on an inhale and I had to thump him on the back several times before he could wheeze out, "Gwaenchana, I'm fine."

"I just hope you like my brain as much as you like my body." I repeated his words back at him sympathetically as tears streamed down his face.

An hour later we were floating in the pool, our new temporary tattoos proudly adorning our skin. I'd chosen to place mine on the inside of my right forearm, since no one I knew would care if I had ink on display, temporary or not. I couldn't stop looking at it though, it seemed so perfect.

"Do you think you'll ever get a tattoo in a place people can see?" I lazily waved my arms trying to keep myself from floating into the edge of the pool.

"Mmm," Jihoon hummed before he answered, "I want to, but it's a lot of hassle."

"When Sungmin got his, the managers were so mad."

I almost rolled over in surprise and had to quickly get my legs under me.

"Lee has a tattoo?" I spluttered. I still didn't feel comfortable using their given names. It made them like real people – which they were – just not to me, so I mostly used their stage names when we spoke about them.

"Yes, he has a tattoo of the moon on his hip," Jihoon replied, tapping his hip bone.

I let my legs float back to the surface to resume my carefree passage around the pool.

"Did you get in trouble for the feather?" I asked, remembering the way he'd pulled up his shirt to show me, that day we'd had breakfast in his hotel room.

Jihoon made a humming sound. "They were not happy, but by that time, it was too late."

I thought about this while I watched the clouds overhead. His body was so regulated, from his weight, to his hair colour. He kept reassuring me they all had so many more freedoms now, so how strict must it have been when they were trainees?

"Will you get more?" he asked, shaking me out of my reverie as he swirled his hands near to me.

"I kept meaning too," I said thoughtfully. "But every time I thought about it, something would come up that stopped me."

"Like what?"

"Uni work, no money, the annual blood-drive on campus. Just life things." I shrugged, not easy to do while partially suspended in water.

We were quiet for a while, enjoying the peace of the garden, the warm sunshine tempered by the cool of the water and the shade of the trees.

"Did you always want to be an idol?" I realised we didn't really talk about his life. I'd always been too wary of seeming too fan-like, but I hoped we were past that now because I really did want to know. It was such a large part of his life; it didn't make sense to tiptoe around it.

Jihoon was quiet for so long I wasn't sure he would answer.

"Yes, and no.

"I always wanted to sing and perform. I knew I didn't want the same life my parents have – always moving around and chasing business deals." He sighed.

"They didn't support you?" I guessed.

"Not at first. That's why they sent me to New York. They thought that if I was further away from Korea, I'd lose interest and want to do something else.

"But my imo and imobu, they saw how determined I was to be a trainee and they wanted to make sure I at least had a chance, so they flew us all back to Korea and took me to the audition for ENT. I was accepted and moved into the dorms and by the time they told my parents, it was too late. My parents couldn't take me out without embarrassment, and that's something they will avoid at all costs."

He laughed, but it was a bitter sounding thing. My chest hurt for him, especially when I think about how my own parents would do anything to support something I was passionate about, without a second thought.

"You proved them wrong though," I said with complete conviction, because he had.

"I proved I could do what I set out to do, but I don't think they see it that way. They would not have chosen this life for me."

"Would you make the same decision again?" I feared that I may be digging too deep, but he answered anyway.

"Yes. The life I have is hard, getting here was even harder. We were always tired, always hungry, always hurting, but when I see our fans, it's all worth it. All the suffering was worth it to know we make people happy. They make us happy. The feeling we get from them when we meet on stage is... I can't describe it."

I could hear the emotion in his voice, and I could only imagine his world – so far removed from mine and most other people's.

The sincerity in his tone was undeniable. He really felt that way, and even though this seemed like a vulnerable moment, I could tell he drew a lot of strength from the relationship he and his group had with their fans. "Do you think you'll do this forever?"

"I hope so." His answer was so immediate, it was either practiced or deeply sincere. Both possibilities gave me something to think about as we lapsed back into calm silence.

Later, I stood over the massive stove top after finally figuring out how to turn it on.

"That smells so good!" Jihoon moaned, coming up behind me and leaning over my shoulder to see what I was doing. Ordinarily, if someone did that whilst I was cooking, it would have been reasonable grounds to be swatted with a spoon, but I somehow didn't mind when it was Jihoon. His still-damp hair tickled my cheek as he leaned in, inhaling the fragrant steam.

Neither one of us had bothered showering after getting out of the pool, both agreeing we'd be going into the hot tub after dinner, both of us fully aware of the clock counting down the hours until we had to leave. Jihoon had a car coming to pick him up at 5:00am for a red-eye back to Korea. Our time was limited; we wanted to make the most of what we had left, so hot tub it would be.

"It's nearly ready." I stirred the contents of the pan, smiling at his enthusiasm. It wasn't as if I'd made anything as fancy as I'm sure he was used to, just a chicken and broccoli stir fry with a honey, soy and garlic sauce. The soy sauce had been in the fridge, the other ingredients we'd picked up from the corner store. I'd practically had this exact same meal every week whilst I'd lived about that corner shop in Clapham last year.

While I was at the stove, I directed Jihoon to cut up some of the bakery loaf we'd picked up on the way home. I'd tried explaining the concept of buttered bread alongside a meal to him, but he hadn't really gotten it, until I'd jokingly said it was the banchan of northern England.

We decided to sit at the kitchen island for the sake of ease. There was something so domestic about preparing a meal together and then sitting down to eat it. It made my heart swell to watch him take the first bite. He groaned and pretended to slide off the chair and onto the floor, making me laugh as I pulled him back up by the arm. Maybe it was the ingredients we'd used today, but that simple meal tasted far better that day than any of the times I'd made it last year.

"I get it now," he said around a mouthful of bread and butter, "this is so good."

"I told you," I laughed, taking a bite of my own bread after using it to mop up the excess sauce on the plate.

"If all food tastes like this in your hometown, I want to go."

I laughed even harder. "That'll be pie'n'peas and a sausage then."

Jihoon cocked his head to the side, "I don't know what you just said."

I howled with laughter.

The sun was finally beginning to dip below the edge of the tree line, bathing the garden in an orange glow that reflected back off the windows of the house. A slight breeze had rolled on through, making the leaves in the trees rustle peacefully as we made our way across the lawn, each carrying a beer in hand as we headed towards the hot tub.

We'd managed to find the indoor switch that activated the bubbles and the heat and we'd waited about half an hour for it to warm up before heading out, giving us enough time to clean up after dinner. We were still wearing our swimming things from earlier, so we hadn't needed to change.

Jihoon reached the tub first, which was bubbling merrily away, wisps of steam coiling up into the cooling air from the warm water. He carefully stepped down into the writhing water and set his bottle down in the holder on the ledge before holding his hand out to me. I slid my palm against his as I gingerly stepped in. Water almost too-warm slid up my calf and then my thighs as I stepped onto the seat in the tub. Holding onto Jihoon, I stepped down again so I was submerged up to my navel. We sat down and I instantly groaned at the feel of the water, so warm and bubbly swirling around my chest and shoulders. I leaned my head back against the side and closed my eyes, letting any tension left in my body just evaporate.

"I need to get me one of these," I mumbled.

Jihoon huffed next to me. "Me too."

Without moving the rest of my body, I opened my eyes and turned to face him. Like me, he was leaning back against the padded edge of the tub, eyes closed and looking so serene it made me smile.

"Do you still live in a dorm, or do you have your own place?" I couldn't seem to stem my curiosity about his life today.

His lips curled up; some joke I wasn't privy to. "We all moved out of the dorm in 2016. Minjae and Woojin each have an apartment, but I live with Seokmin and Sungmin."

"Do you live close to them?"

He laughed. "You could say that. We all live in Hannam-Dong."

The name sounded familiar. "Is it nice there?"

He shrugged. "It's where a lot of idols and actors live because there's a lot of security there."

He made it sound like an enclave.

"But do you like it?" I pressed, turning more fully to him now. Jihoon opened his eyes and turned to face me.

"So many questions today," he murmured, reaching for his bottle and taking a pull.

"Am I being too nosy?" I cringed, absurdly still self-conscious, despite everything.

"No, not nosy. It's just..." He looked thoughtful, like he was trying to think of the words.

"Normally people just know certain things about us. We get asked the same questions in interviews and have to answer in different ways every time, but when it comes to our lives, the small details, people usually already know.

"It's strange to be asked about my life by someone who doesn't already know." He smiled at me and it was a smile that pulled out my own. It seemed like a relief, but I didn't know why it would be, just that I was glad I wasn't annoying him. I hastily pushed that thought aside, choosing not to dwell on the imbalance in... whatever this relationship was.

"To answer your question, yes, I do like it there. It's close to the city so we don't have to spend so much time in the car, but it's safe enough if we want to ride our bikes or go for a run, we can.

"A lot of our friends live there too, it's like a full-page spread of Dispatch," he rolled his eyes and I giggled.

"There's lots of cool places to go too, lots of trendy clothes shops and art shops, coffee places, good food to eat. It's a different planet from the dorms." He scrunched his nose.

"Wow, it sounds kinda awesome. I'd love to see it someday." The comment was a bit of a throw away one, but his eyes laser focused on me like I'd said something important. He said nothing though, which made me think I'd said something wrong. I chewed on my lip, trying to think of a segue, but he beat me to it.

"What was it like where you grew up?"

"The Lakes?" I said in surprise. He nodded.

I blew out a puff of air as I considered the question.

"In some ways it was everything you could wish for as a kid. It's such a wild place, there's always somewhere to explore and get muddy. Freezing cold rivers, forests that go on for miles, hills to run around on all day.

"But then, as I got older, I found it too slow. I wanted to see the cities. I didn't want to run around in the wild anymore."

"You miss it now?"

I guess he must have read something in my expression. I smiled, wistfully.

"I think you always miss the place you call home.

"But then, when I was 18, I moved to London for university and I lived there for four years until I moved to LA this year. The rest is history." I shrugged.

We lapsed into silence again, the jets of the tub being the only sound for so long I wondered if he'd fallen asleep. But then I saw him reach for his bottle again, and I decided to ask the thing that had been in the back of my mind for a while, something that felt like it might shift our... 'situationship' one way or the other.

I cleared my throat and tried to ignore the way my pulse thumped against my throat.

"Joon?"

He turned to look at me and opened his mouth, and then closed it again, a line appearing between his eyebrows.

"It must be serious if you're calling me 'Joon,'" he quipped.

"I call you 'Joon,' sometimes," I muttered, eyes downward.

Jihoon slid towards me until he was right in front of me, one elbow leaning on the edge of the tub, holding his head, his intense stare focused entirely on me.

"What is it?"

"It's not a big deal..." I bit my lip.

"Kaiya."

"I was just wondering... if you'd told the other members, you know, about me. About... Us." I couldn't bring myself to look up at him, but with him being so close, that limited my options to either pointedly ignoring him by looking at the sky, or fixing my eyes on his pectorals. Which were very nice and in any other circumstances...

So instead, I pretended to scan the sky for... birds? Planes? Courage, a heart or a brain?

Jihoon gently pinched my chin and brought my face back down until he was looking in my eyes.

"Is this what you've been worried about? If you're my secret?"

Well, when he put it like that...

"I would understand if you hadn't told them, I mean, it's not like you can announce-"

"They know." He cut me off. "They've known for a while."

My heart skipped a beat, my chin trembled, and I wondered if he could feel it under his fingers. He held my gaze for several more seconds before he nodded to himself, released my chin and unexpectedly stood, water sluicing off him as he climbed out of the tub while I sat there, cocking my head like a confused pigeon to see him exit the hot tub.

"Wait, where are you going?" I cried.

"Be right back," he tossed over his shoulder before jogging towards the house. I watched him re-enter through the French windows, the gauzy curtain billowing around him before resettling.

I ran through our brief conversation, trying to find hints of what could have possibly just occurred, but I came up blank. He hadn't seemed upset...

I didn't have to sit there confused for long though, as barely a couple of minutes later, Jihoon re-emerged from the house, striding purposefully towards me. He climbed back into the tub, sitting so close to me that his slick skin brushed against mine, raising goosebumps in the wake.

"Where did you go?" I tried very hard not to sound as confused as I felt.

"I wanted to get this." He held up a small, wooden box with a metal clasp, making sure to keep it above the bubbling water.

I stared at the box for a long moment, ice cubes slipping into my stomach just as my rational brain was panic-pressing the 'do not panic' klaxon.

It was a small box, but it wasn't small enough. It's absolutely not what it looks like.

"What's this?" My voice was a breath above a whisper as I looked into his eyes, trying to gauge his expression, but he just smiled enigmatically at me.

"Open it."

I lifted shaking hands to the tiny, silver clasp holding the two halves of the box together and flipped it open. I took a breath before I lifted the lid, almost flinching as it opened easily.

One half of my brain translated the image in front of me, while the other half tried to interpret the meaning of it.

Sitting on a purple velvet cushion, were two rings, one of which I immediately recognised from the jewellery stall we'd stopped at today in the market. It was a braided band of silver holding an amethyst that sparkled with the reflected shine of the little lights in the trees. Next to it was a plain band of twisted silver, a companion to the one with the gemstone.

I looked up at Jihoon, searching his face for answers.

"In Korea, it's normal for couples to exchange rings," he explained, shrugging one shoulder up like it was no big deal, but red spots appeared on his cheekbones as he spoke.

"We missed our 100-day anniversary, but I wanted to get you something..." He looked away and frowned.

"Couple?" I aimed for a teasing tone, but with my heart in my throat, it sounded as hopeful as it was.

His eyes collided with mine. "Isn't that what we are?"

"It's just... we've never talked about what we are."

Jihoon looked... I didn't know. His eyebrows were furrowed, his mouth a thin line, but he held my gaze.

"I don't want you to think you're not important to me, just because we can't be open.

"When we signed our contracts, we all knew we wouldn't be able to live normal lives, and even though we don't have a dating ban anymore, it's still... difficult to have relationships." He floundered, and even though I understood what he was trying to say, I could tell how difficult it was for him to say it.

"Hey," I placed a hand on his cheek, gently turning him back to face me. "I may not understand your life, but I do understand it's not the same as mine. I'm just happy to have the pieces of you that I can, however I can. This is enough. You are enough."

His chin trembled under my palm and I watched as he blinked away the sudden shine in his eyes as I tried to swallow past the lump in my own throat.

He looked down at the box in his hands and plucked out the one with the amethyst, putting the box on the ridge of the hot tub.

"Did you know my birthstone was an amethyst?" I asked.

He looked up at me, eyes widening. "No."

I nodded, dropping my hand from his jaw and holding it out for him. "Yup, my birthday is February 21st."

He huffed a laugh, "a Pisces."

"Yup," I grinned.

"The universe has plans for us all." He shook his head, ruefully, before reaching for my other hand, gently lowering the hand I held up for him. "Your left hand," he murmured, "we put couple's rings on our left ring fingers."

My next breath caught in my throat as Jihoon gently slid the ring onto my finger. It fit as perfectly as if it'd been made for me. Jihoon brushed his thumbs across my hand, looking down at the ring now settled there, before raising my hand to his mouth and placing a kiss on the back of it.

I reached for the ring box and carefully pulled the twisted band free from the secure cushion.

"Your turn," I tried to joke, but I could barely get the words past the lump in my throat. Compliantly, Jihoon held out his left hand,

and I slid the ring onto his finger. It went on easily, the pale metal complimenting his skin tone so perfectly.

I held onto his hand, our rings a complementing set that glinted in the dusk, the physical presence of them a comforting thing.

Jihoon pulled me towards him, wrapping his arms around me as he held me. I rested my head in the crook of his neck, my arms tight around his waist and just breathed in the reassuring presence of him, somehow more solid than ever before.

"Just so you are certain about it," he said, "you are my girlfriend. Yes?"

I could only nod, my words had been stolen away by the butterflies in my stomach.

Chapter 31

I t was getting late by the time the movie ended and we'd finished off the six-pack we'd bought earlier. We'd both showered after getting out of the hot tub – separately, before setting down to watch a film, though I could barely recall what it had been about; we'd spent most of the time talking through it, laughing and kissing. Yes, there had been lots of kissing. I was currently too comfortable to move as the end-credits rolled. We'd eventually made it back to the sofa and I was now sprawled across it, my feet in Jihoon's lap, where he was absently rubbing my soles. I was so blissed out that my eyes kept closing, even though sleep was the last thing I wanted to do. That countdown clock was now hovering somewhere around six hours until Jihoon had to leave, and although I tried not to think about it, bouts of melancholy kept creeping in, aided – no doubt – by the beer.

I dimly registered that Jihoon had turned off the television, and when he moved my feet off his lap, I weakly protested. But then I felt his arms scooping me up as I was hoisted against his broad chest. My eyes flew open and I swung my arms around his neck, probably a little too tightly.

"Whoa," I protested, "I can walk."

"I know you can," his voice sounded like a thundercloud from where my ear was pressed to his chest.

"But I want to carry you."

And so, he did, all the way up the stairs to the bedroom we shared. He gently put me down at the foot of the bed, face hovering so close to mine I could count every one of his eyelashes. My arms were still wrapped around his neck, stretching my body out along his, being that much taller than me.

"You can let go now," he smirked.

"No, I can't." I was breathless at even the thought of letting him go, in any sense of the word. He smiled down at me, his face soft in the dim glow of the bedside lamp.

I pulled him down and brushed my lips against his, just an impression of a kiss really, but he responded with such passion that it stole my breath. He grabbed at my hips and pulled me against him – hard, until I went limp in his arms. He ran his palms down my backside and then pulled me upwards so forcefully that it was either wrap my legs around his waist or... I don't think there was another option.

Lips, tongues, and teeth clashed in a fervent need that felt without end, a lit match so close to burning my fingertips that I couldn't let go, and then suddenly a loss of gravity as my back hit the mattress. I hadn't even felt us move across the room.

Jihoon pressed me into the soft bed, his hips pinning me down while his hands softly cradled my face. I know it sounds cliche, but it really felt as though he was my oxygen tank. Nothing we did brought us close enough, this constant pawing at skin and pulling of clothes, wasn't close enough.

I groaned when Jihoon tore his mouth from mine, but silenced when I saw the dark look in his eyes, the intent written so plainly upon his face, his parted mouth damp from our kisses. Slowly, he crawled down my body, running a hand from my throat to my heaving chest. He rose up on his knees, straddling me fully, and assertively placed his hands on the bottom of my ribs, hooking his fingers underneath my thin t-shirt. Holding my gaze, he slowly pushed the fabric upwards, dragging his fingers lightly into my skin and not stopping when he reached my breasts.

My head fell into the pillows, my mouth parted on a sound-less gasp as his palms grazed my bare breasts, his thumbs rubbing across my peaked nipples with maddening pressure. My t-shirt was scrunched up above my chest, baring me completely to his hungry gaze as he looked his fill.

"You're so fucking beautiful," he ground out, eyes wild. His hands trembled slightly as he reached for me, gently cupping me, running his fingers over me as I watched the shadows play over his face. I was like a musical instrument under his hands, every touch felt like he was strumming a chord, the vibrations playing all the way down my body to echo in my core.

I arched my back as he ran his fingertips down my chest, almost dislodging him as my hips bucked underneath him. He chuckled before he dipped back down, inching further down my body so the weight on my hips no longer pressed me into the mattress. I rose up onto my elbows to watch as he bent down to trail soft kisses down my skin, swirling his tongue around my navel and nipping at my hip bones. I squirmed under him.

"Shhh...," he cooed, looking up and holding my gaze, perhaps gauging my reaction as he hooked his fingers into the band of my shorts. I could only pant as I watched him slowly peel them down my hips, down my thighs until he eventually dropped them to the floor.

He now knelt between my thighs, absolutely nothing between him and my skin. Despite the way I was utterly bared to him, it never once occurred to me to feel embarrassed. I shivered, both in anticipation of the unknown, and also at the slight breeze of his breath upon my inner thigh. He kissed me there, peppering soft kisses up and down until I ached.

"Jihoon," I whimpered. His eyes flicked up to meet mine, and it was without a doubt, the most erotic moment of my life. My chest heaved and I couldn't bring myself to look away. He wrapped one arm around my thigh and pressed my hip down with his other hand, keeping me so firmly in place I couldn't move, even if I had wanted to.

Keeping my gaze, he moved his lips away from my inner thigh and I bit my lip, nervous energy thrumming through me, and I wondered if he could feel it.

Half a heartbeat later, all thoughts utterly scattered at the first touch of his mouth. I threw my head back, a silent cry parting my lips, breath frozen in my throat, until the next heartbeat where he flicked his tongue against me. Air whooshed out of me in an exhale so hard it felt like a scream.

After those first few tentative touches, Jihoon seemed to unleash himself; delivering long, deliberate strokes that made me cry out. He licked his way up until he got to that point where all the tension in my body seemed to be gathering, and he pressed a soft kiss there, before engulfing me with his mouth, the heat of his tongue further fracturing me. And when he slid a finger inside of me, I felt it in my whole body, an implosion of feeling that seemed to be radiating inwards in sweeping waves, all rushing towards that small piece of flesh Jihoon was currently fixated on, until–

I cried out, a frenzied exhalation torn from my chest that brought my whole body with it, rising up off the bed independent of my own control or intention, and had it not been for the way Jihoon held me so securely, I would have surely dislodged him.

I hung there for a second, frozen in movement, my body bowed like a violin string, before I collapsed back onto the bed, ragged gasps sawing in and out of my open mouth. My head spun, my body vibrated, everything was a cacophony of sensation, my brain trying to interpret and translate, but falling short.

But eventually, I felt myself sink back into my body, a gradual settling of body and mind, and I became more aware of myself. I looked down to see Jihoon looking up at me, everything about him a study in smug satisfaction. The way he rested his head on my thigh, the hand he had placed over me, palming me in a soothing, but claiming way.

I took in a shaky breath and let out a small giggle, covering my face with my hands. I felt Jihoon make his way back up the bed, but no longer above me. Gently, he pried my hands from my face.

"Don't hide."

Any mirth I might have felt died the moment I looked at him. He was smouldering, and though I could see that self-satisfied crook to his lips, it made his expression no less proprietorial.

I sat up, so close we were almost chest-to-chest and my t-shirt fell back down to cover my top half. Jihoon watched the fabric fall, but otherwise remained motionless. I pulled my legs up under me, rising up onto my knees, crowding Jihoon now but he still did not move. He just watched me with that predatory glint to his eyes, the sharpness of tension that hadn't been released with my own.

I ran my fingers up his jaw to cup his cheek and brought his face closer to mine, so close our lips brushed, but did not touch. I could feel his breathing panting over me, a careful restraint. I could sense he was close to a breaking point. It made me smile. I softly ran the very tip of my tongue over his bottom lip before I lightly nipped it. Jihoon made a noise that sounded like a growl before his hands shot out to grab my waist, fingers digging in almost – but not quite – on the verge of pain.

"My turn," I breathed against his lips, and he groaned a moment before his lips crashed against mine, a forceful insistence I matched with my own fervour, until I was done with playing. I tore my lips away from his, pulling back when he tried to follow and instead pushed against his chest to force him down on the bed. I knew he allowed it, because with his strength, he easily could have resisted, but he allowed me to lay him down and, just as he had with me, I lay a knee on either side of his hips, lowering my weight down on him, feeling immediately the evidence of his arousal.

Seemingly like he couldn't resist, his hips surged upwards and nudged against me, sending a unique kind of sensation through my body. My head lolled to the side, and I had to forcibly remind myself of my own intentions, bringing my gaze back to his, where I saw that masculine smirk curling his beautiful mouth up again.

I tsked, and his grin grew wider.

"Let's get rid of this, shall we?" I tugged at the hem of his t-shirt, and he obliged me by rising up and swiftly pulling it off and over his head before lying back down, a reminder to me that he only lay prone because he wanted to.

Looking down at that teasing smile, I wanted to turn the tables a little bit. I leant down and kissed his ridged abdomen, moving my mouth slowly, feeling the way his skin jumped under my caresses. I looked up at him through half-lowered lids, my mouth slightly open as I moved my body against his, arching my back as I pushed against him with my hands on his chest, rubbing against him like a cat. Jihoon hissed a breath out between clenched teeth and now it was my turn to smirk at him.

"Ah cheon-sa," he rumbled, you're playing with me." I just hummed in response, pressing down on him with my hips, having to widen my stance to do so. He twitched beneath me.

Just as he had, I inched my way down his body, leaving a trail of kisses, until I was kneeling between his legs. I reached for the zipper on his shorts and, swallowing my fleeting trepidation, I pulled it down. I couldn't stifle my gasp when I saw that beneath the shorts, he wasn't wearing another layer.

"Jihoon!" I said in mock admonishment. He just shrugged and put one arm behind his head, the ultimate picture of masculine satisfaction.

Conjuring up my determination, I hooked my fingers into the waistband of his shorts and pulled them downwards, freeing him. Trying not to let my burgeoning nervousness get the best of me, I focused on the task of pulling off the shorts. Jihoon arched his hips, helping me so that I was able to work them off his legs and drop them to the floor.

But before I could do so much as move my hand, Jihoon had sat up and was holding my wrists in his hand.

"Hey," he said softly, forcing me to meet his eyes.

"We don't have to do anything else."

"But-"

"I told you yesterday, this isn't an exchange. I know you've not done anything like this before. You don't have to be nervous with me."

"I'm not," I said, finally finding my voice. "I want to touch you, not just because of what you did. Because I want to, and I want to do it with you."

He held my gaze for long enough that I could see the conflict in his eyes, the warring emotions of trying to do what he thought was right, versus whatever his body was telling him. I wanted to ease that inner conflict.

"So, Baek Jihoon," I raised my eyebrow at him as he smiled at the use of his full name.

"You're going to lie back and enjoy yourself. Understood?" I pushed against his broad chest until I felt his muscles relaxing and he allowed himself to be pushed back down.

"Yes ma'am."

It was true. While I wasn't confident I wouldn't muck this up, or look foolish, I wanted to experience things with Jihoon that would be ours and ours alone. If all we could ever have was secret rendezvouses in between packed schedules, I didn't want there to be anything off limits. I didn't want my own trepidation to be the line I wouldn't cross.

I took him into my hand and saw how he startled at the contact. His skin was warmer than I expected, softer, which was a surprise to me. I expected to feel awkward, but seeing the look of vulnerable need on his face made me bold instead.

I dipped down and put my mouth on him.

He jerked and bit out a rasped, "Fuck!", and I couldn't help the giggle that escaped. Not easy to do, considering.

It didn't pass me by that there didn't really seem to be a way to do this badly, so I just followed his lead and tried to observe what he liked, but he seemed to like it all, judging by the way he had balled his fist in the sheet.

I ran my tongue over him from tip to base, and he almost jumped off the bed, so I did it again.

He was too large to hold in my mouth completely, so I compromised by gripping the base of him with my hand.

"Jagiya, fuck, I won't-" he panted as though in pain, before groaning something in Korean.

I took that as a good sign and kept doing it. He then reached a hand down and cupped my jaw, making me pause to look up him. His eyes rolled back in his skull a moment before meeting my gaze.

"Ky," he panted, "I – you're going to make me..." He couldn't seem to finish the word, but I knew what he meant and what he was saying. It took me less than a second to make up my mind, and without breaking eye contact, I carried on, with perhaps a little more pressure than before.

Jihoon groaned, an incoherent string of sounds just before he jerked one more time, and then lay still, gasping. I rose onto my knees and delicately wiped my mouth, my turn now to look so smug, I could feel the way my face looked in that moment, the self-satisfaction practically glowing from every pore. I got it now, why he had looked at me that way before.

Finally, he opened his eyes and looked at me. I waggled my eye brows at him.

"Good?"

In the space between one heartbeat and the next, he was sitting up and had grabbed my face in his hands. He crashed his lips against mine, so much feeling poured into that one simple action that it seemed to pull me into him, though I did not move.

Wordlessly, we pulled apart, just looking into each other's eyes and I smiled shyly. The silence seemed to stretch between us, a fluid thing that filled all the gaps, but it was a warm, fuzzy kind of silence and together, we settled; heartbeats slowed and breaths collected.

Eventually though, we had to move and Jihoon was the first to, as he kissed the tip of my nose and smiled.

I placed my hand on his chest, feeling the way his heart beat so soundly under my palm, almost audible in the silence of the room. Jihoon lifted it to his mouth and placed a delicate kiss against my palm, and then my inner wrist. My heart swelled at how softly he held me, like I might break if handled carelessly.

After a brief bathroom break, I slid back into bed, the sheets cool against my flushed skin.

"Come, it's late," Jihoon said, lying back down on the bed and pulling me with him to settle in the circle of his arms, resting my head on his warm chest. Instantly I felt drowsy, the weight of sleep hovering at the edges of my mind, waiting to pull over me like a blanket.

I sighed with contentment, but then remembered something I wanted to know. Without moving my head, I asked, "What does 'cheon-sa' mean?"

He'd explained to me earlier that 'jagiya' meant something like, 'baby,' or 'darling.'

Jihoon inhaled deeply underneath me, saying as he exhaled, "It means 'angel.'

Goosebumps broke out over my body and my smile felt tremulous as I snuggled closer to his warmth.

Chapter 32

M orning came sooner than either of us wanted, the shrill alarm of Jihoon's phone was an unwelcome interruption to what had to have been one of the most peaceful night's sleep I'd ever had.

But, it was 4:00am and the driver would be coming for Jihoon by 5:00am, so it was with reluctance that we both got out of bed and went about putting back together the shards of the real-life we were returning to, by doing normal things, like getting dressed, brushing our teeth, and packing away the meagre possessions we'd brought with us here to this oasis we now had to leave.

As I had only my rucksack and the bag Becka packed for me, I was done before Jihoon and headed downstairs to make sure we had tidied up as much as necessary before vacating, but once that distraction was over, I had to come to terms with the fact that our time was up.

Jihoon came downstairs just as the doorbell rang, startling me so much that he came over to ask if I was okay.

"Just on edge, I guess," I mumbled, hiding behind my hair as I looked down.

Jihoon gently pushed a lock of my hair behind my ear before nudging my chin up with his fingers and kissing me softly, but briefly.

Moving over to the door, he opened it to reveal the same driver that had been there that day we visited Santa Monica, five months ago.

He bowed to Jihoon, "Annyeonghaseyo, Baek Jihoon-nim," and turning to me he nodded his head and said, "Good morning, Kaiya-ssi."

I returned his polite greeting and, turning back to Jihoon, "Are you ready?" He nodded, and together we walked out the door to the black SUV waiting in the driveway.

At this time in the morning, it didn't take long to drive back to Glendale. Jihoon had assured me he'd factored this detour into the commute time to LAX for his red-eye, from which he was flying commercial – but still in first class, of course – back to Incheon airport.

We were silent the whole ride there, just quietly sitting with our thoughts, hands entwined, until we pulled up outside my apartment building.

I knew I wouldn't cry this time, I knew better what we were to each other and though the future remained as uncertain as it had back in the spring... well, I'd take what I could, for now.

I leaned towards Jihoon and kissed him softly, not wanting a long goodbye. I didn't want to act like this was the last time we'd see each other, so instead I pulled a smile onto my face and told him, "I'll see you soon."

"I'll call you when I land," he assured me, and I slid out of the car, clutching my backpacks to stand on the pavement and watch him drive away from me again.

Becka had been asleep when I got in, of course, it being not even 6:00am on a Sunday morning. I tiptoed in and debated going back to bed, but decided against it when I saw my laptop on the coffee table in the living area.

So, instead, I made a coffee, opened my laptop, and went online to read.

"Oh, fucking crap-on-a-cracker!"

"Well, good morning to you too," I smiled at Becka from over the rim of my mug. She had her hand pressed to her chest, dramatically leaning against her bedroom door post for support.

"When did you get home?" She pushed away from the door and stumbled into the kitchenette to pour herself a cup of coffee from the pot I'd brewed earlier. I looked at the clock on my laptop.

"Couple hours ago."

"I didn't expect to see you today," she said, taking a fortifying sip of coffee, "I thought you'd be sequestered in your love nest until at least tonight."

"Sequestered?" I rolled my eyes at her.

"It means-"

"I know what it means." I sighed. "Jihoon had to fly out early this morning, he dropped me off on the way to the airport."

Becka scrunched her nose. "That sucks, but at least you got to have this impromptu weekend together."

"No arguments here." I nodded and put my laptop back on the coffee table. "And hey – couldn't have done it without you," I said, turning round from my seat and pointing at her. "Number one secret-squirrel! How long were you keeping that from me?"

Becka chuckled and pushed off the counter, coming round to plop down on the sofa.

"Literally the night before. He called to tell me he was getting on a plane to come see you, and could I help him out?"

"How did he even get your number?" I wondered aloud.

"Hell if I know," she shrugged. "I dropped the phone when I realised who it was.

"Anyway, he asked me to make sure you had a change of clothes, and gave me the address for the Uber – which he paid for, by the way."

"The Uber?"

"Everything," Becka nodded, "the Uber, the clothes, everything."

"Wow," I murmured.

"Yeah, 'wow,'" Becka agreed. "Rich sonofabish."

After a moment of contemplative silence, Becka prodded me with one manicured nail.

"Ow!" I protested.

"Do I have to yank it out of you? Spill!"

"Which part?" I grumbled, rubbing my arm.

"Literally the whole fucking thing, what do you think?" Becka rolled her eyes.

I sighed a long-suffering sigh, but it only hid the gleeful smirk. So, I told her. I started at the beginning, how it had just been so stunning to see him I couldn't let him go, to frolicking in the swimming pool (the PG version), pizza and a movie, to sharing a bed that first night-

"Hold up, hold up, hold UP!" Becka held up a hand, halting me in my tracks.

"Did you," Becka glanced around theatrically, before holding her hand up to her mouth and stage whispering, "do the deed?"

"What?"

"You know, do the deed, the 'horizontal mambo,' 'bump uglies,' 'ride the bony pony.'

"For the love of all that is pure in this world, please stop," I choked out.

"The 'bony pony'? Good grief, Becka, have a word with yourself!" I covered my face with my hands as my shoulders heaved with embarrassed laughter.

"Okay, okay, calm down Prudence." Becka waved her hand dismissively. "But did you, though?"

"NO!" I cried out, trying very hard to be done with this conversation.

"Aw, come on!" Becka jumped up from the sofa, "did you even wear the lingerie I got you? That was good stuff!"

"Yes, because you neglected to put any normal pyjamas in my bag!"

"Well, either Jihoon is a complete saint, or he's blind, because those babydolls would have tempted an angel to fall off his fluffy cloud." Becka slumped back down onto the sofa, pouting.

I gave her a sideways glance before saying, "I didn't say they had no effect."

Becka jolted back upright as if a bolt of electricity had shocked her in the arse.

"Bish, don't you play with me!" she cried, pointing a finger at me, "I only just came round to this relationship. I deserve a pay off!"

I rolled my eyes. And then obliged her, but only with the very minimum of information, but seemingly enough that she grabbed my laptop and pretended to fan herself with it.

"Give that back here, you tech savage." I wrestled my laptop back from her, tucking it protectively under my arm. "This costs more than your annual Sephora spend."

"Pfft, it does not." And I silently conceded that point.

I was just stroking my closed laptop, when Becka suddenly shrieked, again pointing her finger at me, but this time her eyes were fixed on the hand comforting my laptop.

"Whatthefuckisthat?" she garbled at me.

"What?" I said innocently.

"Youfuckingknowwhat!"

"Use your big girl words," I crooned, standing up and taking my laptop with me – just in case. I walked towards my bedroom, but Becka jumped up and hounded my heels like a yappy dog, following me inside my room as I put my laptop safely on my bed.

Becka raised her hands in a placating manner and took a deep, sonorous breath in a visible effort to chill the eff out as I folded myself to sit on the bed.

"I'm only going to ask you this once," she said, still holding those hands up, but now looking more like the dog whisperer. "Are you, or are you not, engaged to the idol?"

I laughed. I laughed long, I laughed hard, and then I giggled, tears running down my face all the while Becka stood there, frozen like a supplicating statue.

"Babes," I got out in between giggles, "calm the fuck down. We've only known each other five months."

"You're wearing a ring!" she hissed at me.

"Yeah," I said in the same tone as one might say, 'duh,' "but it's a couple's ring. Don't you know anything about Korean culture?" The joke being, of course, I myself had not until Jihoon had told me.

"Bish," Becka said with forced calmness, "I will end you." Which only started another round of giggles.

"Yeah, yeah," I waved my hand at her dismissively. "So, apparently it really is a thing for Korean couples to give each other rings, kind of like promise rings, I guess?"

Becka put her hands on her hips, mulling over this information. "Does he have to wear one, too?"

"I don't think he *has* to do anything," I pushed back, "but he did get one for himself, yes,"

"Isn't that going to be a little... obvious to anyone who sees it then?" Becka frowned. She had a point, but I replied, a little uneasily.

"Well, I mean, he can take it off whenever he wants."

"Hmm." Becka quirked her lips, but otherwise kept her silence.

"Okay," I finally relented, "out, I'm going to have a nap, I'm hella tired.

Becka made a harrumphing noise as she turned and walked out the door, saying over her shoulder loud enough for me to hear, "I'd be tired too, if I'd had the task of pleasing an international superstar."

"Oh my god," I groaned, throwing a pillow at the door and slamming it closed.

Because I was feeling lazy, I hadn't bothered unpacking my bags immediately, which is why I hadn't found the strip of photos straight away.

Setting down the bikini I'd been about to put away, I picked up the two photos and looked at them, my eyes beginning to mist. Jihoon must have slipped these into my bag this morning when I wasn't looking. It was half of the strip – he must have kept the other two. The photos in my hand were the only physical pictures I had of us, and they felt like our rings: a quiet confirmation that we were real.

Carefully, I tucked them into the corner of my mirror, where I could see them whenever I wanted.

Suddenly remembering the other thing I'd stashed in my bag, I unzipped the side pocket and pulled out the card from Albert's tattoo package. I read over the note the curmudgeonly old man had written:

Kid – You and the pretty boy reminded me of these birds. Swallows fly thousands of miles every year, but sometimes, distance is just a measurement of space. If two people from two different places each fly thousands of miles to a new place and find each other... well, what the fuck do I know? They're just pretty birds.

I laughed, even as a tear slipped down my cheek.

Jihoon called me later on that night to say he'd arrived safely but was going into meetings and staging preparation for the whole rest of his day, because for him it was just after lunchtime on Monday.

I didn't think I'd ever be used to the vast time difference between us. With a sixteen-hour difference, it was like he was living in the future. It warped my mind to do the mental acrobatics every time.

The next time I spoke to Jihoon, it was Wednesday morning – my time – and he was just going to bed.

"What time is your flight?" I asked as I brushed my hair into a ponytail.

Jihoon rubbed a tired hand down his face, and I felt a twinge of guilt that he'd stayed up to speak to me when he probably should have gone to bed earlier.

"8:00am, the car is coming to get us at 4:00am." He yawned widely.

"Joon," I whined. "Go to bed, we can talk later."

"I will, I will," he nodded, "but I'll sleep on the plane anyway."

I'd already Googled how long the flight was from Incheon to Heathrow. A mere snip at fourteen hours.

I winced in sympathy. "At least London is only eight hours ahead of LA; you won't need to stay up so late to see me," I offered a shrug at such a small upside, but he nodded.

"That is a good thing, but it'll probably still be late. Our days are very busy."

GVibes was flying to London for the week to perform at the Hyde Park festival, and while there, they were also going to be appearing on Radio One's Live Lounge, filming two TV segments and a full episode of their Weverse show.

When he'd first told me he was going to be in the UK in September, I'd joked about how he could go meet my parents, and I don't think he'd realised I was joking, judging by the very serious, very uncool look on his face.

I just considered it a joke from the universe that only the second time that GVibes were performing in the UK, I'd be in another country. The first time, I'd just been too poor to go see them live at the O2 arena.

I'd actually considered flying back over to try and attend, but when I'd floated the idea of leave to Jeremy at work, he'd chuckled, patted me on the head and said, "Good joke, kid." I hadn't paid much attention to my internship contract when I'd signed it – too excited to be working in LA – but on closer inspection, I wasn't entitled to leave. So, there's that. I'd figured as much, but it sucked to confirm.

When Jihoon yawned again, I told him more firmly to go to bed, and this time he conceded.

"Yes, alright," he mumbled, before looking straight at the camera and saying, "I miss you, jagiya."

I felt the sappy smile, but went with it. "I miss you too." I couldn't seem to shake the feeling like there were words missing, but I pushed it aside.

"Send me a message before you're in the air, so I know how long to worry for."

He snorted and waved a hand. "Goodnight."

"Good morning." And one shared smile later, we hung up, and I went on with my day.

I was just finishing up for the day when I got the message from Jihoon to say they were about to take off. I wasn't religious, but I sent up a silent prayer anyway. It wasn't public information, but I hated flying. I'd had to dose myself up with Night Nurse before boarding the flight that brought me to LA from the UK, and that had only been about twelve hours.

I shook my head ruefully as I slid my phone back into my pocket. I didn't know how they did it, they seemed to spend dozens of hours every month in the air. I shuddered.

"Everything okay, Kaiya?" Jeremy paused mid-stride to frown at me.

"Yeah boss, just someone walking over my grave."

"Your who-now, what-now?" He gaped at me as if I'd just said I had peed myself.

"Y'know, that weird feeling when your whole body shivers for no reason?" I prompted.

"Is someone walking over your grave?" he said, doubtfully. "Is this an English thing?"

"I-I don't think so, but maybe?"

"Yeah, okay, whatever." He ran a hand over his face. "Listen, we got that band coming in tomorrow, and I already know they're gonna be a pain in the ass. Whatever you got pencilled in, cancel it."

"The Smoking Guns? Yeah, sure," I agreed easily, only planning on shadowing the tech team all day anyway. "What do you think you'll need me to do?"

He sighed, a long-suffering sigh that echoed of early retirement and neat whiskey. "If the last time is any indication, holding sick bags and reminding them this is a no-smoking building."

My eyebrows shot up. "You're kidding."

"The fuck I am," he grumbled, and turned to continue his journey down the corridor, before spinning around, pointing his finger at me and saying, "and for the love of god, do not let them near the fucking proc deck!"

"So, babysitter, then?" I called after him.

"You got it, kid!" He waved a hand over his shoulder, not turning back around.

"Just another day in LA." I muttered to myself.

Chapter 33

On Thursday, I woke up to a text from Jihoon, the time on it was stamped 2:00am, which – I did the maths in my head – 10:00am, London time.

Joon

> *Good morning beautiful. I love London, we have a few free hours today to sight see. Seokmin is making us go to the Wax museum lol. Later we're filming the One Show and then having dinner at the Shard, have you ever been?*

[sent 02:14]

'

The Hyde Park festival wasn't until tomorrow, so I guess today they were piling as much in as much fun as possible. That last bit made me laugh a bit though. The Shard is a massive, pointy skyscraper in central London, kind of like the Empire State building in New York, where you can pay to go all the way to the top and look out over London and yes, there were restaurants in the Shard, but they were way out of the price range of a humble student – now intern.

Me

Hey you! Now you're on my turf! I can't wait to see the pictures you take at Madame Tussauds – bring me a wax model as a souvenir! I'm definitely going to watch the One Show – I can watch it live at work! And no, I've never eaten at the Shard, but I bought a coffee from a street vendor outside it once, that counts! XD Have an amazing day! X

Jihoon's morning message put me in such a good mood, that later on at work, I didn't even mind when Donna at the front desk told me my shirt was inside out, which was actually really nice of her to let me know. Or when I stubbed my toe on a box of coffee pods, which I know I put away the day before.

The Smoking Guns weren't due in until after lunch, so when 10:50am rolled around, I took my happy butt down to the storage cave on the ground floor, which had become my unofficial hang out, and spooled up my VPN so I could watch the One Show on BBC iPlayer.

I was sat there, eating my sandwich, when the show started. I had to watch through the first half in nervous anticipation of being caught, because while I did get a lunch break, it was normally at noon, so there was every possibility someone would come looking for me. But luckily, I didn't seem to be on the top of anyone's priority, as I was left in peace. It wasn't until the final half of the show when they finally brought on GVibes.

As the group's leader, Minjae led them onto the stage, where they bowed before sitting on the sofa and the taller chairs behind.

"Welcome, welcome, give a big round of applause, all the way from Seoul, Korea, one of the hottest bands in the world right now, GVibes!" The presenter led the audience in a round of applause and cheers that went on for so long, the two presenters had to eventually call for order. Clearly some lucky Vibers were in the crowd today.

"Now, gentleman, would you care to introduce yourselves?"

This was a well-practiced routine that the group must have done thousands of times.

Minjae, as the leader, started by saying, "Hi, I'm Jae, nice to meet you."

Then Woojin, the main rapper of the group, "Hello, I'm Woojin, you can call me Jin."

Sungmin, second rapper and the group's best dancer got up, moonwalked across the stage, which made the audience scream and the group laugh, or put their faces in their hands. He sat back down, took the mic and said, "What's up London, you know I'm Lee, who are you?" I laughed – he was such a clown. Next up was Jihoon, who took the mic, looked right into the camera and said, "Hello, you. My name's Joon, good to see you." I fluttered my face with my hand, inexplicably feeling flushed from all of that stage presence turned on.

Lastly was Seokmin, the youngest member of the group – the 'maknae.' He took the mic and said to the audience, not the camera, "Hi everyone, I'm Ace, but you know that already." The cheeky maknae winked, which just about sent the crowd into apoplectic fits, by the sounds of it. They were screaming, and he just grinned. I shook my head. He knew exactly what he was doing, they all did. They were so good at this.

Once calm had been regained in the studio, the presenter led the group in a series of questions that, though pretty rote in nature, managed to come across as both interesting and up to date. Things like, 'what made you want to be a performer?' Vibers, being the answer, of course, leading to yet more screams.

'What's your favourite song to perform? – 'Pulse,' said Lee, 'Fall in Love' said Jae and Jihoon, the other members voted for 'Work Harder.'

"Who said 'Fall in Love?' Was it you, Jae and Joon?" The presenter leaned forward in his seat, all eagerness to pin that word on someone. Jihoon and Minjae gamely smiled and raised their hands.

"Now, it's interesting that you say that, because idols in Korea are famous – internationally speaking – for not being allowed to date." He turned to the camera. "Many idols have so-called 'dating bans' written into their contracts." He turned back to the members. "Jae, perhaps you can answer for the British public here; does GVibes have a dating ban in their contract?"

The audience predictably screamed, and Jae looked over into what I imagined was a crowd of mostly young women, and smiled before answering.

"No, Patrick, we do not." The audience lost it's ever-loving mind over this good news, and the members laughed. I wasn't surprised at the short answer, since while it wasn't a secret that ENT – their company – did apply dating bans for fledging idols, it wasn't a popular policy, especially outside of Korea. And, since they'd renegotiated their contract last year without the ban, the answer was technically correct. Plus, it implied the members were on the market, which I supposed was good fan service.

"Wow, okay, clearly some people happy to hear that!" The presenter waved his prompt cards in the audience's direction. "But tell me, was the song written about someone? An inspiration, perhaps? I think we'd all be interested to know what kind of person could capture the interest of a KPop idol."

For some reason, Seokmin, 'Ace,' laughed, but it was Jihoon who answered this time, giving me an irrational sense of trepidation.

"We all have people in our lives that we love, Patrick. We love our friends, our family, and of course, we love Vibers. Love is love." All the group nodded and Sungmin clapped Jihoon on the back from where he sat behind him.

As he was pushed forward by Sungmin, I noticed the chain he wore around his neck. It was a plain looking silver chain, but it had a recognisable, but equally plain silver ring strung on it. I had already noticed he wasn't wearing his ring on his finger, but then I hadn't expected him to. It was too recognisable of a symbol, even outside of Korea. But to see that he had it and was wearing it after all... it did things to me. Soft, warm things.

"Well, who can argue with that?" The presenter replied gamely, clearly knowing he wasn't going to get a less than diplomatic answer from the group.

"And now, without further ado, here they are to perform their latest single, having recently swept several awards for it, please put your hands together again for GVibes with 'Work Harder'!"

The camera panned away from the interview couch and over to a raised platform where the members now stood in formation, before the backing track cued and as one, they began their complicated choreography.

The audience had started up a well-known fan chant, while others just screamed. I couldn't blame them; the group were enrapturing to behold.

The fans screaming continued for so long after the end of the song, that the presenter gave up trying to calm them down. In the background, the members still on the stage could be seen blowing kisses, finger hearts, waving, clearly just playing up to the crowd and I laughed as Jihoon gave a piggyback to Seokmin, running around the stage like kids.

The presenter had to shout to be heard. "If you'd like to see more of the incredibly talented, obviously well-loved GVibes, you can watch their live set at Hyde Park festival on BBC iPlayer, or listen in live on BBC radio 2, this Friday. Thank you, goodnight!"

The camera panned out over the audience to show the many, many dozens of screaming fans, so many light sticks and signs, all saying variations of 'I love U.' I smiled to see the love and support they had; it was all so well deserved.

But, real life beckoned, so I shoved my sandwich box back into my bag and closed iPlayer and signed out of my VPN. Time to go back to work.

"Is that them?" Becka leaned on the wall near to me, both of us looking towards the massive entourage huddled in the middle of the lobby. Becka had come down to speak to Donna, and had found me creeping back out of the storage cave, just as the revolving doors had opened, admitting a huge group of people, some of which were now arguing with Donna. I didn't fancy their chances, personally.

"Yup," I sighed, equally as fascinated by the scene. A handful of very rough looking men were huddled in the centre of the roving mass of people, who I guessed were the band.

"What's their problem?" Becka actually stamped her foot, a rare break in her professional composure.

"They're booked in. We've acquiesced to pretty much everything they wanted. What could possibly be the matter?"

"Hell if I know," I shrugged, "I just work here."

Becka snorted.

"Oh, thank god," she suddenly grabbed my arm and pointed towards the elevator, from which Celine was just stepping off.

"No one kisses ass like Celine." Becka sighed as she slumped back against the wall.

"It's a real talent." I nodded.

But our observation of the group was cut short as Celine spotted us, and pointed at me before crooking her finger at me.

"Better go before she releases her flying monkeys."

I hunched my shoulders and rasped, "Yes Master, coming Master." I heard Becka snorting behind me, but I carried on over to Celine, walking normally.

"This is Kaiya, she'll be shadowing you today to ensure all your needs are met." Celine's smile was sickly sweet as she stared at a short, balding man wearing a leather jacket over a serious pair of dad jeans.

"Hi," I smiled.

Dad jeans gave me a slow once-over before he landed back on my face and treated me to a sneer that I was pretty sure he intended as a compliment.

"Well then, darlin,' lead the way."

From that moment on, it went steadily more downhill in various different ways. The band themselves were a modest five-man band comprising of lead and bass guitarist, drummer and two singers, a pretty standard setup. But for some reason, they'd brought not only their manager, but also their publicist, stylist, financial adviser, three bodyguards, their girlfriends and inexplicably, a person dubbed their 'wellbeing officer,' who as far as I could tell was in charge of dispensing little drops of something from a brown bottle under the band member's tongues once an hour.

I'd had to insist to the manager that only the actual band and himself could be in the room, other members of the entourage had to wait upstairs in the hospitality areas. I'd had some pushback on that, but once the producer had threatened to cancel their booking, they'd reluctantly complied.

Thankfully, at least it wasn't Trevor Kyle working with the band.

The vocals actually went okay, but when it came to recording parts of the band's backing track, the lead guitarist was nowhere to be found. A building-wide search was initiated – and by that, I mean that I was ordered to search the whole damn building on my own – which was when I found him upstairs in the lounge, completely unconscious in the lap of one of the girlfriends. I was still unsure if it was *his* girlfriend, but honestly, they all kind of looked the same.

The 'wellbeing officer' at least had the grace to look embarrassed when he told me the guitarist wasn't likely to wake up anytime soon, due to an overindulgence in 'herbal remedies.'

It was with this information that I stormed into Jeremy's office.

"Boss, there's a passed-out guitarist in the lounge and the manager won't stop calling me 'babycakes.' I need a personal day."

He didn't even bother to look up from his computer screen, but he did sigh to let me know he was listening.

"Do we need to call an ambulance?"

"Not according to his 'wellbeing officer.'"

That did get Jeremy to glance up, and frowning he asked, "His what now?"

I opened my mouth-

"Never mind, I don't care." He put his head down on his desk, and I winced at the thump.

"Look, just... goddamn bands." Another thump. "You play guitar, right?"

"I-er, what?" I asked, stupidly.

Jeremy pulled his head off the desk to stare at me, the stare of a man who has truly had enough of these goddamn bands.

"I mean, yes?" I said, cautiously.

"Good. Go offer to play for them."

"Boss... Shouldn't we ask tech?"

He snorted. "Good luck. They're downstairs with the orchestra doing the soundtrack for that new movie with the things in that place with the..." He waved his hand around vaguely.

"I guess I can offer..."

"That's the spirit! Go get 'em, girl."

I'd lost him, he was already eyeballing his screen as if it held the lotto numbers necessary to buying his ticket out of this place.

"And that, my friend, is how I ended up playing the guitar on three tracks of Smoking Guns' newest album, available in all good stores, this winter."

Becka howled as I finished up the story of my shitty day, culminating in the bassist giving me his number in front of his girlfriend, who it transpired had been the girl the lead guitarist had been using as a pillow. Messy, messy, messy.

"Truly, my friend, your life has been raised up to the stuff of legends in the few short months you've lived in LA. It's the dream!" Becka declared, waving a beer in salute at me.

"Yeah, yeah," I grumbled. "Truly the stuff of dreams."

Chapter 34

I didn't get to talk to Jihoon on Thursday; by the time I got home on Wednesday it was well after 2:00am London time, and on Thursday when I'd woken up, he was already out in London filming for Weverse, but I had sent him a message to tell him how much I'd enjoyed their performance on the One Show and how much I'd liked his necklace. He'd responded with a selfie of himself sitting on a park bench, surrounded by a leafy plant. He was holding his fingers up to his face in a 'V', the band of braided silver clearly visible on his finger.

Joon

> *We get to go into the city today to film for Weverse and I know exactly where I'm going, I hope you'll enjoy it*

[Sent 07:43]

Very mysterious. I knew that each of the members was out filming their own separate episode. He'd told me Minjae was going to the National Science Museum, because he'd tried to persuade Jihoon to go with him, but I didn't know which landmark the other members – or Jihoon – had chosen.

I'd thought we might have more opportunities to talk – with London and LA only eight hours apart – but the opposite had proven to be true, as again when I'd gotten home from work, it was in the small hours for him.

Friday had rolled around and today was the day GVibes was playing the Hyde Park Festival. They were headlining and were due to go on stage at 8:00pm UK time, which was noon LA time. It was a two-hour set though, so I couldn't get away with hiding in the storage cave again, but I had already planned ahead for this.

I'd strategically sneezed and coughed in Jeremy's presence all day on Thursday, to the point where he'd even ordered me to leave his office, lest I "fling my germs around like candy at a Macy's Day Parade."

So, it wouldn't have been a big surprise to him when, at 7:00am, I called in sick. I'd felt a twinge of nervous guilt leaving the message. So far, of the three times I'd called in sick to work, two of them had been fake and due to me wanting to spend time with Jihoon – even if it was over an Internet connection this time.

"Did he pick up?" Becka yawned as she moved past me into the kitchenette to get a cup of coffee from the pot I'd just brewed.

"No." I sighed.

"What's the problem, then?" Becka frowned at me.

"I guess I just don't like lying," I said honestly. "He may be the Oscar Grouch of the company, but he's a solid boss."

Becka waved it away. "It's not like there's anything on today."

"Yeah, I know, I guess I just feel like one of 'those' girls."

Becka gave me a weird look over the rim of her mug. "What girls?"

"You know," I said, flopping back onto the sofa, "those girls who suddenly drop everything in their life when they get a..." I hesitated over the word, but Becka helpfully supplied it for me.

"A boyfriend?"

"Yeah, one of those."

"Babes, I don't think three sick days in six months counts. Besides, you don't get leave, paid sick days are basically your leave. Take 'em."

She had me there. I hadn't believed it when Becka told me that some companies in the US treated sick leave as vacation days, like, you could bank them, or use them all up in one year. Bizarre. Back home, we just took them if we were really ill. Or wanted to stay home to watch our famous boyfriends perform in international music festivals. No big deal.

"Yeah, I guess."

Becka hesitated, chewing on her lip.

"Spit it out, Becka." I sighed, already feeling a thrum in my head.

"Look, I'm no one to judge a girl for a personal day." That was a good thing, considering the last sick day she'd taken, she'd spent recuperating in the nail salon.

"I just sometimes think you're maybe not fully embracing your life here."

I blinked at her.

"Hear me out," Becka began again. "I know interning isn't the most satisfying thing you could be doing. I get that. But... in the scheme of things, interning at Pisces is kind of a big deal. And I just think that maybe you've forgotten that. In light of recent events."

Every word she spoke sounded painful, like she was chewing glass just to get it out.

"Anyway, I'm going to get dressed. Some of us are actually going into work today."

She turned to head to her bedroom before I could even open my mouth. Not that I had a response. Her words lay heavily on me, covering me with guilt and discontent. I promised myself I'd examine her words... just not right now.

I reached for my laptop. I'd started a blog recently, just little entries about my life in LA, the music scene in general, bands I liked, that sort of thing. Barely anyone read it, just a few of the followers I'd amassed over the past couple of years, but it was kind of cathartic for me to interact with music in this way. Being at Pisces was... well, it wasn't quite the experience I'd naively expected in many ways, even as it exceeded them in others.

I'd tried talking to Becka about this – how my experiences had changed my thoughts about my future career. She'd seemed alarmed at my change of heart, so I'd downplayed it since then. Perhaps not as much as I'd thought, judging by that speech a few minutes ago.

In some ways, I was glad for the reality check, but in others, I mourned. For years, I'd believed I would go into some form of music production. I'd worked toward it, studied for it. Hell, I'd dedicated years of my life to building the skills I'd need. And honestly, I'd built a pretty decent following on social media because of it – not that I'd spent much time cultivating that lately.

I grieved the life I thought I was going to have. Recently, whole days passed where I couldn't shake the funk of disappointment and disillusionment.

At the same time, I was grateful I'd figured out so early that this wasn't the career I wanted anymore. I'd thought about it a lot, and, to quote Marie Kondo: it didn't spark joy.

At first, I'd chalked it up to seeing the unglamorous side of studio life. But after working with producers – rarely, but enough – I realized it just... didn't spark anything in me, let alone joy.

I'd gone over it in my head dozens of times, trying to figure out why I'd enjoyed it so much at university. The only conclusion I came to was this: learning about something and actually doing it are two very different things. I still loved learning about the process – how music came together behind the scenes was beautiful. But the actual mechanics of it? No. It wasn't for me.

And all it took to figure that out was seven months of interning at one of the most famous record studios in the U.S.

So, while I was grateful to know what I *didn't* want to do, I was no clearer on what I *did*.

Becka left by 8:00am, leaving me by myself. I whiled away the morning with my blog, eating a breakfast of granola and berries, showering, and plucking away at my guitar, and then my eyebrows. I felt restless, and the more I tried not to think about it, the more my mind tried shoving to the forefront the idea that I was pausing my life in pursuit of... what? Watching my boyfriend on TV? Not being able to be there, not even being able to see him regularly, and certainly not being able to publicly be with him.

Though I told my brain not to, it stubbornly posed the question of, 'What can this ever be, and do I want it?' It was a nothing-burger question; borne out of restless energy and frustration, I knew, but there it was; a niggle in the back of my mind like an ever-present headache I couldn't seem to shift.

Thankfully, the time was approaching where I would be able to see Jihoon. Albeit, on TV. I'd already connected the Smart TV to my

VPN so I could access iPlayer. I was armed with a bowl of popcorn and a healthy sense of entitlement – as a fully paid annual TV licence holder and British Citizen, I felt no guilt at streaming the 'beeb' from outside of the UK.

The view on the TV panned away from the crowd just as the live band on stage started an extended introduction to one of their most popular hits, 'Pulse.' The massive screens surrounding the stage began to flash with images and flashing colours, designed to whip the crowd up into a frenzy. It went on for several minutes, until a line of smoke machines suddenly expelled, shrouding the stage in grey mist. The band stopped playing for so long that the screams of the crowd began to die down, until the smoke cleared and white spot lights shot up into the sky, illuminating the stories-tall shadows of five people standing on the stage. The crowd lost its ever-loving mind.

The band began to play again, the first refrain of 'Pulse' pounded out and the members began to move around the stage as they sung. Not the normal, smooth choreography of music shows and music videos, no, this was pure performance, designed to involve the crowds. The stage had been designed with a long walkway that reached out into the crowd, so the members could run up and down it, getting closer to the thousands of screaming fans. And as they moved seamlessly from one song to the next, I could see how much they seemed to enjoy the performance. In between their iconic dance breaks, they were playing with each other, and the crowd; catching gigantic beach balls thrown on stage by someone in the audience and chucking them back, spraying water from their bottles into the hot crowd, pointing at signs, waving, even taking the phones of some fans and filming themselves before handing them back. Just general chaos, and I laughed regularly.

It was amazing though, because like most KPop bands, GVibes never lip synced when they did live performances, so not only were they singing with live mics whilst running around being chaotic, they were still hitting their choreography when they were dancing. The stamina was eye-watering. It made me think I should probably get a membership to the Planet Fitness that was down the street.

The energy of the two-hour performance never faltered, though the members were visibly panting and sweating, and by the end, once night had fallen in London, they performed 'Work Harder,' the most complicated choreography of the evening. It was clear this was the one where they wanted to leave the strongest impression. Woojin bounced as he rapped, eyes clenched shut and the crowd responded in kind by jumping and waving their arms, fully there with him. When the pyrotechnics all went off at the end, bathing the night in showers of purple, red, and green, the crowd screamed one, long refrain that went on for so long that GVibes had already started to file off the stage, after running back a few times to throw more finger-hearts and shouting 'We love you, London!".

The stream ended and it felt like my small living room echoed with the sounds of the concert. It was weird to see sunlight bathing the room in warm light. I was half-expecting to see the smoke-filled night of London streaming in through the windows. For some reason, seeing my side of the world all lit up after being completely immersed in the ever-darkening side he was in, made me feel... empty.

Out of place. Like my whole life was a world apart from where it should be. I pushed the feeling down, to join the other thoughts I wasn't allowing myself to think about these days.

I immediately reached for my phone to send Jihoon a message to say I'd watched the whole concert and how amazing they'd been.

I kept waiting to hear back from him, even if it took a while, but I didn't hear from him the whole rest of that day.

The next Friday was the Chuseok festival in Korea and GVibes was taking the whole week off once they flew back from the UK. I'd spoken to Jihoon briefly the day after Hyde Park, but between the time difference and appearing on Radio One's Live Lounge, it had only been during the fifteen-minute car ride from the BBC Maida Vale Studios to the restaurant they were having dinner at. It hadn't been as much of a conversation as I would have liked, but I did get to wave at Woojin during the video call, which was cool.

I'd asked Jihoon to tell him how cool he'd looked during the rap for 'Work Harder,' but Jihoon had jokingly frowned at me and said I wasn't allowed to compliment other men. I'd laughed and Jihoon had passed on my message anyway, which made Woojin look over Jihoon's shoulder and show me a finger-heart, which in turn made Jihoon shove Woojin.

I hadn't spoken to him since he'd flown back to Korea two days ago, apart from exchanging selfies – him at the airport, wearing a pillow around his neck and a satin eye mask pushing the hair out of his face, and me in my snoopy pyjamas, sitting in bed.

He'd warned me in advance that he wouldn't be able to talk much during Chuseok because most of his extended family were flying to Busan, where his parents had moved back to, and he would be expected to spend most of his time with them.

While I did feel a little melancholy about not speaking to Jihoon, I actually felt mostly homesick. It was a year now since my graduation and my life was almost unrecognisable. I'd gone from that dingy, little bedsit above the corner shop in Clapham, writing my dissertation, going to lectures and studio time during the day and bar-tending during the nights, to living in LA with my best mate, working for one of the most famous studios in the country – albeit as a glorified fetch-and-carry peon – and I was secretly dating a member of one of the world's hottest bands.

Who even was I right now? The question sounded jokey in my head, but as I sat on my bed one evening after work, it pulled me up short when I couldn't immediately answer it.

When I'd been at university, the question of what I did in the 'after' time, seemed vague, but meaningful. Sure, I hadn't known *what* I would do, but I knew it would be *something*.

I'd write music, or I'd go on tour with a band and do their sound tech, or I'd move back in with mum and dad and write about music from my bedroom.

I wasn't sure what I was doing anymore, and it brought back that feeling of being in limbo that kept creeping in from the corners of my mind.

I felt like I was on standby. It was hard to explain, even to myself. My life was taking place in the gaps in between people and events, and I'd started to wonder when it was going to be my turn to be the main character in my own life.

Chapter 35

The new album, *Tracks of Transition*, was set to release the week after Chuseok, just in time for the group to perform at the Incheon Music Festival. It was one of their last big engagements of the year.

The frenzy leading up to it meant that our video or voice chats were brief – always stolen snippets of time. He was either on his way somewhere or just coming back, and he was always tired.

He did send me lots of selfies, though; a veritable feast of fashion and staging pictures from the group's 'look book,' wherein all the members cycled through dozens of different outfits and staging set ups to be used in the album's visual art, photo cards and other merchandise.

I joked one morning by asking if he could get me Woojin's photo cards, and it led to an entire day of pouting selfies. Photo in the changing room? Pout. In the bus? Pouting. Posing with the other members? Pouting. I'd laughed all day at those, especially as I'd sent him the most aegyo-sickly sweet poses back.

It felt like we were doing the most to stay emotionally connected to each other and to stay present, without being present. Aside from regularly calling me 'jagiya' and exchanges of 'x's, it felt more like a penpalship, and it crossed my mind on more than one occasion that perhaps that's what was happening between us.

Maybe I was expecting too much.

"Long distance relationships are hard." Becka had lamented, when I'd confessed how I'd been feeling recently.

"I'd forgotten that you'd understand that," I confessed with a guilty wince. Now that I thought about it, I remembered that she'd been in a relationship with Ben when she'd moved to London for a year during university. He'd stayed in California and they'd somehow made it work.

"You've been preoccupied," she shrugged, giving me far more grace than I deserved.

"How did you do it?" I was hesitant to ask, given how the subject of Ben was still a sore one, but she considered the question for a moment before she answered it.

"Truthfully, I'm not sure. Going in, we both acknowledged it was going to suck. Our relationship was still so new at that point, like yours," she waved her mug at me. "But we were both so adamant we would make it work.

"I think that's the thing that made all the difference, on reflection." She said, nodding with a conviction I envied. "Relationships are a conscious choice and at that time, we both chose the other, and we made that same choice every day we were apart.

"You didn't question it?"

"Oh, I questioned it plenty." Becka chuckled, but it was a hollow sound. I patted her hand and she shot me a small smile.

"But you know what's crazy?" she asked, and I shook my head.

"I wouldn't change it. Even now, even after... even after everything," she swallowed. "I think it made me learn what I would be willing to do. You know, for someone I loved. Even if they didn't deserve it." After that, we'd each lapsed into silence, each thinking, one of the past, one the future.

The Incheon KPop festival was a two-day event, but GVibes was only performing a mini-set on one of the days. It had fallen on a Saturday, which meant I didn't get to watch it before Sunday, and since there weren't any official streams, I had to look around for decent fan-cam footage of it. It wasn't that hard to find, not since I'd joined some on-line communities for purposes just like this.

It made me feel weird to be lurking in those groups, not because I was dating Jihoon, but because of the things some of the fans discussed in them. Largely, it was all supportive and centred around streaming numbers and posting memes about them – I especially enjoyed the memes – but sometimes the fans posted thirst traps of the members, or had entire threads about which of the guys were in a relationship, or even speculating who in the group was dating who. The popular 'ships' seemed to be either Woojin and Seokmin, or Jihoon and Seokmin; no one could seem to agree.

It felt pretty gross to see these completely open discussions about if the members were gay, dating each other, or dating other idols. There was a very real feeling of ownership in these kinds of conversations. Some of it was pretty harmless, but some of it was pretty intense.

The worst, though, were the threads from people threatening violence on anyone outside of the group who was rumoured to be dating one of them.

There had been a stylist of the band who had been photographed standing next to Minjae backstage a couple years ago, and even though it had been her literal job to be there, waves of 'netizens' had hunted her down and found out her name and harassed her so badly that she'd left the entire company. Well, rumour had it that she'd been fired, which was perhaps even more frightening. I would prefer to think any company would support one of their employees in the face of such vitriol. But either way, the rumours died down.

Ever since then, the company blurred out the faces of all of the staff members, if they happened to catch them on film while taping the group.

In the 'before Jihoon' time, I'd known how toxic fandoms could be. It wasn't exclusive to KPop by any stretch of the imagination, but it seemed somehow more amplified. There was a sense of ownership that I couldn't understand. It went beyond hero-worship. But luckily, for all the toxic fans who took it too far, there were whole legions of other fans who were quick to shut it down, who loudly insisted that they were grown men and they could date, or not date and it wouldn't be anyone's business but their own. Those were the posts I took courage from.

It wasn't a surprise that most of the footage I was able to find of the festival was of the individual members, what was referred to as 'solo stan fan-cams.' I watched some of the Jihoon footage before someone finally shared a compilation of footage. Honestly, some fans do the absolute most and are the unsung heroes.

It was Sunday evening by this time, so I dragged Becka into the lounge to watch it with me.

"It's not long," I cajoled, pulling her down onto the sofa with me.

She sighed, but sat down with me gamely, and together we watched the set. I had to credit the fan; she'd done a great job of compiling the various camera angles to form a pretty cohesive one-take.

"They're just all so pretty," Becka said for the third time.

"I know, right?"

"Who's that, and why do they keep cutting to them?" Becka asked as the view once again cut back to a view of the audience where a group of three or four girls were clearly watching the show. They were all super pretty, even under the caps and layered clothes they wore. They must have enjoyed the performance, because they were giggling and pointing excitedly at the stage, just like I would have been. Something about them did look familiar though.

"I don't know," I said, frowning. "Let me look at the comments."

"Already doing it," Becka said, taking a long sip from her massive drink bottle while flipping irreverently through her phone.

"Who's Lee Hyejin?" She wrinkled her nose.

I thought for a moment, trying to remember why the name sounded so familiar, until finally, I offered a silent apology to GVibes and Jihoon and pulled out my own phone, quickly tapping in the name. Immediately my screen was covered in pictures of a group I was aware of, but not familiar with.

"Ah," I said, nodding my head, "she – and I'd guess the other girls – are members of a girl group also under ENT, PrettyYOUngthings." I scrolled for a few moments more, reading the relevant information. "She's the group's maknae. She's the lead dancer and rapper, apparently."

"Good for her," Becka garbled through a mouth full of ice.

Just then, I saw a thread that paused me like a tape deck. I hovered my thumb over it, giving myself the option of not opening that can of worms, but almost compulsively, I pressed down and watched as the page loaded.

First a picture of Lee Hyejin, a woman so blessed with good looks it was difficult to look away, and then to a picture of Jihoon, a still from one of his on-stage performances. He had his head thrown back with his eyes closed as sweat glistened on his skin. It was an undeniably sexy photo, and in this context, an undeniable implication.

Chapter 36

'ARE BAEK JIHOON AND LEE HYEJIN DATING?'

The headline was as subtle as a brick to the face, so I had to hand it to the author for grabbing a reader's attention.

Rumours are once again flying around the internet after eagle-eyed fans attending this weekend's Incheon KPOP music festival spotted none-other than Lee Hyejin of Pretty YOUng Things in the crowd. Her disguise was not enough to hide her beauty, and even less so her obvious enthusiasm at Baek Jihoon's solos during GVibes' performance.

No official statement has been released by either group, or their shared management company, ENT. Let's not forget though, fellow netizens, this is not the first time this pair have faced speculation over their romantic relationship! Both GVibes and PYT were trainees at ENT before their debuts and have been spotted in the crowds for each other's performances. Given this most recent spotting, Vibers and Beautys are left to wonder: is this more than the simple friendship between two company members?

I couldn't stop reading the article, although I wanted to. It was like prodding a cold-sore with your tongue; you knew it would heal faster if you just left it the hell alone. I just couldn't seem to.

"Girl, just call him," Becka waved her hand at me dismissively.

"I can't," I whined. "It's mid-morning on a Monday, he'll be doing stuff."

Becka rolled her eyes at me. "Call him. If he doesn't pick up, he doesn't, but give the guy a chance."

"Wow, you've come a long way from being suspicious of everything about him." I observed.

"Yeah, well, that wasn't getting me anywhere, and he seemed like a decent enough guy, so I changed my mind." She shrugged. "Which is why I'm telling you to call him now, instead of stewing in the gossip of people who don't know him."

I nodded. She had a fair point. I got up from the sofa and walked towards my room, pulling up Jihoon's number on Kakaotalk and then anxiously listening as the call went through.

"Kaiya." The sound of his voice made my knees weak, and I shakily sat down on the edge of the bed.

"Is everything alright?" he asked when I didn't say anything.

"Yeah, um. Are you busy?" I immediately felt stupid for calling over a rumour.

"No, just surprised. Are you sure you're okay? You sound different."

I tried to pep myself up, but the more I thought about asking him about a dating rumour, the sillier I felt.

"Yeah, you know what? I just called to tell you I watched the Incheon festival just now."

"Oh, you did? How did you like it?"

"You guys did a great job. I'm just sorry I had to watch it on a TV screen and not in real life." I could see Becka through my open door, miming, 'ask him,' with big, expansive hand gestures. I kicked the door shut and flopped back down on the bed.

Jihoon chuckled, "Next year we tour North America, you'll see us then."

We'd spoken about this just after he was back in Seoul after Chuseok; the group was going on a world tour next year, kicking off in April in Korea and then other countries in Asia, before heading to Europe, South and Central America and lastly, North America. There were currently 67 dates booked over nine months.

I wasn't sure what was going to happen next year. My contract with Pisces was up in April. I'd either have to fly home to the UK, or try to find a job in LA and get a work permit. I already knew Pisces wasn't going to renew my contract.

While there was a lot of online speculation about GVibes going on tour, they weren't going to officially announce it until November, after they released the next single off the new album; a collaboration they were going to be doing with American singer, Kylie Morrison.

"I hope I get to see you before then," I said quietly.

"Are you sure you're okay?" Just then, I heard someone in the background calling his name, and the person sounded impatient.

Jihoon sighed, "I'm sorry Ky, but I have to go. Speak to you later?"

"Sure."

"Okay," he hesitated. "Jagiya?"

"Yeah?"

"I'm glad you called. Bye." As the line went dead, I had to decide if I wanted to think about these mixed emotions, or put them back in the box I'd created for them, and kick the can down the road.

I chose the can.

Chapter 37

Time seemed to be flashing past now, a blur of days and weeks made relevant by whatever event it was that GVibes was doing at that time. I'd started to feel like a ghost, drifting through my own life, holding on to some unfinished business just out of reach, promising some kind of fulfilment.

Becka had banned me from spending any time in the fan groups online. She said it was bad for my mental health and honestly, I couldn't argue that point. It was like falling down Alice's rabbit hole, every other post was some kind of perceived drama. I never commented on a single one, but for every post I read, I couldn't help but construct a reply in my head. It sometimes got to be like a constant mental narrative, an argument with imagined opponents. Honestly, I was exhausted.

"Enough!" Becka cried one Saturday morning in early October as we were sat in the kitchenette. My spoon clanged against my bowl of Wheebles as I looked up at her in surprise.

"The eff is your problem?" I mumbled through a mouthful of artificial sweeteners masquerading as a nutritious breakfast cereal.

"I asked you three times if you wanted to come with me to the exhibition, and it's like you're not even here. You've not been here for weeks, Kaiya."

I looked at her, shocked to see the way her chin trembled, her eyes that shade of red just before tears spilled out.

"Becka, I'm sorry, I didn't mean to ignore you," I stammered, "we can go, if you want."

"It's not about the fucking exhibition!" She pushed away from the counter and dumped her bowl into the sink so roughly I wouldn't have been surprised if the ceramic was cracked.

"It's about you." She spun on her heel and pointed at me. "It's about who you are these days. Do you even know?"

"What are you talking about?" I dropped my spoon into the bowl, appetite gone.

"I mean," she began, and I could see she was working with a whole head of steam; I braced myself. "When was the last time your entire day was just about you?"

"Eh?" I wasn't sure what I'd been expecting, but it hadn't been that.

"When was the last time you went through a whole day doing what you wanted, when and why you wanted?"

"Literally every day." It felt like my whole face had scrunched in confusion. "I go to work because I choose to, in clothes I like, I eat what I want, I watch what I want, I listen to what I want, I talk to who I want."

"But you don't!" Becka is really impassioned now, her arms flung out wide, as if to bring the whole world into our conversation.

"You wake up and speak to Jihoon, you go to work, but do you even want to anymore? I sure as shit can't remember the last time you actually enjoyed it–"

I opened my mouth to cut her off–

"And don't say it's because it's boring," she waves a stiletto nail at me, threateningly. "You played backup guitar on an album currently charting on Billboard, and you've mentioned it once! Last week THE Sherry Taylor asked you to go to lunch with her! She has three Grammys! It's not. That. Fucking. Boring!"

"What do you want me to say?" I cried, trying to push my point across through the volume of my words. "You want me to be impressed by the constant stream of celebrities? You're upset that I'm not more interested in a job that's 90% grunt work?"

"No!" Becka is shouting by this point, splotches of red across her cheeks as if she's been slapped.

"I want you to remember why you came here in the first place! I want you to wake up, and realise that what you have here, the comical intern role is what you wanted. Your funny year-long side step for experience and a good time. I want you to remember that you WANTED this."

I spluttered, baffled and angry but hardly knowing why.

"I'm allowed to get bored!"

"But it's not just that, Kaiya. You're not you anymore, you're an intern in your own fucking life!"

She might as well have punched me in the face, and I recoiled as though she had, rocking back on the stool and having to stand up in case I fell.

"What's the play here, Becka? Hmm?" I was starting to feel light-headed, a tingle that started in my fingers was now steadily working its way up my arms. "Just say whatever you're beating around the bush about and tell me what you expect to get out of this. Because, from where I'm standing, my best friend is yelling at me because I'm not excited all the time."

To my surprise, instead of yelling, Becka burst into tears. She turned away from me, her shoulders heaving as she tried to take big, gulping breaths of air to calm herself down. Eventually, once she'd settled, she turned back to me, her face streaked with tears, but her eyes still blazed. Fire trapped behind glass. Despite the gulf between us, I couldn't help but want to close the space that kept us apart.

"You don't see what I see." Her voice wavered, but she persisted. "You don't see how small you're making yourself."

I frowned.

"But I do. I see how you fold in on yourself to accommodate him and his life. Your whole life has become about him, Kaiya. Everything you do, everything you plan, or don't plan. Everything you want for yourself is based on him. You've stopped making plans for yourself."

There was a buzz in my head, a persistent, but dull vibration behind my eyes. I had an overwhelming urge to defend myself against the accusation, but when I went to open my mouth, the words died on my tongue, the stunning realisation that I couldn't disagree.

Wordlessly, I sat back down at the counter, looking up at Becka, seeing the way she'd wrapped her arms around herself, as if expecting me to lash out, but all the energy had been sapped out of me.

After several moments, Becka sighed and moved back over to the counter, leaning her elbows on it.

"Look, I'm not telling you to break up with him." It sounded very much like she was suggesting it though.

"I just need you to understand that you're just as important as him. Your life matters. What *you* need matters." She reached across the counter and clasped my hand, squeezing it tightly.

"I do hear you, and I won't sit here and pretend like I don't know what you're talking about." I chewed on my lip, trying to think about what I was trying to say. "Perhaps I've been going about this the wrong way. I've been so preoccupied with trying to fit myself around his life, that maybe I have made that my priority.

"I don't know what I'm doing," I laughed, but there was no humour to it.

"I don't know when it stopped being about us, and started being about him and the group, but sometimes I don't feel any different than those hardcore fans that spend their entire lives following their every movement."

Becka nodded along, her face more open and expressive now. I could see I was starting to make sense to her again. The funny thing was, the more I said, the more it was making sense to me as well.

"When we're together, and it's not about the band or their schedules, it's good. It makes sense."

Becka hummed, looking away as she tapped her fingers on the counter-top, agitation clear in the sharp staccato of her fingernails on the stone top.

"The thing is, babes," she eventually said, "you're hardly together. No, listen," she grabs at my hand as I'd been about to pull away.

"Listen to me, I'm not criticising you. You need to hear this, because it's the truth. You are hardly together. You barely know each other, even you must agree that's true."

I didn't disagree, if anything.

"What's the end goal here? You're here, he's there. He can't openly be with you, or if he does – let's say that happens – are you prepared to deal with what that looks like?"

The truth was, I didn't have an answer. I'd seen the fallout from when two idols were found out to be dating, and it often wasn't pretty, to say nothing of someone... ordinary.

"I don't know," I answered honestly. "I don't have answers, or a plan. All I know is how much I feel for him, and even that scares me, because it feels too much. I know this isn't normal, I know that. I know I don't fit into his world, but I also know I don't want to not try to make this work."

Becka hung her head, her shoulders slumped forward as she took several deep breaths.

"I get it, babes, I do. And I'm not going to try and persuade you otherwise. But this isn't healthy. If you're gonna be in this, you need to remember yourself and put her first. Let Jihoon worry about Jihoon. Be his girlfriend, not his groupie."

I nodded, silence falling between us for so long I began to hear street noises drifting up from below.

"Couldn't this have waited until after breakfast?" I quirked a smile, a peace-offering.

"No." Becka straightened and took my bowl over to the sink, the contents now a mushy mess. "The exhibition is at noon and you weren't paying attention to me."

I snorted. "I'll go have a shower then."

Over the next week, I was more intentional with the way I interacted with GVibes. I completely stopped looking at the fan groups, turned off notifications and muted them. I made sure to be more present at work, even when it was just grunt work. Becka had been right about this, at least. I had chosen this life, this side-step to a future I hadn't mapped out yet. I couldn't waste it.

I still spoke to Jihoon when I could, evenings or mornings, but I now made sure to talk to him about things outside of his group activities. I tried to share more about myself, my hobbies, my opinions, even if it was only on stupid crap like what TV shows should never have been cancelled (Firefly), or what vegetable was objectively the worst (the radish).

And though I almost didn't want to admit it, I noticed the difference. I felt... more awake, less stressed. I was able to enjoy spending time by myself again. I played my guitar more often, and though Becka complained, I could tell she was just relieved I was doing something, other than blank-facing my phone.

Which was why she looked nervous when I told her I was going to watch the interview the group did with Jimmy Fallon the following day. We were sitting in the lounge at work, eating lunch together.

"It's cool, don't worry," I reassured her, "I'm actually going to watch it with Jihoon. They're flying to New York today for the taping tomorrow. He's going to video call me just before it airs and we're going to watch it together. You could watch it with us." I raised my eyebrows at her until she relented, reluctantly smiling at me.

"Someone clearly needs to chaperon you two."

"Yay!" I threw my arms around her neck, spilling my tub of grapes over the table.

"Yeah, yeah, get off me before I squeeze you like a pimple." She pried my arms off her, but couldn't hide the pleased look on her face.

True to his word, Jihoon called me the next day, just after 11:30pm. The group had just gotten back to the hotel after taping the show, which was due to air any minute.

"Hang on, hang on, I'm coming!" Becka rounded the kitchen counter with a bowl of popcorn, throwing herself dramatically onto the sofa.

"Hi, idol," she called in the direction of the phone I was setting up in a tripod so it faced the sofa.

"Um, hey, Becka." Jihoon waved uncertainly. She'd taken to only referring to him as 'idol' or 'the idol,' or occasionally, 'the good-looking sonofabish.'

I just rolled my eyes so that he could see, making him laugh good-naturedly.

"Oh, it's starting!" Becka shushed us, and together, we watched the show start, Jihoon watching the TV in his hotel room.

"I want to take a moment to talk about your newest album, Tracks of Transition, because I hear it's going to be quite a bit different from your previous projects, is that right?"

"I've always loved Jimmy Fallon," Becka says through a mouthful of popcorn.

The mic gets handed to Minjae, who answers the question like the professional he is. "With our new album, we wanted to take the chance to explore the themes of adulthood and the challenges that come with being an adult. The different sound and styles we've used – which you'll be hearing soon – are a reflection of that."

"Such a good answer," I murmured in approval.

After all the serious questions, they moved onto a quick-fire round.

"Okay, let's do a quick round! I'll say a word, and you give me the first thing that comes to mind. Ready?"

The guys all nodded, or gave thumbs up signs.

"Okay, Success."

Woojin slapped the buzzer first, crying out, "Daesangs!" Which made the others in the group laugh, leaving Jimmy to explain to the audience that a Daesang was like a Grammy.

"We're getting those too," Piped up Jihoon, which made me choke on a sip of soda until tears streamed down my face.

"Okay, fellas, when I say, 'home,' you say…"

This time it was Seokmin who hit the buzzer first. "Stage!" Earning him several loud cheers from the audience as the other group members ruffled his hair or patted his back.

"He's such a sweet kid," Becka cooed.

"Becka, that is a full-ass adult." I pointed out, hearing Jihoon laugh from the phone beside me.

"Anyone under twenty one is a kid."

"Unpopular opinion, says 'huh?'" I muttered.

"Huh?" Becka turned to me, shovelling another handful of popcorn into her mouth as I just laughed and waved her off.

"Okay, okay, last one." Jimmy turned to GVibes after several more rapid-fire questions, a serious look on his face.

"Now I need you to think about this one, because there is a follow-up question," Jimmy warned.

"What is the word – or the person – you think about, when I say... love."

The audience erupted in cries of 'oooh,' as if this was the most salacious of gossip. It took so long to die down, the camera kept panning back to the group, who were all pretending to shyly hide their faces, or just giggling. The cameras focused in on Jihoon for a moment, who, when he noticed, held up finger hearts next to his face as he winked.

"Flirt." I hissed at him, though I smirked at the same time. He just shrugged, but had the good grace to look a bit embarrassed. Now that I knew the real Jihoon, there was such a noticeable difference between the man I knew, and the person he was when he was on stage. It was a complete personality switch.

Finally, Jimmy was able to quiet the audience down enough for Sungmin to take the mic and walk a few steps away from the group. He had such a serious look on his face that the audience's response was to quiet further, almost leaning in and I swore there was a collective intake of breath as he raised the mic to his mouth, and said...

"Vibers."

The audience exploded with screams and cheers, and moments later, the fan chants erupted – those synchronized shouts that filled packed auditoriums and stadiums. I could just imagine the sound technicians scrambling to equalise the chaos.

On the stage, Jimmy threw down his pack of prompt cards and leaned back in his chair, clearly understanding there was no point trying to calm the crowd.

The rest of the group all stood up, acknowledging the audience in one way or another, most notably was Sungmin, 'Lee,' who started an impromptu dance to the beat of the chant. Becka and I laughed.

"I like him the most," she said after a few moments, wiping away a tear.

"I'll be sure to tell him that." Jihoon piped up.

"You do that, idol, you do that." Becka shrugged, but I saw the way the flush crept up her neck.

"Okay, okay!" Jimmy finally called for quiet, the noise from the audience gradually dying down, helped along by the group holding fingers to their lips to help Jimmy.

"It's obvious that your fans feel very deeply for you, so I want to stay on that for one more question. So, I have to ask – there's been a lot of buzz about you, Jihoon, possibly dating Hyejin Lee from PrettyYOUngThings. Is there any truth to those rumours, or is it just wishful thinking from the fans? Come on, give us the scoop! I need to know if I should be planning a wedding or just following you both on Instagram!"

"Oop, there it is." Becka took a loud, obnoxious pull from the straw in her soda.

I rolled my eyes, but couldn't ignore the sudden acceleration of my heartbeat.

The mic was passed down through the group until Jihoon was able to take it. He paused a moment before answering to look directly down the lens of the camera, the studio lights illuminating the bronze tone of his irises before he turned his full attention back to Jimmy Fallon.

"Well, Jimmy, while I always appreciate the warm feelings from our fans, Hyejin and I are not dating."

The audience let out a combination of disappointed, "aww's", and relieved cheers.

"It sounds like some members of the audience today aren't too sad to hear that." Jimmy turned his attention back to the crowd, his grin wide.

"But if not Hyejin, then is there anyone out there? I mean come on, have you guys looked in a mirror? You're not that hideous."

The group either laughed or held their hands over their faces, Minjae eventually took the mic back as the audience quieted back down.

"We think you're very handsome as well, Jimmy, but what has that got to do with our music?"

As the audience, Becka and I laughed, Jimmy looked into the camera, eyes wide as he shrugged.

"Well, that's us told, folks. Speaking of music, I think it's just about time for us all to watch the guys perform their recently award-winning single, 'Work Harder'! Put your hands together as they take the stage. GVibes!"

The camera panned over to a raised platform just as all five of them hopped up on it, quickly taking their places before a few seconds of charged silence. Then the opening beats of 'Work Harder' pounded out and they began to move, falling into formation in a well-practiced routine, modified for the smaller stage.

"I take it back, Woojin is definitely my favourite," Becka said speculatively, as we watched the aforementioned man during his dance break solo.

"He'll be delighted with your praise," Jihoon commented.

I turned to him and said, "Don't worry, you're still my bias." I blew him a kiss and watched him lift a hand to catch it out of the air.

"You can give him my number." I turned to Becka, eyebrows raised. She doesn't look at me, but that doesn't stop me from seeing the blush creep over her cheeks.

"He wouldn't know what to do with you, Becka." Jihoon says. I pinched my lips together, slouching further down into the sofa, but instead of the spicy come back I expected, Becka just sighed.

"He might. Right, well, if we're done watching your boyfriend hip thrust, I'm going to bed."

I barked out a laugh, but Jihoon just shrugged. "The fans like it."

"I'm sure they do. Goodnight!" She took the few steps to her room, waved over her shoulder and closed her bedroom door behind her.

In the sudden silence that fell as I turned the TV off, I felt the pressure of the question I was now determined to ask. All part of my plan of putting myself first. I pulled my phone off the tripod and brought it closer to me so it was just me in the screen now.

"You must be tired." He and the rest of the group had flown to New York to film the show just this morning, they were traveling so much at the moment.

"I slept on the plane, and then we had some time to rest this morning." But despite that, I could see how spent he was. It was in the way he rubbed his hand down his face, how deep his voice was and how quiet he was overall.

I chewed on my lip, but before I could lose my nerve again, I found the words. "I know this is going to sound jealous and all sorts of other silly emotions, but I have to ask..."

"You want to know about Lee Hyejin-ssi?"

I must be easy to read. I nodded, even as I cringed.

He nodded, as if he'd expected the question. "The media has always liked to pretend that we're a couple, every time we're even in the same city," he scoffed, hanging his head so that his hair obscured his face.

"We were trainees at the same time, before we debuted. Her group debuted after us, and since then, there have always been rumours about us." He raised he head back up to meet my eyes. "I barely know her, we met because we're in the same company. We were at the same assessment performances, but girl and boy groups are always separate.

"We didn't train together, we didn't eat together, we only ever spoke to each other at award ceremonies after we debuted. I don't even have her number." He lifted his hands before letting them fall. I felt relieved, but at the same time I felt bad that he even had to justify something that clearly never happened. Dating scandals could, and did, ruin idols' careers, even ones so well-established as GVibes.

"I'm sorry I asked," I murmured, but he shook his hands, leaning forward in his chair.

"No, I understand why you did, and I don't mind.

"It's not even me that gets it bad. Hyejin-ssi gets a lot of hate online, and I think netizens are more cruel to her than they ever are to me."

Immediately I recalled some of the hateful things people were indeed typing about Lee Hyejin. I'd been too deep in my feels about Jihoon in that dynamic to give much thought to how it was affecting her. Now I felt like an ass.

"People suck!" The words popped out of my mouth before I could moderate them, but Jihoon just laughed, nodding vigorously.

"Except for us." He winked at me, causing me to giggle. The effect this man had on me.

"Yeah, not us."

I yawned suddenly so wide that it cracked my jaw.

"Go to bed, jagiya."

"I want to see you," I whined.

"You'll see me next week," he promised. Warmth rushed through me at the thought. GVibes was heading to LA to film their music video with Kylie Morrison, and Jihoon had managed to convince his management to let him stay in the city for his birthday, October 29th, which just so happened to fall on a Friday, meaning he was going to spend Halloween weekend in LA. It made me breathless just to think about it.

"Okay," I agreed after another yawn. "Hey Joon?"

"Hmm?"

"You looked super sexy tonight."

He covered his face with his hands, making me laugh at how cute he was.

"Goodnight, Joon."

"Goodnight, cheon-sa."

Chapter 38

October

"Okay, stop, is that *another* Halloween shop?" I stopped, pointing at the shop across the street that was most definitely a Kombucha pop up the week before, but was now either badly infested with ghosts, or had turned into a Halloween store.

Becka followed my finger, then burst out laughing.

"Welcome to LA in the fall, babes." She adjusted her burgundy infinity scarf in the mirrored front of an office building, yet again, discreetly patting her matching beanie hat to make sure it was still artfully in place atop her sandy blonde highlights.

I looked down at my cargo shorts and front-tucked t-shirt. I didn't get it. It was still averaging at about 23-28 Celsius. Why were people wearing knitwear?

It had happened almost overnight, it seemed. One minute people were still wearing shorts and tank tops, moaning about how hot and dry it was, now those same people were sweating under layers of wool, ordering Pumpkin Spice Lattes, but still moaning about how hot and dry it was.

Becka had walked on ahead while I still gaped at the fifth Halloween-themed shop we'd seen this morning.

"How can you tell the difference between summer and autumn?" I grumbled, catching up to her.

"LA has three seasons; Not Summer, Summer, and Fire Season."

"What the eff is 'Fire Season?'" I asked with some alarm.

Becka waved a hand dismissively. "It's whatever the Santa Ana wants it to be." As if that answered my question.

"Remind me again why we're walking through the streets of LA on our lunch break?"

"I want to get my steps up before I go home next weekend. I won't be walking farther than the distance between the front door to the porch, and my mom will stuff me like a turkey the whole weekend."

"Since when do you care about getting in your steps?"

"Since Celine said my ass filled out my pants nicely." Becka's pace increased.

"Is that a bad thing?" I had to jog to catch up with her.

"They were palazzo pants." She growled.

I didn't really mind getting out of the building today, truth be told. It was becoming abundantly clearer as the days passed that my employment was becoming unnecessary. Jeremy had less actual work for me, so more often than not I was sent to dogsbody for other teams. I was learning a lot though, so there was an upside. Mentally, I was preparing to go back to the UK in the new year, especially since I didn't really know what I wanted anymore.

On the down-low, I'd asked Jeremy to put feelers out to people he knew in the industry. He was well aware of the terms of my employment and knew as well as I did that my contract wasn't going to be renewed. I hadn't shared my change of heart about music production with him, but it wasn't like he'd be able to land me a producer's chair anyway. Still, it might be cool to do sound tech for a venue. At least that way, I might be able to stay in LA.

Everything was still so up in the air that it was hard to feel relaxed about any future plans I tried to make.

I was enjoying how the city had suddenly cloaked itself in the disguise of Autumn. It was bizarre; the way people were suddenly draped in scarves and wearing knee-high boots, sweating underneath it all just for the 'aesthetic.'

It wasn't just the clothes, though. The whole city was suddenly bedecked in autumnal foliage, fake orange and red leaves draped all over store fronts, pumpkins and hay bales crowding pavements that now smelt like pumpkin spice and vanilla, instead of... well, hot trash.

It was like the whole city and everyone in it was trying to live out their Gilmore Girls fantasy. I was kind of here for it.

"Is it today they're filming?" Becka's question brings my focus away from a chihuahua dressed as a hotdog and back to her.

"Yeah, today and tomorrow, done by Friday."

"In Long Beach?"

"In some industrial park, yeah." Jihoon had sent me some selfies last night, but as far as I could tell, it was an abandoned lot. The magic of post-production had a lot of work to do.

"And you remember I'm heading out right after work on Friday?"

"Yes, Mother, I remember." I rolled my eyes at her. She'd reminded me every day this week that she was taking the bus up to Oakland to spend the Halloween weekend with her parents.

"I'll mother you in a minute." Becka shot back at me as we crossed over the street to head back to work, the lunch hour being nearly up.

"Oh, you already do." It was probably lucky she hadn't heard me, already half-way across the road. Sighing, I increased my pace to catch up with her.

I said goodbye to Becka as she took the lift back up to her office. I didn't have any assigned tasks left today, so I lingered in the reception, fiddling with my phone.

"Haven't you got anything better to do?" I looked up in surprise. The only person in the bright lobby was Donna.

"I'm sorry," I started, "did you say something?" I really don't think she'd ever addressed me before.

In answer, Donna rolled her eyes and sat back down on the tall office chair behind the desk. She picked up a nail file and began to shape her already-perfect nails.

"You seem like a little duckling, these days, kid. Lost your mama, you?" My eyebrows furrowed so deeply I felt the muscles in my forehead straining. How have I never heard her accent before? She spoke with such a distinct not-quite-French twang that her words took a hot minute to filter through to my brain.

"I guess I'm just feeling a little useless, these days," I admitted.

"Smart girl like you needs a purpose." Donna nodded sagely, not lifting her gaze from her nails.

You could have knocked me over with that nail file. First, she speaks, then she calls me smart?

"Moi?" I said, holding a hand to my chest, as if I couldn't believe my ears.

Donna halts her nail file and looks up at me, raising an eyebrow. "Tu parle francais?"

"Oui," I responded automatically, "un petit peu." I'd gotten a B in my A-Level French, although I'm sure much of it had already fallen out of my brain.

Donna smiled at me, but it wasn't the normal smile I'd seen her give to clients; there was something a bit wolfish about this smile. She seemed to have entirely too many teeth.

"Knew you was a smart girl, you. Now git." She jerked her head and went back to filing her nails, a dismissal as clear as day.

Needing to go somewhere, I headed towards the storage cave. I could always alphabetise the music sheets left over from the orchestra we'd had in a few weeks ago.

I was just tapping out a message to Becka to tell her about my encounter with Donna, sitting on the floor and surrounded by different musical arrangement sheet music when the door creaked open behind me.

"There you are," the voice so unwelcome that it slithered down my spine. "I've been looking for you."

I spun around on my ass to find Trevor Kyle standing in front of the now-closed door.

The storage cave was not small, by any means, but with me on the floor and him at the door, it suddenly felt cramped.

"How can I help you, Mr Kyle." Keeping my voice even was an effort.

"Let me help you up, Kayla." He extended a hand to me, but I shied away from it. He might as well have been holding out a fistful of snakes, for all the inclination I had to reach for it. Instead, I scrabbled to my feet, swiping my finger over the screen and pocketing my phone.

"It's Kaiya. What can I do for you, Mr Kyle?" I reiterated.

He leaned back against the door and crossed his arms, a smirk pulling at his lips.

"How long have you worked for us, Kaiya?" 'Us', as if he didn't work for Pisces just as much as I did.

"Since April, Mr Kyle." I kept expecting him to ask me to call him Trevor, as I'd seen him do with pretty much everyone, but he never did.

"And do you have aspirations to work in the music industry, Kaiya?" It was a simple enough question, but when he said it, it sounded like a proposition.

"I don't know career I'm going to pursue, yet." I answered, careful to keep my tone neutral. All too aware of that closed door.

"I could help you with that, you know." He grinned. "It's so important to nurture talent from within our ranks. I've seen your Youtube channel. You have some promise."

I was so taken aback that I momentarily forgot to be apprehensive in the face of a well-respected producer telling me I had promise.

"T-thank you." I slicked my hands down my jeans.

Trevor Kyle pushed off the door behind him and took a step towards me. "Why don't you spend some time shadowing me? I could show you the ropes. I'd be happy to break you in a little bit."

I blinked, going over the words in my head. Individually they were fine, but altogether, they were... not.

"It's who you know in this business that opens doors," he continued. "You need friends you can look up to. We could be friends." He shrugged, as if this wasn't a big deal, but the next step he took closer to me felt a whole lot like a big deal.

He looked like he was going to move again, where the door loudly opened, slamming against the wall.

And there in the doorway, standing like an avenging angel-

"You okay, cher?"

I heaved a sigh and moved around TK, holding my breath to avoid breathing in the smell of his cologne.

"Did you need me to sort that thing for you, Donna?" I chirped as I joined her at the door, my eyes wide. Her eyes narrowed as she flicked a glance over my shoulder. I didn't turn around, so I don't know what she saw, but it obviously didn't pass the vibe check.

"Yes." She grabbed my arm and pulled me into the too-bright reception, dragging me all the way over to her desk, where she forced me to sit in her chair. Imperiously, she pointed at her computer screen and ordered me to "fix this thing, you."

But there was nothing on the screen, and if there had been – I was not that kind of technician. That didn't stop me from clicking open a bunch of windows, and tapping away at the keyboard like I was doing something when TK strolled past. He looked over at the desk, trying to catch my eye, but I kept my focus on my 'task', until I heard the lift doors closing, the reception lobby suddenly silent, save for the quiet whir of the industrial aircon.

"Thank you." I said quietly as I tried not to cry.

"Be smarter, you." Donna clapped me on the shoulder, her nails digging into my shoulder in a firm, but strangely comforting way.

"For the final time, Becka," I banged my head against the kitchen counter, "I am not going to open the door to strangers wearing costumes. I am not going to leave my phone at home. I am not going to walk down alleyways as a shortcut, and I am not going to go down to the basement to investigate any strange noises." I'd added that last one as a goof, but if she made me repeat the other list of 'do nots,' one more time...

"I lived in London for three years on my own, just fine, and Londoners can be feral, so give me some credit, yeah?" I peeled my face off the stone counter-top to look over to where her suitcase had exploded all over the living room floor. And by 'exploded,' I mean where Becka had pulled everything out of it again, for the third time.

"Becka, you're going for a weekend, not the whole month. And it's your parents' house!" I cried, "I'm pretty sure they'll have a hairdryer!"

Becka chewed her lip as she looked over the eviscerated suitcase. Then, moaning loudly, she flopped forward on top of it, like a sacrifice flinging itself onto the rocks.

"Ow," came her muffled groan.

"Hairdryer?" I winced.

She pulled herself up, wielding the appliance. "Yup."

"Help me close this thing before I put anything else in it!"

I obliged, getting up off the stool and walking over to her, taking the hairdryer and throwing it back in her room. Together, we managed to close the hard-shelled bag and, with me sitting on it, we got it zipped up.

"There," Becka huffed a strand of hair out of her face, "no big deal."

I swallowed my retort, mentally repeating a mantra of 'inner peace,' until I could safely respond. "When's your Uber getting here?"

She looked at her watch. "Any minute now. Help me get this downstairs?"

I closed my eyes for a count of five, trying to remember that she gave me a place to stay in LA and that I loved her.

The Uber driver had pulled up outside our building by the time the two of us managed to get her case downstairs. I cringed as I watched him struggle to put it in the boot.

As the driver got back into his seat, considerably redder in the face, Becka turned to me, grabbing me in a tight hug.

"Ooft," I grunted, "you're only going upstate for the weekend."

She only grabbed me tighter, whispering in my ear, "In my bed-side drawers, there's a whole box of Trojans. Promise me you'll use them."

I wriggled out of her tight embrace as she laughed. "Get in the damn car, Mother."

Becka held up her hands. "I'm going, I'm going."

As I watched her drive away, I stored the information, just in case.

I spent the rest of the day fitfully cleaning the apartment, doing my laundry, clearing out the fridge, doing a food shop; just picking up the errands and tasks I'd added to my list all week, so by the time evening had rolled around, I had dinner in the oven, the whole apartment sparkled and smelled like cinnamon apples – because try as I might, not one single cleaning product in the store had anything that didn't smell like some kind of Autumnal treat. I had a stack of clean clothes ready to put away and I'd even washed the shower/bath curtain. But still, nervous energy thrummed through me, the constant buzz of my internal alarm clock, reminding me that tomorrow morning Jihoon would be here. In our little apartment.

Today was his birthday and I knew that somewhere, right now, here in the city, GVibes had gone out to dinner to celebrate his 25th birthday party. I'd spoken to him today, around lunchtime when the whole crew had paused filming for lunch. He'd said they weren't doing anything too crazy, just dinner downtown before going back to their hotel to film a Live, which is something all of the members did on their birthdays as a way of including Vibers in the celebration. I'd tune in later, just for a little bit.

I decided to shower while dinner was cooking, and even though I played it down, didn't even dare think it through in my head, I still made it an everything-shower. Just in case.

I ate dinner in front of the TV, hair wrapped in a towel, catching up on Married at First Sight. Then I painted my toenails a pretty cerulean blue I'd pinched out of Becka's room. Then I put away the leftovers. Then I took out the trash. Then... I was at a loss, that nervous thrum still going through me. There really was nothing left to do, but the feeling persisted.

Finally, I just decided to lean into it and took myself to bed so I could watch the birthday live in comfort.

It was already in full swing by the time I signed in, the cake already cut. As always, the chat was scrolling by so fast from the thousands of viewers typing messages, mostly in Korean, some in English. Jihoon was sat on the floor, wearing a birthday crown on his mop of newly dyed dark blue hair, cake smeared around his face as the others laughed. I couldn't catch what they were saying. Whilst I had been diligently doing my Korean language lessons on the app every day for weeks now, I wasn't beyond catching the occasional word in casual conversation. It was frustrating and I once again marvelled at how anyone managed to learn a different language, much less fluently.

Minjae was reading aloud something off his phone that made the other guys laugh before he translated to English.

"Someone asked what you're doing for your birthday weekend in LA, Jihoon-ah."

I laughed, until Jihoon looked straight into the camera and said in English, "Going Trick or Treating."

Now I was certain I wouldn't sleep a wink all night.

Chapter 39

Thankfully, my prediction turned out to be wrong, as when I awoke the next morning, I felt rested and more clear-headed than I had the previous night.

It was still early. Jihoon and I had agreed he would get here around mid-morning, so I took my time having a shower and blow-drying my hair.

I'd just sat down in the living room to read a book when a knock at the door sounded, echoing so loudly in our small apartment that I startled, dropping my book on the floor as I jumped to my feet.

It couldn't be – no one had buzzed from the street.

The knock came again, and I hurried towards the door, remembering at the last second to check the peephole, hearing Becka's stern voice in my head, but a moment later, opening the door with so much force it was a wonder I didn't pull it off its hinges.

I threw myself at Jihoon, who caught me with a winded 'oof.' I buried my head in the crook of his neck, inhaling deep, shuddering breaths. He chuckled quietly as he wrapped his strong arms around me more firmly.

"Did you miss me, jagiya?" he murmured, pressing a kiss to the side of my head.

I could only nod, no space yet for words.

"Come on," he said, "let's go inside." He moved his hands down to grip my thighs before hoisting me up. I wrapped my legs around his waist as he walked us into my apartment, kicking the door shut behind him. I marvelled at his strength as he carried me into the kitchen, koala-style, before gently depositing me onto the counter that separated the kitchen from the living room.

Face-to-face now, I ran my eyes over every inch of him, greedily taking in the details I'd missed so much. The way his hair curled around his ears, how his nose scrunched when he grinned, the smell of him – like clean laundry and soap. His dark blue hair was covered by a beanie, which I swiftly took off, running my hands through his longer hair.

"I like this."

"I think it makes me look like a peacock," he said, making me laugh.

I frowned then. "Wait, how did you get in?"

"A nice man and a very old chihuahua let me in."

"That's Carlos and Milo," I grinned. "They live downstairs."

"Milo was very fond of me," Jihoon casually pushed my thighs apart, moving closer between them as he ran his fingers across my cheeks to tangle in my hair.

"Hmm, he's not the only one." I sighed in contented relief as he pressed his lips against mine, a slow, exploratory kiss, the kind you fall into and just stay awhile in. I wound my arms around his neck, drawing him so close to me that his chest pressed up against mine, our breaths mingling until I could no longer tell when each of us inhaled or exhaled.

But eventually, one of us, I wasn't sure which, pulled back. Jihoon rested his forehead against mine, both of us content to just... be still.

"Oh wait!" I gently pushed Jihoon back so I could jump off the counter, leaving him standing there with a dazed look on his face as I dashed into my bedroom. I grabbed the parcel off my bed and walked back to the kitchen, trepidation building with each step.

"What's that?" He nodded at the brightly coloured thing I held so tightly.

I bit my lip and I debated playing it off, but then, cheeks colouring, I thrust the crinkly thing at him.

"Happy birthday." My face burned as I ran through all the reasons why it was a stupid present, now that I came to think about it.

But Jihoon just held out his hands, taking the wrapped gift and looking at it as if it was the best thing he'd ever received. A smile stretched across his face so wide, that on anyone else it would look affected, but on him it looked joyous.

"Can I open it now?" His eyes pinned me to the spot. I nodded, fiddling with the ring on my finger.

KATE ALEXANDRA

He carefully peeled off the hastily applied sticky-tape, folding back the edges of the wrapping paper until he was able to slide out the thing inside. He looked at it for so long I thought he was going to ask me what it was.

"This is the book you told me about." Not a question.

"Yeah. I found a Korean book store in the city and they had a translated copy, so... I wanted you to have a copy. I know it's not-"

"It's perfect. Thank you." He put the book on the counter – a Korean translation of the Time Traveler's Wife – my favourite book, and pulled me in towards him. He kissed my forehead and smiled down at me, the kind of smile that made everything else disappear. The apartment, my job, his job, the weeks of separation. Everything outside the bubble of this moment right here.

But just like Clare in the novel I'd given Jihoon for his birthday, I was all too aware of the passage of time so, reluctantly I pulled back just enough to ask; "Are you hungry? I made pastries."

He grinned and kissed the tip of my nose. "Starving."

We ate breakfast together at the kitchen counter, barely letting go of each other, even as we ate. We held hands, or stroked each other's arms, and my heart even skipped a beat as he put his hand on my knee, so casually it was as if it had always belonged there. My cheeks ached from smiling so much while trying to eat, and when I said as much to Jihoon, he laughed and said he had the same problem. We ended up rubbing our sore cheeks, laughing together.

The laughter came easy, the kind of light-headed giddiness of first dates and exceeded expectations. The bubble of joy that seemed so unpoppable.

When we moved over to the sofa, it seemed natural to fall into him, leaning back against his chest as I doodled my fingers up and down his strong arms while we talked about everything, and nothing.

He told me what it was like to film music videos – surprisingly repetitive, hot, uncomfortable and not nearly as much fun as it seems, apparently. I told him all about filling in for the guitarist for the Smoking Guns. He laughed so hard that I jiggled up and down, which made me laugh until we were both crying.

Eventually, we settled. His heartbeat against my ear lulled me into a calm so still I almost fell asleep. I might have actually fallen asleep, even if only for a little while. I was loathe to move, feeling more peace in this moment than I had in so long.

But I had plans. And they were *good* plans.

So, I reluctantly peeled myself off of him, smiling to myself at his groan of disappointment.

"I know my apartment is super entertaining, but how would you like to celebrate Halloween in LA?" I raised an eyebrow at him, at the same time appreciating the image he presented, reclined on the sofa, one arm behind his head. I mentally shook myself. Focus.

"What did you have in mind?" His voice was rumbly, and judging by the way he was looking at me, he had seen the way I'd checked him out. So, to not get any more distracted, I stood up and put a couple paces between us.

"Carnival." Just one word, but so many images.

Jihoon sat up. "I'm listening."

"Stay here."

I walked into my bedroom and stripped down to my bralette and boy shorts, making sure my bedroom door was firmly closed. I pulled out the bag I had tucked into a drawer and took out the costume from inside, pulling it on as carefully as possible, grateful it was essentially a soft, stretchy jumpsuit. Once in, I spared a glance at myself in the mirror on the back of the door, giggling as I turned from side to side.

When I opened the door, I peeked my head out to make sure he was where I'd left him. But it was better. He was slouched on the sofa, head lolled back, mouth slightly open and clearly asleep. I tip-toed back into the main room, closing my bedroom door behind me to minimise the light coming in through the window, then padding over to the window in the kitchen and closing the blinds. I winced at the soft snicking sound they made as they clacked together.

Once I'd eliminated all the light I could, I crept back over to Jihoon. I stood in front of him, pulled my mask down over my face and flipped the small switch on the box in the small of my back. Then I gently ran a finger down his nose. He twitched, but didn't wake, so I did it again. When I saw him stir, I pulled back and posed.

His eyes blinked open, once, twice. On the third time they focused on the image in front of him, causing him to jerk and let out a startled cry.

I laughed and began to do a silly dance, making the colourful tube lights on my jumpsuit jerk around, like I was a fluorescent stick man.

Jihoon soon recovered and began to laugh. He stood up and closed the space between us until he could reach out and touch the costume I wore.

"This is so cool!" He grinned, tracing the colourful tubes up my arms, across my collarbone and down the centre of my chest.

Suddenly breathless, I was fascinated by the play of colour across his face, the way the light reflected in his eyes, broken apart like a fractured crystal.

"I have one for you, too." I said, my voice muffled under my mask. I pushed it up my face so it held back my hair on my forehead.

"Oh really?" he raised an eyebrow.

"It's on my bed. Wait here, I'll get it for you." I spun on my heel and quickly retrieved the second costume from my bed, trying to calm the way my pulse raced. This man barely had to look in my direction and I was panting. I shook my head at myself and rejoined Jihoon in the living room.

"Here," I said handing him the folded costume. "It's a jumpsuit, you just pull it on," I explained, pulling at the material to show him. "You can get changed in the bathroom, or my room or... here." Jihoon pulled off his shirt in the middle of my living room. Going by the look on his face, he knew exactly what he was doing, and hell if I was going to turn around. Let him tease, I wasn't mad about it.

He smirked at me, while I just hoped I wasn't drooling. Surely the shock of his overwhelming sex appeal would wear off at some point, but clearly not today.

He dropped his t-shirt on the coffee table, the muscles in his arms flexing. I drew in a shallow breath as I stared at him, unable to look

461

away. His toned stomach tapered to a narrow waist, where his jeans hung low dangerously low. Heat flushed through me, and I realized I hadn't exhaled.

Jihoon wasn't done. As his fingers reached for the buttons on his fly, I squeaked and slapped a hand over my mouth. Jihoon laughed, a rich, velvety sound I could have wrapped around myself.

It made no sense that I was still this affected. I'd seen him in less before. Considering the things we'd done in that villa in August. You'd have thought I'd be capable of being a bit more brazen by this stage, but, nope.

"Breathe, Kaiya," he rumbled, a second before dropping his jeans to a puddle on the floor.

"You know exactly what you're doing," I accused, my words more breath than speech.

He chuckled. "Yes."

"Cruel, beautiful man."

He cocked an eyebrow at me, then took two steps towards me that were more prowl than walk.

"Oh, but I can be so much nicer." He reached out a hand, and hypnotised by the promise of sensation, I swayed towards him. Then, coming to my senses just as his fingers grazed the skin of my throat.

"Nope, stop that right now!" I hopped back a step, putting some much-needed space between us.

"Stop casting your sexy-magic on me and put your damn costume on. I want to go to the carnival!"

A WORLD APART

"Sexy-magic?" Jihoon snickered, picked up the costume, and stepped into it, grinning at me the whole time.

"Yes. Sexy-magic. I will not elaborate further. Would you like some help with that?"

"Please." He turned, presenting the broad expanse of his back to me where the wires of the lights were tangled in the fabric. I deftly untangled them before testing the battery pack for good measure. As the lines of his body lit up like a Christmas tree, he laughed in delight.

"This is so cool. Thank you for getting this."

I smoothed my hands over his back. To straighten the fabric, obviously.

"You're welcome. Shall we go now?" I looked down at my watch. "It might take us a while to get there in traffic."

"Where is it?"

"In West Hollywood."

"West Hollywood?" He turned around to face me and waggled his eyebrows at me. "I have very fond memories of that area."

"Me too, so let's go make some more." I lightly shoved him towards the door, making sure to grab my backpack and his mask on the way out. Jihoon chuckled, the sound warming my heart.

463

Chapter 40

We decided on taking the bus, instead of an Uber as the app was showing wait times similar to the bus journey anyway. I'd asked Jihoon what he'd rather do, and I guessed that the mask made him brave, because the idea of taking a bus in LA in the middle of the day seemed somehow exciting to him.

We walked to the stop a few streets over just in time to get the next bus. We sat together and watched the city out of the window, laughing at each other's silly jokes and pointing out the weird and wonderful things to be seen. Just two aliens in the city of Angels.

We weren't the only people on the bus in full costume, so we didn't stand out. I openly admired Conan the Barbarian sitting a few rows over, fully committed to his pelt game, until Jihoon grabbed my face and turned it away, saying, "if you want to stare at a man, stare at me." I laughed and grabbed his hand in mine.

"I stare at you plenty," I assured him. His eyes twinkled through the mask obscuring his face.

"As you should." He squeezed my hand.

We began to hear and see signs of the carnival. The closer we got, it seemed to spill out into the entire surrounding area, so we got off at the next stop, content to follow the crowd and the pulsing music until we were really in the thick of it. Everywhere we looked, people were dressed up, from the more basic costumes like ours, to one guy dressed as a man-tree-thing, with a sign around his neck/trunk that said, "Don't forget to take a sip from your trusty Vault 13 canteen." Obviously, some in-joke I couldn't decipher, but the man's makeup was scarily good.

There were bed-sheet ghosts, zombies, creepy dolls, furries, even a whole group of people dressed up a deck of cards, all holding hands as they walked down the street.

There were also costumed dogs everywhere; small dogs, big dogs, dogs in bags, dogs on leads, one dog on a bike.

It was a lot to take in, my eyes didn't know where to look first. Stalls lined the street, boutique vendors selling everything from Halloween-themed jewellery, bags, clothes, food, to creepy paintings and even an entire stall selling nothing by gas masks.

But through all of the things assaulting my senses, what I was most aware of was the firm grip that Jihoon had on my hand as we walked down the street together, so different from the last time we'd been in public at the flea market. I still remembered how it felt when he'd moved his hand away from mine. I'd understood at the time, as

465

I understood now – the whole 'just in case' of the situation, – but man, it had stung.

Now though, he held on to me like he was never letting go. It made my whole body light up brighter than the fluorescents of my costume.

We came upon a small stage – definitely wouldn't pass a health and safety inspection – constructed mainly out of barrels and pallets, by the looks of it. A band was playing some kind of country-style music, but the kind of band you might have seen playing at a country wedding on the frontier. Four women were really going to town on a guitar, a violin, some kind of drum, and a flute, somehow managing to stomp their boots at the same time. Without giving myself a second pause, I grabbed Jihoon and pulled him into the crowd of people already spinning and dancing along. He didn't even hesitate, just followed my lead, wound his arm around my waist and together we spun in circles until we were dizzy, laughing so hard I was breathless by the end of the song. As the women bowed, we clapped and yelled our appreciation, but moved on.

Afternoon was progressing as we meandered through the streets, stopping often to look in wonder or confusion. Everywhere we turned there were new and interesting spook-themed attractions, stalls, food and people. We'd eaten so many things, my stomach was fit to bursting. My favourite had been the ghost-shaped bubble waffle with purple ice cream and chocolate sauce. Jihoon and I had shared it whilst we watched a man on stilts dressed as Beetlejuice spit fire.

We'd gone into a scare-maze, just a small one, hastily constructed out of a handful of shipping crates, but it had been the kind with actors that jump out and try to scare you. Jihoon talked a big game, acting like my protector, but the second the Nun from The Conjuring jumped out and brandished her rosary at him, he'd collapsed into a heap of half-Korean-half-English expletives. I laughed so hard I thought I was going to puke that bubble waffle straight back up. Even the Nun had looked a little apologetic.

"No more spook houses," he said weakly. I just laughed some more.

The sky was darkening to a pretty shade of pinky-orange when we came to a gated park. Signs on the gate announced, 'Open-Air Horror Movie Screening, $5.' By this time my feet were starting to ache from all the walking, so I suggested to Jihoon that we go catch a movie. He readily agreed and we headed on in. At the end of a wide-open lawn, a massive, white screen had been erected, alongside a tower of speakers, more of which were dotted back from the screen around the grass. There were already a couple hundred people sat down, talking and laughing while the screen silently displayed a slide-show of various stills from horror movies.

We headed to the nearby stall with a large 'tickets' sign above it and handed over our money to a bored looking teenager.

"Look," Jihoon pointed, "they rent blankets." A stack of rolled up picnic blankets sat in a big box next to the stall.

I shrugged, "seems like a good idea." I handed over more notes to the teenager, who had cocked her head and was looking at Jihoon strangely, even though he had his mask pulled down over his entire face. He had alternated throughout the afternoon, lifting it higher up his head to expose his mouth and nose, or pulling it down to his neck to air his forehead, but now he was fully covered up. It was possible the teen was just questioning his choice to wear a full mask in in mid-20s sunny weather, but I was also cautious enough to not use his name right there.

"Come on, let's go pick a space." I took his hand and together we moved further into the crowd of sitting people until we found a decent spot about half-way in, a speaker pole not too far away. We spread out the blanket on the ground and sat down, the relief of getting off my feet was immediate, and I groaned. Jihoon opened his legs wide enough to pull me in towards him so I could lean back against his firm chest. I sighed contentedly as my senses adjusted to this slower, less overwhelming scene.

It was in this calm, relaxed manner that we passed the time in silence until the movie came on not too long later. The sky was starting to properly darken when the screen flickered to black, and the opening credits began to roll. The distinctive song, 'Right Red Hand' blared out across the park, met by a wave of cheers from those sat down, waiting in anticipation, then shushing suddenly as a young, blond Drew Barrymore picks up the ringing phone.

"A classic," I said with a grin.

"I've never seen it."

Eyebrows raised, I turned to look at him over my shoulder, but he just shrugged.

"I was very busy for many years."

I snorted and turned back around, snuggling back against him and settling in to enjoy the movie.

"Well, what did you think?" I asked as we rolled up the blanket to take back to the stall. We'd sat through two movies, but it was getting late now and though we'd grabbed a tub of 'Mac&Scream-Cheese' and a cup of 'Cauldron Soup' to share in the intermission between 'Scream 1' and 'Nightmare on Elm Street,' I was kind of keen for home.

"Mmm." Jihoon frowned as he considered the question. "I preferred Scream."

"Okay, solid choice. Talk me through your reasoning." We walked over to the stall, arm in arm, the crowds of movie-goers behind us chatting amongst themselves as they waited for the next movie to play.

"To tell you the truth, Freddy scared me too much," he admitted, smiling as he shook his head."

"Billy and Stu didn't scare you?"

He made a 'pfft' sound. "If everyone in that movie had more common sense, no one would have died. Plus, I could outrun them very easily."

"If people in horror movies had more common sense, it would make for a very short movie."

Jihoon hummed in agreement as we returned the blanket, a different person now sat there, thankfully, as I hadn't stopped wondering if the teen from earlier had recognised Jihoon's voice.

Outside the gates of the park, the noise of the ramped-up nighttime activities hit us like a wall of sound. The crowd seemed to have doubled in size as more adults had come out to play. We walked down the street, now lit by neon signs and flashing lights, thumping music coming from all directions from competing sound systems, all vying for people's attention to their particular stall.

But when we came upon one horse-box style van selling handmade figurines, we both faltered, hearing the so-familiar opening refrain of 'Fall in Love,' the collaboration GVibes had down in the spring with Haley. I laughed and took a step forward to move on, but Jihoon tugged me back. I looked over my shoulder at him, and though I couldn't see more than his eyes through the mask, in the twinkling neon lights, I could see the mischief there.

He let go of my hand, took a few steps back before reaching behind him to flip on the battery pack, at once illuminating the fluorescent-coloured wires that, against the black jumpsuit in the night that had now fallen entirely, made him a multi-coloured stick-man. He began to dance, the routine from 'Fall in Love' coming easily to him after weeks of repetition and practice. But it wasn't Jihoon dancing, it was a very talented stick-man.

I burst into delighted laughter as I clapped my hands. More people seemed to take notice, stopping and pointing. Some even took out their phones and pointed them in his direction, presumably recording. I felt a twinge of nervousness before I reasoned with myself that he was completely unidentifiable. I tried to relax and just go with it, after all, that stick man sure could dance.

The song ended though, and the stick-man held the final position as the dozen or so people who had stopped to watch began to clap and cheer, asking for another one. He bowed, but shook his hands before jogging back over to me. He pulled me into his arms and I felt his chest heaving as he pressed against me. I leaned up on my tiptoes, carefully rolling his mask up to his nose so I could press a kiss to his mouth. He seemed hesitant at first, probably because a few people nearby catcalled us, but then he pulled me to him tighter, deepening our kiss. The first kiss we'd shared in public.

I melted in his arms. Out of all the overwhelming sights, sounds and smells around us, I only felt him.

Chapter 41

K nowing it was probably quicker to wait for the regular bus than wait for a taxi on Halloween weekend, Jihoon and I left the main thoroughfare of the carnival behind and headed back to the stop we'd arrived from.

On the way home, I rested my head on Jihoon's shoulder as we both looked out the window at the night-time transformation of the city, made somehow even more vibrant in the dark of the night, illuminations chasing the shadows into the alleys we all knew instinctively to avoid.

"I wonder if I'll be here to see all this next year." I murmured, giving voice to the anxious uncertainty I'd blithely pushed aside for months now.

Jihoon shifted under me, but made sure not to jostle me where I had settled against him.

"You're going to leave LA?"

"I think I'll have to," I sighed, briefly explaining. "The studio isn't going to renew my contract, and without them, I don't have a Visa."

He was silent a moment before he said, "Where will you go?"

"Probably back to the UK, maybe London. I'm not sure yet, I haven't made any decisions."

"Will you miss it here?"

I thought about the question, taking my time before I answered. "I don't think I'll miss the city. I mean, I like it well enough, but it's not really that much different from any other city.

"I'll miss Becka. She's the whole reason I'm here, she got me a job, gave me a place to live. She's my best friend. It'll suck not seeing her every day." I swallowed past the sudden lump in my throat.

"But I think I'll really miss the opportunity of LA. I can't describe it, but in a way, it feels like all things are possible here.

"I mean, look at my life." I huffed out a laugh. "Fresh out of Uni, not a penny to my name and I somehow work at a crazy famous studio, meet crazy famous people every other day and... y'know, there's you. I met you here." I ran my hand down his chest, feeling his heart solidly beat against my palm.

"LA has been single-handedly one of the best and most bizarre experiences of my life. I will miss that most of all."

Jihoon pulled me closer to him, offering me comfort in the support of his arms. I snuggled into him as we watched the city outside the window blur past.

The apartment building was quiet as we made our way up the stairs to our floor, only the sound of our footsteps to break the silence.

I put they key in the lock and pushed the heavy door open, almost calling out to Becka, but catching myself. I flipped on the light switch and moved out of the way to let Jihoon enter, closing and locking the door behind himself.

He pulled off his mask with a relieved sigh.

"I'm glad to finally take that that off," he said with a wry grin, tossing it on top of the shoe organiser we had in the small hallway. I copied him, but with less relief, given that I'd had the freedom to take mine off whenever I'd wanted.

"I'm sorry about that," I pulled a face, "that can't have been fun."

He waved away the apology. "It was worth it."

"Can you pull out my battery pack?" I turned around, presenting my back to him, pulling my hair around my neck. A moment later I felt his fingers working at my lower back as he unplugged my battery pack, tossing it down on top of the masks.

"Me, please," Jihoon said turning around so I could unplug his pack. I tossed it on the shoe organiser next to mine.

"This thing is so warm," I said, fanning myself.

"Want some help taking it off?" He waggled his eyebrows at me. I rolled my eyes at him, but then he started pulling the neckline of his jumpsuit, freeing his arms, then his chest, until he had stripped down to his waist.

It felt voyeuristic to watch, but I couldn't take my eyes off him, especially not when the narrow confines of the corridor meant that he was three feet away from me.

"Ahh, that feels so much better," he grinned at me.

I narrowed my eyes at him. Two could play that game.

"Oh, really? Let me try." Just as he had, I pulled the stretchy fabric of the suit down until I could slide first one arm, then the other, until I'd pulled it down to my waist, leaving me bare, but for my black, lacy bralette. Jihoon had been right, having some air on my skin after being in the synthetic material of the jumpsuit was a relief.

But relief was not what I felt when my eyes raised up to meet Jihoon's. He wasn't just openly staring at me, he was looking at me like I was everything he'd ever wanted, but been denied. The naked hunger in his eyes inflamed something in me that I hadn't felt since that weekend in the villa, a reckless kind of abandon, a need to throw caution to the winds.

He felt like a cliff I wanted to throw myself off.

One moment he was standing there, and the next, he was against me, his body pushing mine into the wall. The force straightened my back, but before I could process the impact, his hand cradled the back of my head. Despite the intensity of the moment, I felt protected. Cherished.

"What is this that you do to me, jagiya?" he murmured, looking down into my eyes, wide and... almost fearful.

"The same thing you do to me."

I lifted my face to his at the same moment he lowered, our lips meeting so softly it was like the first time – gentle, exploratory, waking the butterflies in my stomach and soothing them all at once.

I melted into the kiss, winding my arms around his neck for support as my legs trembled. I don't know who deepened the kiss; maybe we both did at the same time. I moaned as he parted my lips with his tongue, pressing his hips harder into me.

The kiss became more frantic, a clash of tongues and lips in a desperate bid for closeness, and when Jihoon ran his hand down my thigh, I shuddered. He pulled my leg up, hooking it around his waist as he pressed me harder against the wall, a build-up of some unnameable tension seeming to seek out all the areas that we touched, a magnetism drawing us together.

Jihoon tore his mouth from mine with a small cry as he leant his forehead against mine, looking into my eyes as he panted.

"I'm sorry, I don't want to get carried away if you don't want this. You drive me crazy, cheon-sa." He closed his eyes, panting heavily.

"I do want this." My heart pounded in my chest, but my words were clear. Quiet, but intentional.

Jihoon opened his eyes, looking at me for so long I wasn't sure if he'd heard me.

"Are you sure?" His voice wavered, though from disbelief or nerves, I couldn't tell.

But, I was sure. I'd been sure for some time. I lowered my leg from around his waist and put my hand on his chest, gently pushing him away. He took a step back, his arms falling to his sides, his gaze never leaving mine, as if I'd disappear if he looked away.

I reached for his hand and, holding it firmly, I led him down the hallway to my bedroom, the door slightly ajar. I turned on the lamp next to the bed, illuminating the room in a soft, ambient light as Jihoon closed the door behind himself.

Seeing him there, standing in my tiny bedroom should have made him seem larger than life, this internationally famous idol, but instead it had the opposite effect. It made him more real somehow, and for the first time since I'd locked eyes with him in the lobby of Pisces recording studios, it felt like perhaps he could fit into my life, instead of me changing my shape to fit into his.

He looked at me like I was the sun, erasing any feelings I might have had of self-doubt, or self-consciousness. As he watched, I pushed the jumpsuit down the rest of my body, letting it pool at my feet as he did the same. My bra went next, no gimmicks, no nervous smiles, just a simple shedding of clothes. I walked towards him, sliding my hands up his chest, feeling the way his muscles jumped under my touch.

"You are so beautiful," he murmured, the words and scene a near mirror of the last time we'd been this close. It made me smile to remember how nervous I'd been then, to compare it with how certain I felt now.

Once again, I took his hand. "Come to bed with me."

He swallowed, but allowed himself to be led. I crawled onto the bed, backing up until I could comfortably lay down. Jihoon followed me, but remained kneeling, looking down at me with a clear mix of want and nervousness playing across his face. I reached up a hand to pull his face down to mine, silencing his unspoken words with a kiss. With my other hand, I brought his to my breasts, a silent encouragement which he scarcely needed.

What started as gentle, exploratory caresses became more urgent, less finessed, a need to have skin meet skin. My mouth tore from his in a cry as he traced patterns over and around my breasts, the skin there tightening in a way that I felt lower in my core, that building anticipation, and I shuddered. Jihoon trailed his mouth from my jaw, down my throat and then to my breasts, making me cry anew. The sensation of his tongue as it scraped gently across the sensitive peaks, coupled with the way he breathed upon my wet skin was incendiary. I arched my back, pushing my chest against his in a desperate bid to increase the contact.

Fingers danced down my abdomen, drawing lazy circles around my navel until finally they dipped beneath the underwear I still wore.

"Jihoon," I gasped as his fingers moved down that most sensitive part of me. He groaned and pressed his lips against my neck, moving his hand in a way I thought I might go mad from, the coiling tightness gathering in my centre so acute now. When he dipped a finger inside me, I swore, bucking against his hand.

Too impatient now for the promise of more, "in my drawer." The words were wrenched from me, I couldn't have been clearer or eloquent if I'd tried.

Jihoon raised his face to look at me, his eyes searching mine, looking for any lingering doubt. He would never find any. He removed his hand and leaned over me to open the bedside drawer that I had stocked late last night, as per Becka's thoughtful instruction.

Jihoon sat back on his heels, still wearing his boxers, his own arousal evident. I sat up slightly to lean back on my elbows, watching with a kind of interest as he held the small, foil square. He hesitated a moment before getting off the bed. I was momentarily confused, until he pushed his boxers down, letting them drop to the floor with the rest of our clothes.

He knelt back on the bed and ran his hand softly over my pelvic bone, the slight tickle made me giggle breathlessly.

Putting the foil packet down, he hooked his hands into the waistband of my underwear. He looked up to meet my eyes. I wordlessly nodded, watching as he slid them down my thighs and then off my legs to join his on the floor.

My heart pounded a staccato beat against my throat, only adding to the feeling that I couldn't get enough air in, but it wasn't nervousness that made me breathless; it was the sight of Jihoon as he moved to kneel between my legs, carefully nudging them wider with his knees, the stretch aching in a way I had not expected.

He picked up the little gold packet, decisively ripped it open and withdrew the circle from inside. I tried not to stare as he deftly rolled it onto himself, but the interest of a thing unknown was hard to resist.

Then, finally, nothing further awaited, no more preparations to be made. It was now, or it was never and that was unthinkable.

His eyes flashed up to meet my own, a slight frown pulling his eyebrows together.

"Are you sure?" And I knew if I said 'no,' he would stop, we would put our clothes back on and he would be fine with it, because it had always been my choice with him.

But I didn't want to say no. I wanted to say, yes. So, I did. "Yes."

He lowered himself until he was leaning over me, holding himself up on one elbow, his face so close to mine I could see the way his eyelashes fanned his cheeks.

I felt him then, pressed against me, a strange but not unpleasant sensation. His face was so tense, his eyebrows furrowed together, jaw clenched. I reached up a hand and smoothed my fingers between his brows.

"So serious," I murmured. He exhaled like he'd been holding his breath, turning his face to kiss my fingers as they trailed down his cheek.

I felt him move, pressing into me, stretching, but not uncomfortable. Not yet.

Jihoon stilled above me, his body shivered against mine, just a pause though, as on my next breath, he withdrew slightly, a sensation I felt more acutely. I gasped, and his eyes shot to mine.

"Are you okay?"

"Yes," I said firmly, if breathlessly. "Don't stop."

This time, when he moved again, he pushed further in, the stretch becoming more uncomfortable this time, but before it could register as more than that, he withdrew. His other hand had trailed up to my hip, holding me gently, but firmly as he continued pushing in and withdrawing. The gentle rocking motion began to feel good, much to my surprise, having heard and read no shortage of experiences to the contrary.

My hips began to move of their own volition, matching his pace, each stroke going deeper until, finally, it did begin to hurt; a pinching sensation that verged on the edge of a burn, but by now the other sensations Jihoon had begun to wring from my body were equal in intensity, the conflicting feelings building within me.

Jihoon moved his hand from my hip to gently rub his fingers just above where we were joined, the sudden sparks of pleasure making me gasp. My head tilted back and I felt him slide in deeper, less resistance now until finally, finally our bodies were flush with each other.

He paused above me, his head hanging down as he trembled. I ran my hand down his face, soothing him even as my heartbeat thundered in my chest.

When he lifted his face, he pressed his lips to mine in a kiss so achingly sweet that I felt my eyes prickle. It was as he kissed me that he began to move inside me again, with less hesitation now, his strokes surer. He gasped against my mouth, a breathy moan that I echoed with one of my own.

Jihoon raised himself up slightly, his movements still gentle, but intentional, especially as he increased the pressure of his fingers, wringing moans from me, even as I marvelled at this new and foreign feeling of him moving within me. It wasn't long until I felt myself cresting that peak, the sudden and climactic pulse that had me throw my head back and cry out in surprise and pleasure, swiftly followed by the feeling of being too tight, too full.

Above me, Jihoon's thrusts became erratic, his breathing harsh and only moments after me, he cried out, partly my name, and partly some words I did not understand. He stilled for a moment, frozen before he slumped onto me, but only partly so as to not crush me.

His breathing was ragged, his shoulders heaved as I ran my hands down his back. Eventually though, his breathing evened out. He lifted his face to mine, peppering kisses over my lips, my cheeks, my nose until I began to giggle, batting at him ineffectually. He adjusted his weight and in one swift movement, he pulled out of me, eliciting a sharp inhale, not quite pain, but not comfortable either. I reflexively pulled my legs together, wincing as my muscles ached.

Jihoon rolled off the bed, his back to me as I saw him dispose of the condom in the small rubbish bin. He got back into bed swiftly, sliding against me and pulling me into his arms.

"Are you alright?" He pressed a kiss to the top of my head.

I grinned, even though he couldn't see it with my face pressed against his chest. "Yes. Are you?"

He laughed, the sound rumbling through him like thunder. "I don't know if 'alright' is big enough for how I'm feeling."

I yawned so wide my jaw cracked, all the activity and overwhelming sensation of this whole day catching up to me, coupled with the warmth of being pressed against Jihoon, skin to skin.

"Tired, jagiya?" The smile in his voice pulled my own out, though it was promptly interrupted by another yawn.

"It was a big day," I grumbled, "I'll be more talkative in the morning."

"You don't need to say anything," his arms tightened around me, "just listen."

"I've never felt this way about anyone, not in my whole life. It's you, Kaiya, it's been you since we first met."

I leaned my head back so I could see his face, my heartbeat speeding up, despite the fatigue I felt.

"I love you, Kaiya."

My heart stopped, my lungs seized, but despite that, I felt the tears as they spilled out, running down my cheeks only to be dashed away by Jihoon's fingertips.

There were so many buts, so many what-ifs, and so many, very good reasons to hold back, to guard my heart, but I'd decided to go all in, no matter the outcome.

"I love you," he repeated, and I could tell he didn't say it to hear me say it back to him. He didn't say it out of obligation. He said it because it was the way he felt.

The moment my heart restarted, the very second I could get the air out of my lungs, "I love you too." It was a confession, an admission, a wish that needed to be spoken to come true.

He laughed in relief, and perhaps I imagined it, but I could have sworn I saw his eyes shimmering, but it might have been the light.

The whole day and all its emotional roller-coaster seemed to press in on me then, and this time, when I felt the weight of my eyelids closing, I didn't try to keep them open.

Chapter 42

We'd woken up in the middle of the night to make love again, slow and unhurried, a more thorough exploration of what we each liked, but the answer had been everything, so far.

Waking up in the morning in the circle of his arms had been a revelation. The warmth going beyond skin deep feeling and instead being the kind of warmth that makes a person feel that much more kindly toward the world, even when the world in question was at that moment leaning on its horn in the street below.

"Gah, what an asshat," I grumbled, wondering how the driver's horn could blare continuously for so long.

Underneath my cheek, Jihoon chuckled, jiggling me ever-so-slightly. His hand lifted to gently trace the contour of my spine, a decidedly nicer way to wake up.

"He's just letting us know what time it is."

"How can you tell?" I leaned my chin on his chest, looking up at the way his mouth quirked in that way I like.

"No one sounds his horn for that long, unless he's late for work. It must be around 9:00am."

"I admire the skills of deduction that went into that, but it's a Sunday." I smirked before rolling onto my back and stretching my whole body, cracking my spine, wincing slightly at the way the muscles of my inner thighs ached.

Jihoon rolled onto his side to face me as he propped his head up on his hand, his eyes roving over my body uncovered by the duvet.

"How do you feel?"

"Hmm, you tell me how I feel," I grinned, loving the slight narrowing of his eyes.

"I could write an entire album about it, and it still wouldn't be enough to describe it."

My toes curled as delighted tingles coursed over my skin, raising tiny bumps on my arms.

"Or, I could just show you." The glint in his eyes was my only warning before he lunged for me, but quick as a whip, I darted out of his reach and out of bed.

"Not before breakfast!" I giggled.

"But I'm hungry now!" He rose to his knees, arms outstretched to snag me as I passed – not made difficult in my tiny room. I shrieked in delight and dodged him by ducking underneath and pulling my door open, laughing as I danced out into the living room.

"ARGH! ARGH! NAKED FLESH, MY EYES, SWEET BABY JESUS AND ALL THE SAINTS, MY EEYYES!" Becka screeched, dropping her travel mug on the floor, where it pinged and bounced for several feet.

"Oh fuck! Ah, shit! Fuuuuuuuuucccccckkkk!" I cried, darting back into my room and slamming the door closed. I leant against it, the wood cold on my backside as my chest heaved.

Jihoon stood statue-still beside the bed, his hands covering his mouth, eyes wide as saucers as we both listened to Becka on the other side of the door, still shrieking obscenities and garbled nonsense.

Until-

"It's ten in the gods-damned morning, put some clothes on, this ain't no commune!" Becka pounded on my door, hard enough to make me spring away from it, as if it might bite.

As if the spell had been broken, Jihoon puffed out a breath, choked on a laugh and a moan of distress. I pounded him on the back, trying to sooth him as I said, "she's joking." I hoped so, anyway.

A few minutes – and a handful of kisses – later, we hurriedly tugged on our clothes and cracked the bedroom door open, both of us peeking around it. Becka had her back to us, pouring milk into a cup of coffee. As she went to put the carton back in the fridge, she spotted us over her shoulder and rolled her eyes so expansively it was a wonder they didn't fall out of her head.

"Good grief, you two. Like a couple of meerkats, you can come out now."

Holding Jihoon's hand for support, I moved away from the door and stepped into the living area.

Becka stood at the kitchen counter, stirring her mug slowly, eyes narrowed at us as we moved towards the coffee and, by proxy, her.

She pushed a spray bottle across the counter, the water inside sloshing. "I'm not afraid to use this," her eyes narrowed, but I know I saw her lips quivering.

I left Jihoon to sit on the stool facing into the kitchen as I moved around the counter to pour myself a coffee. I knew Jihoon didn't drink caffeine in the morning, so I grabbed him a bottle of water out of the fridge and slid it to him. He grabbed it gratefully, opening it immediately and finishing half of it off in one go.

While I was distracted by the oddly alluring movement of his throat, Becka joked, "didn't you give this poor boy any water while he was here? You're a terrible host."

"I was literally coming to get us breakfast when you interrupted me," I grumbled.

"First of all, ew," Becka commented, "that's just unsanitary. Secondly, no need. I swung past Maria's Cafe on my way back and picked up a breakfast platter. I figured you'd be hungry." She leered at me, waggling her perfectly micro-bladed eyebrows at me.

I blushed, a deep crimson I felt down to my soul. Becka laughed.

"Come on, help me unpack that brown bag," she indicated the large, brown sack I hadn't noticed until now. Before I could move, Jihoon was there, pulling out different sizes of Styrofoam containers and putting them on the counter.

"Oh, that smells so good," I moaned as the scents of pastries, bacon and sugary things wafted out of the boxes.

"Right?" Becka grinned at me, and as a trio, we sat at the counter opening the boxes and helping ourselves, companionable chatter and laughter the soundtrack to the morning.

A car came for Jihoon at 1:00pm, after one of the best mornings I could remember.

The three of us had lain about talking about this and that, catching up on Married at First sight, and discussing Jihoon's upcoming schedule, but with more casualness than I'd managed recently. It now seemed less fraught. The pressure to keep on top of it had eased. It felt so easy to just be Jihoon's girlfriend once I'd put aside the need to follow every move the group made.

Becka and I had painted each other's toenails, while Jihoon reclined on the sofa wearing one of Becka's sheet masks. It had been... honestly, wonderful.

It was within that bubble of happiness that I'd been able to push aside all thoughts of Jihoon having to leave, but of course that time had crept up on us.

"I'll call you when I land," he promised, holding me tight.

I only nodded, not trusting myself to speak. We'd already agreed I wouldn't go down to the street to see him off. He'd said I'd watched him drive away too many times already, which I couldn't disagree with.

Becka had gone to her room to unpack, giving us a bit of privacy, and so it was without an audience, but also without a trace of awkwardness that I leaned my forehead against his chest and whispered, "I love you."

He pressed a kiss to the top of my head. "Saranghae, Kaiya."

I smiled but kept the fact that I'd understood him to myself. I still hadn't told him I'd been learning Korean, not wanting to disappoint him when I kept confusing words like 'milk' and 'cucumber'. It felt important to at least get the basics down.

But 'saranghae'... that I understood.

"You'd better go," I said reluctantly. He sighed, but moved away from me to pick his bag up off the floor before heading to the door. He pulled on his hat and a pair of shades before opening it, turning to give me one last look.

"See you in a few weeks," he smiled.

"A few weeks," I echoed.

One lingering look later, and he'd turned away, the door closing behind him, leaving me in the hallway that still echoed from last night.

"You alright?" Becka leaned on the doorframe to her bedroom, a sympathetic look on her face.

I sighed again. "I'll be fine, but let's talk about it all later, okay? I need a shower."

Becka walked towards me and gave me a brief, but firm hug.

"You're paying for my therapy and my dry cleaning, by the way."

"What dry cleaning," I asked, puzzled, trying to discern any stains on her clothes, but finding none.

"I'll be taking my eyeballs to get bleached."

"Oh, shut up," I bumped her with my hip, turning toward the bathroom. Her laughter followed me, even after I'd shut the door.

Chapter 43

December

The year was rolling to a close now; I felt it every time I stepped out the front door. Christmas decorations were everywhere, and festive shops had replaced the Halloween stores seemingly overnight. Witches had given way to wreaths, candy canes taking the place of candy apples.

It seemed to me that LA measured the passage of the seasons by the cyclical replication of seasonal stores.

November had passed by in a blur, but not for lack of activity. Pisces had taken on a large orchestral contract to re-record the soundtrack for an upcoming movie. They'd blocked out the entire building for nearly three weeks, the sound of ninety-some musicians flooded the whole ground floor for days as they'd practiced, then performed in the massive downstairs studio.

It had made my time in the storage cave a whole lot more civilised, but the addition of so many more instruments requiring stands, music sheets and every other musical paraphernalia known to mankind sure kept little ol' me busy. The tech guys were the leads, but hell if they didn't get their jollies off on bossing the intern around. I'd gone home every night for weeks so exhausted I could barely stand up.

The thought of them having to go back to doing their own grunt work once I was gone made me smile with a touch of malicious compliance.

I'd also begun to feel the hastening of time, now that I was settled on moving back to the UK.

Becka and I had sat down to really talk it through. We'd weighed all the different options, discussed ways I could extend my contract with Pisces. We'd talked about me getting work in other studios in the city, maybe even radio stations, but in the end even the tenacious Rebecca Hanson had to concede defeat. I just didn't think this was the kind of work I wanted anymore. Not enough, anyway.

I eventually told Becka about the conversation I'd had with Jeremy, where he confessed he hadn't been able to find any places taking on technicians right now. "The industry strikes this year have made people nervous," he'd explained.

I'd taken the news well on the surface, but inside, it made me feel sick. Sure, I'd been blasé about whether I even wanted to work in production, but having the option taken away entirely felt like a blow.

Since then, I'd been trying to flip the script in my head. If another technician role had come up, I could see how my life might have unfolded – predictable, unchanging, filled with unremarkable days I'd have to pretend to enjoy. At least this way, I didn't have to lie to myself anymore.

This whole LA thing had been fun for a while. It had served its purpose – it was only ever supposed to be a year-long step out of real life. Somewhere along the way, though, I'd forgotten that and gotten lost in the monotony. I couldn't let that happen again.

Leaving was the right choice. I think I needed to leave to figure out what I truly wanted.

Besides, staying in LA wasn't an option anymore. It was time to start planning for what came next.

I would leave LA in the new year. I just had to decide if I was going to move back in with my folks up North for a while, or dive straight back into London life.

But as these plans had settled, it had made me more keenly aware of the time I had left here, doing this, living with Becka. That had been by far the hardest part of my decision.

After hours of deliberation, we'd both been exhausted and crying. It was horrible, but now that it was out there in the universe, we'd both made sure to squeeze all the enjoyment we could out of every day. We were rarely home on the weekends, always out looking for adventure, or mischief. She'd even talked me into hiking one weekend. An experience neither of us would be repeating again anytime soon.

November had been full for Jihoon as well; packed full of end-of-year variety shows, radio interviews and filming the last of the group's lives, because they were all taking nearly an entire month off around the Christmas period.

But more than that, they'd also attended the MNET Asian Music awards in Japan. This particular awards show was like the Grammys of Asia. They'd won two Daesangs – the highest award you could win – for best music video for 'Work Harder' and Best Male Group. The whole online community had been abuzz for days.

I was so proud of him – of the whole group, really, they all worked so hard – they deserved the rest they were about to get.

Normally, they took the whole month of December off, but this year they had been invited to perform at the Jingle Bell Ball at the Staples centre in LA, along with a whole host of A-List performers. The concert was on December 6th, so the official holiday for the group didn't start until they flew back to Korea on the 8th.

Jihoon was staying in the city one extra day though, because he had a meeting with Trevor Kyle at Pisces about the solo material he'd recorded earlier in the year, which was for a solo mixtape he was releasing next year. It had been pushed back so as not to coincide with the new album GVibes had released this year.

When he'd told me about his meeting with TK, I'd made a face. I hadn't meant to, but it was an uncontrollable reaction. Jihoon had pressed because he'd said he knew I didn't like him – no one did. He'd been worried he'd done something, and while TK was a loathsome toad and he had inappropriately touched me, I didn't want Jihoon to get the impression something bigger, something more lawyer-worthy had occurred, so I'd told him how he'd made me feel, the way he'd run his finger over me like he'd had the right to.

I debated not telling him about the storage cave incident, but in the end I did, including Donna's rescue.

Jihoon had been furious – so angry that I'd had to talk him down from flying over here and beating TK senseless – tempting as that was. But professionally, there wasn't much he could do as he was under contract through his company to finish the project with him.

I'd had to calm him down by telling him I never even saw him these days. I avoided him when I knew he'd be in the building and I was never tasked with being in or around his studios, so whole weeks would pass without us crossing paths. That had helped, but I could tell he wasn't going to let this go.

Now December had arrived and with it, a cooler air flowed through the city, a respite after the dry, hot air that had maintained it's grip on LA for far longer than it had any right to.

"Does this look alright?" I turned this way and that, staring at myself in the mirror.

"For the ninth time, you look fine." Becka rolled her eyes as she reclined on my bed, watching me pick an outfit for the concert tonight.

"You realise they're not even going to know what seat you're in, let alone actually be able to see you, right?"

Jihoon had been able to get me a ticket to attend the Jingle Bell Ball. He'd tried to get Becka one too, but he hadn't been able to get more than one – the venue was fully booked.

"I know, but that doesn't mean I don't want to look nice. Also, it's a practical outfit, it's gonna be hella hot in there."

"True," she tilted her head in agreement.

I'd settled on a pair of denim shorts, my Doc Martens and a black GVibes t-shirt. I felt cute, but practical.

"Don't forget to take your water bottle with you."

"Yes, Mother," I tossed over my shoulder, earning me another eye roll.

"All righty then, I'm gonna head out; you just know the traffic is gonna be hell."

"Don't forget to get off at the stop we Google'd. It'll be easier to get off the bus early and walk the rest of the way." Becka said, following me out of my room and watching as I filled up my water bottle at the kitchen sink before putting it in my rucksack.

"We literally talked about this an hour ago; I remember!"

"Take lots of pictures; I wanna see what I'm missing!" Becka hounded me to the front door.

"I'll be back before midnight."

"Don't turn into a pumpkin!" Becka called, just as I closed the door on her.

Between the bus journey, the queue just to get into the Staples Center and then finding my way to my row, it had taken me hours to sit my happy butt down in this seat, and it wasn't even a bad seat. Not quite centre-seating, a little more off to the side, but on a slope so I would at least be able to see over the heads of the people in the rows ahead of me.

I sent Becka a message to let her know I'd gotten here – finally, and then sent a selfie of myself to Jihoon, who to my surprise, responded almost immediately.

Joon

Nice t-shirt! But who said you could have such handsome men on your chest?

[Sent 16:21]

Me

You weren't complaining the last time I had a handsome man on my chest ;) shouldn't you be rehearsing, or whatever it is you idols do?

Joon

Behave ;) I can't concentrate if I'm thinking about your chest. We don't need to rehearse, we're too good already. Plus, we can't, someone let all the people in the arena already. lol

[Sent 16:23]

Me

How inconvenient for you! Come out soon, please, I'm getting bored, I wanna see my favourite band :D

Joon

You'll be waiting a bit longer, jagiya, we don't perform until near the end. Please enjoy the other performers while you wait for us.

[Sent 16:26]

Me

What if I like them better?

Joon

We'll have to practice harder to win back your heart.

[Sent 16:29]

I laughed, earning me a strange look from the teenage girl sitting next to me. She had a lightstick poking out of the bag at her feet, clearly identifying her as a Viber. She'd probably lose her ever-loving mind if she knew who was making me laugh right now.

Jihoon and I carried on texting until the lights in the arena dimmed, the music getting louder, subtle hints the show was about to start and, despite the fact it wasn't going to be GVibes until later, I began to feel excited about seeing the other artists. The line up this year was fantastic.

Stage pyrotechnics went off, announcing the entrance of the first singer – none other than Haley, the American singer who'd collaborated with GVibes on their runaway hit, 'Fall in Love,' at the start of the year. She was met with loud screams from the crowd and went on to earn every, single one.

Each artist performing at the ball performed a handful of songs. I was honestly having a great time, even if I wasn't a particular fan of some of the artists. But still, I was anxious to see GVibes. I texted Jihoon between each artist changeover, pestering him with '*is it your turn yet?*'

Until finally he didn't respond. It was nearing the end of the night, already after 9:00pm. I knew GVibes were the second-to-last act playing tonight, the closing performance being from an artist who'd swept the Grammys this year. When he didn't message me back, I knew they must be on next. I felt a frisson of excitement and impulsively I turned to the teen next to me.

"They're on next!" The shared connection of fandom seemed to close the generational/stranger gap and she grinned a me.

"I know! My soul is ready!" Dramatic, but I got it. Mine was too.

Despite my feelings for Jihoon, despite whatever emotional growth I'd gone through this year, despite the separation I felt for Jihoon and the group, I had been a fan first.

The lights in the arena suddenly dimmed, the runner lights flanking the aisles and some low-lying house lights the only illumination, until-

The stage spots flashed, once, twice, and then a continuous pulse in time with the beat that thundered from the towers of speakers framing the main stage. The audience exploded with screams and cheers, lightsticks appearing from all over the arena, constellations dotting the darkness, individual beacons identifying the Vibers in the crowd with more precision than the volume of their cries.

The vibrancy of the atmosphere was a tangible, electric thing, sweeping us all up in a frenzy not seen before now. It was enough to make me feel almost sorry for the other performers.

Just then, the music silenced, the strobe lights shut off, cloaking the arena in a sudden hush, the audience obediently quieting, for the most part.

Then, with a thunderous drum beat that I felt through my shoes, the silhouettes of the five members of GVibes suddenly appeared on the stage, the smoke machine and spotlights giving the illusion they stood ten feet tall.

Once again but with more intensity, the audience erupted and from somewhere in there, the fanchant started up, repeating over and over until the opening bars of 'Pulse' began, unfreezing the group and driving them into motion.

Though I was several rows back, I was close enough to the stage to be able to identify them all immediately, my eyes seeking Jihoon reflexively. Watching them perform in real life felt transformative, and I screamed and stamped my feet along with every other fan in the audience, regardless of my personal relationship to the main vocal. Just then, I was a fan. I could be his girlfriend later.

They performed four songs in all, 'Pulse,' 'Work Harder,' 'I'm Gonna Stay,' and 'Fall in Love' – for which Haley came out and performed with them. I might have felt jealous, if I hadn't read that she'd recently married her long-time sweetheart. It was incomprehensible to me how they managed to dance that hard, that fast and sing at the same time. It seemed superhuman to me. Idols were built different.

By the end of their set, I was practically vibrating with energy, the kind of energy that feels like you're never going to be able to come down from. There was an uproar from the crowd when they eventually left the stage, and I half expected them to run back and honour the loud cries of 'encore,' but they did not and instead, the tech crews ran on to reset the stage for the next and last performer.

Breathing hard, I slumped back down in my seat and pulled out my phone to send a text to Jihoon:

Me

Come back out! I demand more!!!

He didn't reply for a few minutes, which I expected, but I was still impatiently biting my inner cheek when he eventually did.

Joon

Did you like it? I worked extra hard for you.

[Sent 22:22]

Me

It was amazing! I might pass out. hahaha I want to come to all of your shows from now on! I'm furious I've missed so many

Joon

503

Don't pass out or I won't get you tickets to any of our future shows. I'm glad you liked it! I wish I could watch the rest of the show with you. Don't enjoy it as much as our performance, okay?

[Sent 22:25]

Me

I'm not staying, I wanna get home early before the streets get too busy.

Joon

Let me know when you get home

[Sent 22:27]

I got up to leave and so did the teen girl next to me. We locked eyes and she said, "I'm done here now." Well, okay then.

We headed out of the arena going in the same direction – to the main doors at the front of the building. On the way, I loaded the Uber app and luckily there were several in the area, probably trolling for fares leaving the Ball. I had to walk a little distance from the centre itself, but it sure beat having to get the bus, or beating traffic when everyone else left at the same time. Sliding into the back of the Tesla, I congratulated myself on a smart decision.

The traffic still doubled the drive time, and it was well after 11:00pm by the time we rolled up outside my apartment building. I gratefully tipped the driver and tiredly pulled myself up the stairs, looking forward to my bed, the anticipated post-concert crash well in effect now.

The apartment was dark when I put my key in the lock, Becka must have gone to bed, so I quietly locked the door behind me and toed off my boots. I walked into the living area and flipped on the light.

A man I didn't recognise popped up from behind the sofa. He was very, very naked, a fact not at all disguised by the hands he clutched over his... well.

"WHO THE FUCK ARE YOU?!" I screamed, grabbing the closest thing to me, a hefty Stanley tumbler from off the counter, holding it aloft like I was prepared to brain him with it.

"Kaiya, stop, it's ok!"

"Becka?? What the fuck is going on?" I didn't take my eyes − or my aim − off the naked guy, or Becka − also very naked − I noticed as I glanced in her direction. Confusion made my arm sag a little, the Stanley tumbler lowering to my side.

"Ben, put your pants on." Becka turned to the naked man, holding an arm out to him as if to, what, comfort him?

Hang on a minute.

"BEN!?"

"Ky, stop shouting," Becka pulled a t-shirt on to cover her nakedness; not her shirt, I noticed. "This is... well, this is... Ben."

"Um, hi." Ben waved at me awkwardly after hurriedly pulling on a pair of blue jeans.

"THE Ben?!" I aimed this at Becka.

She nodded, a little sheepishly, while 'the Ben' waved at me again. I narrowed my eyes at him. "You motherfucker!"

Chapter 44

"I think I should go," Ben said, nervously eying me.

"Wait-" Becka reached out to stop him, "your shirt-"

"Keep it, I'll put my jacket on." He moved around the sofa, never turning his back to me, grabbing a leather jacket I hadn't noticed when I came in off the counter next to me. I followed his movements, turning to keep him in my line-of-sight watching as he pulled on a pair of sneakers.

"I'll call you," he said to Becka over my shoulder, before looking me in the eyes for the first time. "Nice to meet you, Kaiya." He opened and closed the door faster than I could think of anything appropriately threatening to say.

As the door snicked shut, I turned back to Becka, slamming the tumbler down on the counter.

"You got some 'splaining to do Lucy."

She rolled her eyes. "Oh chill out, I was much cooler than this when I caught you and Jihoon butt naked in here."

"That's not the same, and you know it!"

"It's not that much different," she muttered, pulling her trousers back on.

"There are a couple glaring differences," I said, argumentatively.

Becka held her hands up to cover her eyes as she took a deep breath.

"Can we talk about this in the morning?" She slid her hands up into her hair and it was then that I saw how red her eyes were.

"Have you been crying?" I asked, horrified. "What did that fucker do to you? I'm calling the cops-"

"For fucks sake, Ky!" Becka shouted, startling me and pausing me in the process of pulling my phone out of my pocket.

"Just... fucking stop. He didn't do anything. Nothing I didn't want him to do, anyway." She sat down on the sofa heavily. I moved round the sofa, but opted to sit on the coffee table in front of her. Because, well. Ew.

"Tell me so I understand. Because I thought we hated him."

"We do!" she cried. "I think. I don't know anymore." She started crying, shoulders-heaving, ugly crying sobs. Ignoring my ick, I moved to sit beside her so I could pull her into my arms.

It took her a while to get it all up, or at least as much as she had the reserves for right now.

Through her sniffles, she began to talk.

"He just showed up, not long after you'd left. Jose must have let him in, you know how much he always liked Ben. Or, I guess you probably don't know that, because you weren't here," she smiled, but it was watery and weak.

"So, when someone knocked on the door, I thought it was you, that you'd forgotten something. I opened the door and almost fell on my ass when he was standing right there.

"I was just so shocked, you know? I haven't seen him in more than a year, and he's just standing there, like he never left. He asked to come in and I... I didn't have it in me to say no." She hiccupped and wiped her face, the tears coming slower now.

"I didn't know what to say, I swear. The first thing to come out of my mouth was, "Where the hell have you been?" She laughed.

"And then, I don't know what happened. We just talked. For ages. He's been living with his mom and he started up his own business and he just kept saying he's not the same Ben anymore, whatever the hell that means.

"And then we opened a bottle of wine and... I don't know, it was like it was before. We were talking about the old days, and he kissed me. It just felt right, and believe me, I know that's crazy, but I can't explain it. One thing led to another, and then I guess we fell asleep." She shrugged, and I could tell she was trying to make light of it, but her eyes were pinched from all the thoughts she was trying not to have. I knew her well enough to know when she's doing mental gymnastics.

But, now was not the time. It was late, we were both tired. There would be time tomorrow to dissect this.

"Come on," I stood, "bed."

She looked up at me and nodded, rising to her feet and shuffling off to her bedroom. At the door to her room, she turned. "Hey," I turned to look at her. "Did you have fun tonight?"

I smiled at the memory. "I really did."

The next morning, we both got up late. I'd woken to several messages from Jihoon asking if I'd gotten home safe, and then to say he was going to the after party and then several selfies of him with multiple celebrities. I especially liked the photo-booth of all five members of GVibes, four members of a punk-rock band and Haley all shoved into a space designed for maybe half that many people. All wearing props, hats, or some kind of mask.

At least they'd been having fun, whilst I'd come home to find some dudes junk all over my sofa and my best friend in tears. I felt my ire rising again. I had to take several deep breaths just to be able to get out of bed. I needed to be cool about this. Becka had never told me much about their breakup, but I now suspected it was because she didn't really understand what had happened. One day he was here, the next day he wasn't.

I don't know how a person gets over that.

I decided right then that I would be the supportive friend she needed, and only maybe make occasional comments about the sofa.

Becka wasn't in the living room when I opened my bedroom door, but a quick glance round the corner into her room confirmed that while she was still in bed, she was sat up, reading a book. I knocked on the door to get her attention.

"Knock-knock. Room for one more?"

She looked up at me before putting down her book and patted the empty side of the bed. I walked over and flopped down next to her.

"Clumsy oaf," she said, smiling down at me.

"Sofa slut," I replied with an easy smile.

Becka groaned and threw her head back against her pillows as I snorted.

"Odds of you letting up about that this side of the apocalypse?"

"Not high," I admitted with the kind of smile you might see on a TV presenter's face along with the words, 'and here's what you could have won.'

"That's what I get for riding the forbidden pogo stick on a shared sofa." She sighed. I just nodded.

We were silent a few moments more before I said, "Wanna talk about it?"

Becka looked up at the ceiling, taking her time to answer. "I've been thinking about it. And while I don't know how I feel about actually feeling it – I'm big enough to admit that the love is still there." She shrugged. "I... still love him. I do. I thought I was done with it, I wanted to be done with it, you know?" She looked at me, frowning.

"I just can't get there. I'm still pissed, oh man, am I royally fucking pissed, but it doesn't override the annoying fact that I love the bastard."

"Do you want to try again with him?"

"I don't know," she said, cocking her head to the side, eyebrows furrowed. "I'm vengeful, you know?" She offered a half-shrug. I didn't try to disagree with her. We all had our character flaws and this was one of hers.

She was like Mr Darcy; once her good opinion has been lost, it is lost forever. Usually. Maybe not in Ben's case, as it was in Mr Darcy's case with Elizabeth Bennet.

"He needs to tell me what the fuck happened, that's for damn sure," Becka said decisively. "And then I think, maybe, I need to see if that makes a difference."

"What if it's something unforgivable, like he cheated?"

She winced before slowly saying, "I think that would make it easier for me to decide, but I don't think it would turn it off. Not immediately, anyway."

I nodded, understanding what she meant. Emotions are not appliances.

"When are you going to see him again?" I didn't try to pretend that she wasn't going to, we both knew she'd decided to long before I came in here this morning.

"He said he'll call me, so let him do the leg work. For once," she added darkly.

I sat up and shrugged. "You're a big girl, Becka. But if you need me to break his legs, give me some advance notice so I can get my alibi straight, yeah?"

Becka snorted. "Yeah, you and my Stanley cup, a formidable pair."

I nodded seriously. "Proper insulation is no joke."

We shared a look before dissolving into giggles. I don't know which of us reached out first, but we ended up in each other's arms all the same, the laughter giving way to the silence of shared space.

"I'm going to miss you so fucking much."

"I know. You're going to clean that sofa."

"I know."

Chapter 45

"Annyeonghaseyo, Youngsoo." I inclined my head to him politely, trying to hide my smile at the way his eyes widened. Jihoon was on the other side of the lobby, talking to Celine and Trevor Kyle. I knew he hadn't heard me.

"Annyeonghaseyo, Kaiya-ssi," he muttered, reflexively bowing, but only a little.

I caught Jihoon's eyes for a split-second before he looked back to Celine, who was speaking. I was probably crossing a line being down here at all, but I couldn't help myself when Jihoon had texted me to say they were arriving.

Trevor Kyle was staring at me, his head tilted, one side of his mouth quirked up. I didn't like the way his attention made me feel; like I had bugs under my clothes, crawling around my skin like they owned the place. I forced myself to tear my gaze away and headed back over to the stairwell, looking over my shoulder just once to look at Jihoon, to admire the way his hair fell down past his ears, the way he smiled slightly when he talked, the way he held himself.

He caught me looking again, and I could see the faint tug of a smile he was trying not to let show. It felt like we were sharing a secret, the kind that swells in your chest like a warm, fizzy bubble. The kind that's part delight, part bittersweet ache, teetering on the edge of something more.

I shook my head, consciously grabbed the door handle, pulled it open and walked back upstairs, gaining more clarity with every step that took me further away from him.

It had been near unbearable these past few nights, knowing damn well where he was in the city, but being unable to do anything about it. I wondered if this would ever fade, it felt so acute now.

I headed to Jeremy's office. He'd been dodging me lately, I think he felt bad that we both knew I was out of a job in a few months, but I'd made my peace with it. I hoped that made it easier on him. I entered his office and he was exactly where he should be; sat in his chair, scowling at his laptop screen like it had offended three generations of his family.

"Sup, boss," I said cheerfully. He flinched, like I'd shouted the words at him.

"Oh, hey Kaiya. What can I do for you?"

"That's not how a job is supposed to work, boss. What can *I* do for *you*?"

He sighed and looked up from the screen. "Kaiya, we both know damn well I got nothing for you. I ran out weeks ago."

"I'm too efficient is what you're saying?"

He groaned. "Tell ya what, why don't you pick a department to hang out with today. Get some hands-on experience. It'll be good for you."

For when I have to update my CV, is what he doesn't say, but we both know. Honestly, I could probably get away with taking a book down to the storage cave and just chilling out, but call me a glutton for punishment, that's just not who I am.

"Ok, I'll hang out with the office today, I've been wondering how they do all the marketing crap in-house." Not strictly untrue. I'd had some thoughts about my blog recently, and Pisces had had some excellent viral marketing lately. Plus, you know, hanging out with Becka didn't suck.

"You do that, kid. Go with my blessing."

"Thank you, Godfather." I saluted, grinning when he groaned.

"Hey babes," Becka briefly looked up as I walked into her office before going back to typing away at her computer.

"Sup, delinquent."

She just rolled her eyes at me. This was not the first joke I'd made about public indecency, defacing public property, etc. True to her word though, she had thoroughly cleaned the sofa.

"What do you need?"

"Somewhere to hang out today, Jeremy is starting to admit defeat. I've been too good at my job, Pisces is now so thoroughly ordered, tidied and otherwise catalogued into it's correct place that I've made myself redundant."

"Please, take a seat and welcome to the valley of broken toys," Becka motioned to the chair opposite. "With AI on the near-horizon, we'll all be obsolete in a few years anyway."

"Don't say that!" One of the other office girls cried, looking up from her own computer.

"I'm kidding, Clara-Beth, we all know the Government will implement labour laws to protect the jobs of office workers before that happens." Becka said with so much authority I looked at her in surprise. The illusion shattered the moment she rolled her whole face back to look at me, and I had to muffle my sudden giggle as a sneeze.

"Gives me the creeps, that stuff does," said Clara-Beth. "Machines thinking for themselves."

"Don't say it," Becka muttered, giving me a hard side-eye.

Ignoring Becka, I turned to look across the office, meeting the eyes of the pretty blonde with the ceramic puppy figurines on her desk. "Don't worry Clara-Beth, 'The future is not set. There is no fate but what we make for ourselves.'" My face was as dead pan as if I were delivering the news. Clara-Beth nodded, albeit uncertainly, like she knew there was a joke in there somewhere, before she shrugged and turned back to her computer.

"Done, John Connor?" Becka leaned her head over to one side, one eyebrow raised.

"For now," I grinned.

Despite my sass, I really was interested in the social side of things, so I spent the morning hanging out behind the desks, looking over Becka's shoulder, mostly, but also sometimes Celine – once I'd convinced her I wasn't interested in any kind of espionage.

Then, sometime around midday, just before Becka and I were due to get lunch, Celine got a message on her laptop that made her click her tongue in annoyance.

"Mr Kyle wants one of us to clear out the conference room." Becka and the other girls in the room groaned.

"God forbid he do it, with his own manly hands," Becka sighed, pushing back her chair.

"I'll do it," I offered, "not like I'm doing anything useful right now." No one objected, which was fair, but also... ouch.

"Thanks!" Celine trilled, giving me a wide view of her veneers before turning back to her computer.

"Be right back," I said to Becka as I got up and walked out the office door. The conference was a straight shot down the corridor from the main office, past the corridor on the right that led to Jeremy's office, the lockers and the tech suites and the elevator on the left. I walked past the tech corridor and the elevator and then the employee lounge on the right, briefly looking in, but it was empty.

I pushed open the door to the conference room, not bothering to check if it was empty before entering.

"Oh-" I pulled up short at seeing one of the chairs occupied. "Sorry, I-" The chair spun round and sat there was Jihoon, who grinned and stood up as he saw me.

"Hey, you." I grinned as he approached. "I didn't know if I'd see you before you left."

"I was waiting for you. I just sent you a message." He reached out to run his hands up my arms, leaving a trail of goosebumps in his wake.

I patted my pockets. "I must have left my phone in the office." I shrugged, even as I reached for him.

"I'm so happy to see you," I leaned into him, inhaling deeply, just content to be in the circle of his strong arms.

"Me too. I have to fly back tonight." He leaned his chin on my head as his arms tightened around me.

"So soon?" I grumbled.

"Yes. I wanted to ask if you'd come to my hotel tonight. Our flight isn't until late." He pulled back enough that he could look at me, his eyes crinkled at the side, a very slight blush on his cheekbones. When would the novelty wear off, I thought. I kind of hoped never.

"Are you asking me to sleep with you, Baek Jihoon?" I replied, scandalised.

"Yes."

I laughed and ran my hands up his chest, delighting in the feel of his firm muscles, before I looped my arms around his neck, pulling him down for a kiss.

"I would be delighted to," I murmured against his lips a moment before he claimed my mouth with his.

"What the hell is going on in here?"

I tore my mouth from Jihoon's and leapt away from him like I'd been burnt.

Celine stood in the open doorway, one hand on her chest like she was having a heart attack. Beside her stood Trevor Kyle, and he was grinning from ear to ear.

"I'm sorry, are we interrupting something?" Trevor Kyle somehow made the question sound like an indictment.

Celine pointed at me, her long, red fingernail that she'd claimed only an hour ago was 'festive,' now might as well have been tipped in blood.

"You," she seethed, "out, now."

"Ky-" Jihoon reached for me, but I shrugged him off.

"It's okay, I'll call you later." I tried to give him a reassuring smile, but I felt the way it trembled; I was quite sure it wouldn't reassure anyone.

I had to move past Celine and Trevor Kyle to exit, but while Celine jumped out of my way as though I was contagious, Trevor Kyle didn't move an inch, forcing me to squeeze past him. Every point of contact filled me with revulsion. Once out the door, I saw Youngsoo heading towards the conference room, his face set in a mask of professional anger, the way his mouth pinched told me he knew what had occurred, which only begged the question, how did anyone at all know?

He glanced at me briefly as he passed, sparing me no expression or word, only heading into that conference room with the purpose I imagined he'd been hired as a manager for. The door closed and I didn't dare linger.

I headed towards Jeremy's office with a strange kind of detachment. A sort of certainty that made me almost giddy as the adrenaline pumped through me.

I didn't bother knocking.

"The shit is about to hit the fan, boss," I said by way of greeting.

To his credit, Jeremy only looked up at me and frowned. "Tell me."

Internally shrugging, I said, "Celine and TK just caught me kissing an idol in the conference room." No point beating around the bush.

Jeremy blinked. Once, twice, a third time before he put his head down on his desk with a thump. "For fuck's saaaaaaaaaake."

I laughed, only a slight edge of hysteria to the sound.

"They FIRED you!?" Becka screeched, and I winched.

"Becka chill," I slid a glass of wine across the countertop to her. I was already on my second one.

"CHILL!?" she screeched again as she snatched the glass of red, taking a gulp I would have choked on, for sure.

Coming up for air, she panted as she said, "How are you so calm? What the fuck are you gonna do? They FIRED you!"

"Technically, I resigned." I held up my hand to pause Becka's oncoming barrage. "Drink your wine and I'll tell you all about it," I soothed.

Eying me, she raised the glass to her mouth, but only sipped at it this time.

"Okay, so there I was, trying to peel Jeremy's head off his desk when Celine comes in, looking mad as a bag of cats. 'You,'" I said, doing my best Celine impression by holding my nose to emulate her nasally voice, "'follow me.' So, all three of us go back to the scene of the crime, only Jihoon, Youngsoo, and TK are gone.

"We all sit down and then Liam Fenway comes in, looking pissed as hell."

Becka gasped. "The Chief Operations Officer? He never comes in, not for anything!"

"Lucky me then, because this is the first and last time I'll ever see him," I chuckled, taking a swig of wine.

"Kaiya," Becka groaned, "be so for real right now."

I waved her off. "Anyway, so Celine starts in, treating the whole thing like a witch trial and I'm the harlot accused of casting seduction spells on the men of the town. Meanwhile, Jeremy is sat there with his head in his hands."

"What does Liam do?" Becka asks through bloodless lips.

"He's just sat there with his hands like this," I lean my elbows on the counter and steeple my fingers together, "like he's one of the businessmen on Shark Tank.

"Eventually he tells Celine to shut her beak and asks me what happened, like anything I say at this point is going to make a difference." I made a 'pfft' sound and sip my wine.

"What did you say?"

"I told them the truth." I shrugged. Becka groaned and put her head down on the counter. Lot of people doing that today.

"Liam asked how long I'd been seeing Jihoon, I told him the truth. I mean, two people literally caught us in the act, what was the point of lying?" I forced a devil-may-care smirk on to my face, but I couldn't force the nervous jitters away as they still coursed through my body.

"Oh babes..." Becka's eyes started welling up as she looked at me.

"Becka, it's okay. I was going to be leaving in a few months anyway, this just... accelerated things."

"But they let you resign?"

"Yes," I jumped on the sideways topic before I thought too much about the rug that had been pulled out from under my feet, three months early. "Liam was all about to kick me out, but Jeremy piped up to argue that considering I'm not a US citizen, that would be terrible for me as I wasn't entitled to claim unemployment and I'd have to leave the country sooner than I planned." I took a fortifying gulp of wine.

"He convinced him to let me resign so I wouldn't have the black mark against my employment record back in the UK. I think he sold it on the basis that it would be less paperwork for the studio."

"And he bought that?" Becka's eyebrows shot up so high, they almost touched her hairline.

"Well," I hedged, a nervous smile pulling up my lips. "Not at first."

Becka blinked. "At first?"

"Did I mention that TK was also in that meeting?" I took a generous gulp of wine.

Becka frowned. "Why the fuck was he there? What's he got to do with anything?"

I shrugged. "He seems to feel entitled to do a lot of things he has no business to," I said darkly. "Anyway, so then TK pipes about, spewing some absolute crap about the studio's reputation and suing me for-"

"SUING YOU!?" Becka screeched so loud I almost dropped my wine glass.

"Ow, ears!" I cried, trying to steady the hand holding my glass to prevent any wine sloshing out.

"Sorry," she said contritely, a hand held to her mouth. "Then what happened?"

"So TK launches into this disappointed mentor routine, going on about how suing me is the only way to protect the studio's reputation and make an example of me – yada, yada." I gestured with my hand and rolled my eyes.

"Oh, fuck, Ky... what did you do?"

"Pfft. I pulled out my phone."

"You-you did what?" Becka frowned, cocking her head to the side as I just grinned.

"I put my phone on the side like this –" I pulled my phone out of my pocket and put it on the counter, where Becka looked at it with a blank expression.

"And then I pressed play, like this." I slid my finger up the screen and played the audio recording, Trevor Kyle's voice filling our small kitchenette.

"It's Kaiya. What can I do for you, Mr Kyle?"

"How long have you worked for us, Kaiya?"

"Since April, Mr Kyle."

"And do you have aspirations to work in the music industry, Kaiya?"

"I don't know career I'm going to pursue, yet."

"I could help you with that, you know. It's so important to nurture talent from within our ranks. I've seen your Youtube channel. You have some promise."

"T-thank you."

"Why don't you spend some time shadowing me? I could show you the ropes. I'd be happy to break you in a little bit."

"It's who you know in this business that opens doors. You need friends you can look up to. We could be friends."

"When did that happen?" Becka is so pale I'm worried she'll faint.

"Sit down." I pulled out the chair at the counter and helped her into it.

"Ky, why didn't you tell me?" Her chin trembled, and I can't help but wonder if perhaps I should have done.

I shrugged. "It was weeks ago and what would I have said? 'TK made more gross passes at me'? I was trying to focus on just being present here, at Pisces, in LA... It seemed immaterial."

"Immaterial," Becka murmured through bloodless lips. "Did he touch you?"

"What? No!" I insisted. "Donna came in and interrupted him."

"Donna hates everyone – but she sticks her neck out for you." Becka started to giggle, but it was a strained sound. "What the fuck is it about you?" Becka threw her hands up in the air. "An idol, a producer, and now the world's most dangerous receptionist."

"I'm not sure how I feel about all those people being lumped together," I reflected.

Becka closed her eyes, pinched the bridge of her nose and took a deep breath in. "Okay, tell me what happened next in the meeting."

"Oh, yeah. Well, as you can imagine, TK blew his top." I grinned. "He tried to grab my phone, but Jeremy pulled it away before he could reach it. Very dramatic." I waggled my eyebrows at Becka, who just took a gulp of wine. "Then, TK tried to downplay it. 'That's bullshit.' He said, 'that recording doesn't prove any wrongdoing.' But he looked nervous as hell." I chuckled.

"I just said, 'maybe not legally, but I wonder what the court of public opinion would think.'"

"Oh, holy fuck," Becka groaned.

"So then he tried to throw the non-disclosure agreement in my face," I added, "but that's when Liam Fenway pipes up to point out that the NDA only protects clients, not 'dumbass producers.' Honestly, Becka, you should have seen TK's face. It was glorious." I sighed, leaning back against the counter and taking another sip of wine.

Becka gulped her wine like water, grabbed the bottle, and poured herself another. She held it up silently, asking if I needed a top-up. I held out my glass, and she poured in the rest, the bottle now empty.

"What happened then?"

"Not much. TK stormed out, Fenway told Celine to get my paperwork printed and then he just told Jeremy to finalise the 'exit interview.'" I huffed and then took another sip form my glass.

Silence fell between us as we each collected our thoughts.

"So you've officially 'resigned'?" Becka asked eventually, a crease between her brows.

"Technically," I agreed, "Jeremy even told me afterwards that if I ever needed a reference, to email him directly and he'll do it for me. Damn good of him."

"He may be on the verge of a stroke, but he's a decent person," Becka agreed.

"How are you feeling? That was a lot, babes." Becka held my gaze, that unnerving stare she sometimes pulled out when she knew you were withholding something. I fidgeted, playing with my ring as I considered my answer.

"Honestly, I'm kind of relieved. The whole thing with TK was more of a weight than I thought – and yes, you're absolutely right, I should have told you."

"Why didn't you?"

I chewed on my lip before answering. "I was so busy trying to convince myself it wasn't a big deal, that I think I convinced myself it wasn't.

"I mean, who the hell am I?" I spread my arms. "Just a foreigner in a country that isn't all that interested in keeping me here without the backing of my employer. An employer I would be potentially implicating in a sexual harassment scandal.

"So, yes. Relief is the thing I mostly feel. And I think I didn't tell you because you've been so invested in me, and my time here. And I've been feeling like an arsehole for not being more into it. You went to so much trouble to get me here and put me up. And it only took me a few months to realise I didn't want this anymore."

I was so worked up, that I almost didn't realise what I'd just said, until Becka held up her hand to pause me.

"Hold up – what did you realise you don't want anymore?"

Ah fuck. Oh well, in for a penny, in for a pound.

I sighed. "Becka I... being here has been such an enormous, wild adventure, and I really mean it when I say that I have loved it. But of all the things I've learnt since being here, the biggest is that... I don't want to do music production. It's just not something I love anymore."

I fell silent and just watched her, watching me. Until she blew out a breath, dropped her head and said, "Finally."

Not the response I was expecting. "Beg pardon?"

"Babes, I get that that was probably a big, dramatic moment for you. But you've forgotten who's sitting next to you right now. I know you, and I've known for a long time that this was not going to be where you ended up. Well, careerwise, anyway."

I gaped at her. "But you've been pressing me to really lean into LA, into Pisces..."

Becka rolled her eyes at me. "Well yeah, because you had a year-long contract, how hard is it to suck it up for a year, make the connections, get the experience and live in frickin' LA? Babes, if you'd been less of a whiney baby deer, we could have done this ages ago and planned on how to get you into an industry you actually wanted. I knew you didn't love being behind the music; even back at Uni. You always talked about the music itself, never the process of putting it all together. You wouldn't shut up about the artistry of it all coming together. You never did that about doing it yourself. You hated practical work. I never knew another student who'd rather write the dissertation than do the practical."

I laughed, even as my chin wobbled.

"Why the fuck didn't you tell me that, months ago!"

"Well, hell babes," Becka grabbed my face in her hands, "I thought you'd figure it out, eventually. I didn't know it would take a sexual harassment allegation and a breach of contract to get you there!"

We laughed for a while, until the mirth subsided and we fell into silence, each of us letting the enormity of the afternoon sink in, before Becka quietly spoke. "What will you do now?"

I sighed, a big gust I pulled all the way up from my stomach and tried to exhale out the demons of the day on it. "I guess, I go home.

"Oh fuck, Kaiya." Becka's voice broke and she put down her wine glass to cover her eyes as her shoulders began to shake, crying in earnest.

I hurried round the counter to wrap my arms around her shoulders, rubbing her arms, trying to impart comfort I wasn't sure I even had for myself.

"Sshh... it's okay," I murmured, "it's going to be okay. This changes nothing for you and me, you know that right?"

"I don't want you to go," she wailed.

I had to swallow thickly before I spoke. "Me either, but it is what it is. This is just the way it was meant to pan out, you know?"

Becka had nothing to say to that. We each held each other, Becka crying, me trying not to, both of us just feeling our way through this, until eventually Becka's cries turned into soft snuffles.

We'd been silent a while before a knock came at the door. I looked at Becka, and she looked at me.

"I'm not expecting anyone," she shrugged, "but I bet Jose let someone in again."

"We really need to tell him to stop doing that," I said darkly, walking towards the door to look through the peephole.

"Oh!"

"Who is it?" Becka called from behind me. I didn't answer before I threw the door open.

"Jihoon," I breathed, walking into him. His strong arms encircled me, and I took the first full breath in what felt like hours.

"Are you alright?" He pressed a kiss to the top of my head and I shook my head, all my bravado having fled the moment I saw him outside our door.

"No, but I will be." My voice was muffled against his chest.

He moved us back into the apartment, closing the door behind him. I reluctantly let go of him, but kept hold of his hand and led him into the living area.

"Hello, Becka." He greeted her politely.

"Sup, idol." She lifted her wine glass to him in salute. I rolled my eyes.

"I'll give you two a minute," Becka said, sliding off the stool and heading to her bedroom, closing the door behind her. I leaned against the kitchen counter, rubbing the hand not currently entwined with Jihoon's down my face.

"What happened?" He didn't need to elaborate on what he meant.

I repeated the same thing I told Becka. A tic started in his jaw and his eyes narrowed when I told him about my 'resignation.'

"Surely, they can't make you leave. It may have been unprofessional, but-"

"It's literally against the terms of my contract," I sighed, interrupting him before he could get a full head of steam on. At his confused expression, I went on; "my contract states relationships with clients of the studio – you –" I gestured at him, "are strictly prohibited and cause for immediate termination, if not legal action. Luckily, they're happy to keep it out of court."

"That's not fair!" His raised voice took me by surprise. I don't think I've ever seen him mad before. Well, except for when I'd told him about TK. Wow, Pisces was really pissing him off, these days. I decided right then to tell him another time about what had happened in the meeting, about TK and the recording.

I shrugged, kicking my toe against the floor. "It's to prevent people taking jobs there who only want to hook up with celebrities."

When he'd been able to look me in the eye, Liam, the COO had explained that even if my relationship with Jihoon was genuine, the contract was watertight to protect Pisces. My job had been forfeited the moment we'd exchanged numbers. Not that I would have changed the events, had I known the outcome.

"I already signed a non-disclosure agreement when I started working there. They were very clear they would sue if I talked about any of this."

I pinched the bridge of my nose, thinking about my next words.

"They said if it ever came out that we were... you know, a 'couple,' the only thing I'd be able to say is that we met during the time I was employed there, but not that we began dating at the same time you were recording, which I guess would be true anyway, not that we can ever go public." I chuckled, but the sound was forced and weirdly high-pitched.

Jihoon's face crumpled as he took a slight step backwards, almost as if I'd physically pushed him.

"Jihoon..." I reached for him like I could snatch the words back out of the air as they lay between us.

Jihoon shook his head, whether to brush aside my concern, or to shake off the words, I couldn't tell. My hand dropped to my side just as he said, "What will you do now?"

I blew out a breath, then turned around and grabbed my half-full glass of wine. I took a sip as I considered my response. Honestly, I hadn't laid any firm plans, it had only been a few hours ago that I'd had a job – a reason to stay here. Now...

"I have 60 days to either find a new job, or... or I go back to the UK."

"Come with me."

"Where?" I frowned. "Back to your hotel? Now? Lemme grab a bag first-" I pushed off the counter and took maybe a couple steps before Jihoon grabbed my wrist. He looked down at me, the intensity in his eyes almost like a physical touch. A tic feathered along his jaw.

"Come with me to Korea."

Chapter 46

"What did you say?" I whispered, half afraid I'd misheard, half-afraid I hadn't.

"Come to Korea with me. Tonight, you can fly over with me." His face softened, the line between his brows smoothing, his mouth quirking slightly at one side. But his eyes – they held mine in a way that made looking away impossible. His thumb rubbed circles on my wrist, pulling me back to the here and now.

I opened my mouth to speak, the 'no,' or 'I can't' forming, and then re-forming before being wiped away like words on a chalkboard. Because, after all, why couldn't I?

Why wouldn't I?

"What the fuck did you just say?" Becka's voice burst through the bubble of my introspection a moment before her physical presence.

Her footsteps stomped on the floorboards with such force I just knew that Jose downstairs would be able to hear it.

"Becka-"

"No, no, not you." She held up a hand to silence me as she stared up at Jihoon, her face as severe as I'd ever seen it, all the softness somehow transposed to sharp angles and shadows.

"You," she hissed, pointing at Jihoon, "what did you just say?"

"Becka, stop." I slid over the wooden floor to put myself between them. "Not okay." I put my hand on her arm and lowered it, but only because she allowed it. She slid her gaze to me, and I could see the pain there.

Over my shoulder I said, "Jihoon, I need to talk to Becka. Can I call you later with my decision?"

I heard him blow out a breath and could imagine the expression on his face, but I kept my eyes on Becka.

"I'll be waiting," he said, "don't take too long, jagiya."

I waited until I heard the door click behind him before I said anything, but I didn't get the chance.

"You can't go with him."

"Becka-"

"I'm serious. Go back to London, stay her for two more months. Whichever, but you cannot go to Korea with him." Her eyes were wide, her jaw set in a tight line as she gripped my hand.

I extracted my hand as gently as I could, because she was hurting me slightly. "Let's sit down and talk about it. You're my best friend; I want your opinion." I offered her a smile and though she didn't return it, she did nod. We both retrieved our wine glasses and the bottle from the counter and took them over to the sofa. I topped us both up. Becka didn't hesitate to take a sip from hers.

"Okay," I began, "you've obviously got some thoughts, and in respect of our years of friendships, you have the floor."

"I don't know how else to say, 'don't go,'" she snapped, and my own temper flared.

I felt the tic in my eye, but pushed it down, muffled it with a deep breath and tried again.

"Tell me why you think this is such a bad idea."

"Did you not SEE yourself this year?" Becka shouted, leaning forward like she would try to press the words into me. "We literally just talked about this, like two months ago!"

"This is not the same thing; don't you see that?"

"It absolutely is! Once again, Kaiya has to compact herself to suit Jihoon the Idol's life. It was bad enough when you had to follow your boyfriend's life online, but now he gets to take you with him so he can take you out and play with you whenever it suits him? How convenient!"

"I'm not a doll, Becka," I spluttered, bewildered by the barrage of accusations, of how Becka saw this.

"Exactly! But he treats you like one!"

"No, he doesn't!"

"Oh, grow up, Ky," Becka scoffed, rolling her head back on her shoulders like she couldn't stand to look at me. "How do you think this is going to end? Hmm? You're going to go over there, he's going to constantly be away, doing idol things, and you're going to be alone in a foreign country, with no one you know, just waiting for him to come back. And then one day, he won't, he probably won't even bother to call you, he just won't bother coming back!"

Becka burst into tears, her whole body shaking with the force of it. She slammed her wine glass down on the table and grabbed a pillow, shoving her face into it to muffle her cries while I just looked on as my simmering anger vanished like a candle being snuffed.

"Becka... Jihoon isn't Ben." I wanted to reach for her, but the divide felt too big.

Finally, she raised her head, her face was splotchy, but she was still one of the loveliest women I'd ever seen. It hurt to see her in this much pain.

"Isn't he?" She wiped at her cheeks. "Because Ben wasn't that man, until he was. We had plans, you know. We were going to live together for a few years before we'd get engaged, get married, buy an apartment. It was the plan." Her chin trembled as she spoke.

"But all our plans turned to shit. Babes, you don't even have plans. You don't even have an official relationship." I flinched. I knew she hadn't said that to hurt me, but hell if it hadn't.

"What will you do when he leaves you? You can't even talk about it to anybody. Because I'm telling you," her shoulders heaved as she tried to force her words out, "don't come crying to me when he does."

A tear slipped down my cheek, but it wasn't for me. I reached for her, finally, scooting forward until I could wrap my arms around her, half-expecting her to push me away, but she didn't, and she never would.

"I will always come to you, and you will always be there for me," I murmured, rocking her slightly, "and I will always be there for you. That's the deal, that's always been the deal."

Becka wound her arms around my waist, holding me tight enough to bruise, but I didn't complain.

We sat there for who-knows how long, just being with each other, feeling the tension seep out until, still holding each other, we slumped against the back of the sofa.

"I'm going to miss you so much." She pulled back to look at me, her face now dry but the sadness written on it remained.

"I'm going to miss you too." What else could I say?

"You better go pack. Good thing you didn't bring much."

I laughed, but it quickly turned into a sob, the mix of emotions swirling through me like a carousel. Which one was driving it – who could tell?

"Now?"

"Yes babes, you can't wait any longer."

"Will you help me?"

"Of course, babes."

Becka stood up, holding her hand out to me to pull me up. I slid my fingers against hers and together, we went into my little LA bedroom and began to pack up my temporary life.

Me

Jihoon. I'm coming to Korea.

End of Book One.

Epilogue

I rode to the airport alone. Becka hadn't been able to face the trip.

"I can't say goodbye to you twice." Her voice wavered on the words. "Just once; a clean break."

I chuckled, but it was a hollow sound that fell to the floor. "Becka, we're not breaking up. I'm just relocating."

Becka nodded, her chin wobbling. "I know that up here." She tapped her forehead with one delicately manicured nail. "But here," she said as she pressed her other hand to her chest, "it feels like you're leaving me forever. I guess I got used to the idea of you always being here." Her eyes fell to the floor, but though they were lowered, I saw the way they glistened.

"Hey." I grabbed her hand, forcing her to look at me. "I have been and shall always be your friend."

Becka stared at me for one beat, two, three.

"Are you fucking kidding me right now?"

I burst out laughing, so forcefully I had to bend over as tears rolled down my face; at least half of them bittersweet.

It took me a hot minute to calm down enough to stand back up, meeting her stern, but also somehow soft expression.

"I thought for a second you hadn't recognised it."

Becka rolled her eyes at me. "You lived here less than a year and yet we somehow got through every Star Trek film ever released. Obviously, something stuck."

Impulsively, I grabbed her, pulling her towards me so tight she had to take a step forward or risk falling. "I love you," I whispered, my voice hoarse with all the tears I refused to shed.

"I love you, too." She rubbed my back and for a time, we just stood there in each other's embrace, until headlights illuminated us and a car pulled up to where we stood.

Reluctantly, I pulled away, turning around just as Becka raised a hand to her face, swiping under her eyes.

A car idled behind me, and as I bent down to the window, it rolled down.

"Kaiya Thompson?" The driver, a woman of indeterminate age leaned over, glancing behind me to where my two rucksacks and a larger duffel bag sat. The sum total of my life in LA.

"That's me." I confirmed.

"I'll pop the trunk. You need a hand with those?"

"Nah, I got them. Thanks."

I turned back to Becka, who was now staring down the street, as if mentally following the route I would be taking.

"You should go back inside. It's cold." My hands felt suddenly useless, so I shoved them into my pockets.

Becka looked at her smart watch. "It's 60 degrees."

I looked at my own smart watch. "That's 16 degrees Celsius. That's cold."

She looked at me, smiling, though a tear trailed down her cheek. "You've gotten soft."

"I'll always be soft for you." My own smile trembled, but I yanked it back into place through sheer force of will.

"Come on," she said, "I helped you lug these downstairs; I might as well help you put them in the car." She grabbed my duffel, and I followed, grabbing my two rucksacks, and together we dumped them in the boot and closed it.

"Get in, I'm not standing out here all night." She jerked her chin towards the car door. I obliged, barely hesitating before I slid onto the back seat.

Becka closed the door behind me and I hurried to put the window down. "I'll call you when I arrive."

Becka scoffed. "Wait until it's at least decent LA hours though, ok?"

I huffed, "Yeah, ok."

We were both silent a moment, and I was grateful that the driver – Janice, according to the ID on the back the seat in front of me – seemed to understand that we needed a second.

"Did you ever know that you're my hero?" Becka deadpanned, crossing her arms over her chest.

"You're everything I would like to be," I said, nodding.

"I can fly higher than an eagle," Becka suddenly burst into song, making Janice jump.

"AND YOU ARE THE WIND BENEATH MY WINGS!" I joined in, our voices unlovely and clashing, sound forcing past the lumps in our throats and both of us heaving with sobs, the tears I'd been trying not to let fall, now falling freely down my cheeks.

"Go," Becka urged, hitting the top of the car twice.

"Yes, please, can we go?" I directed this to Janice.

"Sure." She put her indicator on and we pulled away from the kerb.

I spun around in my seat, unable to take my eyes off my best friend as she wrapped her arms around herself, openly sobbing as she watched me drive away. I clapped a hand over my mouth, trying to stifle my own cries.

"You're gonna be okay, honey," Janice said kindly, holding a pack of tissues behind her shoulder. I gratefully took the box.

"I know," I said wetly.

The song on the radio faded away as the host began speaking, his voice a vague rumble until Janice nudged the sound up a couple clicks.

"As Christmas swiftly approaches, I hope we can all get some well-deserved rest. Doesn't it just feel like this year has been such a trip, folks? I know some of you have had a real challenging year, with the US GDP expected to fall further as we head into the New Year.

"But here's my prediction; I really believe the next year is going to be such a monumental year. I mean, just think of it, it's such a milestone year.

"Something tells me that 2020 is going to be the year that changes everything.

"What do you think, folks, are you going to be sorry to see the back of 2019? Call in and let me know. In the meantime, let's have some more music. Here with a song we just couldn't get away from this year, the runaway smash hit from the South Korean super band, GVibes. Here's 'Fall In Love'."

I smiled as the first notes played, filling the car with voices so familiar to me as I watched the glow of the streetlamps as we passed. The background of LA's frenetic pulse almost like a lullaby as we sped towards the airport; towards the next chapter of my life.

Acknowledgements

To my husband, my biggest supporter, without whom there would be no love to draw inspiration from, and who—despite my dedicated pursuit of self-betterment—still won't let me win at Mario Kart.

To my kids, who make me a better person.

To my parents, who always gave me the room to grow and were (usually) gracious about it when I messed up. Thank you for letting me make my own mistakes and always helping me clean them up.

To Charlie and Emily, who make the world a better place every day and are the other two sisters I always wished lived closer.

To my whole family, half of whom probably don't even know I wrote a book but would go to war for me any day of the week. For all the washing during uni, for all the ways you made me feel welcome, for all the ways you stood up for me, and for the way you saw me. For all the "that's what family does." You all know who you are.

To my editor, Susan Dize, whom I loved immediately and who never seemed to get bored of correcting my muck-ups. I'm still getting you a box of en dashes for Christmas. I look forward to my box of buts.

To Ieva Uloza from Virtual Booklore, for taking a punt on a baby author and providing the kind of insights that are worth their weight in gold. Your kindness is inspiring.

To my beta reader, Alana, and those who wished to remain anonymous—I appreciate you all for your enthusiasm, grace, kindness, and, of course, the insights into Korean language.

To Mary, who took one look at me and decided immediately – and with no evidence – that I could do this, long before I ever believed it.

And to Mrs. Walton, in memoriam. She knew I would do it, so I did.

To all the fans around the world – the Armies, Stays, Blinks, even the Little Monsters and the Beyhive. Without you, we wouldn't have so many truly outstanding artists. Without you in their corners, we would all be worse off.

And lastly, but never least: to you. Yes, you, my reader. For picking up this book and giving it a go, for looking forward to it, for being the reader I wrote this story for. I am grateful to you, and I hope you'll follow me, Kaiya, and Jihoon into the next book to see if Two Worlds really can Collide. ;)

Until then babes,

Kate xoxo

Hey babes.

I really hope you enjoyed reading A World Apart. I'm enormously proud of it, but it wouldn't have been possible without the support of good folks like yourself.

If you enjoyed reading this book, I really hope you'll consider leaving a rating, or a written review. I cannot express quite how much that would mean to me, and how much it helps my exposure as an author. You'd be doing me a real solid.

Love you, bye!

About the Author

Kate grew up in Jersey (the Island, not the city) before moving to the UK for University to study Classic Studies; a super interesting degree, but completely useless in practice.

Kate moved back to Jersey and now lives there with her husband, their children and an assortment of animals.

In another life, Kate always used to write Fantasy romances, but Kaiya and Jihoon's story popped into her head sometime during the summer of '24, almost fully formed. It seemed rude not to oblige them with their book, so here we are.

When Kate isn't writing, she's usually reading, wrangling kids and/or animals, or singing loudly along with Alexa.

You can connect with Kate via her webpage: www.katealexandr a.co.uk, where you can sign up to her newsletter to hear the latest release information, sneak peeks, etc.

You can email Kate via: kate-alexandra-author@outlook.com